LUCKY IN LOVE

by

Lori Avocato

THE CREEK
Whiskey Creek Press
www.creekpress.com

Published by
THE CREEK
Whiskey Creek Press
P.O. Box 726
Lusk, Wyoming 82225
307-334-3165
www.thecreek.com

Names, characters and incidents depicted in this book are products of the author's imagination or are used fictitiously. Any resemblance to actual events, locales, organizations, or persons, living or dead, is entirely coincidental and beyond the intent of the author or the publisher.

ISBN 1-59374-022-0

Printed in the United States of America

Dedication

To my fellow writer, Kim Peterson Zaniewski for all her help and those long lunches where we talk "shop."

Chapter One

Lucky Santanelli glared at the six-foot tall chipmunk and silently cursed her father—once again.

She spun around to see that her limousine had already left, then groaned. Nothing in sight except this dump of an amusement park glaring before her… Red, yellow, and what she guessed was one time orange lollipops bigger than the palm trees back home lined the entryway. They looked half licked or more like partially bitten off by rats, she thought, leaning over to see if the limo may have parked in the lot. No such luck. "Damn it." Now she was going to be stuck here longer.

Behind, a giant roller coaster clanked upwards toward the sky on a whitewashed wooden frame chipping paint like falling snow. When she looked back toward the admission's booth, no one was around except the annoying chipmunk that kept asking her if she wanted to buy an all-day pass or a book of coupons to Funland Amusement Park.

"Look, lady," the chipmunk said. "I haven't got all day…" Who would have thought a chipmunk would have such a sexy voice?

"Why?" she questioned, "you have to start squirreling away nuts for the winter?" She couldn't help but laugh at her stupid comment, until she looked past him to the dilapidated buildings inside the gate.

Funland. Yeah, right. It looked like it may have been a fun place in its heyday, but right now it looked more like it needed to be put out of its misery.

The sight quickly took all humor from the moment.

"Pass or coupons, lady?"

She shook her head although she doubted if he could see

through the black mesh screen on the giant chipmunk head. "A silk suit isn't exactly amusement park attire, kid."

He leaned near. She stepped back but not before inhaling a wonderful, spicy scent. Wow. She would have thought sweating under all that fur would smell...more natural. For a teenager-who the hell else would be desperate enough to dress up in a getup like this-the kid had a very deep voice. "Look, son, I don't want a pass for all day or one minute. I want to see the owner..."

The chipmunk groaned. "You a bill collector?"

"I have business with the owner." She set her briefcase down on a nearby ledge. Her feet were killing her in these heels, never should travel in Italian leather with skinny straps and spike heels, her body cried out for a cool shower and a line was forming behind, making her feel as if every eye shot daggers at her. Especially from the kids.

"What do you want?" the chipmunk asked.

"I have no intention of discussing why I'm here with a boy who keeps harassing me about a ticket." She tried to push past him. A giant brown furry leg blocked her from moving through the gate. "What the hell do you think—" She poked at his bristly chest. He stumbled backwards. Obviously his paws weren't his correct size.

"Mommy, that mean lady is hurting Alvis Chipmunk!" a small boy screamed from behind.

Lucky turned to see the kid, red-faced, eye's glaring and yanking at his mother's hand. The family of four came closer, as if ready to pounce on her and save the stupid chipmunk.

"That's Alv*in*, sweetie," Lucky corrected although she'd rather have told the kid a few choice words.

"No it's not! No it's not!" he whined.

The chipmunk moved his leg. "Kid's right. Alvis.

Combination of Alvin and Elvis…"

"He plays a guitar and sings. Nah! Nah!" the kid chanted.

Lucky caught the mother's eagle eye and shrugged. "Whatever." In order to get his attention and maybe see some human features, she leaned near the face of the chipmunk, ignoring that he smelled good and not like the inside of some teenager's locker and said, "Find me the owner. Now."

"Look, lady. There's a line forming. Wait over there and I'll—"

"Alvis Chipmunk. Alvis Chipmunk," the kid started to sing. "The mean old lady hurt Alvis Chipmunk!"

This was one time Lucky was thankful that her ex-bodyguard had taught her some deliciously naughty curse words in Sicilian. After muttering them under her breath, she turned to the kid. "Your Mister Chipmunk started it—" Cripes, now she sounded like some eight year old.

This fool amusement park atmosphere had a successful businesswoman like herself, a woman who only yesterday closed a multi-million dollar real estate deal in downtown Vegas, sounding like a snotty kid. Oh God how she wished she were anywhere else on earth except Seagrove, Connecticut home of the once famous and now dilapidated Funland Amusement Park.

May her dear departed father roll over in his grave from the vibes she was sending him right now.

After several minutes of watching the chipmunk sell tickets, Lucky yanked off her jacket, slung it over her shoulder and sat on the nearest seat—a mushroom, painted chartreuse. Chips of yellow-green stuck to her black skirt. Frederic, her tailor, would die. But right now Lucky could care less what stuck to the material. All she wanted was to present the owner of this ramshackle amusement park with the legal papers in her briefcase and get her limo back to JFK Airport for the next flight home.

She looked up in time to see the chipmunk hightailing it out of the back of the ticket both!

"Hey, wait!" She slung her jacket over her shoulder and ran after him. The nerve of the creature trying to sneak off as if she wasn't here. She hurried her pace, feeling much like Alice chasing after the stupid rabbit. She'd be damned if this furry jerk was going to make her feel like some fantasy character though. She was a grown woman for crying out loud.

"Stop this minute!" she called.

He turned around. "Almost forgot." He waved a furry hand and turned back, slowing his pace while he walked down a path of psychedelic plastic flowers and bees the size of jet planes. Two wings were missing from one of them.

"Yeah right, you almost forgot." She hurried along, not wishing to lose him in the crowd of whining kids. Granted, it wouldn't be easy to lose a gigantic chipmunk. Actually, his fur hugged his butt so tightly, she wondered how he even fit into the damn outfit. If she made it close enough to strangle his furry neck, she'd probably pass out from heat exhaustion, over exertion from the run, or anger first. This pounding in her temples couldn't be a good sign.

At a gingerbread house with a sign that read "office," he walked up what she guessed was supposed to be a sugarcoated sidewalk although the "sugar" was chipping just like the chartreuse mushrooms, and the house looked like the one where that witch wanted to eat those kids. Lucky wasn't up on her fairytales.

This place needed a hell of a lot of work was all she could think.

And she had no intention of sinking a penny of her hard-earned money into it. Let the other owner have at it.

LUCKY IN LOVE

Lori Avocato

"Hey, wait—" The door slammed behind the chipmunk before she could get inside. "Insolent varmint." She made a mental note to report this employee to the owner, but not before she finished her business with him.

The door opened, nearly knocking her into the plastic lollipop bushes. "Forgot you were behind me."

"Sure you did. You're avoiding me, sonny, and I'm not going to go away. Seems manners aren't a teenager like you—"

He lifted the chipmunk head off as he stood in the doorway. Holy shit! This guy ain't no teen, she thought.

Sweat from the hot costume beaded on his forehead beneath unruly black hair that hung down past his eyebrows. He looked like half-chipmunk, half-Tom Cruise having a bad hair day. Then again, a man this good looking, and Tom of course, too, could get away with any kind of hair day they chose.

"Look, lady, inside this getup it's about a thousand degrees. I don't think straight past nine hundred ninety nine. Spit out what you want." He unzipped the back, and before she could blink, a puddle of fur covered his feet—and he stood there in some black silken boxers. "I said I'm listening."

What the hell did she fly across the country for anyway?

With a snap to her mind, and a yank to her vision before she made a fool of herself, she looked at a picture of an old wooden roller coaster on the wall in order not to look at the...well, she could no longer call him a chipmunk. The coaster looked familiar. Oh well, she must have seen one in her travels years ago. No, wait. Daddy had told her about one like it. Or was it the one outside? Quickly erasing that thought, she said, "I need to speak to the owner of this place—"

"Have a seat." He turned toward the door.

"Wait a minute! Not again!" she yelled. He sauntered out the backdoor before she could say anything else. The latch didn't catch, no great surprise. The door swung open with a gust of the sea's breeze to reveal the man diving into the water behind the gingerbread house.

A feeling of déjà vu had her grab onto the chair's arms. The place looked familiar.

The seashore setting was a perfect spot for an amusement park, she thought. At least Daddy did one thing right building this place.

The man arose from the waves like some sparkling Adonis. Lucky wondered if chipmunks could swim. "You're losing it, Santanelli," she said to herself.

Long powerful strokes had him cutting through waves that she knew would suck her out to sea. And after daily swims in her condo's pool, she was a damn good swimmer. This guy's arms worked like oars, she thought as he dove under. She leaned forward, waiting for him to resurface. Nothing.

She got up.

Still no sign of him.

A mouse clock with black gloved hands that pointed to the numbers ticked away, reminding her that she had a return flight to catch in a few hours. Where the hell was the fool? Never taking her eyes off the spot where he dove under, she moved closer to the door.

Nothing.

Walking out the door, she cursed and hoped she wasn't going to have to rescue him.

Seagulls squawked outside, the sun burned into her black suit like some solar clothing and a sharp odor tickled her nose. The marshes, their scent, pungent, almost salty, that too, seemed familiar.

Increasing her step, she hurried down to the shoreline. She waited. Shielded the sun from her eyes. No sign of him. Wait.

LUCKY IN LOVE

Lori Avocato

Was that his head? She squinted, ignored her heart beating faster. No. Only a pile of seaweed floating by. He'd been under so long. Her heels flung off to the left, her jacket the right. With nylons soaking up the sand, she ran forward and dove in.

And slammed smack dab into him.

They surfaced together. "Jesus! What the hell are you doing?" he yelled, grabbing her before a wave smashed into them. "You could have drowned us both!"

After a second of debating whether to spit her mouthful of briny water in his direction, she turned her head and spit the other way. "Me?" she said after coughing out, "you were under for so long—"

"And you thought you were some 'Baywatch' babe trying to save me?"

"Believe me, I wouldn't do it again," she shouted above the crashing surf now at its peek of high tide. The guy didn't let go. She looked down at his hands on her arms and wished she'd worn long sleeves. The water temperature had to be in the sixties, but her arms were warm where he held her. Beneath, her body trembled, ankles, feet, fingers all of her hurt from the cold. She yanked free. "I should have let you float out to Long Island." A wave pounded into her back. She shoved up against him then tumbled to the side.

He grabbed her arm and lifted her up. She coughed and choked on the saltiness again. "Come on before you do drown us both," he ordered.

She wanted to pull free again, but her clothes must weigh a thousand pounds wet, making walking difficult. No wonder bathing suits were so skimpy. At the water's edge she managed to stand by herself and shrug loose. "Leave me alone."

"Only trying to help...save *you*. You know, one hand washes the other."

"Shut up."

"Look, sorry you felt the need to rescue me. I happen to have good lungs and can stay under a long time."

Good lungs? Who the hell noticed lungs with a body like his? With a shove, she pushed wet hair from her face, cursing that her styled hairdo must look like...wet chipmunk fur.

He, however, looked adorable.

His hair clung to his forehead in a sheen of black, making his eyes stand out, wide and intriguing. The cold water gave his cheeks a healthy pink color. He licked at his lips most likely tasting the same salty flavor as she. His action had her running her tongue across hers.

"Okay, you have good lungs and swim like a tuna—"

"Years of practice. I grew up here. Come on. Let's see if we can find you some dry clothes." With a hand to her lower back, he guided her up the beach and toward the gingerbread house.

And she didn't feel like pulling away.

What she felt like was collapsing into the sand. What a damn day. Her skin was freezing, grainy sand stuck to her feet, and the sun burned into her suit. Hot outside, freezing inside.

Because she wanted to take her mind off of how miserable she felt, she said, "You didn't even introduce yourself, you know."

"Everyone calls me EZ." He guided her up the beach.

"Odd name."

"Name's Edmund Zachary." EZ couldn't move his hand from her back—just yet. Whatever the material of her suit, it felt like wet skin. Warm. Soft. Skin. He swallowed and nearly spit; tasting the damn water she'd caused him to choke on.

"I see why the nickname."

The water always did the trick of cooling him to his gut, but her smile suddenly had him itching for another dive.

LUCKY IN LOVE

Lori Avocato

"I'm Lucky—"

"Odd name."

She turned around, rolled her eyes. "It's not my real name, merely a nickname my father gave me at birth."

He leaned near and said, "And are you? *Lucky* that is..."

She glared at him. Took him by surprise when she didn't pull back. Damn, the woman had spunk. Guess she had to in order to dive in to save his sorry butt. Hmm, an independent lady. Hell. Too bad he'd have to get rid of her soon. He smiled at her.

She curled her lip.

At the office, he shoved open the door. A blast of air conditioning had him shiver. "It's freezing in here when you're wet. You'll really need to change."

"I wasn't planning on staying," she said through clenched teeth, "so I don't have any clothes with me." Her eyebrows drew together.

What were the odds that look was because she was cold, not pissed? After she walked in, he shut the door. "Still, you need to change. Thing is, you're not exactly my size."

"I'll be...fine." Her bottom lip trembled.

"You'll catch pneumonia and probably sue." He lifted the chipmunk suit from the floor.

"Oh no you don't." She pushed at his arm as he held it out toward her. "No way in hell am I going to put that thing—"

"Shut up before you get sick. Just stick it over you like a blanket."

She scowled at him and grabbed the costume. "Don't you have a real blanket?"

"It's July, Lucky. We Yankees pack away our woolies until the winter." He leaned near. "I'm guessing you're not from around here."

"Finally got one thing right."

"Hey, I'm a college grad. Some would say astute. Some would say laid-back, too." He leaned forward, grinned. "And, some would say too sexy. Too damn sexy for my own good."

She clucked her tongue.

"By the way, Lucky, what's your real name?"

"Doesn't matter." She had no intention of telling him that only her father had ever called her by her given name of Lucy—and only when she was very young and in need of comfort. That didn't last long, though.

Early on she would have given anything, even her favorite Barbie doll, her collections of old Nancy Drew novels for him to call her Lucy one more time.

He shrugged. "Okay, Lucky it is. Let me get changed, and I'll see what else I can come up with to cover you."

"Probably some other stupid costume." She sank into his red leather, torn in most places, chair and pulled the moth-eaten fur over her. "Can this day get any better?"

"Turn around." He grabbed a towel from the shelf, ran it across his chest then wrapped it around his waist.

She swung around. "Why should I turn—" He pulled his wet boxers off.

What a lovely shade of red, he thought, looking at her cheeks.

"Don't you have any modesty?"

He shrugged.

God, hopefully the towel wouldn't slip.

"I told you to turn around. You're the one who went the wrong way." She didn't budge as he slipped on dry boxers beneath his towel, dropped it and yanked on jeans—then laughed. "'Spunky' might be a better nickname for you. You're quite a pistol when wet."

"Not much bothers me," she said, ignoring the fact that she really wished the towel had fallen. "I'm a big girl—"

He whistled. "I'll say." Did the big girl realize that the way her wet top clung to her breasts made a man...notice?

She curled her lip again.

"Didn't your mother ever tell you not to make faces, Lucky? You could freeze like that. Be a shame, too."

"How about those dry clothes?"

"Maybe we can throw yours into the dryer over in my trailer—"

"Silk?"

He shrugged. "I'm not up on my fabrics." He pulled a tee shirt over his head.

"Anyone who wears fur in July must not be."

"Summer help's been dwindling. Robbie Hathaway, the chipmunk, got some stomach virus and spread it to nearly half the group. Linda, the saloon dancer, has been out on and off, too. So if you came for money, I'm pleading mercy. On top of that, I've got three rides closed today." He shoved his foot into a very worn Nike running shoe. "Patrons don't much like that."

"I see."

He leaned near, "Then you also see that I get a bit testy when I have to do 'chipmunk.'"

"Is that a fact? I hadn't noticed. Anyway, speaking of patrons—"

He waved a hand at her. "I have no intention of speaking of patrons, chipmunks or anything to do with this place right now." He yanked open a drawer of the nearby filing cabinet and pulled out his trusty aspirin bottle. Without a thought, he swallowed three, dry. "Maybe you should come back another day."

She wrinkled her nose. "Don't you use water with pills?"

He looked at her, told himself she wasn't nearly as gorgeous as his hormones were telling him, that her nose must have been fixed cause no one was born with perfection and said, "I'm a big boy."

"Very funny, and I'm not leaving—"

She'd kept talking, he knew. But he'd been too busy looking at her face, that nose, the skin that made him want to reach out.... Jesus. What the hell was he doing ogling her? She was obviously some bill collector or maybe, by the look of her, the owner of one of the concessions he dealt with. Either way, he more than likely owed her money. "Wrap up. I'll be right back."

* * *

Lucky watched EZ strut out of the office, and mentally let out a curse of her ex-bodyguard's nastiest Sicilian words. "What a jerk." She pushed the stupid costume off and walked to the window.

After lifting the control's lid, she turned the air conditioner up to eighty. "I'm not about to sit here with that creature on me." But when she bent to pick up the costume, she inhaled his scent imbedded in the fur; she told herself that was not the reason she didn't want the warmth covering on her. It was too *furry* feeling. Lucky Santanelli didn't do fur or fluff.

She grabbed her purse, opened it, and took out cell phone, but the "out of area" feature wouldn't let her make a call. No great surprise. Taking her daily planner, she looked up the number for the limo company then glanced around the desk. There had to be a phone here somewhere. Even a guy like him had to communicate with humans outside this place and not carnie workers all the time. She lifted a stack of papers and noticed they were all bills. Bills marked 'past due.' All the more reason for her to get out of this mess.

The chipmunk was probably the manager, too. An even

better reason to get out—fast.

With a shrug, she let the papers fall to dig under three more piles until she found an old rotary phone. This guy was too much. Not even a cordless touch-tone. She dialed the numbers and waited for a dispatcher to answer.

EZ walked in to see Lucky'd helped herself to his phone. Hopefully not long distance, he thought. Before he questioned if it was, he paused, leaned against the doorframe. Damn, she was a looker, but he'd rather donate his corneas to science right now than to keep staring at her. He paused without the intent to eavesdrop but couldn't help hear her say, "Hi. I'd like to be picked up right now."

She was leaving. Great. He didn't need anymore bill collectors hassling him. One problem solved.

"This is Lucky Santanelli—"

Jesus, he thought. "*Santanelli?*"

She swung around toward him. He couldn't move from the doorway. Didn't trust himself if he did.

"Of course, thank you," she continued into the phone. "I'll be at the front gate."

"Santanelli," he said to be sure. "As in Rosario Santanelli that cheating gangster?"

She glared at him. "No," she said, slamming the receiver with such force two bills flew off the desk. "As in Rosario Santanelli, my *father*."

LUCKY IN LOVE

Lori Avocato

Chapter Two

Lucky stuck out her hand, ready to shake EZ's, but he only glared at her and said, "I wish the hell you were a bill collector, but now, Santanelli, I can finally get what *my* father has coming to him."

"Excuse me?" she said, pulling her hand back from him. Obviously he wasn't going to shake it as any kind of gesture of introduction. By the look of anger on his face, he must have been thinking of another kind of gesture. Rooted on the spot, he looked her up and down.

"You heard me." He leaned near. "I'm surprised I didn't recognize you."

"We've never met."

"Sure we did. You came here as a kid."

"I..." That's why the beach looked familiar, but she didn't remember.

"Besides, from the pictures of your old man that I've seen around here, you have his...a look about you that resembles him." No way would he tell her that her chestnut hair, deep brown eyes and silken skin looked like a gorgeous version of Rosario Santanelli.

Damn, he couldn't look at this woman like *that*.

Lucky Santanelli, the enemy, he reminded himself.

"I look more like my mother."

She shut her eyes. What a dumb thing to say, but his reaction to learning who she was, his reminder that she'd been here as a kid, and the crack about the truth took her by surprise.

Confused her. Besides, she wasn't used to such rudeness. No one who worked for her treated her this way and certainly the men who'd worked for her late father had more respect for women—even if they didn't have any regard for each other. "Look, it doesn't matter who I look like. I've come here to talk to the owner of this place—"

EZ stopped glaring at her, walked to the torn leather chair behind his desk and sat. With a glance at the door, he propped his feet on the desk as if that was her invitation to exit.

"First of all, I'm not leaving. Second, I don't know who your father is, but I have business to discuss with the owner of this place. I'd appreciate if you'd call him—"

"Dalton?"

"Why, yes. Daniel Dalton."

A smirk covered his face as he looked at her. "Did I forget to mention my last name?"

She let out a sigh. "I don't care what your last name is. I don't know who you are or what you have against my father." Conversations about her father's dealings were old hat. How many times did someone in some Vegas casino accuse her old man of some wrongdoing? She'd learned as early as her teen years, to refer them to his lawyers. If they knew how little she had to do with him, they wouldn't have bothered with her.

After all these years, though, she thought it had all gone away. Guess she was wrong.

He dropped his feet to the floor, stood and came near. "Don't be too sure that my last name doesn't matter, sweetheart."

She gritted her teeth. "Lucky."

He sucked in a breath and continued, "Yeah, right, *sweetheart*. Guess names really do matter. Did I tell you that my father started calling me EZ at the age of two? Seems I was easy to get along with—"

"You could have fooled me." She looked at her watch. An hour and a half wasted here. Was it the time or the company that made her want to bolt out the door? Firming her stance, she said, "My limo will be back shortly. That's great that you are easy to get along with and your names coincidentally had *E* and *Z* as the first letters. Fascinating." She lifted her jacket from the chair. "Still, none of my concern—or interest. Any dealings you had with my father—"

"Never met the guy."

She sucked in enough air to fill her lungs for a long slow sigh. Pungent sea air reminded her of the dive in the water to save him. Shouldn't have wasted her time. Before she could remember how his touch had warmed her, she blew the air out. "If you never met him, what have you got against him?" Damn. She had no intention of continuing that conversation.

"Seems, Ms. Santanelli, that my father knew yours—"

"Then tell him Rosario Santanelli passed away seven years ago—"

EZ's smirk faded. "I had no idea. Sorry."

"Why? You didn't drown him."

"Of course not. Oh, I get it. Sarcasm. Look I didn't know—"

"It wasn't exactly national news." Around Vegas, though, the press had had a field day. "He...he fell overboard from his yacht." And escaped every creditor west of the Rockies, every enemy after his ass.

"I'm sorry to hear that."

She nodded at him. "So, if you'll get me the owner of this place, I can do my business and leave."

"Dalton."

"Yes, as I said before Mr. Dalton."

LUCKY IN LOVE

Lori Avocato

"Dalton is *my* last name."

She caught herself against the doorframe as she looked into his eyes. "EZ Dalton?"

He held out his hand.

She refused it.

He laughed, ran his hand across his chin.

"*You* are Daniel Dalton's son?"

"The one and only." He leaned near. "You didn't recognize me either from when we were kids."

"I...no." Not that it mattered, but she'd repressed so much of her youth, obviously the memories of meeting this jerk were long gone. No loss. She looked at her watch, wanting to be anywhere but here. "Then you know were I can find your father."

"Sure I do."

"Good."

"Not for you."

She curled her lip. "I really don't have much time. If you'd get your father.... Oh my. Is he..."

"Alive and kicking."

"Fine. Then if you would take me to him, I can do my business and get the hell out of here."

* * *

He waved a hand toward the chair across from the desk. "Sit. Anything to do with Dad's business...I handle."

Lucky looked at the man who'd tricked her from the minute she looked into his chipmunk eyes. Great. Now she was going to have to deal with *him*. Well, she'd had a lifetime of dealing with her father's shenanigans, so she was rather an expert on that kind of stuff.

"Fine," she said as she sat down and opened her black eel skin briefcase. "My father left me his half of Funland in his will.'"

"Will? Why the seven year time span?"

"Legalities. Look, I have no desire to own any of this place, so my lawyers drew up a very reasonable, actually overly generous, price for you to buy out my share." She set the papers on the desk. "Please read and sign it in the three places marked. We can set up some liberal terms of payment, too." She dug around in her purse. "By the looks of your desk, I'm guessing you won't be able to find a pen for several days." She grabbed her engraved ballpoint and held it out to him. "Here." She waved the pen several times.

He looked down as if she held out a rattlesnake.

"I only have a short time before my ride comes. My flight leaves in two hours—"

"All neatly planned. Seems Lucky Santanelli takes after her father in the business department. One hell of a businesswoman. Make that one hell of a cheating businesswoman."

The hairs on her neck rose. In her firmest voice she said, "I'm *nothing* like my father. The deal is more than fair," she swallowed, gained her composure. "Please read it all before you sign."

He sat on the edge of the desk, still not taking the pen from her. "Out of morbid curiosity, you know the kind like when you drive by an accident and have to look to see some blood and gore, how much we talking about for the buyout?"

She pointed to the figure on the contract. "It's all clearly stated—"

He bent near. The dip in the ocean hadn't washed off his scent, or he'd reapplied whatever made him smell so spicy, so appealing. She swallowed, pulled her gaze to the wall, to the safety of the old roller coaster picture. Now she remembered why it looked so familiar. Didn't Daddy once say it was one of the oldest in the country that still worked? Without turning to

EZ, she said, "Please hurry, Mr. Dalton."

"My dad's Mr. Dalton. I'm plain old EZ." He stood up, walked to the side.

"Fine." She gritted her teeth. "Please hurry, plain old EZ."

She felt him move and guessed he'd stopped looking at the contract. From the corner of her eye, she watched him approach. Not able to help herself, she turned in time for him to reach up and take her head into his hands. With a gentle tug, he had her looking directly into his face.

Normally she had great reflexes. Years of Karate training and more recently TAEBO, but in his hold—she froze.

"Just to make sure you don't miss a word, Santanelli. No…way…in…hell."

Lucky yanked her head free. "It's very cheap. I'm not making a fortune on it. The entire park will belong to you."

"To my father you mean. And that's the only part of this contract that I agree with. Should have belonged to him years ago. He never should have trusted your old man, built it with him."

"You'd be a fool not to take this offer."

"Then, Lucky, I'm a fool."

Obviously her business tactics were wasted on this guy. Before she found herself inclined to using some feminine wiles on him, like the ones she'd witnessed the bimbo female executives doing but had always refused to stoop to using herself, she decided to tug at his emotions. Emotions she could do. Had years of training with her family. In fact, she was a veritable roller coaster of emotions.

She cleared her throat, summoned every ounce of compassion she could manage. It wasn't an easy feat. Not that she wasn't a caring person, although some might call her cold. But she was human and could act the part. "Sorry for whatever my father did to yours, EZ. I can't answer for him, nor would I want to."

"My. My. Sounds as if someone wasn't exactly 'Daddy's Little Girl.'"

A pang of guilt touched her heart. "My relationship with my father is none of your concern."

"True, but his relationship with my old man is."

"Then buy me out and have him own this place. What better way to get back at my father than to own the entire park? Obviously you've been running it…trying to run it anyway."

He leaned near. She'd faced enemies across boardroom tables all over the country fixing business deals gone bad. Then there were the looks, from supposed mourners, at her father's memorial service, but she'd never seen such hatred as she saw now in the eyes of EZ Dalton.

Years ago she'd said her token prayer that her father's soul was taken care off, but now she knew she'd never forgive him for all of this.

And, damn it, she was sick to death of paying for the sins of her father.

"I won't give you a penny, Ms. Santanelli, for what your father stole from mine."

"I'm sorry if your dad was hurt years ago. Sorry about the money."

"Money isn't everything. Oh wait, maybe it is to you Santanellis."

Because she had to make this all stop, she shut her eyes. It killed her to be about to offer such a stupid business deal when her life's career was making sound real estate dealings, but all she wanted was out of this one so she opened her eyes and said, "Have your lawyer write up a contract buying me out for…one dollar."

He stared at her. "You must really want to end this partnership."

She stood, looked out the window. "My limo is here." She grabbed a business card from the pocket of her briefcase. "Express mail me the papers and your check. I'll have my lawyer work out the deed—"

His laughter took her by surprise.

She pulled back, grabbed the doorframe. "There's nothing funny here."

He walked to within inches of her face. "Then your sense of humor and mine are very different, sweetheart. You see, I find paying even a dollar for something my father should already own humorous. Boisterously entertaining. So hilarious that...I have to turn you down."

Lucky tried to ignore the fact that his laughter made her head pound. She even chose to forget that her damp suit clung to her and smelled of seaweed. But what she couldn't disregard was the threat of revenge from this man.

He had some axe to grind with her father and even though Rosario was deceased, EZ, it seemed, had no intention of letting bygones be bygones.

Because she'd worried all her life that she may be like her father, she'd made a point to make all her deals sound, honest ones. Oh, she fought when attacked as he would, but never dirty, never dishonestly. This time, however, being attacked by EZ, she'd known what it felt like to be a target of someone's hatred.

"As I said, I don't know why you seem to dislike—"

"Hate."

"—my father so much, but my recommendation is that you take this offer to your father. *He* is the other owner of Funland. Actually," She put her hand on the doorknob. "I don't know why

I'm discussing any of this with you. I demand to see Mr. Daniel Dalton."

This time his laughter came out an eerie chuckle. "I handle all my father's business, Lucky, as I said. He gave me power of attorney exactly for offers like this one. But you see, Ms. Santanelli, I have no intention of buying you out."

"You'll never get another offer like this. I'll take you to court, sue you for letting the place run down, and you'll end up giving me your half." That sounded like an empty threat, even to her. Not being a lawyer, she wondered if what she said was true, or even made sense, or if any part of it could sound true enough to fool a carnie worker. Christ, her head pounded. Here she thought coming to Funland would be so cut and dry. Sell off the last reminder of Daddy. "Then," she said in her most businesslike voice, tucked her briefcase under her arm to hide her hands in her pockets so he wouldn't see the trembling, "I'll sell it to some developer. This seaside property has got to be worth millions."

EZ cringed. It wasn't as if he didn't know the value of the property. But no way could money tempt him into selling out his father. "You'd need my okay to sell it, so that's a mute point.

Damn him. The guy looked like some "carnie" but underneath the ruffled, too-long hair, must be some brain. At least a devious enough one to ruin her offer. "I haven't been here long, but I can see this place needs work. If you buy me out, you could earn all the profits. Fix up the place." She set her briefcase on top of a cluttered bookcase. "Are you aware that my father had been receiving earnings for some twenty years—"

He pounced at her, grabbing her arms.

"Ouch!"

"Like I need reminding of that." His hold loosened but he didn't let her go. "You do fight dirty, Santanelli. Shoving your old man in my face."

"I...that wasn't why I mentioned it." She wiggled her shoulders, debating whether to knee this guy but instead straightened her posture, glared into his eyes and said, "I mentioned it so you'd see that all his profits could be yours. Your father's."

"Profits?" He laughed. "Take a good look outside. Your old man's the only one who ever got any profit out of Funland."

"But, there are some people here. You must make some money. Don't let revenge get in the way of you father's income."

He let go. "What the hell do you care about my father?"

"I've never met him but—"

"Sure you did."

"I have a photographic memory. That's why I'm so damn good at business deals. I would know if I'd met him."

"Even if you were about five years old?"

To buy herself time, Lucky looked out the window. Did she ever meet Daniel Dalton? She'd never been so confused. She'd always prided herself in her quick mind—until now. The limo driver had gotten out and was heading to the door. She leaned near the opened window and said, "I'll be out shortly."

He nodded. "Yes, ma'am."

As she watched the driver head back to the limousine, she shook her head. "No. I would have remembered."

"You were here. I remember. Your old man had hair dark like yours—"

"Any picture would show that."

"Yeah, right. Well, a picture can't show how you used to rock yourself to sleep while he played cards with his buddies...."

She knew EZ was still talking but her mind had traveled back some twenty-five years. Every Friday night, Daddy played cards, her mother would be working a show, and he wouldn't even put Lucky to sleep. She'd sit in her little rocker and doze off. That is, whenever he spent time with them.

EZ remembered.

"Big deal. You saw me asleep one time. I don't remember your father, though and that was the point of this conversation. So, let me meet him now. Let me make my offer since you seem to have a chip on your shoulder bigger than Mt. Rushmore."

"I repeat. No way in—"

"Hell. Yeah. Okay, then where does that leave me?"

"I'd like it to leave you back in Vegas in some plush condo, but that ain't gonna happen."

"I am leaving shortly."

He strolled across the room and lifted the top of her briefcase. Before she could slam it shut, he said, "I'm not looking at your stuff, merely making a point. You must be some businesswoman. Looks like you have a lot going on. Actually, you must—" He looked at her from head to toe. "—earn a damn good salary to dress like that. So, I'm gonna go out on a limb and say you're some kind of executive—"

"I'm Vice President of Hartwell Holdings in charge of their real estate section."

"Oooweee. Isn't that that billion-dollar company that buys and sells just about the entire country? Hm, Daddy must have had some decent connections...oh wait, organized crime folks don't need connections. They damn well get what they want—"

"I *worked* my way up without anyone's help."

"Maybe. Oh wait. I did read about you a few years ago in *People*." He looked at her, trying to forget she was a woman, realizing the perfect opportunity for revenge just fell into his lap. Businesswoman of the year. He'd read it in black and white. On her way up the corporate ladder. This woman used her skills, abilities, it'd said.

LUCKY IN LOVE

Lori Avocato

Lucky Santanelli didn't sleep her way to the top.

She had the brains, the guts, the abilities.

Unfortunately, she was his only saving grace.

"Right. You worked your way up. My point here is, though, you must have some property of your own. Maybe a house or two. Maybe even a casino since you live in Vegas."

She looked out the window. "Make your point, Dalton. I have a plane to catch."

"No, actually you don't."

She shoved the top of her briefcase down, grabbed it, saying, "I've had enough of this." Then, she walked to the door. "I'll have my lawyer contact your—"

"You can contact whomever your little heart desires. But if you leave, you could lose everything—or at least a big chunk."

At the doorway she stopped. This guy was a pain in the ass, an annoying pain. All she wanted to do was get away from him, from stupid Funland, from reminders of Daddy.

But his tone had her stop dead in her tracts.

Again his eerie chuckle filled the room. "Thought that'd get your attention."

Without turning to look at him, she said, "Make your point."

His footsteps clicked on the worn wooden floor getting louder as he obviously came closer. His hand touched her shoulder. She stiffened but remained facing away. She'd be damned if his touch would intimidate her.

"My point, Ms. Lucky—" His grip tightened. "You said you were always lucky. I'm guessing today is going to change that streak."

A chill, colder than the one she'd felt when she had plunged into the freezing water outside, shook her body. His hand remained. A hot breath burned into the back of her neck. She tried to take a deep breath, but couldn't with him so near. If she screamed, the limo driver would hear, but she knew nothing would come out. Fear had her paralyzed under the hold of EZ Dalton. But she'd burn in hell before she'd scream.

"Yep. You may have to change your nickname, *sweetheart*. You see, if you leave without settling this, as part owner, all your holdings will be affected—when Funland goes under."

LUCKY IN LOVE

Lori Avocato

Chapter Three

This was enough.

Lucky wasn't about to take anymore of EZ's bullshit. She yanked free of his hold, turned and glared at him. He walked away, settled himself at his desk, feet propped up on a pile of papers as if he hadn't a care in the world.

He'd certainly gotten her attention.

After his revelation, she'd been mute with shock, very uncharacteristic for her. Could he be right though? A horrifying thought. What did this, this pompous, angry, chipmunk alter ego and obviously a sloppy, non-bill-paying son of the half-owner of this place, too, know about real estate laws?

She pulled her thoughts to the reality that he could be right, and looked out the window. The day looked beautiful with the sun's rays glistening on the water behind the park. The limousine stood at the entrance, the driver waiting patiently in the hot sun. She could see her expenses piling up. No matter, she told herself. She could well afford it, yet, old ways die hard. "Would you mind waiting a few more minutes?" she called to the driver.

As the man nodded toward her, EZ said, "Gonna take a lot more than a few minutes to settle all this—"

She spun around. "Look, if you'd buy my share for the stupid dollar, no, make that a penny. One measly penny. I'll leave and be out of your life forever."

He hesitated, glared at her.

She had him. Only a fool would pass up an offer like that.

"As tempting as the latter part of that sounds—no way in

hell."

It took a gigantic deep breath to control her from screaming that he was a jerk, a fool. Oh hell. She blew it out and shouted, "You are a fool!"

"That very well may be, Ms. Santanelli, or, it may very well be only your opinion." With that, he settled back into his chair.

He really wasn't called EZ for nothing. It irked her that he could remain so calm, look so relaxed when her insides were gripped in a knot just staring at him.

How in the hell was he capable of running this place? From this view she noted the paint chipped mushroom, the sugar coating peeling beneath the visitor's feet and heard an awful clanging sound that she guessed was some ride in need of WD40 oil.

He *wasn't* capable of running this place.

For a second, she thought of what she'd do with it if she could get free-reign of Funland. Don't go there, Lucky. She had more irons in the fire back in Vegas than she could handle and taking on a monumental task like saving this place was absurd.

What benefit would it be to her anyway?

Besides, after forcing herself to come all this way to get rid of this place, she'd vowed that no way would she consider keeping anything that her father left her. Except, of course, her mother's jewelry. That, she rationalized came from Mamma. She looked down at the sparking ruby on her ring, but couldn't even force a smile.

Even though her business-juices were flowing, she wanted no part of saving Funland. Daddy could turn over in his grave, if they have graves in Hell, but she'd get rid of what was his and go on with her life.

"Howdy, folks." A scratchy, rather weak voice pulled her back to the messy office.

LUCKY IN LOVE

Lori Avocato

Lucky swung around to see an elderly man dressed in Western attire saunter in and seat himself in front of the window air conditioner. He wiped at his brow, took a deep breath, leaned near and inhaled. She thought she noted a wheeze in his breathing, and his color was rather flushed. She gave a quick look at EZ who was already hurrying over to the old man.

"Hello," she said.

EZ took the man's hat off. "You know better than to wear that get-up when it's so hot, Doc."

The old man growled at EZ, sucked in what had to be a much-needed breath, then, winked at Lucky! She smiled at him. He was adorable for an older man she supposed. There was something in his face, a look that kind of captured her. She felt a bond trying to form, so she turned away. She didn't want to bond with any old carnie worker, but his eyes... They held an appeal that sucked her right in. The deep brown, watered by the years, held some kindness and something else. Sadness?

She'd be leaving in a few minutes and couldn't let herself care.

Besides, she could be wrong about him since she wasn't much for reading people. Lucky dealt in reality. She let that body language crap up to the airheads. Like some of the women at the office. Ones who put relationships before work, before success. Not her. Nope. She was going to be the first president of the West Coast office of Hartwell Holdings before she turned thirty-five.

And she'd do it with her brains.

The old man coughed. She walked to him as EZ started taking the man's jacket off of him. Some gesture of concern. Ha. He probably didn't want to fill in for the old man if he got sick like the chipmunk kid. The thought of EZ in Western gear had her hesitate, grab the back of a nearby chair. Tight jeans, threadbare in all the right places. Two, maybe three day's worth of beard. Red plaid shirt hugging firm chest muscles. She'd noticed them when he stripped to take his dip in the sound. Damn. Those kinds of thoughts were exactly what she always avoided. In all her business dealings she'd seen handsome men, many better looking than EZ, too. But she never put the moves on any of them. What the hell was wrong with her now? She had to stop this, so she reached her hand out to the old man and said, "I'm Lucky—"

The man whistled. "I'd say old EZ's the lucky one with a woman like you—"

"She's not my woman!" he yelled.

"I'm not his woman!" she yelled at the same time. It'd be almost humorous how the two of them proclaimed the statement at the same time. But nothing was funny about her and this lazy, fool belonging together.

"Whoa. No harm meant." The old man waved his hands in the air. "But me thinks Yee two doth protest too much."

"You're the Medicine Man this month, Doc, not Shakespeare. This is Lucky Santanelli. She inherited part of Funland when her father passed away."

"Lucky Santanelli...." Doc's eyes seemed to water more.

She wondered if he had cataracts and that was the cause.

"Howdy, ma'am." He gave her a polite nod.

She shook his hand and though his grip firm, but there was no mistaking a weakness of many years gone by. "Nice to meet you, sir—"

"Shoot. Call me Doc like everyone around here does." He winked again, followed by a fit of coughing.

EZ seemed concerned about the man as he turned the air conditioner up higher and bent to tell Doc something. She wasn't one for eavesdropping, but had EZ turned the air conditioner higher so she couldn't hear him? This mess was getting to her.

No, the jerk was getting to her.

What secret could he be telling the Medicine Man that would have anything to do with her? Shit. She was getting paranoid, something else she refused to let herself become. With her family's past she could have easily grown up thinking someone was out to get her every second of the day. But she refused to think like that and lived her life damn well the way she wanted to.

Right now she damn well wanted to go home to Vegas.

Doc leaned further back into his chair. "You two go on about what you was discussing. I'm gonna catch a bit of shut eye until my next show." He smiled and nodded toward her.

"Nice to meet you. I'm actually leaving—" His eyes shut before she could finish her sentence. He looked so at home. Obviously Doc came here quite often to cool off and rest.

Not certain what to do next, she looked at EZ. If she brought up her offer, he'd most likely start an argument that might wake up Doc. So, she stood a few minutes and debated whether to ask EZ to go outside. The clock behind the desk said she didn't have much time or she'd be spending the night at some noisy airport hotel. "Look, could we take this—"

EZ took her arm, leading her toward the other end of the room. "I don't want him woken up."

"I didn't intend to—"

"You better not."

She grabbed her arm free. "You didn't have to say that," she whispered. "I can see he's elderly and in need of rest."

For a second she noted something lighten in EZ's eyes. She expected an apology, but instead, he said, "He does. He'll be seventy-seven next month and insists on working two shows a day."

"Seems a lot for a man his age. Couldn't even *you* hire a replacement—"

"Sure I could if I wanted to break a friend's heart. Loves this place. Been around since day one. He's talked me into hiring every senior citizen east of New York City for the last year, too. He and the new fortuneteller, Zos, are a real pair. Became close friends right off the bat," he said as if not really speaking to her. She didn't need information like that, nor did she much care.

Caring led to pain.

She looked at the man and thought of her own father. Not thinking of Daddy was something else she'd promised herself she would do. He'd be about seventy-eight himself if he.... She still couldn't believe Daddy was gone. Literally. Not that she was filled with such grief that she couldn't accept his death, missed him so badly.

Hell, she thought, you can't miss what you never had.

Coming to Funland was the biggest mistake of her life. The barrier she'd so carefully built up around her heart was now threatened.

"Lucky?"

"Hm?" She turned to EZ. Obviously he'd been talking as she'd drifted off in thought. Never the sentimental type, she brushed off the thoughts of her father, as he'd want her to do. After all, that's exactly how he treated her, too.

"Lucky? You all right?"

"Did you say something?" she asked.

"I said, we need to discuss your not leaving."

"Leaving. I can't stay here." My heart couldn't take it. She craned her neck to see the limo still waiting outside. "And speaking of leaving, I really have to go or I'll miss my plane. I'll have my lawyer contact—"

Doc waved his hands wildly about as a fit of coughing had him turn redder than the chipmunk's felt tongue. She and EZ ran over to him.

"Oh God, is he all right?" She'd never been one for first aid, nearly fainting at the sight of her own blood. Her strengths were in her brains for business, not her abilities to mother or nurse anyone.

EZ took Doc's arms and raised them over his head. In a surprisingly calm tone, he said, "He's fine. Aren't you, Doc? Merely an old man trying to get attention."

She pushed at EZ's side. "What a horrible thing to say. He could have choked—"

"He wasn't even eating anything." He let the old man's hands go to settle on his lap.

The coughing stopped. She should have turned and walked toward the door, but something, had her run a hand across Doc's forehead, brushing some curls back. The texture wasn't right. Obviously he wore a wig as part of his costume. She did, however, suspect the handlebar mustache was real. This was getting ridiculous, she thought, as she fought off the urge to tweak it.

The old man was someone you just wanted to hug.

She couldn't remember ever meeting anyone that she wanted to hug.

Doc grabbed her hand, pressed it to the paper-thin skin of his cheek. "Thanks."

Lucky's hand stiffened. "I really have to go—"

He pulled her closer. "Come here."

"But…I—"

When he had her ear near his mouth, he said, "Stay for lunch. You'd make an old man happy."

"That's very nice of you to ask, but I have a plane to catch."

And nothing was going to get her to stay here to have these damned emotions stirring inside her. Her barrier shifted.

"Planes run all day long. I'm—" He started coughing again.

EZ rolled his eyes.

Lucky curled her lips at EZ and heard herself say to Doc, "Maybe just for lunch." Oh damn! She hadn't meant that, had no intention of staying, but he'd caught her off guard. Or was it EZ's look that had her agreeing? The urge to one-up him was so strong, she'd agreed to waste more time here. Damn him.

"Great," Doc said, chuckling.

She caught the grin on EZ's lips and cursed to herself. If the old man hadn't looked at her like that to begin with, she could have refused his offer. Now here she was staying for lunch when all she wanted to do was get away from Funland and from EZ. Well, at least she'd have Doc as a buffer between herself and the fool. "Let me first call to make sure I can get a later flight."

"Good idea," Doc said, smiling.

She phoned the airline, managing to inquire coherently, which seemed an impossibility since EZ glared at her all the while. Never good at lying, she thought of trying to say she couldn't switch flights, but it never would have worked anyway when she looked at Doc. "All set," she heard herself say.

He smiled.

EZ groaned.

Lucky went outside to tell the driver to take a break for a few hours. She offered to pay for his lunch and the extra hours he'd have to wait, then headed back inside the gingerbread house. As she came near, she heard EZ's voice at the same time Doc was trying to say something. She tapped lightly at the door and opened it.

Silence met her with the two men smiling in her direction.

The phoniest smiles she'd ever seen—and living in Vegas—

she'd seen some doozies.

* * *

EZ leaned back in the red vinyl kitchen chair of his trailer, propped his feet on the seat of the empty chair next to him and watched. Lucky Santanelli was a hell of a show to watch. Vegas must be in her blood, he thought as she leaned back her head and laughed.

Of all accounts she was exactly like her old man in business, but she must have a gene or two from her mother. He could remember seeing pictures of her mother in show costumes. Funny how certain images stuck in a person's brain. He had to be about ten when he had seen them in Lucky's suitcase once when she had come here as a kid.

Doc had her in stitches through the entire meal while bile flooded EZ's gut, preventing him from eating a bite. And he loved leftover corned beef. He had to like leftovers since he ate plenty of them.

"You know, girl, that suit of yours is beginning to smell like the bottom of EZ's closet," Doc said, then chuckled.

Lucky's face reddened. Hm, the woman of steel does have some feelings. Apparently Doc had embarrassed her, broken through part of her facade—making her seem human. Before EZ could revel in the enjoyment of her discomfort, she lifted her arm to her nose.

"Oh, God, Doc. You're right on that one. I smell like the marshes." She joined the old man in a chuckle while the bile made its way up EZ's throat.

"Don't you have nothin' this lady can change into, boy? She's got to be uncomfortable in damp silk."

She reached over and touched Doc's hand. "Thanks for your concern, but I'll be leaving shortly." She squeezed his hand. With a laugh, she said, "I'll buy a new outfit at the airport. I can't believe you recognized silk. You're a real doll."

She turned toward EZ and smiled. It wasn't a "come hither" smile or a friend teasing one another-type smile. Nope, it was a this-old-man-can-even-recognize-silk-type smile and you, you jerk, couldn't.

EZ let his feet fall to the floor with a thud, pushed away from the table and headed to the kitchen cabinets. Somewhere in this trailer had to be a bottle of Maalox tablets. As he rifled through the drawers and cabinets, he listened to them make small talk, chuckle, all out laugh, but what annoyed him most was the fact that each time he looked around—she was watching *him*. Damn.

She must think he was a slob. He looked at the clothes covered furniture, the countertops filled with stuff, and the sink, hell, who had time to wash dishes when they had to run an amusement park? Well, okay, he wasn't the neatest guy on the block, but he had other more important things on his mind. Like Funland.

Finding something in this trailer wasn't important, he'd buy himself some new Maalox or whatever else he couldn't find. As he went to shut the cabinet, a pile of unopened mail fell to the countertop. Behind stood a bottle of Maalox tablets. Hopefully it hadn't expired years ago. He took it down, snapped open the top and poured out a handful without checking the date. Lucky watched him. He shoved back half and chewed up the rest.

Why the hell did he care if she watched him anyway?

She was merely his target for revenge—his hope for Funland, his hope for his old man.

"You gonna find something for her to change into?" Doc asked as he turned toward EZ.

"Haven't had the chance to look yet," he managed through the chalky lemon mouthful.

Damn the woman again, he thought, when she grinned.

"I'll be fine," she said.

"Shame. That's what it is. How'd you get yourself all wet anyway?" Doc leaned over and rubbed a hand across her sleeve.

EZ took two more tablets, chewed and swallowed as he waited for her answer. He'd hoped Doc wouldn't bring it up, but well, that was hoping a lot where the nosy old coot was concerned. "She fell into the water—"

Doc furrowed his brow at EZ. The look had his heart momentarily stop. The old man had power in his pale eyes. EZ felt about five years old.

"No one falls into the ocean from shore," Doc said.

She pushed away from the table and stood. "I...someone looked as if they needed saving. So, I jumped in—"

"And ruined your pretty suit." Doc's eyes softened. He gently touched at her arm.

She covered his hand. "I'll have my tailor do something with it. The man's a genius where fabric is concerned."

EZ leaned against the counter and shook his head. She looked him in the eye.

"He'd have that chipmunk suit air conditioned with tiny fans inside," she informed him.

He curled his lip. "You can keep your tailor's ideas to yourself, sweetheart."

Doc stood and walked toward him. EZ readied to duck if the old man pulled a punch. Instead he glared at EZ and said, "Mind your manners, boy. Ms. Santanelli is a guest here." He squinted at him. "You wouldn't have been swimming underwater like some fool fish again? Would you?"

Lucky looked from one man to the other. EZ suspected the way her gaze darted from side to side that she was confused. Well, Doc was the type to get away with anything he wanted to at his age. EZ smiled at him. "Don't you have a show starting in ten minutes? Wouldn't want to have to fire your ass, old man."

Doc looked at the clock above the stove. "Hellfire if I don't." He turned and took Lucky's hand. "Nice to meet you and don't rush off. Come see my show. You'll get a kick out of it. Out of the whole place," he said with such enthusiasm, she cringed. "Even get your fortune told by my friend."

She leaned forward. EZ thought she was about to kiss Doc's cheek, actually expected it, but she pulled away. That didn't surprise him.

Bitches were often cold-blooded.

"I'd love to, but you know I have to go. It was wonderful meeting you, Doc."

Doc stuck his hat on before he hurried out the door. EZ smiled to himself. The woman had the old man so flustered; he'd forgotten his manners. Poor old Doc! Bamboozled by a drop dead gorgeous woman whose face would sell a million copies of any magazine, which had her on the cover.

He, however, was not taken in by her looks.

"I wouldn't make my 'good-byes' too permanent if I was in your spike heels, sweetheart." He leaned onto his elbow, resting on the counter.

"My limo driver has waited long enough. Besides I'll miss the last non-stop to Vegas if I don't leave soon." She picked up her briefcase and pushed past him.

The trailer had always seemed roomy enough for a single guy when he stayed here. Heck, he'd never felt claustrophobic in it or missed the open spaces of his real house. But, right now, with her brushing her damp silk suit against his arm, he felt as if they were in one of The Great Handini's secret boxes that the magician used for his act.

And EZ didn't much like the feeling.

"Please talk to your father, have your lawyer at least look at my proposal and consider it."

It took a second, but he pulled his staring from her suit, blinked himself into reality and said, "Nope," when the only thing he desired right now would be to work directly with some gray-suited lawyer instead of her. That is if he intended to buy her out—which he didn't.

He couldn't let her off so easily.

She sucked in a deep breath and before she could let it out, he noticed how her breasts pushed against the damp fabric of her white blouse. Damn, they must be soft and round and—

Why the hell couldn't Rosario Santanelli have had a son instead of her?

"We've been through that, Lucky. I have no intention of buying you out. If I were you, sweetheart, I'd send the limo driver packing and…well, I'll look for something dry for you to change into—"

"No way."

"Then, you better have that lawyer look into what effect a foreclosure on one of your properties—Funland that is—will have on your personal finances."

She slammed her briefcase against the counter, jarring open an overfull cabinet. Papers, boxes, who knew what other kind of junk, sailed onto both of them.

"Christ!" She pushed at the litter as he reached to grab it. Their hands collided in a grasp. EZ watched the snowfall of mail as Lucky glared at him through it. For a second, the moment seemed like a scene from a romantic comedy. He had the urge to laugh. Then, her eyes widened. A frightening sight if he'd ever seen one. Anger was not an attractive emotion on Lucky Santanelli.

She yanked her hand free. "Get out of my way!" She

grabbed her briefcase, pushed whatever had fallen onto the counter right into the sink full of dirty dishes and turned toward the door. "You may want to reconsider tangling with me, Mr. Dalton."

Before he could remind her that only his old man was called by that name, she'd slammed the door behind her.

"Welcome to Funland, *partner*."

He leaned against the counter, watched the screen door swing on its hinges. He'd never tell her, he thought. Never would he let her know the truth about his father. A gutsy corporate ladder-climber like Lucky Santanelli would no doubt badger his father to buy her out.

No way in hell would EZ let that happen.

LUCKY IN LOVE

Lori Avocato

Chapter Four

Lucky threw her briefcase into the backseat of the limo as the driver, thank goodness, opened the door just in time. The poor man. He must think she's nuts. Well, right now she couldn't worry about that. Nuts? Sure, she might be. It wouldn't be the first time someone thought that about her anyway. She flopped into the seat and refused to look back to see if EZ was watching. Who cared anyway? The man was a jerk. A fool. A foolish jerk who couldn't run Funland if his life depended on it. Hell, he couldn't even keep a one-bedroom trailer in order. He'd have this place bankrupt before she got home to Vegas.

Bankrupt.

She couldn't deal with that. A mess. A pain. An embarrassment to say the least. Knew what it was like, she did, after watching Daddy go through it several times years ago. Several? At least three that she could remember. Probably repressed the others. Something she'd gotten very good at to keep her sanity. If he'd only left her alone to her life. Hell, she thought, he'd never even sent her a birthday card.

Even though he'd moved out on her mother and her when Lucky was a kid, Daddy'd managed to snare her into some of his business deals—the ones that were legit—despite the fact that he never came to see her, never even took her out for a stupid dinner. Why'd she do it? she wondered. Why'd she make any attempt to help him? With a shrug, she decided a kid never did get over that childish need to please a parent—even when they'd deserted her. Look how abused kids never wanted to rat on their parents to the authorities. Looking back on it all now, she wondered yet again why she, after becoming an intelligent adult, never refused, especially when Daddy had kept all their visits so secretive. That, she rationalized each time they met, was because of his "career" choice.

Hell, she really couldn't worry about their failed relationship anymore.

Bankruptcy was something else.

The driver started the engine, turned to see if anyone was coming and pulled out. When they passed under the exit of Funland, she yanked open her purse and pulled out her cell phone. A sense of relief after leaving the place should be flooding her right now, but it wasn't.

Through the tinted window, she watched the park sitting there like a wounded animal. Although, in her opinion, it needed a hell of a lot of work, the parking lot was about a third full. There was no accounting for taste in some people. Admittedly, her views of the park were colored by her past. She turned back toward the driver.

"Take me straight to the US Airways terminal," she said to the driver. "Oh, and thanks for your patience." She jabbed out a phone number as he nodded.

"We're only about a hundred twenty miles north of New York City. Barring any traffic backup, we should get you there in about two hours. No problem, ma'am."

There is too a problem, she thought, and his name is EZ Dalton. "Great. I'll need to make a few calls so, again, thanks." There was no time for chitchat with the driver. She needed to talk to Mark. Why didn't this limo have that window in between the front seat and back? Even if it did, though, she wouldn't have used it. Too impersonal. Too much like she was superior to the poor driver. Too much like Daddy used to be. Her foot tapped lightly on the floorboard as the dial tone sounded in her ear. A few beeps. A connection. A voice. Her foot tapped faster.

"Attorney Mark Braddon's office," Hilda said.

"Hi, Hild, it's Lucky. Is he in?"

"Yes he is, Lucky, but he's with a client. Shall I have him—"

"Interrupt him! I... sorry, Hilda. It's rather an emergency—"

"Oh, my. Are you all right? You're not hurt?"

She could see the older woman ready to dial 911 while yanking a pencil from the purple bun she always wore.

"No. No. I'm fine—physically." But this jerk of a guy I own property with has me mentally crazy. "It's business, but I'm in a limo headed for JFK Airport and I need to ask Mark something."

"I'll connect you. He's with Mr. Jackson from that new casino on the end of the strip. The man's a pest so I don't mind interrupting. Besides, Lucky, Attorney Braddon always has time for you."

She groaned out her, "Thanks." Hilda had to be doing arthritic cartwheels at the prospect of Lucky needing to talk to Mark. The woman had been his advocate for fixing Lucky up with him for the last four years. No chance. Still, he was her closest friend even if nothing sexual could ever come of it as far as she was concerned. No animal magnetism. He was too nice a guy for her anyway. Too Ivy League. Too white picket fence. The line crackled. She pulled out the antenna in time to hear him come on the line.

Besides, she could take care of herself. Didn't need a man.

"Lucky? What's wrong?" Mark asked.

She pushed the phone closer to her ear. "Oh, hey, Mark. I need some legal advice."

"You do?"

He stressed the words as if she'd gotten herself into some

kind of trouble. Mark had been asked to be one of Rosario's lawyers but he'd refused. He'd done his homework on her father, and her, too, no doubt. He never could hide his opinion of Daddy and believed the old adage that an apple doesn't fall far from a tree. His behavior always made her think Mark had a romantic interest in her. That and the way he'd acted. But he'd been one of the best in Vegas, and she sought out the best for her deals.

She knew it wasn't true about her doing business like her father, but everyone that knew her and her father must have thought it about them. Mark never let her forget it. Sure, he more than likely was trying to protect her reputation, but she could handle herself she'd always tell him. Still, he'd brought up her father on one too many occasions. Maybe that's why there was no animal magnetism.

"Look, I don't have much time to go on about this. I'm heading home now."

"The contracts all signed?"

She looked at the traffic piling up in front of the limo and hoped she'd make her flight. The farther away from Connecticut she got the better. "No."

"Now isn't that what I told you to do?"

He sounded like a schoolteacher questioning a student. She'd ignore his tone this time and not argue. "This jerk, who also happens to be the manager of Funland, and happens to be Dalton's son, won't sell."

"No problem. We'll drop the asking price down a few grand. He'd be a fool—"

"Is a fool. I dropped it already. He wouldn't bite. The stupid fool." Mark would crease his navy pinstriped trousers if he knew about her last-ditch offer.

"Then we'll go lower. You have to get rid of that place,

Lucky. You have too much going on here. By the way, I bought that condo unit for you outside of Vegas. You'll have no problems renting since it's so close to Nellis Air Force Base. Oh, and the deal for Hartwell went through."

"Great. Mark, I dropped the price to a ridiculous amount."

"How much?"

"Ridiculous." She shoved off her shoes and curled her toes. Slowly she rubbed her foot against the plush interior of the limo, watched a dusting of now dried sand fall off. Why hadn't she noticed how these shoes had been killing her feet? Too damned pissed about the whole thing to worry about her feet. "What matters is the guy is a jerk and has some vendetta against my father."

"Jesus. Is that guy still haunting you from the grave?"

She pulled upright ready to defend her father. Defend him? From Mark? He knew Daddy all too well. Besides, she really didn't care what anyone said about him and truth be told, it was usually true. "He was a powerful man, Mark. Guess he'll haunt me as long as I have any ties to him, his life. That's why I need to dump this Funland place. It's the last connection I have to him."

"That and the financial statement we have on it. I can't understand why an amusement park can't make it in that part of the country. It's so near those casinos that are racking in the bucks, on the coastline of Connecticut and only hours from New York City. What's the problem?"

"EZ."

"I'm not being easy. I'm being honest. Are you really all right, Lucky?"

Oh God, not *that* tone. Whenever Mark spoke to her like that, she knew he was playing his surrogate father roll. Why'd all the men in her life think she needed protecting? Hell, she showed them, over and over, by how well she did for herself—

all on her own. With a shiver, she thought of how if she'd married Mark years ago when he'd begged her to, she'd have gotten a father figure and husband all rolled into one.

She wanted a lover, though. Too many lonely nights. Damn. She shouldn't be thinking like this. That EZ Dalton had her all messed up.

"I am fine, Mark. Hold on." She sat upright and leaned forward. Red taillights greeted her like the Vegas strip running all the way down the lanes as far as she could see. "Damn." She leaned forward toward the driver. "Can you see how

far the traffic jam is?"

"Hm?" He turned toward her for a second. "Oh, sorry, ma'am. Wasn't sure if you were talking to me."

Lord, he could hear her entire conversation. Well, at least he couldn't hear her thoughts.

"We're approaching Westport, and I'm guessing there is an accident ahead. I can't see too far though."

"Great."

"Sorry, ma'am."

"It's not your fault." She lifted the phone to her ear. "Mark, we're stuck in traffic. I may miss the final flight out tonight."

"What was your last offer so I can draw up new papers?"

She hesitated, shut her eyes. EZ, feet propped on the desk, damn chocolate eyes grinning at her came into view. She blinked him away and said, "A penny."

For a second she thought she'd lost Mark. Then a near scream came across the country. "A *what?*"

"A goddamned penny, Mark. One cent and the guy turned me down."

"There's more to this than meets the eye."

She wanted to say, no kidding Sherlock, but her grudge wasn't against a good friend like Mark. She had too few to antagonize even one. "Look, he's furious with my father, doesn't want to let me off the hook. And, here's why I called, Mark. The place is in bad need of repair. He stinks as a manager and—" It was too hard to get the real issue out. If she said it, it would, or could be true. Mark would know, and she really didn't want to find out.

"You're legally responsible for your half, Lucky. If things are as bad as you say—"

"Of course they are!"

He hesitated.

She felt like a jerk. "Sorry, Mark—"

"Then he might be nearing foreclosure on the place. The lender will get a hold of it and...well, loss and liquidation usually go hand in hand."

She held the receiver away from her ear. It didn't matter what legal crap Mark went on about. She knew what the facts were. Funland could swallow up her assets if EZ had let it get that deep in the arrears. The ton of past-due bills came to mind. Damn him. "Mark, I'll talk to you when I get back—"

"I'd get this settled immediately, Lucky," was the last thing she heard before shoving the phone shut—and cutting off her only friend.

* * *

EZ walked around the side of the old stagecoach almost knocking over some kid who stood there screaming that he wanted the Rainman, Doc playing the part today, to make it rain. "Sorry," he managed although it must not have come out sincere enough by the looks of the kid's old man. Great. That'd be one way to end this farce of an amusement park. Piss off all the patrons. He forced a smile and kept walking.

He felt a fool after he'd waited nearly fifteen minutes for Lucky's damn limo to drive back into Funland. He thought for sure she'd head back after he'd refused her offer, then planted the seed of worry in her adorable brain. Worry? Nah, she wasn't the type. Adorable? Nah again. Too savvy. Too cold. Too gorgeous to be considered adorable. Adorable was for his kid sister, Chloe. Who, by the way, he reminded himself, was past due coming home from her visit with her boyfriend in New Orleans. EZ'd have to give her a call and a chunk of his mind. She could lend a hand here for the summer before going back to UCONN this fall. He wondered if she'd fit into the chipmunk suit.

His head hurt.

This was all way too much for a guy like him to deal with. He should be sitting in some plush Hartford office, feet propped on desk, waiting for some sexy secretary to bring him a cup of Joe. Yep. That's exactly where he should be instead of this place. He looked up in time to see Doc's arm vigorously shaking some cowbell. The audience anxiously waiting, and Doc shouting, "Let it raaaaaain!"

Water pelted EZ's head.

"For crying out loud!" He stepped to the side of the sprinklers hidden in the trees and shook his head. Oh, hell. Why shouldn't Doc's imaginary rain pour down on him? He deserved it. If he hadn't been so hell-bent on revenge, he'd have signed those fool papers, and his old man would own this entire place.

And EZ would be responsible for saving it for him.

And he knew he didn't have a clue of how to.

He walked under the sprinkler. Wet clothes were too good for him. He'd tried to take the easy way out, making Lucky have to deal with saving this place. All he wanted was her expertise and business experience and, if need be, some financial backing. He leaned against the tree beneath the sprinkler despite a group of nearby kids getting their jollies off of the sight and told himself she deserved the revenge. Look what her old man had pulled. Doc always said nothing was fair in life or love.

Since her old man was gone, she had to inherit the responsibility.

Just as EZ had to for his father. After all, what were families all about?

"Shower's not working?"

EZ swung around to the sound of a female voice. If it were any old guest, he'd have laughed and moved on to drier ground. But when he saw her, standing there in her still damp, wrinkled black silk suit, just outside the perimeter of the "rain," he remained rooted on the spot.

"Don't want to waste precious water."

Lucky eased to the side so as not to get wet herself. "At least that's a start for saving some money." She waved her hands around as if to encompass all of Funland. "You could use the extra cash around here."

Remaining in the water, he said, "Speaking of here, I see you've come to your senses about returning. Took you long enough." That got the rise he'd expected. Red complexions go quite well with raven hair, he told himself. His body warmed beneath the cold water. Damn. That wasn't the reaction he expected or wanted.

She remained near enough to hear, but far enough not to get wet. "One month. I'm giving you one month to get this place in the black. I want a signed statement that you'll buy me out for my original asking price at that time. No deal if you don't sign it."

"Just how am I supposed to accomplish that?"

"With a pen, you fool."

He lifted his head upward and let the water hit him square in the face.

She clucked her tongue.

"The black, smart-ass. How am I to get this place in the black in one month?"

"Oh." She gave a fake laugh. "Guess I failed to mention that I get managing control for that month—"

"Ha!"

"Fine. Then no deal. Take me to court—"

Lucky had to look away. There was something so sexy about a soaking wet, still clothed guy. Okay, so maybe he wasn't ugly as sin, but he sure wasn't making her life any easier..

Sucking in a deep breath, she admitted, hell, he wasn't ugly as anything. A family moved past, staring at Lucky and EZ who nodded toward them. The little boy yanked a small Dachshund along on a leash.

"Court? You'd like that wouldn't you. Something tells me you thrive on legal stuff. I'll bet you don't even own a pet."

"What the hell does that have to do with—?"

He looked her square in the eye. "You should get yourself a dog, Lucky. Like that little kid." He tilted his head toward the family. "It could loosen you up a bit. Have something to talk to and not be so cold." Before she could curse him out, he finished. "One month, you manage, I get final say on things and you pay off the back debt—"

"No way!"

He glared at her. "You'll get it back with interest when Funland shows a profit. I'll sign a contract stating as much."

"Ten percent interest."

"Crook."

Lucky's hackles raised. He could have called her anything else but that. The connotation always struck too close to home. Beneath the droplets of water he must have read her expression. Damn how she wished he hadn't noticed.

With a softened voice that bugged the hell out of her, he said, "Sorry. That was out of line. Write up what you want. Eight percent included—"

"Ten." Before the word came out, she wished she hadn't fallen for his baiting. "I'll have my lawyer fax over the papers."

"Sounds like we've got ourselves a deal."

The "rain" shut off as she turned on her heels and forced herself not to look at how he must look with that stupid shirt clinging to his chest.

* * *

EZ swiped his hand across his face. Drops of water splashed to the side. The woman was infuriating, he thought, as he watched her walk to the limousine and take out her briefcase. No luggage. Of course, she hadn't planned to stay.

Well, at least he got a commitment from her. That should help and if he'd done his homework right, her business savvy could be the only hope for Funland. He thought of the *People* magazine article that had been done on her a few years back. He smiled to himself, wondering what she'd thought of their calling her the "Don's" daughter. Of course, no one could prove her old man was embroiled in organized crime, but if a skunk smelled like a skunk as Doc always used to say, he sure as hell must be a skunk.

The reporter had touched on Lucky's business dealings, and her record wasn't anything to sneeze at. She'd managed to outsmart several male contenders for VP of Hartwell Holdings so EZ figured he could use her smarts for this place. He leaned against a giant mushroom and watched her walk toward the gingerbread house.

It irked him.

The sway of her hips in the stupid silk skirt, the legs that ran miles above the sinful spiked heels, and the wind, his beloved sea's comfort, snatched her dark hair about as if Methuselah were her nickname.

It wasn't only her physical presence, he noticed, although that was the major part that had his hormones buffeting him inside like the waves crashed onto the shore. Nope there was an air of authority, no, independence that settled around her like a cloud. Make that a halo. Lucky was a hell of a confident woman, like none he'd ever seen before.

Because he stood here noticing, it all irked the hell out of him.

"Then stop it, you fool." He pushed up, nodded toward a family of four heading into the Funhouse, and walked toward his office. Might as well get started on his precious month.

* * *

Lucky chose to ignore that EZ's hair, slicked down from the outside shower he'd just taken, made him look damned handsome in a rugged, devil-may-care sort of way, and walked toward the side of his office. His hair wasn't the only thing she didn't want to be drawn to. To fight, to ignore. How could cologne still be so strong after getting so wet?

Once inside she walked to the wall and, with a finger, gently straightened the photograph of the old roller coaster. "I need a place to stay that's close—"

"Trailer number seven's empty."

"A trailer. Perfect. Why am I not surprised?" His chair scraped the floor. She refused to turn. Reflected in the picture's glass, she could see him sit down, prop his feet. Typical EZ. "What number's yours?"

"Eight."

For a second she readied to protest, but that'd be exactly what he'd want. So, Lucky was learning the ropes where this jerk was concerned. Instead, she gave a perky, "Fine" and moved on to the next picture. It, too, needed straightening. Daddy, looking very young, and a man whom she guessed was Mr. Dalton although his face was covered in shadow stood with shovels poised for the photographer. It had to be the day of the initial groundbreaking ceremony.

That one, she left crooked.

"Where's the nearest mall? I need clothes and a rental car."

He chuckled. "You'll have to settle for either an expensive chic boutique, which I'm sure you could afford, or family department store, which you more than likely wouldn't set foot in. Seagrove is not mall territory. Small New England beach towns like this have some kind of ordinance for things like malls and movie theaters—"

"How the heck did an amusement park ever pass then?"

Reflected in the mirror, he shrugged. "Guess our fathers were smarter than the city fathers. Or," he said, leaning near, "*one* of our fathers managed some kind of crooked deal."

She wasn't going to get into a discussion about her father with him, ever. Because so much of her young life was spent defending him, or at least trying, she'd given up on that in her late teens. When the subject came up, Lucky had become rather an expert on avoidance. "I can live with a small boutique, but I'm not going to be marooned here—"

"I have an old car you can use—"

"I'd rather a rental."

"Then you'd rather have to find yourself a lift into New Haven cause I'm guessing that's the closet city with rental service. The car is my sister's. She'll use it when she commutes to college and that isn't until fall."

"You have a sister?" It hadn't been meant to sound as if that were an impossibly. Her nerves were pushed to their limits with the guy around. She shook her head and asked herself how she got into this mess, and more importantly, how she was going to live here an entire month.

"No, I was found all alone in a patch sugar coated mushrooms."

"I...it's that you hadn't mentioned a sister." Her neck was starting to hurt, facing away from him as the tendency to turn toward his voice had her keep shifting. What the hell. He wasn't going to scare her or make her neck hurt anymore than it already did. She turned. "I don't remember you mentioning having a sister or any other siblings."

His grin was the first thing that caught her attention. He'd made a joke and like a cat with a feather sticking out between its mouth, he was thoroughly enjoying himself.

"Actually, I didn't mention anything to you about my personal life. That, Ms. Santanelli, is why it is called 'personal.'"

"Bastard."

His feet slid off the desk as his laughter, annoyingly boisterous filled the small office. "Maybe. But take the frigin' car. You wouldn't be putting me out."

It was too hard to look at him and feel as if her guts were knotting up like some rope. "I wasn't concerned about putting you out although now that you mention it, that wouldn't be such a bad thing. In fact, to see you 'put out' as you say might bring a little laughter into my life." Lord knows I could use it. "I'll take the car, and I'll be long gone by fall."

"One could only hope."

She spun around, no longer caring how good he looked, how much he might make her warm inside, or how the light had a way of catching the sparkle in his eyes. "Look, buster, I'm here to help. *H, E, L, P.*"

"Is that *R, I, G, H, T*?

She pushed past his chair and sat across from him. Suddenly

her shoes pinched her feet again. Obviously his annoyance kept her from noticing that she must have blisters the size of lemons on her heels. "Yes, that is right." She shoved off her shoes.

"And here I thought a keen businesswoman like Lucky Santanelli was only here to save her own butt."

She leaned across the cluttered desk, ignoring the reams of paper that sailed to the floor. "That, you have right. My first concern is always saving my own butt—"

He bent further, looked her up and down. "Not a bad job I'd venture."

She refused to budge, as a matter of fact, she even pushed out her chest when she straightened her shoulders and ignored the sexual innuendo. "My second concern is not having my hard-earned investments touched by your inadequate running of this place since I've been cursed with inheriting it."

"Half of this place."

She curled her lips. "Believe me, Mr. Dalton, nothing would make me happier than to forget that I own half of Funland or one stupid mushroom. Unfortunately all my faculties are intact."

"So, where do we start, sweetheart?"

This time she stood, leaned so far over, "If you ever call me that again, I'll have to kill you."

"Okay, partner. Don't take a contract out on me."

She cursed at him then suddenly her stocking feet slipped on the linoleum floor. Catching herself in time, she landed face to face with him. His gaze caught on her chest as she ordered, "Don't *ever* refer to me like that again either," and let him have an eyeful.

EZ knew she was saying something; hell her voice couldn't sound anymore annoying or perturbed. But his attention landed on the way her blouse stretched across her breasts as she caught her balance.

The fabric, obviously dried by now, retained its silkiness, its ability to stretch over what had to be firm, pointed nipples. Oh God.

Why the hell did such a pain in the ass have to be blessed with a chest like that?

More importantly, why the hell was he cursed with noticing?

LUCKY IN LOVE

Lori Avocato

Chapter Five

Pungent salty air stung Lucky's nostrils as she walked down the cobblestone sidewalk. She'd driven here in the car EZ had leant her and used the directions he'd written out. When she looked around, she wished she were looking at Vegas high-rises instead of the quaint buildings surrounding her. Seagrove was what one might consider an adorable coastal town. Classic New England, she thought. Snowy white church steeples climbed above the maple trees lining the town green in the center of what consisted of four or five downtown streets.

Passerby's faces reflected their typical Yankee keep-to-yourself unfriendly attitudes. As far as she was concerned, that was fine. No way did she want any friendship with someone from around here since never in her life would she return.

Once in awhile someone would crack an attempt at a smile. Those she labeled as tourists. There had to be a huge amount of them around. These little beach towns attracted tourists most of the year, except maybe the winter months. She thought, though, it was a great place for Funland. In its heyday, she remembered hearing that Daddy and Mr. Dalton had made enough money when the weather was good so they could take off the winter months. If she wasn't mistaken, she remembered how Daddy said that was so he and Mr. Dalton could spend time with their families. Yeah, right.

Before she could find a clothing store, she noticed a man on the other side of the green. He seemed to be staring at her. Following her? Jesus. She thought she'd gotten over the old paranoia. One of Giacopetti's men? It wasn't long ago that she'd read how he was in financial ruin, and even after all this time, blamed her father.

Daddy was long gone, she told herself. No reason for any of his past "acquaintances" to go after her. After all, she had nothing left of his except Funland. She readied to shout out to the guy he could have the place, or at least her half, in a heartbeat, but before she could, two little boys ran up to him and jumped into his arms. A local. She shook her head and told herself that the past was long gone—forget it.

Across the street, mannequins stood dressed in sporty outfits in one shop's window. EZ had been right about there only being boutiques around. Well, she'd never been a clotheshorse, owning mostly tailor-made business suits. Now she would only need a few things for one month. It wasn't even worth sending home for what she'd need.

She looked down at her rumpled skirt and thought that a suit was not proper amusement park attire. Geez, even her style of dress was affected by being trapped here.

Actually, she'd been so busy these past few months, shopping hadn't been on her to-do list. This was kinda fun. Like a much-needed vacation, something she'd never allowed herself.

The atmosphere was quaint. The people standoffish, the way she'd prefer them to be. And by the smell of something cooking from the little bistro next to the candy shop, the food was going to be decent.

She crossed the street and headed toward the mannequins. A bell clanged as she opened the door to "Yolanda's Boutique." The sales clerks turned in unison, scrutinized her from head to toe and continued on with the customers they were waiting on. Lucky ignored the clerk's looks, knowing that she must appear like some bag lady. Elderly customers, expensively dressed, hair coifed to perfection and skin wrinkled as prunes couldn't take their eyes off her either. Locals.

Because no one rushed to help, she started to browse on her own. Expensive was an understatement. As she passed to her size, she caught a glimpse of herself in the mirror. Good Lord, no wonder the clerks snubbed her. Her suit looked like a wrinkled prune. And smelled like a rotten one.

"May I be of service?" asked a young girl coming from the backroom.

"Thanks. I need a few things for…as you can see, my suit has been ruined. My tailor will die." She had no idea why she added that last part. It wasn't like her to care what others thought. Being here was draining her sanity, her self. That, she blamed on EZ Dalton whether he was around or not.

"Dressy or casual?"

"What the hell would I need dressy—" She smiled to the confused looking girl. "Sorry. Casual. I'll need a few jeans, shorts, a jacket for nighttime if it gets cold around here—"

"You're not from here." It was more a statement than a question as if Lucky exuded outsider. Well, that was fine with her. No way did she want "in" around this snobby little town. All she wanted was to fill Funland with sucker tourists for the next month to get the hell out of her inheritance.

She mentally cursed her father yet again. Not one of the juicier curses, those she'd save for EZ, but a bad enough one her bodyguard had taught her nonetheless. Well, it was more an annoying one like how the hell did you get me into a mess again?

She refused to try on anything except the one pair of white shorts and nautical-styled red, white and blue shirt, which was befitting of the little seaside town. At least it felt good to get out of her suit. The other clothes she told the girl to package up and shoved her MasterCard toward the clerk. It was then her stomach reminded her that she should get a bowl of clam chowder before heading back. Food. She hadn't thought of how she'd need to feed herself now that she was staying in the stupid trailer.

Damn it. Cooking was never an interest or an ability she possessed. Even her mother had never attempted to teach Lucky to cook. Of course, Mama had been busy with her career and didn't teach Lucky much. Except, of course, how to fight off drooling men. Mama'd had her share when she did a show and Lucky'd been cursed with guys trying to jump her bones all throughout high school.

Until they found out whom her father was.

Because the name Rosario Santanelli was linked to organized crime, the boys often only made one attempt.

"Oh, my, Ms. *Santanelli*, not a common name," the clerk said.

Lucky leaned over the counter. "What? Something wrong with my credit card?"

The poor girl's hand shook. "No…er…I'm sorry. There is nothing wrong."

Recognized the name. Oh well, she must think Lucky was going to shoot her at pointblank ranger here in Yolanda's. The girl had been nice enough, nicer than the old coots so Lucky laughed. "No relation to that mobster. Roman? Was it? You know the one in Vegas."

The girl gave a weak, albeit relieved laugh. "Oh. Rosario, I believe. Yeah that was it. I once saw a show on PBS about the Mafia. He was…."

Lucky knew the kid was talking, but she tuned it out. She'd heard enough of that kind of crap to last a lifetime so she plastered on a smile and waited until the girl's lips stopped chattering before she tuned back in.

LUCKY IN LOVE

Lori Avocato

The clerk handed Lucky the shopping bags full of what she'd need for one month. "Enjoy your stay in Seagrove." Obviously because Lucky had reassured the poor kid she wouldn't whack her on the spot, she added, "Where abouts are you staying?"

None of your business held on the tip of her tongue. The kid couldn't be more than eighteen. A tender age. An age where peer pressure rules and ruins lives. An age Lucky wanted to forget. "Funland."

"Funland? You mean in one of the hotels off the service road from Funland?"

"Nope." She turned to go. "Thanks."

"You're welcome." The kid followed her to the door and opened it.

Lucky nodded to her.

"I didn't think there was anyplace to stay on the park's property."

"Trailer number eight," came out before she could think of how stupid she felt.

"I know they hire a lot of summer help, but wow. A woman like you working there. Imagine?"

Lucky leaned against the wall. The kid held the door open wearing a stupid look of interest on her pretty face. "No way am I working there…no way. Managing it. I own half—"

"With EZ?"

Lucky straightened. Seems that name did that to her.

"You know him?" Lucky asked.

Now she knew what swoon meant. The kid's eyes glassed over as if Lucky had mentioned either Tom Cruise, Ricky Martin or one of the Backstreet Boys.

"Everyone in Seagrove knows EZ Dalton. Well—" Her blush deepened. "Knows *of* him that is."

She should go. She should say goodbye and go get her clam chowder even if it wasn't dinnertime yet. She should but she looked at the kid. "So, why's that?"

"Oh, he's the cutest, most gorgeous, most eligible bachelor around."

Not what she cared to hear. "Well, bye."

Before she could shut the door, the kid added, "He's the smartest businessman in town, too."

She couldn't help it. Because the absurdity struck her, she let out a howl that had every passerby turn and stare. Controlling the urge to stick out her tongue, she instead turned toward the girl. "That park is a mess and near bankruptcy."

The kid looked scared. Lucky's businesslike tone must have done as much. "I...sorry. He is great. Mom owns this store and my uncle owns the bistro two doors down. Mr. Dalton's been on the Chamber of Commerce for several years."

Lucky's appetite for clam chowder deteriorated. No way did she want to strike up any conversation with someone who knew Dalton. "Well, everyone is entitled to their opinion. Thanks again.

"He is dreamy even it you don't think—"

"Yeah, he's a regular dreamboat." No need to be snide with a misguided teenager who must see EZ Dalton as some idol. Fool. Poor child.

"All the women in town think so."

Lucky paused. Why would she care what the women in town thought of him? She didn't. She could care less so she smiled and started to leave.

"He'd be married and out of contention if Maisie Lawlor had her way."

Lucky froze. What the hell was a Maisie Lawlor?

* * *

LUCKY IN LOVE

Lori Avocato

"What in tarnation are you doing?" Doc asked as he came up behind EZ.

"What does it look like? I'm cleaning out this trailer." He shoved a box full of junk at the old man. "Make yourself useful and take this to the Dumpster."

"I've got a Bingo game in five minutes."

EZ turned and glared at him. "Bingo my you know what. Poker game's more like it. Who you skinning alive today?"

"Zos and Handini, and that cute new lady who sells cotton candy by the Funhouse."

"Millie." EZ chuckled and shook his head. "Nothin' better to do with your money, you old fools?"

"We may be old, but we are not fools," Zos said as he rounded trailer number seven.

"Hey, Zos. You letting this old coot beat you—"

"Zos's a natural," Doc said, frowning. He ran a gnarled hand across his mustache. "I'd swear he could play in the big league."

"Don't you get any ideas like taking him to Foxwoods or any of the other casinos off property. It's one thing to have your group of senior citizens gambling for fun, but going to one of those places, you guys could loose your shirts." He pushed a box at Doc. "Take this on your way out."

"Someone moving in?" Zos asked.

EZ looked at the old man. Years hadn't wrinkled his skin like Doc's. EZ wondered if Zos hadn't spent much time in the sun. He couldn't remember where he'd come from before hiring him. Wasn't it Maine or some other New England state? Wherever, they must have good water because he looked years younger than Doc, although EZ remembered from his job application that they were close in age.

There was no detectable local accent, more a New York

one or something more ethnic. He'd hired him, at Doc's insistence as usual, as the fortuneteller after old man Rodsinsky was diagnosed with prostate cancer. He'd been doing fine but retired to his daughter's farm up in Vermont. Zos, The Great Zosimoff, fit the role and even the nationality. Half Gypsy didn't hurt for convincing the guests to cough up two bucks to learn what their futures held.

EZ smiled to himself. Most of Doc's elderly employee recommendations turned out to be duds. But Zos and Millie were damn fine workers. Who knew how long they'd be around though?

Doc grabbed the box. "So, you didn't say who our new neighbor was going to be?"

EZ's gut tightened. Thank goodness he hadn't eaten supper yet. "She's only temporary."

"Hm," Doc grinned. "Someone we might like?" He winked at Zos.

EZ groaned. "Only if you like 'The Ice Princess.' No, make that 'The Iceberg Businesswoman of the Year."

Doc and Zos gave him confused looks. No, wait. He'd have to say Zos's bordered on anger at first. Then he quickly changed to confused. Hell, EZ couldn't figure out Doc let alone this other old geezer.

"Sorry. Lucky Santanelli is moving in—"

Doc grinned, looked at Zos who'd gone to expressionless.

"Oh hell, didn't your mother ever tell you not to judge a book by its cover, old man? She's a witch in satin—"

"Silk," Doc interrupted.

"Shut up and go play your cards. I've got to get this place cleaned out so she doesn't sue my ass off if she falls on the garbage that gunfighter with the lisp left after moving out of here last month." He watched the old men leave and wondered if he'd ever be able to get this place into the black with the turnover of employees that he had.

Zos paused as Doc shoved the box at him. "Doesn't sound much like your type of woman, EZ."

He laughed. "No. She's not my type. But, she does come highly recommended where her brains are concerned. That's the only part of her fit and trim body I'm interested in, and, damn it all, I'm not opposed to using that brain of hers to help out Funland."

Doc whistled. "So, you noticed her body—"

EZ threw a piece of old carpet at him, landing it smack in the old man's gut. He let out a howl of laughter and turned, scurrying out of the trailer compound with Zos on his heels. "Old coots!" EZ yelled.

"Nice way to talk to senior citizens."

He swung around to see her. Lucky, standing with several shopping bags in hand. She'd changed her clothes was his first thought. "Almost didn't recognize you without your stinking wet suit on." But damn if those shorts didn't show more leg than a man had a right to see.

She shoved a bag at him. "Didn't your mother ever teach you to help a lady?"

He took the bag, turned. "She taught me all right and when I see I lady, I oblige."

Lucky opened her mouth, and shut it just as fast. She'd be damned if she'd stoop as low as him with his comments. Lady indeed. She was more a lady than he was a gentleman. As he walked ahead of her into what was now to be her "home," she ignored worn jeans hugging his butt and told herself she couldn't take away the fact that he was a man, a real man.

Damn him.

At least he held the door for her. She stepped up the last

step and paused. She'd expected a carbon copy of EZ's trailer, and had even prepared herself to be living as if camping.. Instead, she stood and thought her little trailer nice, cute in a homey sort of way. And it was, thank goodness, clean.

A tiny table sat opposite the sink that sparkled as best it could, considering its obvious age. On both side of the sink cabinets hung polished and lemon scented. Blue curtains with little white dots swayed in the gentle breeze since someone, EZ no doubt, had opened the window.

Behind the table was a living room, make that a living area more or less with a brown plaid sofa, matching chair and a rocker that looked as if it had been squeezed in between.

Placed at the center of the room, was a photograph of the old roller coaster—the one she'd been admiring in his office this morning. Interesting. A weak point to use against him?

"Well, you gonna stand there all night?" he asked.

His comment yanked her from staring. "No." She walked in, set her bags on a red vinyl chair. A matching one sat opposite the table. Windex, ammonia, and even some cinnamon scent filled the air. She looked at the stove to see a small pan, bubbling brown liquid.

"Who's been cooking in my trailer?"

"No one, Goldilocks. It's cinnamon in water. Takes the damp smell out of the air, not to mention cigars that the cowboy living here before you stunk the place up with."

"You...you wanted it to smell better for me?" She wasn't sure how that made her feel. Annoyed was what she wanted to go with, but not many people did little "cinnamon" gestures for her in her life. So, it was difficult to muster up any annoyance. No way would she feel touched by anything *he* did though.

"No, I didn't want to hear you complaining about the stink. I did it for me."

LUCKY IN LOVE

Lori Avocato

She sucked in a breath, remembered apple pies but didn't know why, and grabbed onto the red vinyl chair.

Damn him for dredging up memories.

Memories should stay locked away in one's head.

The present, the future were all that mattered to her. She didn't have the time or the inclination to remember—anything.

"That sounds about right for you." She grabbed the bag from him and looked toward the door. "Good night."

He turned to leave. "Office opens at eight. I'm guessing someone like you doesn't waste much time on beauty sleep—" Before he finished, he knew he'd made a major "faux pas." Her eyes burned like two giant bronze gems with fire behind, waiting to burn their heat across his face. "Look, I—"

"I don't give a damn about what you or anyone, for that matter, thinks I look like—"

"I knew you'd take it the wrong way."

"At least, then, we've got each other's number."

"Well this time you've dialed wrong, lady."

She shrugged. "I care less about what you think I look like than what you think my 'number is.' She scrapped the chair across the floor, sat and once again looked at the door. "I've had a rotten day. Just go. What the hell difference does it make what you think about me or I of you anyway? It's all business for us."

He came forward instead of leaving. Damn it.

"No one has to tell you that you're beautiful. You've got eyes. I meant a businesswoman of your caliber must not waste time sleeping but gets up at the crack of dawn to work. That's all."

Because he'd confused the hell out of her, she could only stare. But it didn't take long to pull her thoughts from his height towering over her chair, his hair mussed to perfection or the stubble of beard that had to have grown since this morning.

"God, have I only been here one day?"

He looked at her, a smile cracking at the corners of his lips. "It's been a long one for me, too. Not that you would care—"

"You're right." She'd managed to look past him at the cinnamon bubbling. "I don't care. I'm too tired to care. So tired that I hadn't realized how hungry I am. Leave so I can fix myself something."

He reached over and tilted one bag. "I wasn't certain, but I didn't think Yolanda sold groceries at her boutique."

She leaned back, shut her eyes and cursed him out in her mind. No energy to curse aloud.

"I have a pot of stew on my stove. You're welcome to come over—"

"Can't you do take out?"

He chuckled, shook his head. "You can take the lady out of Vegas, but you can't take the Vegas lifestyle out of—"

"How would you know what my lifestyle has been?"

"Only guessing." He came forward, lifted her hand.

She pulled away.

He grabbed it again.

"Don't touch me!"

"I'm not touching you in any special way. Relax. I'm just getting a closer look at your nails." He lifted her hand closer to his view.

She pulled free.

"I knew you wouldn't have working hands, or better yet, make that cooking hands."

With her hands dropped down to her sides as if she needed to hide them from his stupid truth, she said, "What the hell are cooking hands?"

"All I'm saying is, I'd bet my entire pot of stew that you are no female Emeril Lagasse."

She looked at him. Raised her hands to rest on the table. The nerve. The stinking nerve. Even though it was the truth, this guy had no right to assume she couldn't cook. It only made her wonder what else he thought about her.

And that's what made her blood give the boiling cinnamon a run for its money.

"Go eat your stew."

He turned to leave. "Fine, but I thought you were hungry?"

Her insides grumbled. Or maybe that was a cry for substance. "I'll go get something to eat in a nearby restaurant." Except for the fact that she didn't know of any.

"Enjoy." He reached for the door.

She knew he paused, could see it as his hand grasped the knob and held. He was waiting to continue his incessant bantering, annoying her to no end. Well, she'd sit here in silence and not give him the satisfaction. Her stomach knotted itself into a starving ball.

She bit her lip.

He lifted his hand from the knob, ran it through his hair, and grabbed the knob again.

Maybe the tiny drips of her blood as she bit harder would satisfy her until he left.

He coughed.

Fake, she thought. "And you enjoy that stew, EZ."

The door opened, he stuck a foot out. "Damnedest stubborn woman I've ever met."

As the door shut, she leaned against the chair and let out a laugh that came from so deep inside, it bypassed her balled up stomach.

* * *

Would he ever learn his lesson?

EZ stood outside her stupid trailer, smelling the damned

cinnamon that he now hoped would burn, and reminded himself that he'd probably never would learn.

How many times had he given of himself and gotten kicked in the teeth?

Well, he wasn't about to let Ms. Vegas get to him. He had to clean out the place for whoever would be moving in next anyway. She was only temporary. He looked up to the stars and muttered, "Thank you for that."

Seagulls settled along the fence behind Lucky's trailer. Oh hell. Was he going to have to think of it as hers? She'd ruined his day, was damn ungrateful for the hours of slavery he'd spent to fix up the place and most importantly, she ruined his meal by the smell of it.

Normally he'd take the time to watch the birds, the sun sinking down at the horizon and inhale the sea's scent, but right now he needed to get inside to salvage his dinner.

She could starve for all he cared.

Once inside, EZ yanked the pot off the stove, shoved off the burner. It would only take a few minutes and a big spoon to scrape off the salvageable top of the stew. Damn the woman.

Damn all women as a matter of fact, he thought.

They'd brought him nothing but trouble, more dependence on him. Dependence. He'd have a life of it. That, he decided, was one thing he didn't need from anyone. If Maisie called with one more problems for him to solve, he'd hang up on the woman. That wasn't like him, but he'd reached his limit these last few months.

A drastic change in lifestyle seemed to do that to him.

He looked out the window to see trailer number eight. Thank goodness the windows didn't line up. Still, he could picture her flopped down in the brown plaid couch—and his appetite disappeared. Burnt or not he couldn't eat a thing, thinking of Lucky Santanelli.

He did, however, decide he'd satisfy his hunger for business knowledge by picking her brain bright and early tomorrow.

Seems they both were going to bed hungry tonight.

But he'd console himself in the sweet joy of revenge.

LUCKY IN LOVE

Lori Avocato

Chapter Six

Her stomach hurt. God, she hoped she wasn't coming down with something. Flu. Bugs of all kinds. Those ailments that doctors blame on viruses when they had no clue as to what the heck was wrong with a body.

Come to think of it, every muscle above her toenails hurt. With a groan akin to a wounded animal—and she was certain her mouth was still closed—Lucky shifted her position wherever she was. Her eyes were still shut and didn't want to open.

Fine. She'd give in and lie here exactly like this.

Lying. That's right. She was lying down on something scratchy. That much she knew. Woolen fabric. Yeah, she was on some scratchy woolen fabric. When she rubbed her eyes, she decided they wanted to remain shut a bit longer.

Sleep. She'd been asleep by the feel of it. Of course, she had to be waking up because the fool sun was heating her eyelids and an annoying sound came from what had to be an open window. Where was her silken eye shield that she normally wore to sleep so Jetta, her maid, wouldn't disturb her on weekends?

Birds.

She'd never heard birds from her penthouse before. Damn not just any birds. Seagulls, she guessed. It was then it dawned on her that she was in Seagrove, living in a trailer. Probably twenty feet long. Probably six feet away from trailer number seven. The worse place in the compound she could be.

One eyelid peeked open. Yep. Early tag sale décor right out

of the 70s. Trailer number eight. Neighbor to the hospitable EZ Dalton. That one would have made her chuckle, but it'd hurt too much. With another one of those wounded animal sounds, she pushed up into a sitting position, leaned back and shut her eyes. Should have done that first, but she craved a second of maybe being wrong, of hoping she was wrong.

Maybe she was in her penthouse that overlooked the brilliant lights of Vegas. Maybe that scratchy material was a woolen afghan that Jetta had accidentally left on Lucky's bed. She opened her eyes.

Maybe she was having a nightmare and there was no such thing as Funland.

The roller coaster photo caught her gaze. Pushing off the edge of the sofa with a groan, she walked to the picture, reached out. She ran her finger along the frame. Daddy.

She blew out a breath, pulled her finger away and told herself that she would not think about him. If she did, she might run the risk of being haunted by his ghost especially after he'd heard the things she was *really* thinking. Ghosts? They weren't real...

Funland was real.

Possibly losing a large chunk of her capital was real.

Starving was real.

She looked at the kitchen area to see the pan of now settled cinnamon in water and remembered EZ here last night and that she'd been so annoyed with him that she had laid down on the couch for a few minutes to cool off her temper.

Obviously she'd fallen asleep. Now she had no food. Not even a teaspoon of coffee to burn her insides. God how she'd love a steaming hot cup of black coffee with one packet of Equal. She'd given up sugar years ago, but still needed that sweet taste to knock the edge off the bitter.

"This isn't getting me anywhere." Not knowing what time it was, she looked at her watch. Jesus. EZ would think he was wrong about her being an early riser. Normally she was, but with the day she'd had yesterday, she hadn't slept this late since age thirteen. Anyway, she loved the idea of EZ being wrong about something, anything. No, make that everything. She laughed.

It was a tossup as to what she wanted first. A shower-or food-of any sorts. She looked down at her wrinkled new shorts; top bunched up in creases and knew her hair had to be tangled into a nest. Somewhere in the Yolanda's Boutique shopping bags was new makeup and toiletries. She'd use the grapefruit shampoo and inhale really deeply. Maybe that'd curb her hunger until she looked human again.

Speaking of humans, she wondered why EZ hadn't strolled, and that's exactly the way he walked, over to wake her earlier. Surely he was dying to have her get to work and save his sorry ass from bankruptcy.

"Correction," she said, chuckling, "tight ass."

With that, she opted for the shower and to get to work as soon as possible.

Maybe then she could get the hell out of Dodge in less than a month.

One could only hope.

* * *

EZ looked out the office window for the hundredth annoying time. Damn. Where the hell was she? Not that he was anxious to see Lucky in those sinfully short shorts. He leaned back, took a deep breath. Yeah, right. He'd only imagined, hoped, they were sinfully short. With a squint to jog his memory, he thought that her mother was some kind of dancer. That was it. She was a showgirl. Obviously Lucky had inherited her legs.

Legs?

"Cripes." He pushed himself forward and decided if he kept thinking of her that way, he'd never get this place out of the red. He had to do it and soon. His old man wouldn't be around forever.

"You eat yet?" Doc asked.

EZ swung around to see the old man, box of donuts in hand coming in the door. "Didn't your doctor tell you to cut down on sugar?"

He set the box on the desk, grabbed a cream-filled donut. "Did he? I don't remember any such foolishness. But," he switched the cream-filled with a plain one, "if you say so, I won't have the sugar coated." He gave a smile to EZ, then champed a huge bite.

EZ shook his head. "Coffee's nearly gone." But he stood and poured Doc what was left. After he turned away, he noticed the old man's reflection in one of the pictures. Did he really forget about what Doctor Hattley had said? Knowing Doc, he could be lying to eat whatever the hell he chose. Still, it bothered EZ. He'd seen too much evidence of forgetfulness in the old man lately. The last two months that is. He'd have to watch out for more.

"Thanks, son. You drink far too much coffee you know?"

EZ shrugged. If only Doc knew how much EZ planned to consume over the next month. If he'd been a drinking man, he'd be a candidate for AA before Ms. Santanelli limoed her way out of Seagrove. This way he'd only risk an ulcer or two along with nerves wound like a spring about to sprung—damn if he'd switch to decaf because of her though.

Doc took a sip of coffee, wiggled his nose. "Coulda added at least one spoonful of sugar."

"No, I couldn't. You feeling alright, Doc?" EZ took a sip of his now cold coffee, winced but didn't feel like getting up to stick the mug in the microwave.

Doc shoved the rest of the donut into his mouth as if he feared EZ would grab it out of his hand. "Why?"

Doc was too proud a man to admit forgetting things lately and no way would EZ insult him. He cared too much for the old geezer. "No reason." Settling back in his chair, he propped his feet on the desk. Several papers fell to the floor. He left them.

"Then why the hell the question?" He stood, wiped his hands on his suede vest and bent to look out the window. "Now ain't that a sight for my old eyes?"

EZ didn't want to move. The chair rocked slightly backward, lending itself to the most comfortable position. He loved this chair. Could remember sitting in it, this very comfortable position as a kid when his old man ran things around here. Doc kept gawking out the window. Hell, one of the workers must be prancing around with their costume on backwards or something. It wasn't as if Doc hadn't seen that before with the turnover of employees.

Doc whistled.

That got EZ to at least lean far enough over to see what the hell held the old man's interest. As he did, the door opened.

Doc whistled again.

Lucky walked in and gave him one hell of a smile.

EZ's feet, crossed in comfort, slid on a pile of papers along the desk. He reached out to catch himself, but landed on the floor—his favorite chair left empty, rocking in mockery at him.

Lucky reached over, grabbed a donut. "May I?"

Doc smiled, looked at EZ and shook his head. "Help yourself, Sugar."

Before he'd finished his sentence, Lucky'd nearly

swallowed the Boston cream whole. She licked the chocolate from her fingers.

"Make her some coffee, son."

EZ made a sound a kin to a growl. He'd managed to get himself off the floor while the two of them ignored him. What if he'd broken something? "I couldn't find the pencil I'd dropped," he lied, feeling more foolish than when he fell.

Lucky had to turn to avoid EZ seeing her face. No way could she hide her smile that wanted to be an all-out laugh. Over her shoulder, she watched him.

EZ grabbed his rocking chair and sat back down. "We have work to do. And so do you, old man."

Doc headed toward the door. "Make her some coffee." He yanked open the door, looked square at EZ. "Falling for a woman this early in the morning." He broke out into hysterics. "Shame on you."

EZ threw a wadded up sheet of paper at Doc.

"That's one way to get rid of all your bills," Lucky said, turning back. "However, I suggest you pay them." With that, she sat down. Sugary food made her lightheaded almost gave her a buzz like some people get from caffeine. Since she avoided sugar, her tolerance for it was low. But she'd never eaten something so wonderful before or been so hungry.

"With that kind of remark, there went your chance of having coffee." He leaned over, grabbed some papers off the floor."

"First thing I suggest is change your filing system."

"Ha. Ha." He shoved the papers into a pile. "You want coffee?"

She shut her eyes a second, imagined, no, at this point, craved, the nutty taste. "Um. Please."

"Pot's over there."

Her eyelids flew open.

He motioned with his head. "Grinds are in the can."

He sat there like some fisherman, baiting his hook. Baiting her. Baiting her temper. Well, she wasn't going to fall for that, Mr. Smarty. Nope. She'd make her own coffee and summon every ounce of businesslike qualities she had. And, she had a million of them. More than he had bait, she told herself. "Thanks. I *do* prefer my own."

She walked to the shelf, pulled the electric chord out of the socket and bit her tongue. He was seething. She could almost hear the steam coming out of him. Her life had done a nose-dive since yesterday, but she'd learned at an early age to be a fighter, a survivor.

And she'd damn well survive EZ Dalton.

* * *

EZ watched her making her own coffee and hoped it turned out as bitter as a pill accidentally bit into before swallowing. When she noticed him, he looked at the clock behind his desk on purpose. Nearly ten. "So, you think you're on vacation here?"

She shoved the electric chord into the socket. "My idea of a vacation is skiing in Aspen or sailing in the Caribbean. Not stuck in prison."

He paused, glared at her. "And you are late because?"

"Because I didn't pack an alarm clock, foolishly thinking I wouldn't need one for a day trip."

He headed to his desk, sat and swung around to face her. "Hm. Well, maybe next time you'll come more prepared."

She looked him in the eyes with a stare that could fall a lesser man. He smiled.

"There will never be a next time. Come thirty days, or less, from now, I'll be winging my way back to Vegas. Thank God."

"I'm holding you to your month promise—maybe more if

you keep coming to work so late." He got a chuckle out of the way she rested her hands on her hips. Obviously she thought that emphasized her point. He wondered if she positioned herself like that in the boardroom.

She combed a hand through her hair. Another gesture not befitting her. Too casual. Too human. Maybe her little stay here had unnerved the woman of steel.

"I'll be here at eight tomorrow come hell or—"

"Yeah. Yeah. I know the cliché. Pour me a cup of that. Smells ready." He nodded toward the coffeepot.

Her eyes narrowed into slits. Barely could see the color any longer. "I'm guessing you don't serve coffee—"

With her head raised high, she walked to him, sat on the edge of the desk and looked down.

He figured she liked the top position.

Goddamnit but that thought had him getting hard.

"Let's get things straight. I don't want to be here. I don't want even one chipped frosted mushroom from here—"

"They're scheduled to be re-frosted in two weeks."

She ignored him as if he hadn't spoken and continued, "I'd like nothing more than to be in my downtown Vegas office right now closing a multi-million dollar deal. I thrive on that kind of stuff."

"And donuts, by the way you devoured the poor Boston cream down."

"You can make all your wise-ass remarks, Dalton, but I don't serve coffee to you or anyone else. Nor will I cook, pickup the crap all over this desk, and, I don't answer the phone. I have an assistant who does all that for me. A male one."

She leaned so near he could smell grapefruit. The acrid scent jolted him. She couldn't have gone to the grocery store yet since he hadn't given her directions. He inhaled again. It was better than eating breakfast.

"Clean up this mess or I can't work, Dalton. If I can't work, Funland goes down the tubes—"

"Along with your multi-million dollar deals."

"Maybe." She jumped off the desk. "Maybe not. I at least know I can wheel and deal—successfully—until my assets are restored." She walked to the window, yanked apart the curtains. "By the looks of this place, you, on the other hand, Dalton, couldn't deal your way out of a fixed poker game."

"Don't be too sure of that." He looked at the desk. Okay, he'd give her the part about the mess. He yanked open the top drawer and with one swift motion scraped all the papers and bills into it. "Clean."

She shook her head, wondered if she'd successfully hid her fears. Oh she could act the cool collected female, but worries about her holdings she took very seriously. But she would be damned to hell—most likely joining Daddy—if she'd let on to Dalton. "If that's the way you want it." She shrugged, walked to the shelf, took the coffeepot and filled a cup.

He hoped it was clean. Suddenly he felt as if he was a slob. Okay, he was close to being one, and damn it all if he didn't feel like picking up a few things since Ms. Good Housekeeping had her eagle eyes on his office.

Lucky came over, sat in the chair opposite him. "I'll need the debits and credits for the last...when's the last time Funland was in the black?"

He took a deep breath. Wanted to curse his old man, but loved him too much. Besides, his condition contributed partly to the downfall of the park. At least EZ wanted to think it did. "I've only been running it for two months."

Her eyes narrowed as if she didn't believe him.

Nonchalantly, he straightened the phone and can of pencils

on the desk. "You can check the records—"

"Why two months?"

None of your damned business, lady. No way would he air his family's dirty laundry out for her. "It's...what the hell difference does it make?"

"Give me the files for the last six months. Also, you make a stack of past due bills. Latest to the earliest. I want a list of employees, their hire dates, benefits etcetera."

"You want those etceteras in order latest to earliest?"

She looked at him. "And, I want *that* chair."

He looked down like a kid about to be forced to share his prize Tonka toy. "No way in hell—"

"Way in hell, Dalton. I can't work from this angle." She stood, walked around the desk.

"Why? Is that your bad side?" Not that he'd noticed any bad side, he thought, then wished he hadn't noticed anything about her except her brain like he'd lied to Doc about.

She pushed at him. "Move before I spill this coffee on you. Accidentally."

He stepped to the side.

"And, Dalton, get this straight. I don't have a bad side."

The phone ran as he readied to open his mouth. "Saved by the proverbial bell."

"Yeah, Dalton...EZ here." He looked at Lucky.

She was smiling.

"Damn it. What's wrong with her?" He turned away from Lucky. "Hm. No. No problem. Tell her to drink plenty of fluids. And to call a doctor. Maybe she needs some pills, antibiotics or some quick cure. Sure. Bye." He hung up.

"Well?"

"Well what?"

"Who was that?"

LUCKY IN LOVE

Lori Avocato

"I thought you don't do phones." He sat on the edge of the desk, taking her position of authority, but when he looked down into her face—he figured the desktop didn't do a damn thing for him authority wise.

"I don't *answer* them. Sounds like someone is sick. Who?"

"What if I told you it's my date for tonight?"

"I'd say she was one hell of a lucky gal.

"Oh?" He leaned near, grinned at her.

"—for lucking out with whatever bug attacked her."

He had to laugh. The sound reverberated in the small office. He'd give her credit for a sassy tongue. "Okay. Okay. Santanelli, one. Dalton, zero." He reached over and lifted a strand of hair from her shoulder, fingered it. Inhaled. There was the grapefruit scent. Sassy. Fresh. Appropriate.

She reached up to push his hand away, but when she touched his, she hesitated. Hm, seems Ms. Lucky noticed the chemistry, too. Good.

He'd hate like hell for it to be one-sided.

He let go of her hair but grabbed her hand. "But, Ms. Santanelli, don't expect that score to last for long." With that he dropped her hand, pushed off the desk and walked to get himself a cup of coffee.

Normally he used cream and sugar, but right now, with his insides shifting gears from touching her perfectly-moisturized-with-the-most-expensive-lotion-skin, he figured he'd drink it black.

Anything to take his mind off that luscious skin.

LUCKY IN LOVE

Lori Avocato

Chapter Seven

Lucky swallowed the rest of her coffee. Cold now, damn it, but she didn't much care. It and the donut took the edge off her hunger. She had to get to the grocery store soon, but the fact that she didn't know a damn thing about cooking kept her from hurrying out of EZ's office. That and the fact that she wanted to get to work as soon as possible.

The sooner she finished, the sooner she could leave.

Month or no month.

As soon as she saw even a deep shade of gray in Funland's books, she'd be on the phone to the limo company in a flash. She looked to see EZ staring out the window. She shook her head. "Is that how you spend most of your day managing this place?"

He looked back. "Hm?"

"Oh, brother. Who exactly was that on the phone?"

"Phone?" He rubbed his hand as if it bothered him.

She didn't even want to think that it was the same spot she'd just touched by mistake. Of course it was by mistake, and she didn't plan to be doing much touching with this guy again. Who the hell cared if her heart did a pitter-patter when she did? "Yes, Dalton. The phone rang. You answered it, and it sounded as if someone was sick. Do you need to go help out?"

"No. No. Linda is sick. Only a cold."

He leaned against the shelf in his annoyingly relaxed manner. Someone with so much on his mind shouldn't be allowed to look so relaxed.

The more easy-going he looked, the tenser she felt. "Okay.

Linda is sick. My condolences. But who is she?"

"The gypsy."

"Excuse me?"

He looked out the window. "The gypsy that helps Zos with his act. You do remember that Funland is an amusement park?"

She curled her lip. "Yes, I repressed that thought. So, call in a replacement."

He leaned toward her and glared for a few minutes.

Damn him. "What?"

He shook his head. "If I had a replacement, Einstein, I'd call her." As if he had a wonderful idea, he pushed away from the shelf and came toward her. "Then again—"

"What? Don't touch me."

"I'm not going to." He sat on the desk next to her chair. "Although I'd say you have a phobia about being touched."

"You found me out, Sherlock. Only thing you left out is the touching has to be done by a jerk to cause my phobia."

"Oh, then it'd be all right if I touched you." He leaned over; she glared at him but didn't move. Damn spunky broad. He grinned in spite of the evil eye she gave him. "Okay, no touching. I wouldn't want to upset Linda's replacement."

"You're joking. Go to hell. I don't do—"

"Yeah. Yeah. You don't do coffee, phones or gypsies. Well then, Ms. Santanelli, what do you suggest we do? The fortuneteller booth pulls in big bucks." He grinned at her. "Folks just love to know." He leaned down.

She hadn't noticed before but there were flecks of black, nearly impossible to see except this close, in his dark eyes. Damn. She shouldn't be noticing things like stupid flecks.

"—they love to know what the future holds. Don't you?"

She pushed at his leg to get up. He yanked it away as if she'd burnt him with her now cold coffee. And unfortunately, she had the same reaction as she pulled her hand back faster than she could wish she were back in Vegas. "No. I'm too pragmatic to believe in fortunetellers or psychic crap."

He shook his head. "Not a good attitude for...let's see. Miss Ivana. No. Miss Sonya. Unh-unh. *Madam* Sonya. That's it."

"Get out of my way. I'm going to get something to eat. You can take your Madam Sonya crap—"

"Yeah. Yeah. I know the cliché of where to stick it. But what you don't know, Madam Businesswoman, is that last week Zos and Linda made enough in their booth for me to pay three employees their back salaries. If Madam Sonya is a no-show, he can only make half that alone. Suit yourself, lady. It'll only take longer, much longer than a month I'm guessing, to pull this place out of the hole—"

"That you got it into!"

EZ could argue with her on that one, but he wasn't about to. He still didn't find the need nor have the desire to let Miss High-And-Mighty know about his old man. "What's done is done. If you don't do the gypsy thing—"

"No, I won't do the gypsy thing or anything else except these books." She waved her hands in the air.

He had to smile at himself. She looked about ready to take off in flight and wouldn't he love to point that out. But, he was at the mercy of Ms. Santanelli right now—damn it all to hell. "Suit yourself."

She hesitated, squinted but remained silent. He'd guess that look on her face was one of success, thinking, wrongly that is, that she'd got the upper hand. Well, he'd dealt with his sister for too many years to let a female outsmart him. Still, looking at Lucky, he knew he had his work cut out for him. He'd never faced a tigress before. He shrugged again.

"Okay, back to business. Oh, make sure when you're doing

the payroll for the week that you hold back the checks for the last five employees that you're working on. That should cover our asses instead of facing overdrafts when the bank gets wind of our paychecks being cashed."

Was that a hint of retreat in those deep eyes?

He leaned back, relaxed.

"You can't do that to people. They have families to support—"

With a shrug, he said, "Pick out the single ones—"

"They have to eat too, you jerk."

He merely stared at her, shrugged again.

"If you do that again, I won't be responsible for my actions when you land up on the floor."

He shrugged again.

"For chrissake. I don't have the slightest idea what to do in a fortune telling booth."

"It's easy." He couldn't help but grin again. "Like me."

"If you don't wipe that smirk off you face, I'm outta here. I don't care if Funland falls into the ocean."

"Sound. We're on Long Island Sound. Like a big inlet—"

She punched him in the arm.

"Ouch." He rubbed at the spot. "See. You'd make a perfect hotheaded, swarthy gypsy. You've got the dark hair, the eyes...." He looked at his arm where she'd hit him, paused as if he'd forgotten what he was going to say. "Er...just tell them good stuff. Future stuff with a positive slant. Use your imagination. If you've got one. If they have kids, tell 'em they'll grow up to be rich with scads of grandkids for them. Young girls will find Mr. Right. Couple's will have that happy ever after ending."

"They'd be fools to believe in that."

With caution, he came closer, took her hand into his. She pulled it away. He took it again, holding tighter. "Sounds like you need to give yourself a good fortune-telling, Madam Sonya."

She pushed free with her other hand. "Get me some food first. And groceries. I'll need groceries."

"So, you'll do it?"

"I don't suppose the costume fits you? You did make a moth-eaten oversized chipmunk fool of yourself yesterday."

He sucked in his breath. "Nope. As svelte as I am, it wouldn't fit."

"I get it. You only do varmints."

He laughed. "Atta girl. We love team players around here. Especially ones with spirit. Sorry the costume doesn't fit me. Besides, I'm Sheriff Dalton today. One of Doc's cowhands."

"Don't your employees ever show up for work?"

He started to answer, but she waved away his words. "After you get me all the debits and credits we're setting up a meeting with employees. I'm guessing you don't have a policy to terminate the ones who chronically call in."

"No need."

"Of course there's a need. This is a business, a corporation. You're not here to give free rides to anyone. Absences should demand the employee bring in a doctor's note or these kids and old folks that you hire—"

His insides percolated like the coffee with her accusations. "My employees are reliable-"

"Then where's the chipmunk kid, the gypsy, the sheriff?"

"Sick."

She punched him in the arm again. This time he grabbed her and pulled her close. Before she tried to free herself, she said, "This isn't even cold and flu season, Sheriff. Don't you know when these temporary employees are taking advantage of you. And for every day you or I have to fill in—"

He wanted to strangle her. The close range would be

perfect. He could fit one hand around that milky-white neck. He wanted to, but instead the desire to shut her up had him lean down to her mouth, red, full, and inviting while it kept spouting accusations.

And he kissed her.

She hesitated, pulled back, glared at him as if he were under a microscope. Then, she shoved his chest with the force of a man. "Don't ever do that—"

He grabbed her, and did it again. This time when she pulled, he held tight. She wiggled; he wrapped his arms around her. Slowly, she eased off. Then, strictly in character, she grabbed him and kissed him so hard, his lips burned. Goddamn but he'd never met such a hellion.

Without missing a beat, she pulled back enough to say, "We'll make a list. Yes. That's what we need. A list." Her voice faltered, she caught herself.

He grinned.

"A list of...people. Employees, you know."

"Yeah. I get the gist. People who work here." She hadn't pulled back again, yet. Defiant little thing. Her eyes were much darker at close range. He could imagine himself falling into the depths. One hell of a fortuneteller. That's what she'd make. Right now, he'd love to know what his future held. She wasn't even talking so, no need to shut her up again. Yet, he had to kiss her again.

This time she didn't pull back so fast. He'd made contact with the softest lips he'd ever kissed. She tasted as if she'd eaten the entire box of donuts. Sweet, silky as honey on a bun. Damn it. Not at all what he expected from a glacier disguised as a businesswoman. When the desire to touch her body jumped up and bit him in the ass, he pulled away.

Lucky thought she'd collapse into a puddle of a soon to be

fortuneteller. This feeling, the loss of momentary control was new to her—-and she didn't much like it, nor intended to have it happen again.

Never mind that her toes were wiggling from Dalton's lips kissing her moments ago. "I could have you charged with sexual harassment."

"You're the boss now."

She slammed her hand against his chest, ignored the firmness and said, "Make a list of all employees and their phone numbers. Keep it here so when someone calls in sick or whatever, we call a fill-in. Someone on their day off. We pay time and a half for that day only."

He sat on the edge of the desk and stared at her.

"What now?"

"Nothing. Go on."

"The list…that's it. I don't have anything else to add."

EZ shook his head. "Well, you single-handedly managed to tear my ego, my macho manhood, into tiny bits."

"I wouldn't think you'd have a problem with…go to hell, Dalton."

"I just might. To warm up that is. It's got to be a heck of a lot hotter down there than here in this Ice Palace—even my kiss couldn't warm you."

"By the way—"

"What? You're so bowled over by us locking lips you lost your head?"

"Don't *ever* do it again."

* * *

EZ settled back into his chair behind the desk. Lucky continued to go on about lists, debits, and credits. Was there a nervous chattering to her talking? Damn but he couldn't pay attention after smacking lips with her. Didn't she even feel anything?

That rankled. She knew it.

He'd bet his last penny that should be invested into Funland, that she did feel something but was so cool, so controlled, that she wouldn't let herself enjoy one, make that several little kisses.

He wished he had her fortitude. Then he wouldn't be so pissed at himself that he'd actually enjoyed them. Men were different than woman, he told himself. They could enjoy locking lips with a decent looking woman for the hell of it. That was it. It was all for the hell of it, and no wonder he enjoyed it—got as hard as a teen on a first date in the backseat of a '69 Chevy.

Because he kept ruminating about the stupid kiss, he felt like a jerk for kissing her, but at the same time, he felt glad he could upset her perfectly controlled apple cart. A double header.

Could this day get any better?

He looked up to see her scrutinizing a paper in her hand. Most likely a bill.

Could this day get any worse?

The phone rang, knocking the ruminating out of his head. He looked up at Lucky. "You want I should get...oh, yeah. Boss ladies don't do phones."

"Answer it before they hang up. Maybe someone else is 'sick.'"

"Touché." He grabbed the receiver, rested it on his shoulder and leaned back in his chair. "Dalton here."

Lucky paused. If she had to look at one more unpaid bill, she'd scream. Watching Dalton, on the other hand, could be entertaining in the least.

"Hey, kiddo. Where are you?" he asked.

Because he'd softened his tone, Lucky wrinkled her forehead and leaned closer without him noticing.

"Washington? It's high time you headed back here. I need help...we both do."

He couldn't mean Lucky in that "both." He better not be including her with him. With interest peeked, she lifted a paper and pretended to look at it.

"Okay. Two days tops. And, Chlo, I love you."

Lucky looked down. The paper was upside-down. Who cared when she'd heard him pour out his guts? The guy had nerve. Too much damn nerve as far as she was concerned. He'd just kissed her and now was proclaiming his love to someone else.

Love?

Why'd she even care? She didn't. Turning the bill right side up, she noted the date, amount and time given to pay it--but had no idea what she was looking at. So, she looked up to see EZ watching her.

"Let me know if that upside-down thing works better. I usually read my mail right-side up."

When her fingers tighten on the papers, he heard a tearing sound and smiled to himself.

"These on top are to be paid fist," she said, managing to ignore him or at least pretend to.

"Fine. Well, time to get your costume on—"

"Which one?" she asked.

"How's that?"

"I'm guessing that was another employee calling in. What am I supposed to dress up as?" It killed her that she even wanted to know who he'd been talking to and, damn it, her little question didn't seem to be fooling him.

Was that a hint of jealousy in the depths of Ms. Santanelli's eyes? Nah. Couldn't be. Must be his imagination going wild. Stranger things were known to happen around here. He should let her go on with that line of thinking, serve her right. Knock some of the bitchiness out of her. But he said, "Chloe is my sister. She'll be here to help out in a few days. Don't look so shocked."

"It's just that...I didn't remember your having a sister until you lent me her car. Now that you mentioned her name...it doesn't ring any bells."

"Seems you repressed a lot of things about this place. She's years younger. Still in college, and I intend to have her butt work off some of the bills before school starts."

"Then she can be the gypsy."

He got up, walked to the door. "She'd never fit into the costume. Linda is very well endowed." He turned, grinned and tipped an imaginary hat at her.

Lucky watched the door slam. Then she picked up the closest thing, a Yankee baseball cap, and threw it at him.

He'd noticed *she'd* fit into Linda's costume.

Damn him.

* * *

Doc watched EZ coming into the Old West section of the park. Somethin' on the boy's mind. He could tell by the way his walk slowed, more careless than usual. Course EZ had been just that for so long, it was hard to tell when something was up his craw.

"Something's bothering the boss," Zos said, coming up behind Doc.

He turned to see The Great Zosimoff walking toward the wagon Doc liked to sit on during his coffee breaks. "Seems as much. My guess is we both know what it is, too." He held out his thermos toward his friend.

Zos took it, lifted a Styrofoam cup from the box next to Doc and poured himself some coffee. "Or should we say we know *who* she is." With a deep chuckle, he lifted himself onto the back of the covered wagon.

Doc slammed him on the back once he'd seated himself. "You could say that. How's your morning going?"

"Linda's sick today."

"Cripes. Wonder if our boy is going to take her place?" They howled like the two old coots that they were as EZ came around the side of the wagon.

"Sounds like you two are up to trouble, again." He grabbed the thermos and a cup.

"Didn't you learn to respect your elders as a kid?" Doc asked, chuckling.

EZ poured his coffee. "I learned all right. But you two together always spell trouble. "Zos, Linda is—"

"Millie told me the kid's sick again. So, you planning on fillin' in?"

He looked at Doc, evil grins showing worn teeth. "No, I am not. I'm taking the sheriff's place today as a matter of fact."

Zos took a sip of his coffee. "Pity. You'd look lovely in black."

Doc sputtered his coffee into the air. "Cripes."

EZ shook his head. "Lucky is replacing—"

That wiped the smile from both the old men's faces.

"She'll do fine," EZ said.

"Maybe…no doubt that is. She agreed?" Zos asked.

EZ flung his empty coffee cup into the trash barrel. "When it comes to money, Ms. Santanelli appears to put the almighty dollar first." EZ started to turn, but caught the expression on the fortuneteller's face. Zos had only been here about a month and a half, but EZ'd never seen him upset. EZ's words tilted the man's even keel.

Zos was one of the more flamboyant, yet intriguing

characters that Doc had him hire. Zos'd claimed he had no family around; wife passed away, one kid somewhere. Or was it none? EZ couldn't keep track of the employees as it was. No way could he remember details of their families.

"Hey, I meant no harm," EZ said. "She's a crackerjack businesswoman I hear. All I'm saying is, when she heard how much you manage to pull in, she agreed." He patted the old man on the back. "Think you can show her the ropes? I'm guessing it'll only be a few days that she'll have to fill in."

"No problem."

But EZ sensed there was a problem. Something about Lucky must have rubbed the old man the wrong way. Why else would he have such a reaction to someone coming to help? He didn't get upset when Millie filled in that one time. Odd. Maybe he had a problem with young women. "Oh, speaking of filling in, Chloe's on her way home."

Doc's eyes lit up. "When's she due here?"

"She's in Washington now. I'm guessing with her timing, about three days for a one day trip."

"Now don't you start on that girl. She needs you right now. Too damn young and confused to make her own decisions," Doc said, getting up from the wagon.

Perfect. Just what EZ needed—to have one more person with problems out the whazoo—and he the only one to solve them.

Doc looked down at his pocket watch. "Show'll start in half an hour. Go get dressed."

EZ gave a salute to the old man. "You're the boss here in the Old West."

"I have to go to my trailer...then I'll go show the ropes to Ms. Santanelli," Zos said as he stood and walked toward the exit of the Old West.

"Zos's reaction seem odd to you, Doc?"

He hesitated, watched the fortuneteller until he was out of earshot. "Hadn't noticed."

EZ wrinkled his forehead. "Well, it did to me." And I'd bet this entire place that it did to you too, you old sly fox.

What are you two up to?

LUCKY IN LOVE

Lori Avocato

Chapter Eight

Lucky wiggled her hips to make the fool skirt move up to her waist. This was the stupidest thing she'd ever agreed to do in her life. Gypsy fortuneteller my ass. The damn costume was a size too small. Linda must be petite.

And Lucky refused to give a thought to EZ's comment about her chest.

And especially she didn't want to think about him noticing.

She looked at herself in the mirror. Black skirt flowing over her legs with a waistband that said she needed to take a deep breath in order to snap. The blouse at least fit better with its silken material cooling her skin beneath the see-through arms making the long sleeves bearable.

"Not bad. Not bad at all." Oh God, what was she saying? Of course it was bad! She never even dressed in costumes on Halloween.

Before Millie had left the employee's lounge to work the cotton candy booth, she gave Lucky a brief rundown on how to apply makeup to look the part. It was then Lucky tried to convince the older woman to switch jobs. Selling cotton candy she could handle.

Telling guests their futures—especially happy ever after ones—was going to be a stretch.

She sunk into the chair and looked into the mirror. Really. She looked a mess. Dark circles had formed under her eyes in the short time she'd been here. That, of course, had to come from sleeping on the fool couch. She grabbed a cover-up stick and ran the flesh color over the dark.

"Great. Stooping to theater makeup, dressing like a gypsy, and lying to people." And she blamed it all on EZ Dalton.

Well, she'd gone up against more powerful, certainly more businesslike men before.

And beat the pants off of them.

She'd do it with the lackadaisical Dalton, too.

But first, she had to prance around like a fortuneteller. She'd only do it for today, though. Hopefully his sister would get here and take over if Lucky had her way—and she planned to. If Lucky didn't get going on those bills, she'd never get out of here in a month's time.

And, she predicted to her reflection, she would be home in thirty days or less because no way in hell did she plan to stay longer.

"Now that's a good fortune," she said, pushing up to stand. With one final look, a groan, and shake of her head, she walked toward the door—to get this day over with.

* * *

First EZ noticed the flowing black skirt. Then, and damn his good eyesight to hell, he noticed her waist. Thin. Much thinner than he'd guessed with her other outfits covering it. He could get both hands around her waist and his fingers would touch.

Scarlet O'Hara had nothing on Lucky Santanelli. He should've stayed in the Old West, got too nosy.

He shut his eyes. What the hell was he doing? Noticing black skirts, waists...breasts. Next he'd be going on about her pointed chin or high cheeks or her rear end.

"So, where do I sit?" Lucky asked.

"Perfection," he muttered.

She pushed past him to open the door of the fortuneteller's booth. "You make no sense. What are you mumbling about,

Dalton?"

He'd lost it. "I've got a lot on my mind."

"So do I. This getup, and lying to people isn't part of it. Where do I sit?"

He motioned to a red velvet chair opposite a table. She walked over, ran her hand across the crystal ball on top. "Antie Em. Antie Em. Get me the hell out of here."

He leaned against the wall, smiled. "Good one. Zos should have been here by now. Park opens in thirty minutes. Guests will filter over here soon after." He pushed back the Stetson he'd stuck on for his gig today. "They'll buy a ticket at Millie's booth. You take it, stick it in the container under your skirt—"

"What?"

Shoot. "The skirt. The skirt of the table. Lift it up—" He walked over, bent and went to lift the brocade fabric as Lucky did the same. Their gazes met. Great. He'd soon be losing his grasp of reality, already fragile because of her. If those sexy, ebony eyes looked any deeper into his soul—he'd be a goner for sure.

"I...okay. I stick the ticket in the box." She'd softened her tone, but with a push to his chest that came out of nowhere, she made clear that he should keep his distance.

Fine with him.

He leaned back. "Three minutes. You give them three minutes for one ticket—"

"Three? I can't think that fast."

"A crackerjack businesswoman like you? I'm sure you've cut deals in less time."

"True."

He noticed her tense. One hand grabbed onto the chair's arm. So, little Lucky was miffed but had the control of a cloistered nun. Nun? Jesus. His old teacher Sister Mary

Magdaline would cringe hearing that comparison. A gangster's daughter referred to as a nun? He looked at her and said, "You'll do fine." He started to turn but noticed her eyes. The conviction with which she spoke every word since he'd met her had dimmed. Something, fear maybe, had nudged its way in.

Damn but he couldn't take her being afraid.

He glanced at his watch. "I've got time before Doc needs me. How about a cup of coffee?"

"I don't get—"

He waved her words away. "I'll get you one."

She ran her hand over the glass ball. "Okay. Yes. I could use caffeine. Get me a double-loaded latté."

He shook his head, turned and went out toward the commissary.

* * *

Lucky watched EZ leave. She'd been so foolishly nervous about this fortune telling stuff that she hadn't noticed his outfit. Spurs, leather, and *man*.

Damn he'd have made a great cowboy.

Physically, she told herself. She'd give him that.

A hint of his cologne wafted across the room, only to be devoured by some other scent. Roses? No, some other kind of floral smell. The room was so dark she could barely make out the other end, but could see another chair covered in the gaudy burgundy velvet.. Reminded her of the sleazier sections of Vegas. The wedding chapel like the one she and Vinny...oh cripes, her insides knotted on that thought.

Beneath the table, her foot bumped into something. She lifted the skirt, grinned at the thought of EZ doing the same, then froze when she saw it. Jesus. Dixie Beer. An empty can of Dixie Beer. Daddy's favorite brand. He'd first had it in New Orleans, she remembered him saying. She shook her head. Why the hell did she keep doing this to herself? Why did she let an empty beer can upset her? It must belong to Zos. She kicked the can further under the table, dropped the skirt.

Fake candles, unfortunately, illuminated a mirror on one wall so she could see her reflection. The room swallowed her identity, leaving a gypsy with dark hair, veiled enough to cover only the back of her head and with a look in her eyes as if she faced a firing squad.

Why was telling people happy ever after so difficult?

If she hadn't eaten that donut, she'd blame her gut tightening like a piece of hemp on hunger. Face it, she told herself, this job was the cause.

"Plain ordinary variety black is all I could manage. Obviously Funland isn't as sophisticated as what you're used to. For latté you'll have to head into town. Wasn't sure if you used cream and sugar," EZ said, backing into the booth to hold the door with his foot. "Do you?"

He carried several containers along with two cups of coffee. The aroma had that hemp tighten.

"No. Black." She got up to take the cups from him. "No sugar either. Equal if you have it."

"I should have known that—"

"What's that supposed to mean?"

"Er...you're sweet enough?"

She glared at him.

He set a box down on the table, opened it. Wrapped in cellophane was some kind of biscuit with cheese seeping out of the side. Gooey stuff that would shoot her cholesterol up a hundred points. Not that she had to worry about it with her diet of salads, veggies and fruit.

"You eat eggs?"

"I've been known to." I'd eat the cellophane right about

now, she thought, realizing the donut's relief was long gone. That had to be the cause of her stomach feeling as if a bird had hatched inside and was now taking its first flight.

"Good." He lifted out a sandwich. Smelled like Heaven. "You haven't eaten yet?

"No." She wanted to grab it, eat it in one gulp. But she summoned up as much grace as she could, starving and all, and nodded. "Thanks." Because the word came out too softly, her gaze flew up to meet his. A smile formed on his lips. She wanted to clarify that in no way did his little gesture touch her, but damn it—he'd remembered when even she had forgotten.

"Eat up. There isn't much time left." He straddled a chair, much like he'd do if on a horse, opened his sandwich and took a bite.

Lucky sat opposite him, forcing herself not to eat like a pig despite how she felt. The coffee wasn't Starbucks, but the warmth went down to relax her a bit.

He'd finished his sandwich without a word, ripped a piece of cellophane off the end. "Here."

She looked down at his offering. "Gee, thanks."

He chuckled. "My ticket. Give me my three minutes, Madam Sonya."

"You make me sound like I run a brothel." He opened his mouth but she shut it with, "No sexist comments, Dalton."

He grabbed his chest. "You've once again wounded my fragile male ego."

She curled her lips, shook her head. "I'm certain you'll live."

He looked at his watch. "You've wasted two of my minutes. I demand to see the manager—"

"Shut up." She took in a breath, looked at the damn crystal ball and shut her eyes. "I see—" His hand over hers caused her eyelids to fly open. "What the hell—"

"You can't see into your crystal ball with your eyes shut."

"Oh." She bent over the freaking ball, cursed in her head. "I see happiness—"

"Too general."

She looked up at him. "You're a stranger. How do I know what is more specific? "

"Because, sweetheart—"

He took both of her hands into his. She ignored the fact that the fake candles had this place warmer than a kiln. She ignored that his breath tickled across her skin. She ignored that the bird was doing aileron rolls in her stomach about now—and pulled free.

"—you are the all-knowing, all-seeing Madam Sonya."

"I'll never be able to pull this off."

"Then you'll be here *several* months—"

She ran her hand across the ball. "You are alone at the moment, but will meet a woman—"

"How do you know I'm alone?"

"Because you're a jerk, and stop interrupting me!"

"I'm trying to help. Look, there are a few tips you could use."

"Why didn't you tell me?" She lifted her chin, stared at him, and said, "I'm a fast learner. Spill."

EZ had to smile to himself. She had the spunk to pull the gypsy part off, and with the look in her eyes now, he had no doubt she'd do the fortunes all right, too. "First, look at your mark. Study them for the obvious. Wedding rings. Jewelry that says their lovers gave it to them."

"How would I know who gave them?"

"Easy. The woman lovingly fingers her necklace or ring. Smiles when her fingers touch the stone. Piece of cake."

"You certainly seem the expert where woman are concerned." Over her cup of coffee, she grinned.

"Learned all I know from the charlatans who worked here."

"So," She leaned near. "You saying you aren't the Don Juan of Seagrove?"

"Let's just say I know what I want." Don Juan? Yeah. He couldn't get a date for the prom at the rate he was going. They didn't make woman like they used to.

"Hm. What exactly *do* you want, Dalton?"

She leaned too near. The sickly floral air freshener that Millie insisted added to the atmosphere of the booth was momentarily reprieved by Lucky's pungent grapefruit scent. He inhaled, felt invigorated as if the scent had filled him with vitamin C. Oh, man. He was loosing it.

"Well?" she asked.

"Apple pie, home, hearth, a woman to wait on me—"

"You male chauvinist!"

This was getting too personal. "Five minutes 'til show time, Madam. You ready?"

That knocked the spunk right out of her.

"I didn't think so. As I was saying. Look for the obvious. Start by saying something like, I see a man in your life. Then, and this is the important part, pause. The mark will more than likely start spilling her guts. Take it and run with it."

Lucky pushed up and looked down on him. "You think you know so much about these…marks…these women. But, Dalton, I don't have to be psychic to see that you are alone—and with good reason."

He slid off the back of the chair. "I don't recall asking for your opinion."

She lifted the piece of cellophane up and waved it at him. "Seems you did."

He snatched it from her hand. "That's what I get for trying to help a stubborn, too damn independent woman like you." With that, he turned and headed toward the door.

"I see the too damn independent woman kicking your butt where business is concerned." He walked out the door. She couldn't help herself as she ran to it and called, "Stop living in the past, Dalton. Here's another prediction for you. You'll die a lonely old man with that 'woman to wait on me' attitude."

He didn't even turn, merely waved his hand in the air as if brushing away her words.

"Damn you, Dalton—"

Two teenage girls came around the corner, tickets in hand.

Lucky leaned against the wall and groaned. "Show time."

* * *

EZ leaned against the fence surrounding the Ferris wheel and watched as a blonde no older than fourteen and apparently with her friend walked up to Lucky. He had to smile. The look in Lucky's eyes was enough to make his day. It wasn't true fear as if her life hung in the balance, more a worry that she didn't have every little tidbit of her existence under control. Didn't take a genius to see that the woman thrived on control.

Probably kept up that slender figure with doses of power, too. Yep, he'd guess Lucky enjoyed the upper position. With a smile on his face, he thought of the women of his past. None of them...had the spunk for that position.

Damn, but he didn't much care for Lucky taking over Funland though.

How he hated the fact that he needed her expertise, her money to pull the place out of the clutches of the creditors. Why couldn't Rosario have had a son? At least EZ wouldn't be distracted, feeling torn between lust and disgust.

Maybe revenge wasn't so sweet.

LUCKY IN LOVE

Lori Avocato

He must have been nuts to force her to stay. What the hell was he thinking anyway? Revenge was not his style. Damn but he'd been blinded by the pain Rosario had caused EZ's father—and damn it all, Dad couldn't fight his own battles anymore.

Guess EZ had inherited the job of fighting his dad's battles.

EZ tipped his hat to shade the sun from his eyes and watched Lucky taking the tickets from the blonde. Hope she remembered to keep them under the table's skirt.

Skirt.

He'd made a fool of himself when he'd tried to tell her the tickets went under the skirt of the table. An intelligent man like himself, and didn't a Harvard degree prove as much? shouldn't be that distracted by a woman.

Even if his love life had been on hold for months.

Of course, there were several women in town who'd come so close to throwing themselves at him, he'd considered buying a catcher's mitt. Still, no one had made him want to catch them—until Lucky came to town.

Yeah, he wanted to do more than catch her after them locking lips today. There was no doubting the physical attraction, he told himself. For once he wished he were the type to use a woman for her body. Because damn it all, Lucky had one hell of a body. This was not good, thinking like that. He had to stop. Change of scenery. That's what he needed.

Well, he'd head off to the Old West, help out Doc, and come check on Madam Sonya in a few hours.

He noted the time on the huge clock above the town hall, turned and walked past the cotton candy stand, the Ferris wheel, Haunted mansion and around the bend to the petting zoo corral.

He looked at the watch on his wrist, an accessory that most cowboys wouldn't wear. Too bad he hadn't removed it before getting dressed in chaps and a Stetson. Surely some observant, mouthy kid would notice.

Jesus. Had it only been five minutes since leaving the fortuneteller's booth?

LUCKY IN LOVE

Lori Avocato

Chapter Nine

Lucky forced a smile at the young girl with the blonde hair. She knew it must have come out more like a squint by the reaction of the girl. The kid glared at her. Almost looked as if she'd jump out of her seat and run out. Lucky had to think fast, do something before these kids ran out screaming, and they'd loose money on this booth today. Worse thing was then she'd have to face Dalton.

"Well, I...you..." Think positive. What do teen-age girls want nowadays? Being so far removed from any teens, she had no earthly idea. Her own teenage years couldn't be used for reference either.

Nothing about her life had been normal.

"Did my time start yet?" the kid asked.

"Hm? Time? Oh, no. Not yet. I..." Okay. She was a cute kid. Must have a boy friend. Lucky tried to think of what EZ had said, but all she came up with was his stupid kiss.

Damn what a distraction the fool was.

Okay. Okay. Concentrate. No ring on the kid's finger. Dumb thing to even look for. She couldn't be old enough to be married. Of course, that's what everyone had said about Lucky at the ripe old age of eighteen, too. Wait! A sparkle hanging from the kid's necklace caught Lucky's eye. A ring. Looked like a boy's class ring. Bingo.

The girl gave Lucky an annoyed look. Pretty soon she'd give the kid a bucket-load of bad luck for her fortune if she didn't wipe the annoyance off her face. She decided to cut the kid some slack, ran her hands over the crystal ball and shook her head slowly as if she'd become possessed by the devil.

That, she managed by picturing EZ when she shut her eyes.

"Madam Sonya sees...yes, a man in your life—" She peaked out, waited. Come on, kid, give me something to work with here.

The girl looked at her. "Keith."

Houston, we have liftoff. "Why yes, Keith is your—"

"Brother."

"Of course he's your...brother?" Great. Damn EZ Dalton and his stupid suggestions.

"He can't stand Paulie."

"Paulie. Yes, unfortunately that is true because they are so—"

"Similar."

"You took the words right out of my mouth. Of course, Paulie cares a great deal about—"

"Me. My God, you are good, Madam Sonya."

Lucky's heart did a little jig. Foolish, she knew. But a sparkle had lit up the kid's eyes when she'd mentioned the infamous Paulie, and it didn't hurt Lucky's confidence one bit either.

The day was starting to take an upward turn.

"Hello."

She looked behind the kid to see a figure of a man enter. The dim lighting had her eyesight out of whack. Just as well. Maybe the clients wouldn't ever recognize her once she got out of this getup.

"I'll be right with you—" Lucky said.

"It's me," he said.

She hadn't recognized the voice at first. He'd been so quiet the few times she'd been around him. Not like the gabby Doc.

LUCKY IN LOVE

Lori Avocato

"Oh, hi, Zos...The Great Zosimoff that is."

The kid looked over her shoulder as if afraid. The one on the chair waiting for her turn squirmed in her seat.

"Just call me Zos, Sugar."

Hadn't Daddy called her that, too, before he moved out? The years played tricks on her mind. Of course, she'd been so young naturally she couldn't remember. Still, if she were a sentimental fool, she'd be tearing up. But, the past was long gone. No sense crying over it. She'd been brought up to deal with all kinds of problems—realistically. And Lucky Santanelli didn't waste tears on sentiment.

"No problem, Zos." She leaned closer to see that he'd dressed in a rather elaborate costume, silks, brocades and there seemed not be a shortage of burgundy velvet around here. He wasn't an exceptionally tall man, but costumed as he was, he came across as impressive. But his voice lacked the booming confidence she'd at least expect from a fortuneteller if she were stupid enough to waste her moncy on one.

He looked at the other girl, bowed. "The Great Zosimoff will assist you, my young lady!"

Lucky's eyes widened. His tone had changed in an instant. Maybe he was a shy man who hid behind the cloak of Zosimoff? Of course, she was no expert on old men either. The kid in front of her leaned nearer.

"I'm not paying anymore, you know."

Lucky looked at her. "What? Oh, no. Sorry for the interruption. Look, kid, I'll give you an extra minute—"

"Two."

You'll never live to fifteen at this rate. "Of course. Two. No problem. Now where were we?"

"You should know that."

Lucky looked across the room to where Zos sat opposite

the other girl. He had a smaller crystal ball on his lap, and she wondered if she'd taken his spot. EZ hadn't said Linda sat here. She hoped not as he winked toward her. She nodded and smiled, turned back to the insolent kid. "Of course I remember. Paulie and Keith not getting along. Keith is too protective of you, wants to keep you a kid sister while your heart yearns for Paulie..." Yearns? Great. She was waxing poetic now. If this got out, her reputation as a top-notched businesswoman would be in question.

"Yeah," the kid interrupted her thoughts, "I want to marry him—"

"No!"

Zos's gaze flew to Lucky. Okay, she shouldn't have shouted, but this girl had no idea what she was talking about.

"No, dear. You are too young. Although Paulie is a nice enough guy—" She pretended to look into her crystal ball. If only someone could have done the same for her years ago. Okay, this kid needed saving, needed a good dose of lying to. "I see a man, tall, blonde—"

"Paulie's got brown hair—"

Lucky gave her an annoying glance. "I *know* that. This blonde guy isn't Paulie. He is however...your future. He will be rich, care for you like no other and the two of you will have kids. Three of them, all blondes." She threw that last part in to solidify the future. Shit. That felt good.

The girl hesitated, ran her hand through her hair, pulling out the white scrunchy only to wrap her long curls in it once again. "Blondes?"

I hope you're a natural, kid. "Like their mother and father."

"You mean?"

Lucky nodded and hoped whatever she meant was along the same lines as what the kid meant.

"Then...Timmy Nickels is blonde."

She'd said it with such conviction, such teenage wisdom, such foolish optimism that Lucky jumped on it. "Be aware of Timmy Nickels." She looked at the clock on the wall before the girl could comment. Lucky touched her hand. "Enjoy every minute of your life, kid."

The girl nodded, stood, looked over at her friend who was getting up at the same time. Lucky'd spent way too much time with this one, but, hey, doesn't your first always take longer?

"Nice one," Zos said.

Lucky looked at him. "Hm?"

"Nice ending about enjoying life. Kids nowadays need to be reminded about that. We all do."

Once again he'd softened his voice. Because they were alone, Lucky felt a current in the room that wasn't there before. The guy sure had what it took to pull off a ruse like being a fortuneteller. Her, well that was another matter all together. She could imagine the talk at the local teen hangout about the stupid fortuneteller who didn't know a future from a lie.

Maybe this Great Zosimoff was the real thing.

* * *

After a few hours in the Old West, EZ made his way over to the fortuneteller's booth and hesitated as he stood in the doorway, watching. Lucky continued on as if the words of the future sped from her lips on their own accord.

She *was* a fast learner.

Zos sat at Linda's seat with another mark. EZ had forgotten to tell Lucky to sit over there. Hopefully the old man wasn't miffed. He'd done a surprisingly good job since EZ'd hired him. It was as if the man had a real knack for telling the future, more like he was on the outside looking in. A real gem for Funland, but an odd guy nonetheless.

He figured the guy harmless, but the thought of him working so closely with Lucky had EZ make a mental note to pop in more often. It didn't go unnoticed that Zos's demeanor shifted a bit around Lucky.

Course, so did EZ's, and he didn't have any deviant thoughts on his mind.

Normal male hormonal induced ones, yes, deviant, no.

Jesus. What if old Zos was hot for Lucky?

The steamboat whistle blew, signaling noon. EZ pulled away from the wall and walked inside.

Lucky continued on with her mark, talking non-stop. EZ relaxed into the shadows for a listen. Zos had noticed him, but EZ lifted a finger to his lips to ask the old man not to say anything. Zos winked at him. Fatherly. It came out fatherly. EZ felt his forehead wrinkle in wondering more about the man. Seems he was like a chameleon. Quiet, shy one minute, booming in his charlatan act the next.

Bears watching.

Lucky's laughter yanked EZ's worries from his thoughts.

"So, your children will have two boys and a girl and they'll keep you out of that nursing home you are so worried about by offering their loving care."

The woman seated in front of Lucky grabbed her hands. "Thank you. Thank you. I've needed to hear that after the last visit from the police with my sixteen year old."

"Police?" Lucky nearly screeched as the woman stood, turned and hurried out. "Great. I've just let a future criminal off the hook."

"Not necessarily," EZ said, stepping forward. She jumped. He smiled.

"How long have you been—"

"Not very. And what you told that lady could have actually

helped the kid."

She leaned back, stretched, silken material taught against full breasts.

"Well? What are you talking about?" she demanded.

"Silk…er…the mother. Your prediction that her kid is going to turn out all right might just have her treating him differently."

"Yeah. Until he ends up in jail."

"If she gives him self-confidence, maybe increases his self-esteem by her beliefs, he'll inadvertently turn himself around."

She shut her eyes, sighed deeply, then opened one eyelid. "When you'd become a Dr. Freud?"

"I've always studied people. And I know I'm right this time. Raised my sister and she's a gem."

"You…really?"

He chuckled. "Really. So, how'd your first day on the job go?"

"Only day on the job." She opened her eyes and stood. "Get a replacement for tomorrow if Linda is out."

Zos's client stood and walked out.

"She did a fine job. I'm proud…she did fine," Zos said, getting up and walking to the door.

EZ watched the old man, thinking there was something odd about him again, but couldn't put his finger on it. He didn't scare EZ. No, it was something else. Something psychological that had him notice. Maybe EZ was becoming psychic.

Lucky looked at Zos, waved a hand at him. "Thanks. But I still don't want to—"

"Linda has tonsillitis," EZ said.

Lucky blew out a breath so near, the frayed edges of his vest danced in the current. "Can't she just pop a few antibiotics for that?"

"I'm no doctor, but I'm guessing the fact that they hospitalized her means no."

"Great."

"I'm off to lunch," Zos said, heading out.

"See you later," Lucky said. "You." She pointed a perfectly manicured finger into his chest. The dim lighting wasn't enough to recognize the color, but he suspected someone like her wouldn't wear bright pink. No, she was more the deep red color. More authority. More control. Like a navy business suit.

He reached to take her hand, but as if she'd expected that move, she pulled back.

"You fill in while I go to lunch." With that she turned to go, but three elderly ladies walked into the booth giggling worse than the first teens that were here this morning.

Lucky smiled, but through clenched teeth managed, "Damn."

EZ lifted off his hat and waved it toward the women, inviting them to take the various seats in the room.

"Oh, my, Stella, isn't he the handsome cowboy."

Lucky groaned. "He's a real looker, but actually he's our resident fortuneteller—"

"Dressed like that?" Stella asked.

"He's from Texas. Dallas," Lucky said, flopping down into her chair. "If you'll have a seat here, Stella, one of you can sit with Hop-a-long over there and—" She smiled at the other woman. "He'll be with you in a few minutes."

"Three, Dearie. We get three minutes for our money," Stella said, then giggled more.

* * *

Lucky could barely concentrate. Geez. She'd told poor Stella there was soon to be a new man in her life. It was then the old woman screamed, nearly fainting, Lucky was quite certain, as poor Stella rambled on about her husband of fifty-three years! Did Lucky mean he was going to die soon? Great.

From his seat in the shadows, the way Lucky liked it, EZ cast a glance, grinned.

"No, ma'am, Stella. Your darling is not...I see many years together. The other man—"

"I'm going to have an affair?"

"No!" Lucky wanted to take her by her curly gray hair and pull her out the door. She had no business in the so-called job, and EZ's grinning and snorting didn't help much. The second little lady he'd gotten around to was cooing like a fat pigeon at his every word. "No. That is not what I meant."

Stella grabbed her with a bony hand. "My son? You mean my son is coming back?"

Great. Maybe her son was dead and now she thought he'd be rising from the grave. A major headache suddenly formed like a giant tornado lifts from the clouds to descend on the Midwest, causing Lucky to run her fingers along her temples. She needed a cup of triple-loaded latté.

Before she could finagle her way out of this mess, she looked up to see the two women by the door and felt someone behind her. He leaned so near, she felt the tickle of the frayed edges of his vest on the back of her neck.

"How long has he been gone, Stella?" EZ asked.

Lucky felt ready to swat him and his stupid vest away, but before she could say anything, Stella offered, "My dear has been in Florida for two years."

"Alive?" slipped out of Lucky's mouth, to the shock of Stella and her cronies.

"Of course he's alive, Dearie. Is he really coming back?" But this time she looked at the know-it-all standing behind Lucky. She turned, raised an eyebrow at him.

"He'll be here within the year. Go home and give him a call tonight."

Stella cooed, stood and blew a kiss at Hop-a-long.

Just like that. He'd saved Lucky from having the poor woman suffer the vapors or some such elderly ailment. She should be glad. She should be turning around and shaking his hand. She should be jumping up and even hugging him in thanks.

Because she was Lucky and he was who he was, she pushed up to stand, turned and looked him in the eye.

"If you want me to do this job, then keep your goddamned nose out of my fortunes." Not wishing to get into a discussion with him—and face loosing, she walked toward the door.

"So, that means you'll be Madam Sonya tomorrow?"

* * *

Lucky refused to turn and give EZ the satisfaction of admitting that he had her. Her insides knotted tighter than the stupid tassels holding back the burgundy drapes. She could lie to herself and say the feeling came from hunger, or she could tell it like it was and admit that Dalton made her feel this way.

No matter the cause, she had to get something to eat. Lightheaded, Lucky reached for the wall. Could things get any worse? Here she was facing masquerading as Madam Sonya again, and she didn't even have any food in her trailer for lunch. What she'd give for a grilled chicken Caesar salad right now. The cafeteria at the Hartwell building had the best salads.

"You all right?" he asked.

Before she could finish fantasying about a Caesar salad, EZ had come up behind her. She turned to face him, sucking in a breath to buy time and think of a lie to convince him that she was fine.

He leaned near.

She pulled back so he wouldn't touch her.

With one more step closer, he said, "I don't even have to ask again. You look pale. Hungry?"

"I...yes. I'm hungry. So, if you'll excuse me—"

"That makes two of us needing lunch."

"Fine. I'll go now and eat fast. You stay here until—"

Zos picked that moment to come around the side of the cotton candy booth. Damn. She'd almost gotten away clean.

"Perfect," EZ said as he placed his hand on the small of her back. "We can get something to eat and discuss business at the same time."

"Whoopee. You just made my day."

"Doesn't much matter to me how your day goes, we need to get down to business. Two of my creditors are threatening to sue."

She'd debated about pushing away from him and finding something to eat in this place. Even an overpriced hotdog was sounding good about now, but his words had the exact effect on her that she knew he intended. So, she turned to him and said, "I'll work on business, but lunch is on you and after my shift here, you give me directions to the grocery store."

He looked at her, his chocolate eyes twinkling. "You do have that 'let's make a deal' part down pat. Don't you?"

"That's precisely how I've gotten as far at Hartwell Holdings as I have." She turned to Zos who stood by the doorway, obviously waiting to get in. Obviously getting an earful, too. "I'll be back in a few minutes."

He waved at her, looked around. "We've had a decent morning and afternoons always have a lull from lunchtime until evening when the teenagers come out in full force, Sugar."

For some reason, she remembered how Daddy had used "Sugar" or "Lucky" so frequently, she wondered sometimes if he even knew her real name. As a kid she'd gotten used to "Sugar," insisted he not call her that after she'd reached her teen years, but he persisted. But since she and Daddy always spent time alone, it really never mattered what he called her.

Zos's term had her remembering things she had no desire to. Not that she blamed the old man. Sugar was a common enough endearment, especially where older men were concerned.

Zos came near and touched her arm. She must have looked as if she were daydreaming. More like a day nightmare if Daddy was in it. "Take your time."

Just what she wanted to do. Spend more time with Dalton. He'd already started out the door and turned toward the cotton candy booth.

"So, what do you feel like?" he asked.

She looked at him, curled her lip. "A fool in this outfit."

EZ wanted to say she looked anything but a fool. Actually, she made the outfit that Linda looked mystical in, sexy. Yep, on Lucky the swirling silk, like gossamer wings managing to yank his hormones out of hiding, looked sexy. At least that's unfortunately how he saw her. "I'm talking about food. What are you in the mood for?"

"A Hartwell grilled chicken Caesar salad."

"Well, the saloon in the Old West has barbecued chicken. I can have the cook scrap the sauce off and throw it on some lettuce—"

"Get me a hotdog somewhere."

"You really like to live dangerously, huh?"

"Not a very good vote of confidence for your park's cuisine, Dalton."

"I'm guessing as half-owner you won't spread that around."

"I'm not stupid." She looked around. "Well, maybe I am to have gotten into this mess. How the hell did you let this place get so bad anyway?"

He shrugged. No way would he tell her the truth. Let her think what she wanted. "Hey, the mushrooms are being re-frosted as we speak."

"Goody." She figured she'd let the subject drop. He wasn't going to confess his stupidity or rotten business skills. Didn't need to. It was all too obvious.

They walked past the Funhouse toward wherever EZ was taking her to eat. The breeze today made it quite comfortable. Vegas was always dry, so she'd expected Connecticut to be dripping with humidity. But it wasn't, since being by the water kept it comfortable. Suddenly she remembered coming here as a kid—but, try as she might, she couldn't get a picture of EZ's father in her mind. Did he look like him? she wondered.

She'd forgotten what it had been like since not coming here for so many years. No doubt due to her confusing childhood—years of repressing memories.

Could she ever yank those memories from where they'd been hidden?

Chapter Ten

EZ watched Lucky. The air conditioner hummed in the background of his office. As usual, she'd taken his chair at the desk, leaving him the hard wooden seat opposite.

She ate as if she'd been starving for days. Actually, that wasn't too farfetched an idea, he figured. Unless she ate while she was out shopping yesterday, he didn't know when she would have had the time to grab a bite. Besides, she hadn't asked for directions to any local restaurants, and no way could anyone find the nearest grocery store on their own. The town fathers had seen it in their infinite wisdom to seclude the store on the outskirts of town, as if quaint little seashore townsfolk didn't eat.

He was being too hard on the place of his birth. Of course he loved Seagrove, but lately, maybe since the arrival of Lucky, he started to miss his own place.

Since the arrival of Lucky? He had to be insane to even think something like that. Of course he was. Having this problem heaped on him had taken its toll. Look at the way he watched her? Cripes. What happened to loving to sit and eat on the beach with the seagulls dive-bombing for his scraps?

A drip of mustard sat to left of her lips. A tiny yellow-brown spot hardly noticeable. Yet, he in his unfortunate vision, noticed. Stuffing a mouthful of hotdog into his mouth, he decided his interests had waned lately because she was such a successful businesswoman, and he missed his old life.

He would not wipe off the mustard.

LUCKY IN LOVE

Lori Avocato

"So," she said, after taking a sip of bottled water.

Of course she drank bottled, and her look of annoyance hadn't gone unnoticed when he'd handed her a generic brand instead of the Perrier she had requested.

"Did you get a chance to collect all the debits and credits I'd asked for."

He chewed, slowly. Watched her watching him. Took a sip of his water, which, he thought, tasted generically delicious and swallowed. "I am capable of a certain amount of secretarial work, you know."

She set her water bottle down or at least she pretended to try. Every place she went to put it had stacks of papers on it.

"Point taken. The ones on your left are debits, the right credits."

"And everything in-between?"

Was that a smile threatening to form on the Iceberg Princess's face? "Everything in-between is up for grabs."

She shook her head. "I can't work like this."

He shoved the rest of his hotdog into his mouth, chewed, drank the remainder of water and got up. "Well, Ms. Santanelli, my guess is you'll have to make due with this setup unless you want to hire, at your own expense I might add, some *male* secretary to come in and organize all this shit. I am not secretarial material, you might have noticed. And, I'll be the first to admit, a good secretary is worth every Christmas bonus he or she earns."

"I have no intention—" She reached for the debits, scanned the top few. "—of putting a penny of my own money into anything to do with Funland."

He leaned against the shelf. "That mean you won't be treating me to a cotton candy for dessert?"

"Exactly. I don't eat sugar anyway. Neither should you.

Might make a difference. By the way, I need to get to the grocery store. Write up the directions while I start on these."

His muscles tensed. Her tone had come so natural to her that she probably didn't notice how condescending she sounded. Well he did, and didn't much like it. "Don't I even get a 'please?'"

She'd leaned forward to study one of the bills. "Hm?"

He rolled his eyes. "Pretty please write up the directions, EZ, since you're such a great guy?"

"Look, my mind is...preoccupied here. Either write the damn directions up or I'll go ask Doc."

EZ flinched, wondered if Doc could give her directions? EZ sucked in a breath, walked to the opposite side of the desk and sat down. While she ignored him, he took a pencil that needed sharpening and rummaged through the papers to find a scrap piece.

She looked up. "Do not mess up this wonderful filing system."

"Ha. Ha." With that he started to write out the directions sending her a bit out of the way—say three or four miles. Revenge, at least on this basic level, felt pretty damn good.

When he looked at her, for a second, he let himself feel bad that he'd kept her here out of revenge.

Once finished with the directions, he set them on the pile to her left. "It's open until nine."

She looked up. "Nine?"

"Nine o'clock at night. Seagrove doesn't allow businesses to stay open, except for a few restaurants and us, after nine."

She curled her lips. "I should have known."

He leaned back, stuck his feet on the side of the desk, away from her papers, but her gaze darted to them as if to admonish him for almost knocking her piles off.

"So what time does a career gal like yourself usually go shopping?"

She held one of the bills up to look closer. "Lawlor Foods. I see they're the distributors for all of the snack and restaurants here. Correct?"

"Correct," he mocked her King's English tone and shook his head.

"Schedule an appointment with them. We need to set up some terms to pay them off."

"Maisie Lawlor comes here every Friday."

Lucky looked at him. "Maisie? Don't tell me I'm going to have to deal with some 'mom and pop-type.'"

EZ stretched back. "Maisie's the owner."

"Great. That's even worse. You're dealing with such a small-time business that the owner comes to collect on past due bills?" She'd play dumb that she'd ever heard the name.

He shoved his feet off the desk, leaned forward. "Actually Lawlor Foods has contracts along the entire East Coast all the way down to Atlantic City. Her old man was friends with your—"

That got her attention.

But he didn't like the look it caused. Her eyes deepened, darkened in a way that said beneath lay some secret, maybe even some pain. This level of revenge really *wasn't* his style.

"My old man has dealt with them for years. Maisie comes here…to lunch each week."

Her eyebrows rose. Hm. Either she'd forced whatever pain had cause that earlier expression down or Little Ms. Santanelli actually was human and showing some female side to her. Jealousy?

She'd turned her attention back to the bills. Nah. He had to be wrong about that one. Even after their kisses, no way could she be interested in who he lunched with.

Why the hell had he even thought of that?

"Good. Set up a time after the lunch that I can talk to her…'"

"You can join us." He thought she hesitated, but she was so smooth that he couldn't be sure.

"Fine. And, for the record, I don't do my own grocery shopping in Vegas."

He looked across the desk and watched a smile form on her cinnamon colored lips.

And felt as if he'd been sucker punched.

* * *

Lucky swallowed back her smile. Maisie Lawlor. Great. Now she had to deal with some country bumpkin who, if the clerk at Yolanda's had been right, had a crush on Dalton. Besides, Lucky asked herself, why else would the owner come to this rickety old amusement park? But, of course, Lucky could care less. They could be in the throws of a heated love affair and it was no never mind to her.

Business came first.

Always did. Always would.

"Fine. I'll join you and Ms. Lawlor—"

"Maisie. She doesn't stand on ceremony."

"What's that supposed to mean?"

He got up, leaned over and wiped a finger to the side of her lip. Before she could protest, he said, "Mustard," and headed toward the door. "Oh, and in answer to your question, it means Maisie does her *own* grocery shopping." With that, he opened the door, paused and said over his shoulder, "Lunch break is over," and walked out.

Lucky watched the door slam, sending a breeze to ruffle her piles together. "You jerk!" She looked at the mess and decided he could redo them until she realized he'd probably "dog the job" and she'd be here longer than a month.

She grabbed the bag the hotdogs came in, looked to see if there was any mustard inside, and shoved the bills into it. She'd work on them while waiting for customers in the fortune telling booth.

Before she got up, she couldn't resist the urge to touch her cheek. Mustard indeed. How dare he touch her! How dare he insinuate that she was some hoity-toity and good old Maisie was as down-home as apple pie and mom. Lucky couldn't resist the urge to touch her cheek because she wanted to make sure there wasn't any mustard left on it.

And, besides, the damn mirror was on the other side of the room and she wasn't going to waste any steps just to find out.

* * *

After three days as Madam Sonya, Lucky gave EZ an ultimatum. Either he find a substitute or she packed up and left for Vegas, bankruptcy be damned. Too bad his sister had stopped off to visit friends on the way home and hadn't shown up yet. Then again, he'd said she wouldn't fit in the costume. Lucky'd suggested Millie, but he had every excuse in the book against that idea. At least he hadn't mentioned the costume size again. Come to think of it, Millie wouldn't have been able to get into it if she'd held her breath all day.

That's how she found herself here this morning, engrossed in debits and credits, him on the other side of the desk, making phone calls.

Yesterday they'd had lunch with the infamous Maisie Lawlor. Oh she was a cutie, but no spine. The damn woman looked to EZ for everything she did. Couldn't even open her own Coke can. Jesus. Well, Lucky told herself, looking at EZ, at least the guy had some taste. She could tell old Maisie got under his skin.

Why the hell that made Lucky feel good, she didn't know—or care.

"I see. Well, Nick, when Lydia gets out of the hospital, you give me a call. We'll settle your account then. Give her my best." EZ took the list of phone numbers and started to dial.

She reached across the desk, slammed her finger on the hang-up button.

"What the hell are you doing?"

"What the hell are *you* doing?"

"You sound like a goddamn parrot." He blew out a breath that had her hair dance along her forehead. "I, *boss*, am calling in all the money owed to Funland as per your request."

"Then how come this Nick isn't paying us?"

EZ's face contorted in a way that she'd have to call anger yet she'd also have to admit he still looked damn handsome—foul expression and all. "He's got problems."

She stood and leaned near. "And *we* don't?"

"You've got a few easily identifiable ones, I'll grant you."

"Well, by the look of your books, I'd say you're right behind me—"

"I wasn't talking business."

She pulled back. His words slapped her in the face as sure as if he'd stood and used his hands. Don't let things get personal, she ordered herself. "Look, I agreed to stay and pull you out of the quagmire you've gotten yourself into. But let me make one thing clear, buddy. If you don't cooperate with what I tell you to do, I'm out of here."

"That would make my day, lady. But you keep forgetting that you have a stake in this place, too." There it was again. That look. Pain. Why didn't he just go over and punch her in the gut? EZ once again wished he could pull back his words. Something didn't set right with Lucky when it came to this place, and he wasn't at all certain it was because of homesickness.

He'd watched her yesterday when Maisie was here, hoping he could get a clearer picture of Ms. Santanelli, but the woman was a closed book—or just too damn good at hiding her feelings.

"I…never forget anything to do with business," she said.

"Look, I didn't mean—"

"Yes, you did. I may *want* to forget that this place ever existed, but I haven't."

He hesitated. If he continued on with this conversation he could piss her off and she would leave. Although it ate away at him, he knew he couldn't let her.

He, damn it all, needed her.

New tactic. That's what he needed with this female who one minute looked as if she'd cry. Then, the next minute she had solidified a look of confidence on her face to rival Donald Trump's during a heated business meeting. "Sorry. How can you say you want to forget Funland ever existed?" He stood and came to her side of the desk, looked closely at her. Gingerly he took her by the shoulders. She flinched, started to pull back. He tightened his hold. "Don't you remember the fun we had here as kids?" She remained expressionless. "You've really repressed it. Haven't you?"

"We all do what we need to."

"To survive. From what, Lucky? What has made you forget the time we took that dinghy out in the sound and the offshore breeze prevented us from getting back? Don't you remember how that motorboat threw us their ski rope and towed us back to the shore?"

He should let her go. He shouldn't be trying to make her remember, but he had to. Hell, one thing he didn't want was to get involved with another dependent person. But as much as he didn't want to stick his nose into her business, he couldn't ignore it either. For old-time's sake. Despite what she said, Lucky needed to get some things cleared out of her mind.

Of that he was certain.

"Lucky?"

She looked up at him, remained silent. But didn't pull away.

He chuckled. "Remember that time we found that puppy hiding in the sand dune and we thought it was some monster when we heard it but couldn't see it? You couldn't have been more than six, but you have to remember." Even though she was quite a few years younger than him, the times that her father had brought her here, EZ had hung around with her. Of course, he was called "Eddie" in those days..

"You called him Frankenstein," she whispered.

EZ let her go, sat on the edge of the desk and looked down. "Yeah." He laughed. "I'd read that Frankenstein was the most popular of all the monsters. My dad let me keep him, you know."

She shook her head.

"Yeah. I ended up calling him Frankie. Lived 'til I went off to school. He died at the ripe old dog age of seventy." He looked across the room and remembered the scrawny puppy he had to nourish or it would die, and thought of how early on he'd become a caretaker. "Guess you'd already left by then—"

"My father...had me sent home in a hurry."

EZ looked down. The years had clouded his memory of some things, but he'd had a decent childhood and couldn't complain about what he could remember. But her. Lucky. She'd gotten the short end of life because of her old man.

It sat on the tip of his tongue.

The urge to tell her to go, forget this place, forget him, sat on the tip of his tongue.

But only for a minute.

Because he could remember his old man struggling for years to feed his family, send them to school. He remembered his mother not being able to afford her own car and having to beg rides to the grocery store because Rosario Santanelli had stolen half the profits from Dad.

And, to EZ's knowledge, Daddy never said a thing about it—and worst of all, he blamed himself for Funland's downfall.

"Yeah, well, your old man had sent someone for you from Atlantic City and rushed you back to Vegas before you knew I'd kept Frankie."

She swallowed. He noticed and if he had an ounce of observation in him, he'd swear a tear had threatened to form in her eyes. But, she remained in control and pulled her chin up. "All that wasted reminiscing isn't getting Funland in the black. And I *am* leaving when my time is up."

"Reminiscing isn't a waste, Lucky. It's a shame you feel that way."

"Well, I do. Just as I feel you need to get that Nick back on the phone and—"

"His wife had a heart attack, for crying out loud!"

In her businesslike tone, she said, "Send her a bouquet of flowers. Give him two weeks to pay his bills to us. Most heart attack patients are home by then nowadays."

He looked at her and wanted to grab her, shake her, but instead he stood and walked to the door. "His number's third on the list. *You* call since I don't have the heart to do it. Of course," he said, glaring at her, nearly looking through her, "you'd have to have a heart to be affected by things like this."

"You bastard."

"Maybe. But one thing I know is, I ain't calling Nick again."

On the way out, he grabbed his Stetson but didn't even take the time to shove it on.

Because she'd infuriated him, he needed a swim.

He'd put his hat on later.

* * *

Lucky tasted the salt on her lips and jerked her thoughts, and face, away from EZ as he slammed the door behind him. She shut her eyes and used one of her ex-bodyguard's most vile curses.

It had EZ's name on it. Capital letters.

Frankie. Now that the orphaned dog had a name put to her memory, it hurt all the more to think about him. She told herself not to, but the scruffy little dog wouldn't leave her thoughts. They'd played on the beach with him, took him sailing even. Now she remembered the time EZ rowed them out too far and an offshore breeze kept them from getting back. Lucky had held Frankie, ready to swim to shore and save him. Thank goodness EZ'd then had the foresight to flag down a passing motorboat, which towed them back to shore with their ski rope.

She shut her eyes. He never mentioned the Fourth of July fireworks—the best she'd seen in her life—and how she got to share them with his family on a blanket in the sand. Something else she'd never shared with anyone in her life.

How *dare* he? How dare he try to make her remember what he had no business, no right to.

If she wanted to shut out, repress her past, that was no one's business except her own. Especially shutout not some jerk who'd let his father's business go down the drain like this.

He'd be better off selling it and giving the old man the money to move to Florida or some such thing. But by the sounds of Doc, who could stand to retire after obviously working here for years, and EZ, this place had been engrained in their blood, and most likely in his father's too, and selling wouldn't be an option.

Since it was the smartest thing to do, of course Dalton wouldn't choose it.

She tried to look at the next bill, but noticed the list of phone numbers. She'd call that Nick and tell him the deal. Business was business. With one hand, she grabbed the phone and with the other the list. After she dialed the number, she took a deep breath and cleared the foolish sentimental thoughts out of her head.

Business as usual, she thought. Daddy's motto. "Yes," she said as some elderly man answered the phone, "I am the new manager of Funland, sir, and although we sympathize with your personal concerns for your wife..." Her throat tightened. The finger she'd used to point to Nick's number began to shake.

"Hello? Are you still there?" the man asked.

She blew out a breath, steadied her elbow on the chair's armrest. "Yes, I am, sir. There has been a change of plans...." After laying the deal down to Nick, she ran her hand through her hair and listened to him agree in the feeblest voice, that tried to yank her heartstrings into knots. The receiver clicked as she set it down, spun her chair around to come face to face with the photograph of the two men who'd gotten her into this mess.

It was then that she realized she was, indeed, her father's daughter.

LUCKY IN LOVE

Lori Avocato

Chapter Eleven

"Excuse me?"

The quiet, obviously female voice from behind penetrated Lucky's thoughts. She wasn't quite ready to give them up, though, and kept her eyes shut. The revelation about her being like Rosario Santanelli was too unbearable.

But because she was, in fact, like him, she'd learned to bear just about anything—even the comparison. So she told herself to suck it up and go on.

"Hey, are you all right?"

There was an annoying familiarity to the voice. With the New England accent, had to be a local. Lucky sucked in a breath to cleanse her mind and opened her eyes.

EZ Dalton in drag was her first thought.

No. She's years younger. "Sorry. I was—"

The girl flipped herself into the chair, both legs flung over the side. "You were in La La Land, lady."

Lucky straightened herself in her seat. "It's Lucky, and I was deep in thought."

The kid laughed. "With a face and figure like yours, you *are* lucky." She reached a slender hand across the desk, black nails polished to sparkle. "Chloe. Chloe Dalton—"

"EZ's sister."

The kid laughed again. There was something very youthful, very friendly about her. "So, you've met my charming bro?"

Lucky groaned.

Chloe's laughter had the power to pull Lucky out of the

funk her "bro" had gotten her into. "Yes, unfortunately."

She slapped her thigh. "What'd my darling brother do this time?"

"Managed to get Ms. Santanelli to right the wrong her old man caused," EZ said, coming in the door.

Chloe screeched and jumped from her seat to run into EZ's arms. "Missed ya!" She looked about ready to jump again, but paused, turned and looked Lucky in the eyes. "You're his...Santanelli's daughter?"

"Yes," she blew out the word, "I am."

Chloe pulled free of EZ's hug and nearly ran to the desk, leaned over the stacks of bills, sending some to the floor.

"Careful—" Lucky ordered.

But Chloe scrutinized her and asked, "What's it like? I mean what was it like to grow up as a gangster's kid?"

EZ shook his head. "Cut it out, Chloe. She's—"

Lucky looked at him and waited for him to crawfish his way out of this one. He damn well believed the same thing as his sister. At least she had the guts to voice what she thought truthfully.

Now Lucky wanted to *hear* him say it wasn't true.

If she were being honest with herself, she'd admit that she wanted to ignore it as much as EZ lied about it. At least she was never exposed to that "business."

Because she figured EZ'd change the subject, and she had no intention of letting him, she locked her gaze with his—so he couldn't.

"She's here to help get Funland in the black," he said.

Chloe gave her a confused look. "Why?"

EZ came forward and sat on the edge of the desk near her. One big happy family, Lucky thought, and refused to give credence to the fact that she envied them.

"So we can get it back into shape and not losing money," he said.

"Duh?" Chloe leaned back, much like EZ's comfortable slant although she at least was in a chair. "I get that this place needs to make money or else it has to close or be sold."

EZ tensed. Lucky was certain she hadn't imagined the muscles beneath his shirt tensing. Why on earth did he refuse to take the logical, sensible way out and sell this place?

Chloe turned to her as if she thought her brother wouldn't give the kid a straight answer. "You tell me. Why did you volunteer—"

EZ made a sound a kin to a wounded croaker frog.

Lucky merely looked at the girl and said, "Blackmail. Your brother threatened that I'd loose my hard-earned businesses because of this place—"

Chloe looked annoyed then angry. "EZ's never blackmailed anyone in his thirty-three year old life as far as I know. And why the hell—"

"Watch your language, Chlo," EZ ordered.

She shrugged and continued, "Why the heck would you lose your business—"

He leaned near as if to make it clearer. "Lucky's old...father passed away and left her his half."

"That he never cared about. Oh right. Of course. The part that he stole money from Daddy? That part."

EZ looked at Lucky. "That's the half."

She glared right back at him. "And I could very easily have risked my businesses, Dalton." After she'd said it, she wished she hadn't. It made it sound as if she did, in fact, stay to help because she wanted to.

Lord knows that wasn't true.

Chloe got up and leaned between the two of them. "She

looks damn capable of doing just about anything she plans to, EZ. But can you trust *his* daughter?"

EZ wanted to shake his kid sister. Oh, the desire to protect Lucky seemed humorous at best. Still, it was there deep down in his Parochial school induced conscience. Lucky hadn't given any inclination that she was dishonest like her old man. Hell, anyone who masqueraded as Madam Sonya for three days wasn't doing it out of the goodness of her heart or to hide a swindling ulterior motive.

No. Lucky was honest. He'd give her that.

Damn if he didn't find himself coming to the rescue of someone else yet again. Just like his family. But then again, he told himself, Lucky was the most independent woman he'd ever met. She'd refuse his sticking up for her faster than he could offer it.

"I trust her." He refused to look at Lucky and fixed his gaze on his sister. More than likely, Lucky sat there with some smug look on her face that he'd be tempted to wipe off—maybe with his tongue.

Cripes! Where'd that come from?

Well, he told himself, it didn't much matter where, but what mattered was that he fully intended to ignore the illicit thought and make some small talk with his sister. "So, how was your trip?"

"Fine. Cool. Owen—"

EZ groaned.

Chloe slapped his leg. "Don't start with Owen. We had a great time. New Orleans is the neatest, historic, woo woo, romantic place in the world." She leaned up and gave him a pathetic look. "Yes, my darling brother, I love Owen so romantic places are a part of our lives—"

EZ pushed off the desk. "You're too young."

Like a defiant kid, she shook her head. "Oh yes, New Orleans is *sooo* romantic. Moss covered trees, jazz bands at every door, hot, humid, sticky weather so's you have to strip down nearly naked—"

"Stop that," he ordered.

Lucky smiled to herself.

"Get any foolish thoughts out of you head, Chloe. Linda is going to be out sick for another week. You'll take over for her." He wanted to walk out of the room, cool off his temper. No way did he want to discuss his kid sister's harebrained plans in front of Lucky. Or, God forbid, the kid's sex life. He cringed.

Lucky was, after all, an outsider.

"Have you seen Doc yet?" EZ asked.

Chloe's face lit up. "Nope. How is he?"

Lucky tried to busy herself with the debits and credits, but this "touching" interaction wouldn't let her be. She should wonder why Chloe would be excited about seeing Doc, but figured the old man was like a human magnet. Everyone that met him obviously loved him on sight.

Still, she'd have thought EZ would have mentioned their father first. Come to think of it, in all the aggravating confusion of having to stay here, look at the sorry state of financial affairs, and even become Madam Sonya for a few days, she hadn't met Mr. Dalton. Maybe he didn't even live nearby, although she doubted that. Since EZ's attempt at exorcising her thoughts of the past, she recalled the Daltons had always lived in Seagrove. Her last memory was when she was in college and her father mentioned that Mr. Dalton still lived here.

Why had Daddy mentioned that?

That much she couldn't remember. And with a headache threatening, she couldn't care less.

Maybe, she wondered, Mr. Dalton was sick. Yeah, maybe

even in a nursing home and EZ didn't want to let on.

"Lucky, I'll be back to go over those bills in about an hour," EZ said, interrupting her thoughts. Maybe he'd been bullshitting her all along.

"Where're you going?" Chloe asked.

"Check on things around the park."

She nodded a goodbye to Lucky and said, "Walk me to the Old West to see Doc."

EZ stuck his hat on. Lucky noticed since he'd filled in as a cowboy the other day, he'd taken to wearing a black Stetson instead of his usual baseball cap. Damn, the cap had given him an adorable boyish look while the fool Stetson oozed sex appeal.

She could handle adorable.

Sexy was an entirely different matter.

"Doc and a few friends are at the casino today. He'll be back this evening or sooner if he looses his entire Social Security check."

"Oh pooh," Chloe said. "Okay, then, well, I'll hang out here until you get back and we can talk about Owen—"

EZ tipped his hat toward her and walked out the door.

Chloe ran to the open window and yelled, "Don't you take your time either. We *are* going to talk about him!" She swung around and looked at Lucky. "Owen's my boyfriend...no, fiancé."

Lucky looked at the girl who couldn't be more than nineteen and let her head drop into her palms. "I figured. If you'll excuse me, I have a headache."

"Cool!" Chloe gave a surprising whoop and ran around the desk toward Lucky.

She readied to duck. "What the hell—"

"Don't talk like that around my brother. He likes the old fashioned, stay at home kind of woman. No cursing. Of course, that's the only kind of women he had ever dated. Some were such spineless sponges." She tapped a nail to her tooth. "Maybe he doesn't really like that kind, but hadn't had much choice." She giggled, leaned near.

Lucky peeked out from behind one palm. "I have no interest in what your brother—"

Chloe screeched again.

Lucky winced. "Could you please not be so loud."

"Sorry." She swung Lucky's chair around away from her. "I'm always this pumped. Can't help it. EZ accuses me of being hyper. Even had me tested for ADHD, but I passed with flying colors. I just love life." She leaned down over Lucky's shoulder and said, "Don't you?"

Love life?

She'd never thought like that. Loving life. She survived. She planned, worked hard. And damn well succeeded. But loved life?

No, she honestly couldn't say that.

"Anyhoo. I learned this fab technique to get rid of headaches from this woman in New Orleans—"

"It doesn't involve drugs or incense does it? I can't stomach the stuff."

She laughed. "No. Only pressure points. Here."

The girl had Lucky bending her head forward, and kept pressing a hand along her neck, and up to her temples where she'd press until the pain numbed. Either the annoyance of EZ's sister being here took Lucky's mind off her head, or the damn thing worked.

Once Lucky announced her headache had eased off, Chloe walked to the other side of the desk and flopped down in the chair again.

"You married?" the kid asked.

Lucky didn't think she'd ever met such a forward young person before. "No."

"Ever been?"

"I don't see what that—"

She glared at her. "That's a yes."

"I didn't say that."

"Don't have to. I can see you were as sure as I'm sitting here—"

"Some would argue that your position would qualify as sitting."

Chloe howled. "I like you. Too bad about your old man. Sorry, again. My mouth gets away from me sometimes. I'll cut you some slack where he is concerned, but that trying to sidestep my question like you just did means it wasn't a happy marriage."

Lucky glared at her. "I...we were too young."

"Shit."

"Excuse me?"

"I was hoping for an ally against my brother."

"As much as I'd relish being an ally against EZ, I don't know what you are talking about."

Chloe leaned her head back, glared at the ceiling. "You know. Another female with the same ideas as mine. Someone to support me in my decisions, not be the devil's advocate and challenge everything I want to do. I miss my mom so much some times."

Lucky wanted to reach over and touch the kid's hand, but she didn't have it in her. Besides, she told herself that she didn't *want* to get close to the kid or anyone else for that matter. "I miss mine, too."

"She dead?"

"Over fifteen years."

"Wow. You were younger than I was then. About EZ's age

or a few years younger. Anyway, Owen and I are getting married—"

"Without your brother's blessing?"

"Wow again. How'd you figure that out?"

"I was Madam Sonya for a few days."

Chloe looked at her and smiled.

It was then a bond formed between the two—despite Lucky's shield to protect herself—much like it had when she had first met Zos.

* * *

EZ headed toward the fortuneteller booth and stopped. Millie looked the part all right, and she had a way of telling humorous things to the marks who never complained. But something about the booth was different.

She's not there.

After getting the hang of it, Lucky actually fit right in and did a great job. And, he had to admit, her looks hadn't hurt business. Despite the niggling of envy that started to simmer in his gut, he thought about the line of kids, teens, all male that had formed outside the booth for the days she was Madam Sonya.

Crazy. Nuts. He was crazy with a little nuts mixed in to be thinking like this. Thinking of her for crying out loud. His business partner under duress. That's how he should consider her. He leaned near the cotton candy booth to get a better view then motioned for the girl working the booth to give him a blue one.

He hated cotton candy.

As the sugary sweetness nearly gagged him, he thought of Lucky the first day she'd arrived. Seemed so long ago. But there was something she hid, and something that had loosened her up to allow her to stay.

With a finger full of blue spun sugar, he smiled to himself.

He'd find out what was going on with her before her month was up. It was the least he could do since she did stay here to help—despite that duress part.

The cotton candy melted on his tongue before he could even swallow as the thoughts of Lucky melted into his brain.

Seems independent women held a certain fascination for him. Cosmopolitan. None like he'd ever met before.

A child's shout knocked him out of his thoughts. The kid was having a ball on the Kitty Hawk in the little children's section behind him. EZ turned to watch, to remember how many times he rode that same ride. Sometimes with his friends, with Chloe or alone but always in the red one. He liked it best alone when he could pretend he was actually a pilot flying off to the other end of the world.

Had he really wanted to fly away or were those merely childhood fantasies?

He'd sure as hell like to fly away right now. Away from debits, credits, iceberg businesswomen, his sister's plans to ruin her life and the responsibility that had him up half the night more often than not.

But, just like the Kitty Hawk, he couldn't leave Funland either.

"Hey, bro, penny for your thoughts."

He turned to see Chloe coming toward him. She grabbed the cotton candy out of his hands. "Since when do you eat this crap?" She stuck a handful into her mouth.

"I don't," he said, tasting the sweetness. He grabbed a bottled water from the booth.

She wiped a finger across his lip. "Uh, yeah, right, blue mouth."

He took a napkin from the container on the counter and wiped. "You should go unpack so you'll be ready to work as

Madam Sonya tomorrow. Bring some safety pins to make the outfit fit better."

She leaned near, locked her gaze on him as she so often did in her kid-sister way. Before his teen years, he could ignore her. But after Mom died, Chloe's look had the power to yank at his protective heartstrings. Right now, she obviously was going to hang around and drag him into some discussion.

And Owen would be his guess for a topic.

"I like her."

"You're far too young to ruin your life with—" He leaned near. "Her?"

"Don't tell me you haven't noticed the fab body, or the blemish free skin, I hate the woman for, and those eyebrows that look as if she spends a million dollars on each to have them perfectly tweezed. Not even the world's best Cracker Jack surgeon could accomplish those looks." Her gazed tightened. "Don't tell me."

"I know nothing about eyebrows—"

"Unless you're dead, bro, you noticed all the other parts of Lucky."

He reached for the sickening sweet cotton candy he didn't want. She pulled it away.

"Unh-unh."

He yanked his hand back, lifted his hat and pushed his hair back. "I'm alive."

"Ooowee. I knew it. Then make your move, stupid." She laughed. "By the way, I like you in that Stetson. Gave up that stupid Yankee's hat finally?"

He chuckled. "It's been retired to a place of honor and the Red Socks don't have a chance." The best times he'd spent with Chloe was taking her, the diehard Socks fan, to games. He couldn't help rubbing in every Yankee win though.

"Well, that one looks better, sexier." She giggled.

He shook his head. "Cut it out." Sexier? Had he been trying to look sexier? Was that even something guys did? Well, he just happened to like the hat and the way it made him feel. Rustic. Western. Sexy? Okay, but no way would he admit something like that to his sister. She was still a kid for crying out loud.

Besides, his kid sister was dead wrong with her insinuation that he wanted to look sexy for Lucky.

"So, glad to hear you are alive and notice knockouts like Lucky."

"Come on. I have to see how Timmy Jenkins is doing filling in for Doc." He put his arm around his sister and headed them toward the Old West section.

"How is Doc, EZ?"

EZ paused. Kid's howled in laughter around them, seagulls squawked as they dive-bombed for scraps of snacks the attendees dropped, then a stillness held in the air as Chloe silently waited to hear about Doc.

* * *

Lucky hung back behind the cotton candy booth. The touching scene of EZ and Chloe had her grab for the counter to steady herself.

It wasn't as if she hadn't seen family interactions before. At Hartwell Holding's picnics, kids were the norm for the male executives and most of the clerical workers. It was only the female execs that seem to be childless and mostly single, too.

How could they claw their way up that ladder with outside responsibilities?

At least she had no desire to have little rugrats. Things were just fine the way they were. Chloe had dredged up the failed marriage that Lucky wanted to leave buried as it should be.

Children's laugher had her turn toward airplanes hanging

off giant metal beams that swung around in a circle behind her. Kitty Hawk the ride read.

She watched, but never allowed the laugher inside.

"Care to take a flight?"

"No. Oh, hi, Zos." The old man stood behind her dressed in civilian clothes instead of his costume. He looked much older, she noticed, as if the years of his real life had taken a toll on him. When he'd worn his costume, he looked swarthy, magical, as if immortal. "How was your day off?"

He chuckled. "Well, let's just say I may be working years into my retirement after the loss."

She smiled and hoped he was only kidding. How many times had she seen the elderly lose their life savings at the casinos back home? It was a regular epidemic, and she guessed it spanned the country all the way to Connecticut.

Sometimes she hated Vegas.

"You have to be careful—"

He stepped closer as if he wanted to put his arm around her. He hesitated. She smiled to ease his discomfort.

"Actually," he said, deciding for no contact, "I had a rather good day. Buy you a cup of coffee?"

Because his offer took her by surprise, Lucky merely smiled at him.

"No problem. Maybe another time." He nodded and turned to leave.

"Wait. I...coffee sounds wonderful. My eyes are so tired from looking at paperwork, bills."

Zos hesitated. Shook his head. "Then coffee might perk you up. The little café outside the Haunted House has a decent cup and it's not usually crowed."

"It isn't?"

He shook his head and they turned to walk in that direction.

She wondered why it wasn't crowded and made a mental note to check into it. Not that she was any expert, but scary exhibits should be packed, especially with today's kind of teens.

Along with bill paying and getting debts paid up to Funland, she had to come up with some idea on how to increase revenue. With a place like this, and she was admittedly not an expert on amusement parks, but common sense said they had to increase the number of patrons especially in the summer months. That was another thing, why on earth had her father and Mr. Dalton built this place in New England? Home of winter snowstorms and cold weather. Hurrying her step to keep up, she asked, "Zos, why do you suppose someone would build an amusement park here in the East?"

He looked at her. "It's a highly populated area. With the cost of living, the average income has to be one of the highest in the nation."

Jesus. He sounded like some three-piece suit businessman. "True. But there is winter to contend with."

"Hm." With hand to his chin, he started to rub as if that would help him think. "I'm guessing the owners made enough during the season to take winters off. Maybe spend them with their...families. Think Doc mentioned that once."

"Oh." She looked around, not sure if she bought that family crap, but said, "You may be right then."

He seemed to grow solemn. Maybe she'd touched a nerve about families with him.

"How do you take your coffee?" Zos asked softly.

She looked to see he held a chair for her. Behind was the Haunted House, but no one was in line. "Black. Sugar substitute. Equal if they have it, please."

He shook his head. "Seems to me sugar wouldn't hurt you."

She laughed at his comment as he walked to the counter.

Behind the Haunted House was a ramshackle graveyard that she guessed was supposed to be funny. "Here lies Fred, he died from a bump on his head."

It made her groan. Who wrote that junk? EZ came to mind.

Another mental note: spice up the graveyard.

Hopefully she could fix the place's balance sheets and increase revenue before she had to start redoing parts of the park. She should be long gone before that was needed.

"Here you go." Zos set the steaming coffee in front of her.

"Thanks. Zos, have you ever seen this section of the park crowded?"

He looked around earnestly. "Seems too young-minded, for the teens, too scary for the little ones."

She poured one packet of Equal into her coffee, stirred and took a sip. "Um, delicious. Have you ever been inside?"

He laughed. "I spend my days off outside of Funland."

"I understand. But I wondered why a ride would be so empty in the middle of the day?"

"Well," he hesitated, stirred his coffee almost nervously, and then said, "maybe we should take a look inside, see for ourselves?"

She wondered why she made him nervous, but the idea of checking out the Haunted House seemed necessary if not exactly appealing. "You're right. It might need some sprucing up that we could recommend to Mr. Dalton."

Zos gave her an odd look. Obviously he wasn't comfortable with her. Well, she didn't plan to make the poor man uncomfortable, but, then again, *he* had asked *her* for coffee.

Maybe it was just a nice gesture since she worked with him a few times.

They finished their coffee and walked to the entry of the Haunted House. A few pre-teens, she guessed, had gotten in line in front of them. Thank goodness the wait wouldn't be long. She had much better things to do with her time than ride this thing. Like grocery shopping and finishing bills.

Zos stepped aside to let her pass first. As she walked to get into the black hooded ride, he touched his hand to the small of her back.

She froze.

"I...sorry," he mumbled and stepped aside to get in.

Lucky merely looked at him and nodded. The spot on her back didn't burn like it did when EZ touched her, but nevertheless, she noticed Zos's contact. What a stupid reaction. The poor man looked embarrassed, as if she thought he was coming on to her. But it wasn't that at all.

Still, she couldn't put her finger on *why* she had reacted that way.

* * *

Chloe saw Doc coming into the trailer section at the same time EZ did. She ran toward the old man, nearly knocking him down.

"Whoa!" He grabbed her tightly. She kissed him on his paper-thin check as usual.

EZ shut his eyes, savored the minute, then wished things could have been different—as usual. At least Doc recognized Chloe. But then again, EZ had to give him the benefit of the doubt. He hadn't had many "episodes" lately. Still, it stuck in EZ's mind every time the old man left his sight that he hoped someone would keep a close eye on him. He hadn't stooped to instructing whomever Doc went out with to watch out and be sure he didn't wander off.

It'd only been that one time.

Maybe Doc's blood sugar was low and had been making him confused. EZ listened to Chloe giving Doc a travelogue of her trip and smiled.

The rewards sometimes outweighed the hard work.

"So, got enough to pay your rent after your casino run?" EZ asked.

Doc growled at him. "If you wouldn't charge me an arm and a leg, I would."

Chloe looked about ready to add her two cents.

EZ waved his hand at her. "He insists on paying to keep the books straight."

She curled her lips in the childish manner she always did. "According to Lucky, your books ain't too straight."

EZ wanted to growl this time but merely said, "Let's just say many of our opinions vary one hundred and eighty degrees. I don't want you hanging around her...bothering her while she's working—"

"Ha! You don't want me around her for other reasons, bro. You've got to get up pretty early in the morning to fool a sharp cookie like me." She smiled at Doc. "Isn't that what you always say?"

"I've been sleeping later and later nowadays," Doc said. They both howled.

EZ had no intention of finding out what his sister meant about him not wanting her around Lucky. He knew the truth was that he wanted Lucky to finish her job here and go back to Vegas. What did it matter what his kid sister's take on things was?

Sharp cookie, yeah right. Chloe slept until noon most days.

LUCKY IN LOVE

Lori Avocato

Chapter Twelve

Lucky eased to the side. Not that Zos was bothering her as they rode through the horrible Haunted Mansion. That is, not horrible as in scary, but more ridiculous. She was by no means an expert on amusement parks not having ever been to Disney World.

Family outings were nonexistent in the Santanelli house.

Actually, Funland was the only one she'd ever been to. Zos's presence made her notice him, though, and that annoyed her.

It wasn't the same way she noticed EZ though when she'd brush against him. With Zos it was different. He was non-threatening, non-attractive to her, yet she was so aware of him that she had a hard time concentrating on the stupid ride.

Well, maybe lack of interest in this crap had something to do with it. Still, she had to force herself to forget her odd reaction to Zos. She'd be thinking he was one of her father's enemies like the poor man downtown Seagrove if she kept this up. With a shrug, she decided her father-complex was rearing its ugly head—once again—and she'd have to cut it out.

Zos kept shaking his head as they swung around the corner to see a "ghost" appear on the wall. Make that a film of one. When he'd shift in the seat, she'd ease further over. That damn urge to move away from him wouldn't stop. Hopefully she wasn't insulting the poor old guy.

"This is pathetic," he said.

She looked over to see his grim face in the dusky lighting. "I agree, but have no suggestions for improvement."

"I have one." He turned and chuckled. "Close it down and turn it into a casino."

She started to laugh, then realized he was serious. "I...that might not be a bad idea. You're not just saying that because you had such a good day at one today?"

He smiled. "Yes and no. You should have seen that place. Packed with tourists and locals."

Lucky turned around enough to face him and ignore the rest of the ride, which she'd pronounced hopeless anyway, but not close enough to touch him. "How do you know they were locals?"

"Senior citizens. The bread and butter of the casino. Oh, there're some high-rollers who lose big, but the majority of their capital has to come from the over sixty-five crowd."

Lucky ran a finger along her lip. "I hope they aren't spending over their means."

"Some are. Some aren't. But that's not the casino's worry."

That last comment took her by surprise. He'd seemed like such a nice man; suddenly she had the feeling there was more to The Great Zosimoff than met the eye. "I don't know. I'd feel responsible to a point if someone spent more than they could afford."

He glared at her until she felt so uncomfortable she turned in time to see a headless statue fall from its pedestal. The thing obviously was made out of Styrofoam.

"Seems to me," he said, "someone couldn't get as far in business as you—"

She swung back. "How do you know about me?" The tone came out defensive, not what she'd intended. But, she really didn't like anyone prying into her life nor did she care what other's opinions of her might be. But that fool EZ probably had told everyone about her.

"Doc, EZ. They mentioned you a few times."

"I can imagine what EZ said."

"I don't think you can."

Whoa. What did that mean? As much as her usual interest was peaked, she refused to ask about EZ. So, to change the focus off of herself, she asked, "Where are you from, Zos?"

He hesitated again. It didn't strike her that odd though. Many of these carnie people floated around from place to place and didn't seem like the types to live in white houses with picket fences.

"Around."

Hm. He could have at least said where he grew up. No way did she let anyone evade her like that. But this guy was like a closed book. The challenge had her ask, "Around the East Coast?"

"Lived here. Lived in the middle of the country."

The ride stopped, thank goodness. Lucky stepped out and Zos was close behind, but not close enough to touch her. They walked out into the sunlight. "Geez. That'll hurt your eyes."

He chuckled.

She smiled then said, "Where's your family?"

"Who said I had a family?"

"We all come from someone."

"I have no one left. Well, thanks for the company." He turned to walk away.

Company? Was that all this old man wanted from her? She didn't believe that anymore than she believed EZ was inspecting the goats at the petting zoo up ahead. He was watching her. She ignored him and hurried after Zos. For some reason she wasn't going to let him get away without learning more about him.

"Kids? Do you have kids?"

He didn't turn but didn't speed up either. "One."

"Then you have a wife—"

"Had."

He rounded a souvenir booth. Tacky stuff. Another mental note to sell better junk. "Sorry. My mother died—"

"Look—" He spun around. "I...don't like to talk about some things. Nothing personal, Sugar." With that, he turned and hurried away.

Lucky remained near the tacky souvenirs, hearing "Sugar" over and over in her head. The way he'd said it, the intonation, was so familiar. Zos didn't resemble her father in the least, even had a raspy voice where Daddy's had been smoother, but when he'd called her that nickname—he'd opened a wound that even a tourniquet couldn't stop from bleeding.

Maybe she just wanted to imagine he'd said it as Daddy would have. The man was inches taller than Daddy anyway.

"I thought you said you wouldn't sink any of your money into this place?"

Lucky turned to see EZ standing there. Looked down. In her hand was a stupid plastic skull. She'd inadvertently taken the thing off the souvenir rack when she'd been thinking. "I'm not buying this, you fool." With a shake of her head, she shoved the thing back on the rack. "By the way, this stuff is very tacky."

"Tacky sells in amusement parks, boss. FAO Schwarz we ain't."

Because she was so shaken by Zos, she didn't want to get into any bantering with EZ and face losing her edge. "Yeah, well, I'm going back to the office to work."

"About time."

She readied to say something then realized she must have been gone a very long time. Seems her conversation with Zos and the ride had her forgetting it had to have been a few hours. "I was doing some investigating around here. We need more publicity, maybe some specials in conjunction with local business, you know, coupon specials."

"I *know* what specials are."

They'd ended up walking toward the office, she noted, when she saw the chipped mushrooms and candy canes that threatened to fall off the gingerbread house. "Good. Then you can start working on that. I'll finish up with the bills—"

"By the way, Nick called. The check's in the mail."

That brought an I-told-you-so smile to her face. "Well. Well. Glad to see he had the time to—"

"He found the time in between making funeral arrangements." He walked ahead of her, opened the door, and walked in, slamming it behind.

Lucky grabbed onto a giant mushroom. She'd made ruthless business deals all her career and none had ever bothered her—until now. They'd never felt so personal. She never knew anything about a client's life, their family. It was like dealing with the mannequins down at Yolanda's.

Turning toward the center of the park, she really didn't notice a thing as she wondered if Nick had gotten the flowers first.

* * *

EZ leaned against the door as if trying to keep Lucky out. With a deep sigh, he let out the air slowly and figured his life would return to normal—whatever the hell that would be like at the end of this month.

Even if she didn't get the place in the black, he thought he'd tell her to go home anyway. Then, he opened his eyes, noticed the picture of his father and Rosario behind his desk. Why'd he even keep that reminder there?

"No, she'll stay and finish the job," he mumbled.

LUCKY IN LOVE

Lori Avocato

The door slammed into him before he had time to move.

"Sorry," Lucky said, coming in, her face solemn.

He wished he hadn't noticed. She wasn't one he'd ever figured cried, but the other day.... Who cared if she balled her eyes out? What was poor Nick Zambian doing right now? When the check came through EZ knew he'd feel like sending it back. Would, too, except that would only be an insult to poor Nick. EZ'd given him his condolences and did the best he could to apologize for Lucky.

Damn thing was, Nick said he understood.

Had to be his manners talking. EZ sure didn't understand her ruthlessness. Then again, he wasn't a businessman and now he knew why. Sure he'd had to deal with unlikable problems in his job before coming here, but he never intentionally or otherwise acted so cruelly to another person.

"Are you all right?" she asked.

He shoved off his Stetson, landing it on a nearby shelf. "I'll live. Give me my assignment, boss. The month is ticking away."

At first she hesitated. He wondered if she was going to apologize about Nick, but then again, she wasn't the type to kowtow to anyone and the look on her face earlier said she'd punished herself enough already. Seemed worse than anything he could do or say and he'd never been out for blood, merely financial advice, help for Dad.

"Look, I had no—"

"Doesn't matter." He grabbed the coffeepot of now stale coffee and poured a mug full. "Let's see what you can do to get this place in the black besides squeeze blood out of a turnip."

She looked him in the eye. Then, she straightened to what he figured was about five feet seven to his six feet. "The man owed a lot of money to you. He's a businessman and understood the situation better than you." She walked to the desk, pushed the chair around and sat down. "I see there are several who owe more. How the hell did you let things get so out of hand?"

Oh, boy. She knew how to push more buttons on him than there were in the cockpit of a 737 like the one he wished she were winging her way to Vegas on this very minute. "I—" If he wanted to win this argument, he had to come clean. Did he want to? Did it matter that much to him that Lucky Santanelli know that he wasn't a total mess-up where running this place was concerned? "There are things you don't understand, Lucky. Just do what you can and get on with it." He looked at her and finished with, "Then leave."

She rocked the chair back and forth. Watched him. Maybe she didn't care what he said. Maybe it really didn't matter to her why the place was losing so badly. Maybe she only wanted to see him squirm under her accusations.

"You seem like an intelligent guy. I find it hard to believe that you're such a poor businessman."

She'd thrown out a hook, baited with a nice juicy catch.

Would he bite?

He'd like to bite her right on those cinnamon lips. He'd always been partial to cinnamon since his mother had baked the best apple pies every autumn, heavy on the cinnamon. He walked behind the desk and leaned over.

She pulled back in the chair.

"You have no idea what kind of man I am, Ms. Santanelli." Before she could comment, he grabbed her by the shoulders and lifted her from the seat. The little she did to protest allowed him to pull her closer.

"Let me go," she said, but didn't move.

What were the chances Lucky was too scared of him to fight? Fat chance. She was more likely too stubborn to move. *That* brought a smile to his face. But scared? Nah. She was a lot of things, but scared of him wasn't one of them. Too damn independent to be scared.

"I don't think this if funny."

"No, you are right, Lucky. This isn't funny. It's—" Damn what was it? Lust? Desire? With these primal urges, was he any better than the animals in the petting zoo humping each other? "It's chemistry between us."

She blew out a breath. "There's no damn chemistry between us, Dalton. Maybe mutual dislike. That could be clouding your brain."

She pushed her hand against his chest. Not hard, but enough to feel her fingers on him. He had to swallow. One, to think of something to say, two, to ignore that he could feel her through his tee shirt.

Oh, hell.

Who cared about why? All he knew was she'd gotten him so irritated all he could do was bend down toward her with the idea of biting her lips foremost in his mind.

Lucky wasn't surprised when he kissed her. Nor was she surprised that she didn't pull back. He was, after all, stronger. Sure she was tall for a woman, but she wasn't strong physically. Never had been. So when she pushed against his chest, felt the muscles that held her so close she could see a faint mustache that must have grown since he last shaved this morning, she wasn't surprised.

But she was aroused.

He kept his lips on hers longer than the last time. Not moving, not trying to force hers open. Just staying there, touching, teasing, with the slightest of pressure.

Melting into her skin.

He pulled back, whispered, "You feel it. The chemistry."

She wanted to lie. She wanted to say no way. She wanted to

pull away and run, but Lucky had never run from things in life—although she should have more than once. She looked him in the eye, "Yeah, I feel it, Dalton. I'm a woman. You're a man. There's chemistry here like there is between plenty of men I meet. Only thing is, I don't act on it with guys like you."

The grin was sexy. Probably figured he'd get away with it with his innocent looks. "But you *did* react to it." He pushed himself closer. She felt the hardness against her.

This chemistry lesson was about to explode.

It'd started out innocently, the kiss. EZ reminded himself that it should continue along those lines but his body had other ideas. Who'd have thought locking lips with Ms. Santanelli would have him immobile? He should have known kissing a beautiful, despite her personality, woman would get his hormones flooding, but, truthfully, he hadn't intended to keep up the kiss this long.

It was just that...he really didn't want it to end. When that sobering thought struck him, he pulled back. Away. Bumped into the wall behind him.

Damn her grin.

"Well, professor, seems Chem 101 class is dismissed, for now," she said, the grin nearly covering her entire face.

It was like some live caricature where the artist enlarges the best features. Geez, he wished his imagination had gone for comical.

Looking at her only made him want to advance to Chem 200.

"Okay," she said, moving away and looking down at the papers on his desk. "Time to get back to work." She glanced at the calendar. "You're right about the month seeping away on us." She touched a finger to her lip.

Smiling, he walked to the chair opposite the desk and sat.

Damn but he was having a hard time forgetting the kiss. Not her, though. She seemed to revert to her old self too damn fast. "So, what next?"

"You know—" She leaned near, smelling like damned grapefruit. "—you could come up with some suggestions, too, at least try to get this place—"

He rested his feet on the edge of the desk. "Need I remind you, that's why you're here?" Settling back and staring at her, he finished, "You're the expert. So—" He swept his hands in the air. "Give me some of your expertise."

Lucky's heart did a back flip as she watched the fool. He'd swept his hands in the air as if encompassing the entire room. His words were a double-edged sword. He could be inferring she was an expert in business, but, by his smirk, he had to mean an expert in kissing. Well she was a modern woman despite what he thought. She pulled her gaze from him—the only thing to do to get her mind off the stupid kiss.

Why the hell was she even thinking about it?

"Okay." She paused, cleared her throat and lifted a stack of papers. "Earlier I'd read through these, EZ. You're owed enough money here to cover two months salaries for crying out loud. Surely everyone's wife...." Her throat tightened. She sucked in a deep breath, let it out slowly and commanded her hand not to shake as she held out the papers toward him.

"I look at each case individually—"

"And let them all get away without paying. Well, my first expert opinion is call in all these debts. You've loaned money out, let groups postpone paying their admission. Even some of these rides are sublets and you haven't kept up with them paying you their rentals for the space. Here for example," she waved the bill toward him. "This group of fifty hasn't paid up their admission price since last April."

LUCKY IN LOVE

Lori Avocato

He leaned near to look at what she held. "They've made a payment—"

"One that covers about ten people. Why haven't they paid up?"

"Jesus, Lucky. That group was from a church in Rhode Island. I'm sure they'll pay eventually, and the kids had such a good time..."

If they don't pay, it doesn't matter, she thought. It doesn't matter to him. He'd never make a good businessman, but damn if he wasn't a nice person.

She didn't need nice, she needed savvy business deals that would get her home sooner than the month. With a forced blink, she summoned every professional skill from deep inside and shoved the papers at him. "Call them and get them to pay along with all of these. That alone will get this place thousands toward the black. And don't make that face at me. You started this. I could be home now—"

"Sure. Desert the place like your old man—"

She jumped from her seat, grabbed his shirt as she leaned over the desk, but not before sending his feet flying off the side. "Don't you ever compare me to—"

EZ took both of her wrists into his hold before she could pull away. "Come on, Santanelli. Anyone who could get Nick to pay up must have tougher skin than you pretend to have. From what I understand, your old man would have these poor souls—" He looked toward the stack of past due bills, but never released his hold. "—paid up in a day. And—" He looked her straight in the eyes. "—from what I see, you could do it in maybe two."

"I... Fuck you." She released her hold under his, shoved his hands off hers. It would be so easy to argue, but it would be such a lie. The fool was too close to the truth, too close to the pain, too damn close to the fissure widening in her heart.

Again, she had to admit she was her father's daughter.

* * *

Over the next few days Lucky threw herself into work, starting with setting up a meeting with Maisie Lawlor. Alone. It went well, and she'd made it clear to the woman that, in the future, while Lucky was at Funland anyway, she was in charge. She needed to finish here and refused to admit that this place was getting to her. She'd never become emotionally involved with a business transaction and wasn't about to start now. No way. It wasn't good for her sanity. So, she shoved on her "businesswoman's" hat and plunged deeper into work.

She'd even dressed in her white slacks, the nautical top since it's stiff shoulder pads gave her more a look of authority—and today she wore heels. Tempted to wear her black suit for appearance sake, she decided not to. The smell was pungent. Why hadn't she thought of having it cleaned yet? Maybe facing her tailor's wrath for letting a "generic" cleaner touch his fabric had something to do with it.

With a groan, she decided she'd like nothing more than to kill EZ Dalton for his brainless business tactics.

Before this day was over, she wanted to have at least ten accounts pain in full.

"Head bothering you again?"

Lucky looked up to see Chloe standing above the desk. "I didn't even hear you come in."

Chloe lifted one foot above the desk and held it toward Lucky. Obviously the kid was trying to make some point with or about her foot. The girl had to be double-jointed. She waved that foot at Lucky. "Jellies."

Lucky leaned near to look at the clear purple rubbery looking shoes on Chloe's tiny feet. "Jellies?"

Chloe leapt onto the desk in her usual Olympic athlete-style. "Why I walk so quietly." The kid had far too much energy. "Don't tell me you didn't wear Jellies as a kid...wait, they probably weren't around back then."

Lucky chuckled. "I know you mean well, but I'm not *that* much older than you. And, I just never had much interaction with teens to know about Jellies."

Chloe's face deepened. "That's sad. Hey! Let's go have lunch and you can interact with me!"

Lucky laughed. "As tempting as that sounds, I have a lot of work to do."

Chloe stuck her hand on a paper that Lucky readied to pick up. "You need to loosen up."

"You're not going to give me some massage or something like that—"

Chloe howled. "In some ways you are so like my brother."

Lucky's heart skipped a beat it must not have really needed. "I'm nothing like him."

Chloe winked. "You'll see. In the meantime, you have to eat. Come on."

"Wait a minute. After that comment, I want to hear what you mean."

"You and my brother? Well, you both treat me like a kid, care about people, and...and the rest you have to find out for yourself." She laughed.

Lucky looked at the girl. She was much like a child in a woman's body. Geez! Where'd that mature philosophical statement come from? She had neither the business or the desire to be analyzing EZ's kid sister. After a quick bite, she'd make an excuse to leave, preventing any deep conversations with her. She looked up to see Chloe stretching one arm in the air as if in aerobics class.

Well, maybe deep conversation wasn't the right term.

Chloe looked at her as she put her arm down. "Ready? I'm famished."

Lucky stood and walked around the desk. "You know, I have an awful lot of work to do, so I can't take too long."

"Yeah. Yeah. My brother should be shot for working you so hard." Chloe walked to the door, pushed the screen door and stepped aside. "Come on."

Lucky had to laugh to herself. Chloe sounded as if she were helping some elderly woman out of the door. She looked to see the kid smiling at her. If she were being truthful with herself, she'd admit that it was nice to have someone care.

Normally the brilliant noonday sun would highlight any blemishes on one's skin, she thought going out the door. And her without her usual expensive makeup. Chloe's skin was spotless though. as they passed the second chartreuse mushroom, Lucky, however, felt a new wrinkle form. Now she'd have to invest in some company that sold miracle wrinkle creams.

Amongst the calliope music, kid's laughter and occasional creaking of a rusted ride, Lucky found herself looking amid the guests to see if EZ was headed their way. She told herself that was so she could tell him how far she'd gotten on the bills. "He doesn't work me too hard, you know."

Chloe slowed her fast pace. "Hm?"

"Your brother. He doesn't tell me how to work. No one does."

At the next intersection, Chloe paused. "Barbecue or pizza?"

"Pizza." She really didn't want pizza, but figured EZ might be in the Old West section of the park where the barbecue was served. He seemed to spend more and more time out there with Doc. Her earlier thought about EZ had been foolish. Why should she care if he came around or not? The only time she really needed him was when she could tell him the park was in the black and to call her a limo.

"I figured as much." Chloe walked to the end of the line.

Lucky watched a table of teenage boys ogling an unaware Chloe. The kid was oblivious to the outside world. She really did look as if she loved life though. Standing in the line, she smiled at everyone that walked past, whistled to any worker who went by as if they'd been old friends and smiled at the boys, nearly sending them flying off their benches. If there was a World Class "Chatting" Competition, Chloe'd be a shoo-in. "You figured what as much?" Lucky asked.

"Nothing. Only that someone like you doesn't let others tell her what to do. Not like me."

"Well, I...practically raised myself, Chloe. Nothing I'd wish on any kid."

Chloe's eyes deepened. "But how fascinating to have such a famous...infamous father."

"Not really." She would have given anything in the world to have her father be different. Damn. She'd told herself to stop thinking of him although it was near impossible since it was because of him that she ended up sequestered at this prison.

They moved to the front of the line. Chloe leaned near, staring into Lucky's face. "What?" Lucky asked.

"Let me guess. A savvy businesswoman like yourself must want...veggies on her pizza. No, wait. Not just plain old veggies. Eggplant. Broccoli. And, wait. No. That's it."

Lucky shook her head. "What were you going to say?"

"Onions." Chloe laughed. "Then I decided you were too classy for onion-breath."

Lucky turned to the boy awaiting their order. "Eggplant, broccoli on half and—"

"Onions on the other," Chloe said then howled.

Lucky got their drinks and carried them to the table not trusting Chloe since she just about bounced off every picnic table in her zest for life.

Once the pizza arrived, Lucky studied Chloe. She once again managed to convey her exuberance of something so simple as sticking a piece of stringy cheese into her mouth followed by a giggle. This kid must have had a darn good upbringing to be so happy.

Not that she wanted to, but she wondered how much EZ had contributed to Chloe's upbringing.

"You know why I asked you to lunch with me today. Don't you?" Chloe asked.

Lucky licked a drop of sauce from her finger. "You were concerned I'd starve to death in that gingerbread house that masquerades as an office?"

Chloe gave her a solemn look. "No, Lucky. I wanted to get to know you better. You know, like woman to woman."

Lucky nearly choked on her next bite. Not only didn't she want to remain here a day longer than necessary, but no way in hell did she want to befriend a wide-eyed innocent girl like Chloe. "That's flattering, but—"

"I'm not trying to flatter you. I always say what I mean. I...thought we had some kind of relationship starting. You know, when I told you how I missed my mother and you said you missed yours, too."

Oh God, she's groping for a mother—and in the worst person possible.

"I do. Did. But, I'm not..." A teary film covered Chloe's dark eyes. Lucky hadn't realized before, but they were the same shade as EZ's, but his were more masculine in their deep hue if that were possible. That's the way she saw them anyway. But where Chloe's were sweet, innocent, EZ's were sexy.

Why'd she have to think of that?

"Lucky, please. I want to marry Owen and my father and EZ are opposed—"

Lucky's mind swept back about twelve years. A defiant girl stood before her father *telling* him that she was in fact going to marry Vinny Bivalaqua. In all her damned independence, she had never once flinched at the man who the press had called "Don," while he forbade her to marry Vinny. Whether she believed the presses stories— that her own father were capable of ordering people's lives to end—she didn't care. She had merely repeated that she was going to marry Vinny.

The biggest mistake of her life.

"I'm going to marry Owen—"

"You can't!" The words flew out of Lucky's mouth with such force, the pizza slice Chloe was holding fell to her plate.

"But you never met Owen. He's a doll. He's so sweet. He does everything for me—"

Lucky shut her eyes to erase the past memories that insisted on filtering into her thoughts and said, "Look, kid. Women don't need men to do everything, or anything for that matter." How she wished she could tell her that Daddy had let her marry Vinny, actually encouraged her, most likely to get rid of her.

It hurt too much to think it—no way could she say it.

"I know, but I love Owen."

"I thought I loved—" She sucked in the last of her words, bent her head and took a sip of bottled water. No, she didn't. She really didn't think she'd loved Vinny.

"You loved who? Oh, wow. You were in love...Oh, of course you must have been at your age—" Her hand flew to her lips. "Sorry!"

"Look, Chloe. I was married when I was eighteen. I know what it's like. You are too young—"

"You sound like my brother. What does age have to do with love?"

"Love isn't…there has to be more…I—" She pushed up. "I knew this wasn't a good idea. I am not one to give advice." She shoved her paper dish and remaining pizza into the nearby trashcan. The teenage boys watched her every move. "I…Chloe, I am not—"

"I only wanted you, another woman, to see my side. To be there for *me*."

The years of not allowing herself to feel, the barrier she'd so carefully built, began to crack, threatened to crumble—but she couldn't let it, knowing only pain would come. "I can't be there for you, Chloe. I'm not…I'm not your mother. Damn it."

Chloe's eyes reminded Lucky of the doe's who'd only seconds before had been shot by her father the one time she'd stowed away on his hunting trip to the mountains—and felt as if she'd been shot through the heart when the first tear fell

Chapter Thirteen

She stared at the office calendar. If Lucky didn't know any better, she'd swear time had stopped the last few days. It couldn't be true. She had several weeks to go in this prison. Before she could shut her eyes, she noticed some movement outside the window. Her first thought was to ignore it. That's right. Ignore it. Don't look. You'll only get into more trouble here.

What if someone was watching her?

Damn it, Lucky. You may have enemies across the boardroom tables, but not ones who follow you around. Her thoughts were getting ridiculous. Probably one of the workers, or some kid run off from his parents. The figure moved closer. Lucky, being Lucky, couldn't ignore someone peeking in the window. She got up and moved to the side of the curtain. Not one to frighten easily, she couldn't explain her heart thudding faster than the roller coaster clanging across the metal tracks. Geez, it was the middle of the day, EZ would be around anytime now. She of all people should have learned to live with stalkers or at least enemies of her father who tailed them from time to time. Those fears died seven years ago, she supposed. Or at least they should have.

Talk about a fish out of water. This place, this family-oriented place had her acting nuts.

And no way would she give into the foolish thought that her heart was doing aerobics cause she thought it might be EZ out there. No way.

LUCKY IN LOVE

Lori Avocato

She pushed forward, leaned past the curtain to see a man inches away glaring at her through the screen. "What the hell!"

At the same time, the man, who she now recognized as being no older than Chloe, yelled, "Who are you?"

She would have reached out and grabbed him if the screen wasn't in the way. "Me? Who are you? What the hell are you doing?"

"I...sorry, ma'am. I was looking to see if Mr. Dalton was in—"

She moved to the doorway, opened the screen door and looked at the kid still standing by the window, waiting for her reply. The sea's breeze was having a field day with his carrot red hair, and if he stayed out in the sun a second longer, she'd guess the freckles of his "Opie" looking face would blend into a mass of red burn. "The father or the son?" she asked, trying to ignore how innocent a young guy he looked. "Well, it doesn't actually matter. Neither one is here now. Looking for a job?" Mentally she sized him up for the chipmunk suit. Though a good six inches shorter than EZ, the kid might make due.

"The son, EZ that is. And, oh no, I have a job in town at the boatyard."

"Good for you. I'm sure he'll be around soon. Bad penny and all." She smiled. He looked at her as if she were nuts.

"Excuse me, ma'am?"

"Lucky. Call me Lucky since I'm only a few years older than you." He gave her another are-you-nuts-look. "Okay, maybe more than a few. You can wait inside. Out of the sun that is." His face reddened from embarrassment so she decided against mentioning his fair skin. For some reason it wasn't anywhere as much fun to tease this kid as it was EZ. "And you are?" she asked as he came in and set himself in the chair opposite the desk. The kid had been here before. Looked familiar with the setting. She walked to her chair, sat and looked at him across the mass of paperwork.

"Owen."

Geez! She thought he was going to say Opie.

"Owen Manning, ma'am."

"Owen. Oh, Chloe's Owen. Make yourself at home until EZ comes back. Coffee's over there...if you drink the stuff." Whole milk was more like it.

"Actually, I don't, ma'am...Miss Lucky, I mean. I didn't really come here to see him either. I'm...well, Chloe and I are—"

"About to get engaged." So this was the infamous boyfriend about to steal EZ's baby sister away. Hell, the kid didn't even drink coffee! Well, EZ had told her to keep her nose out of his family's business, and that was fine with her. She had no interest in a family. Years of being alone saw to that.

"Oh, I get it. You were peeking in to make sure he *wasn't* here." She laughed until the momentary fear crossed the kid's face. Poor thing, having to deal with EZ. She wouldn't wish that on her worst enemy—or herself for that matter. "Well, you can hide out...wait in here, but I've got work to do. Oh, and drop the 'Miss' part." He nodded at her. Very polite, she thought. Vinny, he wasn't. But then again, there was no jumping to conclusions where anyone with a "Y" chromosome was concerned.

She'd learned to be wary of each and every one of them.

After what had to be several hours, and a million phone calls, Lucky looked across the desk. She'd forgotten Owen was even here. No wonder. With eyelids shut, the kid slept silently. Didn't even snore. Again, nothing like Vinny.

Well, Owen was none of her concern. Neither was Chloe or Doc or Zos for that matter. And certainly not EZ. When she looked down at the pile of papers on the desk, she was concerned with the number of people that had owed EZ. What on earth was he thinking by letting all these groups delay payment of their entrance fees, renege on rentals, or loan out money he didn't have? At least she'd gotten several to pay up.

She'd also had some success in delaying a few over-due bills—expert business dealmaker that she was. So, what were a few free entry coupons worth anyway?

She smiled to herself with the idea of giving free entry to those who Funland owed money. At the same time, there would be no more freeloading from those who should be paying their way. "Ha. EZ could never have pulled that one off."

"Pulled what off?"

Her head flew up as she readied to tell Owen it was none of his business. But, obviously a characteristic of teens was to sleep through anything. He remained with eyes shut. Behind him, to her dismay, stood EZ, questioning look on his face.

"What?" she asked.

"You said I never could have pulled something off. What?" He walked to the counter, poured himself a cup of stale coffee and came around in time to see poor Owen opening his baby blues. The kid looked as if he'd seen a ghost. He jumped up so fast, his elbow knocked into EZ's hand—the one holding the mug.

As she heard his curse, watched the brown liquid seep into EZ's red plaid shirt, a protective quality came out of nowhere and had her saying, "Give the kid a break. You startled him."

Another side of herself she didn't want to learn about.

She'd had too much of Chloe's attempt at bringing those qualities out. They must have been tucked away, as it should be, in some gene she'd inherited from her mother.

EZ grabbed a tissue from the nearby box and rubbed at his

shirt. "I didn't even say anything yet!"

She motioned for Owen to hightail it out of the office as she said, "You were going to."

"How the hell—" He swung around to see the screen door swing as a flash of red whizzed out. "Where'd he go?"

She shrugged her shoulders when he looked back.

"What was he doing here anyway?"

"Sleeping." She looked down at her papers. At least she pretended to, hoping he'd get what he came for and leave. But, no. That was too easy a wish.

He took Owen's seat and glared at her. "I asked...never mind. I'll find him later. What did you pull off that I couldn't?"

She met his glare, shrugged again. "Guess you'll find out sooner or later." She pushed the stack of papers toward him and explained her triumph.

At first EZ couldn't concentrate. Not that he didn't understand what Lucky was saying; it was the *way* she was saying it. Her usual businesslike tone had deepened to a husky, damn-it-all-sexy tone.

Why hadn't he noticed she talked like that before?

"So, as you can see, we are approaching the black...."

He looked at her and watched her lips moving. Cinnamon sticks. That's what he thought of. She had a way and obviously the means to buy some kind of expensive makeup that made her cheeks and lips somehow match in color. They weren't a cheap pink or reddish shade, no, they were the autumn cinnamon-like shade of fallen leaves dancing about in the breeze. Dancing about? Jesus. He was...

"Well? I asked you a question." She raised her eyebrow at him. More like a scowl.

"I...I agree." Any woman liked a man to agree no matter what she said. But, then again, Lucky Santanelli wasn't any woman. She leaned near, grabbed his shirtfront and curled her lips at him.

"I don't know what the hell you're daydreaming about, Dalton...."

You.

"But I asked if you understand that your precious Funland could be in the black soon according to my figures."

He reached up, took her hands. Okay, he held them a second too long before letting them go. But damn if he didn't like the way she hesitated, even if only with a look, when he touched her. Why? Why did he enjoy this? Well, if he were honest, he'd say he liked having Lucky around—and not for her business brain.

Black!

"I...you said *black*."

With a look of disgust, she said, "Black. As in making money. As in not bleeding red ink all over your spreadsheets. Yes, when these people—" She shoved the stack of papers closer to him. "—pay up. Funland will be about healed."

"Healed."

"Stop repeating things as if you've gone deaf and have to read my lips." She reached a fingertip to her lips.

"Cinnamon."

She hesitated. "Estêe Lauder's Café Latte actually," she whispered.

Oh, God. He'd said that out loud. With a force deep inside him, he pulled his thoughts from lips, cinnamon, and *her* and said, "So, you're telling me we are making money—"

"Not just yet. I have to get some more of these—" She pointed to one pile. "Paid up. You know, though, we'll only be at zero before we start making a profit. Which brings me to another point."

Business. He had to concentrate on business. Isn't that, after all, why he took his coffee break to come here? "Which is?"

"A casino."

He took a sip of what little cold coffee remained in his mug. That made him think of Chloe and Owen. After making a mental note to run the guy off property, he looked at Lucky. "A casino."

"That's right. I can get you only so far out of the red, Dalton. This place is behind the times. Today's families want more than dilapidated rides and Styrofoam heads that fall off pedestals. The Haunted Mansion is outdated. To refurbish it would cost…a hell of a lot more than you have to invest."

"Nothing is a hell of a lot more than I have to—"

She chuckled. "Right. Anyway. That place does have a certain charm in its décor. Today's gamblers don't only go for machines that clang. They want big payoffs, some even with exercise equipment. And, and here's where the Haunted Mansion comes in, they want a neat looking place. I've never been to the Connecticut casinos, but I've seen brochures and Zos says they are packed. We need a theme, trained dealers, babysitting, kid's video games and while the kids play, the parents spend. Funland takes a giant leap into profitability."

He sat opposite her and watched the wheeler-dealer businesswoman in action. It was almost as if he could see her brain churning out dollar signs. But a casino? He'd been against Doc gambling away his Social Security check for years, but, then again, Doc always came back a happy camper. Even if he lost. "I don't know." Doc never left himself destitute, EZ thought.

"What's to know?" He opened his mouth. She shut it with, "There's nothing to know except profit, Dalton. You want this place in the black for your father? A casino, done my way, will do it."

"That would seem to take…." She sat silently looking at

him, a look of her about to call him "shmuck" on her pretty face. Do it her way? That caught his interest. Even she couldn't pull of refurbishing the Haunted Mansion into a casino before her month ended. Then again, if he agreed, it would keep her here longer.

"Draw me up some plans." That alone would take several days.

She reached into her briefcase that he hadn't noticed on the floor earlier. The day she'd arrived she carried it with her, but since then he assumed she hid it away in her trailer. As he pondered how long it would take, he watched her pull out several sheets of papers and thrust them at him.

"We start slow with some slot machines and Bingo. Bingo's a big draw. Then we move into Roulette, Black Jack etcetera. I've got all the preliminaries done including a number to call to find out about training dealers. They could make or break a casino, you know."

No, he didn't know. He'd never thought about a real casino. The closest he ever came was the restaurant in the Old West section that looked like one. But she'd done her homework and now had cut off days, maybe weeks of an extended stay.

His insides knotted as though he'd much rather this relationship went back to being based on revenge.

But one thing he'd learned in life—you couldn't go back.

* * *

Chloe watched the last of her customers walk out the door and motioned to Zos that she was going out for her break. He gave his usual nod as he continued telling some young girl that she'd marry the man of her dreams. Zos hadn't started out doing too good a job here according to EZ, but since no one else had applied for the job, her brother'd kept him on. Of course, Doc's insistence might have had something to do with it.

But, lately she'd noticed Zos was getting quite a knack for telling fortunes. Somehow he'd changed and was even getting repeat customers. She herself thought the entire thing a joke, but he almost took on an alter-personality as he told his tales. He'd make a great actor.

She pushed aside the crystal ball and smiled to Zos's customer on her way out. The sun stung her eyes as usual when she came out of the darkened booth.

"Took you long enough."

She swung around to see him waiting by the fence. "Owen!" With a leap befitting a high-wire artist, she landed in his arms. "I missed..." She kissed his cheeks. "You." Then she moved to his lips. He always tasted like licorice. Owen loved licorice. Of course he would. The child still lived in her Owen!

"I missed you too, Chlo. Ran into EZ a few minutes ago."

She groaned as they headed toward the commissary. "Did he give you *the* lecture?"

"Didn't have time. Lucky—"

"Oh you met her! Don't you just love her? Well, not love since you love me, but isn't she so...different. Classy. Lucky is so classy."

"She's like someone out of a movie. I mean, here in Seagrove we only see those prim, stuffy New Englanders like my mom. Oh, I love her, but she's not a savvy businesswoman like Lucky."

He tickled Chloe beneath her arms and amid her squeals of delight said, "She's not you, not my type that is, but, yeah, she's classy."

"She's more than that, Owen. I...you've known me since fifth grade. You know I don't have any aunts or cousins that I ever could share, you know, girl-talk with. But with Lucky here,

I...well, I feel as if I might be able to."

He put his arm around her shoulder and pulled her close. "That's great, Chlo."

"Well, she...hasn't exactly accepted the volunteer position of her own free will—yet."

He looked down at her. God, she loved those big blue eyes amid the dots of freckles on his face.

"Maybe you shouldn't force her into anything—"

Chloe let out one of her piercing laughs. Owen winced. "Sorry. Next time I'll move away first. Anyhoo, I'm guessing, no, I'm positive no one could force Lucky into anything she didn't want to do. Actually, I'm still bowled over by the fact that she's here to help EZ with this place. Doesn't seem her cup of tea if you know what I mean. Big time Vegas businesswoman and all."

Owen chuckled. "Maybe he's got something on her?"

Chloe grabbed his arm. "Don't ever accuse her of anything like...you do know who her father was, don't you?"

"I...have I ever met him?"

She punched his arm. He winced. "Sorry again." Poor Owen. She made a mental note to remember that her darling wasn't the world's strongest man. What woman needed "strong" when she had sweet, sensible, and wonderfully fabulous with red hair thrown in?

He rubbed at his arm. "You know I bruise easy, Chlo."

"I know. Anyhoo, her old man was Mafia with a capital *M*."

Owens eyes popped out further in their sockets than even she could have imagined they'd do. There'd been a few times, one in particular that she still remembered when she...er...asked if they could sleep together after the Senior Prom when she thought she'd have to catch his baby blues in her palms. But, right now made that time pale.

"Maf—"

"You heard me," she whispered and looked around as if hit men hid behind the chartreuse mushrooms. "Don't say it so loudly. I mean, she's not *connected*, but you know the old saying about blood is thicker than water."

His eyebrows rose. "I don't understand that, Chlo."

Chloe shook her head at him. "Sometimes we aren't on the same wavelength, Owen. Lucky comes from a very interesting family situation, but as far as I can tell, and you know I'm great at people-skills, she is nothing like her old man. She's so nice, albeit a bit distant. That, I chalk up to her not having family. She doesn't even have any siblings, cousins or aunts and uncles. I read an article from a *People Magazine* about her that I found in EZ's trailer the other day. Imagine being that alone in the world?"

"Wow. And imagine EZ having that exact magazine. What a coincidence."

Chloe slammed her palm against her forehead. "Duh, Owen Manning. He obviously got it out of the library recently to read about her. He's nuts about her—"

"Really?"

"Yes, but the fool doesn't know it," she said, grabbing his arm. "But if you tell him, I'll have Lucky find someone to take out a contract on you." She looked up at him. "Gee willies, Owen, I'm kidding. I love you. And speaking of love, here comes my brother. Don't say anything about him and Lucky."

"No...I...hey, EZ. How's it going?"

EZ strolled up to them, his eyes shaded by the Stetson he now religiously wore. If only he knew the reason why, she thought and smiled to herself.

"Fine," EZ said a bit standoffish. "You need to get back to your booth soon, Chloe. Zos needs to take his break."

She looked at her watch. “Holy crow. I lost track of time.” With a peck to Owen’s cheek because she didn’t want to start anything in front of her brother, she turned and ran toward the booth not daring to look back.

She’d feel obligated to go rescue Owen if she did.

Chapter Fourteen

Lucky took a sip of coffee and looked at the stack of bills that now seemed to have dwindled. Seemed? They damn well had better dwindle after all her hard work. Speaking of seemed, Vegas seemed a distant memory right about now. She sighed, leaned back and tried to picture her condo.

Were the walls eggshell or pure white? She knew the furniture was snowy white, but for some reason could barely picture it. Living at Funland had taken away part of her memory. Now when she longed for a good night's sleep, the horrifying picture that popped into her brain was the lumpy mattress in trailer number seven.

"That sucks" she murmured.

A deep chuckle had her head swing up. EZ stood there grinning. "So, you gonna tell me what exactly sucks?"

"As if you didn't know. And, quit sneaking up on me!"

He grabbed the coffeepot and his usual mug with the Yankee's logo on the side. Typical. As he poured, she heard him chuckle. "Okay, I'm guessing since it's your opinion, Funland sucks."

"Bingo. Give the man a Cupie Doll."

EZ settled himself across from her, drink in hand, legs resting on the edge of the desk. Boots worn. A small hole threatening to work its way through the sole. "Speaking of bingo. I thought about the casino thing—"

"There's not much to think about, Dalton. You need a bigger moneymaker than telling fortunes. Granted that's a start, but gambling in this day and age is what you're going to need to stay afloat." She shoved a stack of bills toward him. "And I sure as hell didn't work my butt off to let this place sink after I leave."

EZ lifted his head enough to look over the desk—directly at her butt.

She squinted a warning at him.

"Okay, I won't say the obvious, but what I was going to say before you so rudely interrupted me was that I decided to go along with the casino."

"You...well, oh, good."

He took a sip of coffee, looked at her over the mug. "I called in some favors all on my own—"

"I'm so proud of you, Dalton," she said dryly.

He grinned. "Anyway, Mack Stanton is going to meet me tonight to go over the changes. I don't know where the hell I'm going to get the money for the slot machines though."

"That's why there are lending institutions." She shook her head. "This place is going to fall into the ocean when I leave—"

"Sound," he corrected and chuckled. EZ watched a flicker of emotion in Lucky's eyes. He had to be quick or he'd miss it. Still, it'd been there. Something, maybe regret, maybe sadness at the thought of leaving had given a little insight into the fact that Lucky Santanelli may be human after all. She wasn't only a gorgeous face without a heart.

"Sound, ocean whatever. I've been working on the proposal more in my free time, such as it is, and have written up some suggestions for starting the place, and for you, more importantly, running it." She raised an eyebrow at him with that last part.

"Geez, give me some credit here."

"For what?"

"Well, I—" He sipped his coffee to buy himself time. "Hey,

I had the smarts to get you to stay."

She groaned.

"Okay, not the best example." He leaned near. "I do appreciate it."

She smiled. "At least you are man enough to admit that."

He leaned back, stared at her for several seconds.

"What?"

"Sounds like you've got some smarts, too."

"What the hell are you talking about?"

He'd made her uncomfortable, he could tell. She pushed away from the desk, from his staring and walked to the coffeepot, which he'd just emptied.

She poured out the remaining drops. "Thanks for nothing."

EZ should have stayed in his seat. Sure he knew that, but when a woman, make that a damn good looking woman who'd proven herself to be a good businesswoman on top of everything, says you are man enough for anything, well, that got his hormones peeked. A guy had to make some kind of move. She'd remained with her back to him, but he wasn't opposed to looking at that part of her anatomy—for a minute or two.

Especially in the shorts that let a bit of soft, smooth flesh peek out from beneath. Her butt. Cripes.

She swung around, and slammed into his chest. Okay, maybe he'd been in her space, but she had to know it—and didn't pull away. Instead she took a step back.

Okay, now we're getting somewhere. She didn't walk back to the desk. He stepped closer, leaned against the counter and smiled.

"What?"

"Is that all you've got to say when a man looks at you?"

"I could go with 'get lost, buddy.'"

Was that a slight smile threatening to form on her lips? He

licked his, imagined he tasted cinnamon. "Yeah, you could, but this is my office. Besides, how could I get lost in my own office?"

At first he thought she'd get a look of disgust on her face, but she actually did smile this time. Could The Iceberg Businesswoman be melting?

"Take a look at your desk." She motioned with her head. "You could get lost in that stack of papers if you weren't careful."

He leaned near. Inhaled coffee mingled with the tangy grapefruit. She'd managed to get at least one mouthful out of the pot. "I'm always careful...."

Her hand came up to rest on his chest, her fingers playing with a button on his shirt. He inched forward. She didn't pull her hand away, although he had to admit she barely touched him. But damn if he still didn't *feel* her.

"It's happening again, Lucky."

"What...okay, you're right. Seems I can't come up with anything else to answer your comments except 'what.'"

"Hm, what does that say about us?" He had no idea how big a millimeter was, but was certain he'd moved several of them closer. Today she wore a yellow, canary he'd call it, shirt with shoulder pads that made her look as if she stood at attention. Her shorts, those shorts that said look-at-me to men, reminded him of springtime daffodils with yellow and white pedals.

But she smelled like that delicious, yet tangy grapefruit.

Famished, he decided to stop ogling Lucky—and act on what any healthy American male would do in this situation. He leaned one more millimeter closer....

She grabbed his face and landed her lips on his!

EZ'd been in charge for so long, since his teen years, having a woman take over was a shocker and, he thought as she ran her lips back and forth across his, damn fine with him.

LUCKY IN LOVE

Lori Avocato

Lucky pulled him closer until he was certain the shelf had to be digging into her back. If he took a step back to free her, she might interpret it as him trying to pull away. Well, he thought, as she bit his bottom lip and his jeans felt as if they'd shrunk in the dryer, he'd enjoy until she made the move. Couldn't be too uncomfortable for her.

As he reached up to place his hands around her—the goddamned phone rang. "We could let the machine get it," he said against her cheek.

"You don't have one. By the way," she said, nuzzling his ear, "you need a machine."

Like some alarm that he felt certain would have every park security guard in here any second, the phone insisted on wailing like a siren.

Lucky pulled back. "You have to get it."

He groaned. "That's right. You don't do phones."

She punched him in the back when he turned to get the phone. Amazing how pain and pleasure blended into a wonderful feeling when one was horny.

"EZ here. Yeah. Well, take it easy." Lucky remained by the shelf, her lips reddened. He'd left his mark on her. Boldly she stood with arms at her side where another more conceited woman would be retouching lipstick, fluffing hair. "Yeah," he mumbled into the phone. Lucky's hair was mussed in all the right places. The canary shirt should be singing a damn good tune with her nipples hardened beneath the material too. "Huh? Okay. Take care." He stood for several minutes watching Lucky, dial tone buzzing in his ears until she shut her eyes.

"Which one this time?" she asked.

"What?"

"That's my line, Dalton. Which employee just called in? And by the way, have you set up that list of who to call—"

"Saloon dancer number seven. Lucky number." He chuckled. She wasn't smiling.

"Some coincidence, and no I haven't had time yet."

"No time! Now you have another employee out. Chloe is filling in for Linda, you moonlight as the cowboy, who knows who you roped into wearing that chipmunk—"

"He's back."

"Who's back?"

"The chipmunk kid. He's all better."

"Then he can fill in for the saloon—"

"Very funny. A busload of fifty seventy-five year olds is coming to the park to see a show. And, Ms. Santanelli, they're all paid up. We don't give them a show—"

"Oh no you don't."

"I didn't say anything yet—"

"*Yet* being the operative word. Don't even look at me like that, Dalton. I'm sure six saloon dancers—"

"Won't work. The others only know how to dance with seven. They'll fall all over themselves if we don't have the right number."

"Bullshit."

"It may sound like bullshit, but in fact, I've seen these dancers. They're not professional. They dance by rote memory. We'll have to cancel—"

"Don't start with me." She shoved her hands over her ears. "La la la. Don't you dare," she shouted.

"I know you can still hear me—"

Her la la la las got louder.

He raised his voice an octave higher. "This could set us back, I'll have to give back that money and use—"

"La la la la!"

"The money for the casino, at least part of it to pay the

employees. Either way we lose. So, Lucky, I need you to fill in for—"

Slowly with the precision of a brain surgeon she took her hands down and rested them at her side. "I'll do Madam Sonya, let Chloe dance—"

"My sister!"

"You want me to prance around as a frilly saloon dancer in front of a group of old geezers, but you won't let your sister do it?"

He covered his ears this time. "Ouch. You don't have to scream."

"Apparently I do."

Taking his life in his hands, he figured—what the hell—and walked closer to her. "Chloe is too young anyway. You have to be over twenty-one to be in the saloon—"

"Liar."

"Okay, to drink in Connecticut, but, hey, it was my last shot. You have to do it, Lucky. We need the money."

"We?"

"And here I thought you were beginning to get attached to this place." He blinked and gave her the best boyish grin he could remember using on every teacher before ninth grade when he needed to get out of trouble.

"Go to hell, Dalton."

"I'm taking that as a yes." The cliché "if looks could kill" was too mild for the one she aimed at him right now. Still, he'd never been afraid of a woman yet. Afraid? How about *turned on* by the sassy, independent Santanelli? "I said 'we' as in *you* and *I*, since the ownership of Funland is still in our capable hands."

"*My* capable hands, Dalton."

"Okay. Okay. I admit defeat on this battle, but the war isn't over yet."

That clichéd look turned into one of the most sensual ones she'd ever aimed at him.

He gulped, hard.

"I'll concede this battle, Dalton, but since you mentioned it, this is a first. I believe the war will be over—" She picked up the calendar from the desk. "In two weeks, two days when I step foot on a US Airways non-stop to Las Vegas."

"You probably don't even know if they have a non-stop out of JFK."

She growled at him and shoved the calendar into his chest. "Here, mark the date. I don't care if I have to take the milk-run, I'm going home one month to the day when my sentence here is up."

"How could you say that even after our…you know—"

"Kiss? We're two consenting adults, Dalton, with chemistry between us as you said. Like two animals. Nothing more."

He heard the words, but not with conviction in her voice.

He looked down at the calendar—and wondered how he was going to make two weeks and two days last longer.

* * *

The next day Lucky looked at herself in the giant mirror framed in light bulbs, trying her damnedest to apply makeup like a pro. Well, she wasn't exactly a pro where makeup was concerned. That's why there were salons that catered to woman like her—too busy to fuss over themselves. She couldn't even remember the tips Millie had given her.

"Oh my God! You look fabulous!" from behind Chloe shouted with her usual exuberance. Then, she stuck her face near the mirror to study Lucky's reflection. "EZ said you were filling in for seven, I forget her name, anyway she's out sick and you're filling in—"

"We've established that already. Please do not remind me."

LUCKY IN LOVE

Lori Avocato

Lucky shut her eyes and hoped to open them anywhere else except backstage at the saloon show.

"Open your eyes and let me fix your mascara," Chloe ordered. "You put it on too thin. Haven't you ever heard of theatrical makeup?" She giggled.

Lucky curled her lip. "Yes, and I'm fine the way—"

Chloe swung her chair around so Lucky faced her. "No. No, you need it darker to highlight your gorgeous eyes." She reached for a makeup tube.

"I'm fine, Chloe, really. They won't be looking at me since I plan to stay way in the back—"

"Ha! Ha! Good one, Lucky. No way are you going to be hidden. When they get a load of your legs—" She looked down at the stupid fishnet hose Lucky had on. "Ooowee. Sexy. Has my brother seen you yet?"

Lucky's head swung up from looking at her legs. "Don't you breathe a word of this to—"

Chloe crossed her heart, zipped her lip and threw an imaginary key into the air.

Lucky shook her head. "What are you doing over here anyway?" She tried to swing her chair around, but Chloe's leg held her still.

"Shut your eyes."

As she applied more mascara and insisted on adding more of just about everything, Lucky gave up and sat still. She used the time to daydream. At least she tried to, but the kid insisted on talking non-stop.

"So, I really want your opinion," Chloe said.

Opinion? Lucky hadn't even been paying attention.

She looked into the mirror to see the kid wide-eyed and waiting like an eager puppy. What on earth could this girl want from Lucky? She had no experience in dealing with teens or anyone other than businessmen and women for that matter. Well, she had to get Chloe to understand that Lucky was not some kind of mentor who could advise her on anything about life. And by the kid's look, it was a real life problem she'd been asking about.

"Lucky, please."

"Look, I'm not one to tell anyone about...sorry, Chloe, I didn't hear your original question." She might as well have struck the girl across the face. "Really. I am sorry. My mind wandered. You know, I'm not looking forward to this 'gig.'"

Chloe's face softened. Oh boy, she must really want some advice not to storm off angry.

"You've met my Owen, and, well, I want you to help me convince my brother that we can marry—"

"Whoa, there. I have no business with telling EZ anything. You know that."

"But, Lucky, I...never had a woman I could discuss this kind of stuff with."

Lucky couldn't help her mind this time. How many times had she thought the exact same things after her own mother had passed away? No relatives, scads of nannies and Daddy, well, never a help there. "I understand your need to talk to someone. I told you I was in the same situation myself, but the marriage thing—I can't help you on that one."

Tears streamed down Chloe's cheeks. She sniffled and looked at Lucky in the mirror. It was amazing that she started crying so quickly. Lucky could see it wasn't a put on, the kid was too down to earth for that. In some ways a lot like her brother. Obviously Daltons were truthful people. Chloe sucked in a breath, wiped her hand across her cheek, and shoved down the makeup container.

Lucky reached for a tissue and handed it to her. "I told you I was married as a teen and it didn't work out."

Chloe blew her nose and sat in the chair opposite Lucky. "Why?"

"Why didn't it work out?"

Chloe nodded. "Yeah."

"I...Vinny wasn't right for me for one thing—"

"Owen and I are like matching bookends. We complete each other."

Jesus. What could she say to that one? "Well, that is fine and great, but bookends a marriage doesn't make. It takes work."

"We're willing to work at it. We know that. People change as they age. They mature. All we want is a chance."

"A chance to maybe ruin your lives, Chloe? Why can't you just live together—"

Chloe clucked her tongue. "Come on. We're talking EZ is my brother here. He doesn't even think we sleep—"

Lucky waved her hands. "That, I don't want to discuss. All I can say, Chlo, is that at your ages...you haven't grown enough to know what real life is like. When I married Vinny, I thought it would be a real fairytale." An escape from Daddy.

"So why wasn't it?"

"Vinny treated my as if he owned me. He...was like my father, thinking I was his possession—"

"Owen's, not like that!" Then, she proceeded to spout off qualities of the boy or "man", as Chloe called him, including how much he loved licorice. Black. "So, since he's not possessive like your Vinny—"

Lucky looked at her. "I...see what I mean? I told you not to ask me about this stuff." She shoved herself from the seat with her blood pumping faster, her head throbbing. Why did this kid have to dredge up painful memories from her past? Not for the first time since being here did she feel her wall of security start to crack.

No way would she let that happen. It'd taken too many years to build.

Goddamnit but she liked Chloe, even liked the fact that the kid needed her, but Lucky wasn't in any shape to give love-life opinions. She'd always been lucky in life, but never in love. "I can only tell you this time I agree with your brother. And you've got to know how hard that is for me to admit."

With the wisdom of a person years older, Chloe gave her a dubious look. "We'll talk about it again."

Lucky didn't feel like arguing and saying no way would she ever change her mind. She looked in the mirror at her face. "Are you almost done?"

"You mean with the makeup or my story about Owen?"

If Lucky had to listen to one more story about the redheaded licorice-eating boy/*man* as Chloe called him, she'd shove the mascara brush...well, Chloe was a good kid despite herself.

Chloe motioned for her to sit back down and picked up at tube of lipstick that she applied with a brush like some artist creating a masterpiece. "Makeup's done. Look."

She swung Lucky's chair around toward the mirror. She opened her eyes and squinted against the bright lights. "If I lose all my investments I can head out to one of the Mustang Ranches in Nevada—"

"I didn't know you knew anything about horses." Chloe said as she put the makeup back into its case. "Besides, what would you need so much makeup—"

"Never mind, kid." She wasn't about to tell her the ranches were legal brothels. Chloe was more innocent than she thought. If Lucky couldn't handle marriage at the same age, and her having been so much worldlier, then Chloe didn't stand a chance. "Well, I've got exactly twenty minutes until I make a fool of myself. I don't know how I let your brother talk me into this stuff."

Chloe gave her a look that Lucky could only classify as coy. Who knew Chloe could do coy? Wait a minute, maybe the look was sneaky.

Chloe sat herself on the edge of the counter, pushing makeup containers left and right. "EZ talked you into this?"

"Why else would I be doing it?"

"Right. I thought more for Doc and saving the park."

"True, but, Doc? What does he have to do with—"

"Chloe, I'll take it from here," EZ said.

Lucky looked into the mirror to see him standing there dressed as some bistro worker. White shirt and red bow tie. He looked as if he'd stepped out of "Gay Paree." Adorable.

Chloe gave a grunt of annoyance, hopped down and kissed Lucky on the cheek. "We'll talk again. Break a leg!" With that last comment, she slugged EZ in the shoulder.

Lucky rested her head in her palms and groaned.

"Oh don't mess up your makeup!" Chloe shouted. "You look too good!"

Lucky remained facing downward. "Goodbye and thanks."

She peeked out of the side to see if Chloe had left, hoped her brother had followed.

"She's right, you know."

No such luck. He was still here.

Lucky straightened herself in the chair. Oh, boy. The way her stage makeup made her look sexier than ever, EZ knew he'd have a hard time with any conversation right now. Not that he'd like to see her in it all the time. She didn't need it. But, the saloon outfit, allowing just a hint of cleavage, her hair swept up beneath the black lace headpiece—man, he had to sit down.

He flopped into the chair opposite her.

She swung around to face him. "What did your sister mean about saving the park and Doc? What does he have to do with it?"

EZ tried to look past her. The damn lights were like beacons, though, honing in on her face. Jesus, give me strength. "I...what was she talking about anyway?"

"Don't answer my question with another question. You sound like some shrink."

"You've been to a shrink?" he tired to joke, but she wasn't laughing.

"Several. Look, I don't have much time left. What did she mean?"

EZ hesitated. He'd protected members of his family for so many years, you'd think he'd be better at thinking of a lie right now. But he couldn't. For some reason, he couldn't lie to Lucky. "I didn't hear your entire conversation—"

"You heard the important part. Why did she say that?"

"For Doc and saving the park?"

Lucky took a deep breath and let it out in a whoosh. "Yes, Dalton. What does Doc have to do with—"

"He owns it."

"But, your father owns it. That's what you—" She stood, glared down at him.

Damn, he hated having her in the position of power. He tried to stand. She pushed him back down, paused then stared into his eyes.

"Doc *is* Daniel Dalton," she accused.

It wasn't a question. He looked her in the eye. "The stage name stuck from way back in the old days."

She punched him in the chest. "Why didn't you tell me!"

LUCKY IN LOVE

Lori Avocato

"Because it didn't make any difference."

"I...yes it does."

He shoved her arm away and stood. "How?"

"It just does." She turned away from him and started toward the door.

He grabbed her arm, but she wouldn't turn around. "You're a better linguist than that, Lucky. If you try harder, I'll bet you can come up with a coherent explanation of why it matters that Doc is my father."

She reached for the door. He took her hand and managed to turn her to face him—and wished to God he hadn't.

Like a river forging its path through a canyon, tears streamed down her face, leaving tracts in what had earlier been flawless makeup.

"Because I care about him...." She punched him in the shoulder like his sister had a few minutes earlier. "And now...I can't just leave.

Chapter Fifteen

EZ'd seen women cry before. Hell, he'd caused a few tears in his day, but watching Lucky, the woman who'd never shown a sign of emotion since she'd invaded his office with her request for a buyout, was a whole other ballgame.

He'd made Lucky Santanelli cry.

He'd rather have taken a punch to his gut.

When he looked at her face, he thought, damn if it didn't feel as if he had. "Lucky, I…sorry."

She grabbed for the doorknob. He should let her go. Not humiliate her anymore. He was certain that's exactly how she felt crying in front of him. Her eyes, ringed now in red, were a clear sign of the fact he'd hurt her. The way she pulled her shoulders straight had to be her way of trying to act as if she didn't care, or maybe defiant was more like it.

But he'd been a protector for so long, he couldn't let her walk out. Yet another person needed him. He didn't know if he could take it. For a second, he shut his eyes, willed this mess to go away, but when he opened them a single tear worked its way down her cheek. His gut tightened. So, he reached for her hand and covered it with his. "I really am sorry."

For a second, some force passed between them in the mingling of their touch.

When he felt it, he thought he'd done the right thing by accepting the job of comforter.

Then, she yanked her hand free and swung around, landing said hand in a direct hit on his cheek.

"You liar!"

Damn, it was good to have her back.

Next, she hit him on the shoulder. Good thing she kept her hand open-fisted.

Hell, it might have felt good to have her back to normal, but he wasn't going to be her punching bag for long. When she raised her hand again, he grabbed it. "One more shot is all you get." He held his chin out toward her.

She hesitated, stared him in the eye then pushed at him to try to get buy. He'd have let her go, too, but when he noticed her eyes, he couldn't. Coldness, almost an emptiness had replaced the sadness. He'd rather see the sadness. That he could deal with. Now he felt helpless.

She'd put up some kind of emotional barrier—no great surprise, but still he'd obviously dented it when he didn't tell her about Doc. On closer observations, he realized the pain still lingered in her eyes and he wanted to...no, needed to at least make it go away before she did.

"Move. I have a show to do."

He looked at the clock behind her. "You have a few minutes. Besides, I can't let you go out feeling the way you do."

Well, the pain seemed to dim. At least that's what he thought since anger nudged in to take its place.

"You *can't*? What the hell makes you think you have any control over what I do? Or for that matter, Dalton, know how I feel?"

"I...Jesus, Lucky, a few seconds ago you were crying." Great. Hit her below the belt, you cad. He wanted to hit himself, but she looked more ready to do it than he did. "Don't you dare."

"Wouldn't want to break something before my debut. Now get out of my way. I'm fine—"

"No you aren't."

She blew a breath at him. "Since you are so determined to tell me how I feel—go ahead." She folded her arms and leaned against the wall.

He knew exactly how she felt. Hell, dealing with Chloe for years he'd learned a thing or two about women. Not that he'd become an expert—no man could ever claim that lie. But saying what he thought she felt like would only be rubbing her nose in it. Damn it all, she knew that.

But he knew, too, that he couldn't explain about Doc without betraying his father.

He stepped to the side. "As Chloe said, break a leg."

She hesitated. "So you aren't going to analyze me?"

"No."

As she grabbed the doorknob, she said, "Why did you lie about Doc?"

"I have my reasons."

"So that's the way it's going to be? You lie to keep me here."

"I thought you were staying now because of—" The woman had him insane! He'd never usually fight this dirty. It wasn't in his nature to hurt people. As a matter of fact, he'd been the family peacemaker for so long, it was getting frustrating. Despite that fact, he'd hurt Lucky and had to apologize. "Sorry."

She opened the door, walked into the hallway and turned to him. Because she was back to her old self, he couldn't read any emotion in her eyes once again. "Yeah, you are one sorry man."

EZ leaned against the doorframe and watched her walk down the hallway. "I am, but not the way you mean."

* * *

Zos hid behind the wall outside the dressing rooms and watched Lucky go down the hallway. There'd been some trouble with her and EZ, Zos could tell. He had to hold back and merely watch, not interfering. Not something he was used to doing. Goddamnit how he hated this new role he had to play. When EZ mumbled something to himself, banged his hand against the wall and walked in the other direction, Zos followed Lucky, feeling every deceptive bone in his body.

He told himself he only wanted to see if she needed him.

At the stairwell to the back of the stage, he found her straightening her headpiece. "Don't you look as if you've stepped out of the Old West? Lovely."

Lucky smiled at him. She had to force it, he was certain. What had EZ said to her?

"Thank you, Zos. What are you doing over here anyway?"

"Oh, well, I come here sometimes for lunch. Better barbecue than in the other restaurants."

Lucky gave him an odd look. "I thought the food all came out of the same kitchen?"

"Well, maybe, but tastes better in this atmosphere." He forced a chuckle. He felt he was losing his edge.

She looked between the curtain and the wall. "Then you better go get yourself a seat. Place is filling up fast since that bus-load came in."

"I'll do that. Join me during your break."

"Speaking of breaks. I wish I could break something not too necessary so I wouldn't have to go on."

He laughed, reached out to touch her arm, but pulled back. Lucky wasn't ready—yet. "You'll be fine."

The other dancers came up from behind. One placed her hand on Lucky's arm. "You remember everything we went through during rehearsal?"

"No."

"Then you'll fit right in," another one said, then laughed.

Zos shook his head. "See, no pressure. It's an amusement park not the Vegas strip—"

She swung around, eyes glaring. "How…how did you know I come from Vegas?"

"I…didn't really. That's just a common saying. Everyone knows Vegas is known for its strip." He smiled at her but it felt more forced than natural. "Me, I've never been there. Do you really come from Vegas?"

"Lived there all my life."

"Imagine the coincidence."

"Yes. I guess. My mother was a dancer."

Zos hesitated. "Oh…well then, young lady, you should be a shoo-in as they say. I'm certain every eye will be on you. Perhaps she, your mother that is, taught you some things?"

An odd sensation struck Lucky, standing back here behind the curtain with this man. Not that she feared him, but, hell, she couldn't put her finger on why she felt so weird—almost as if she'd done this before. Lord knows she'd never danced a step in her life, she thought, then said, "Very little. Mother taught me very little."

He looked past her to see the other dancers. "Here, they're getting ready to go on." He pointed to the other girls taking their places on the stage. One motioned for Lucky to join them. "Go ahead."

She smiled. "Wish me luck."

As she took her place behind the closed curtain, Zos smiled to himself. "With your name, you don't need me to say it."

* * *

Lucky stretched her legs like the other dancers were doing although she had no earthly reason why she was doing it. She knew less about dancing than she did about running an amusement park. The dance number was by no means complicated, but she asked herself what the hell was she doing here knowing she could fall flat on her face, actually wanting to. She'd rather be carried off on a stretcher than make a fool of herself in this getup.

Zos's comment had her thinking of her mother. What little Lucky could remember about her, was having to wait for Mother backstage in some Vegas casino. Lucky must have been so young, but there was no doubt that she remembered. Looking at the burgundy curtain, a feeling of déjà vu passed over her.

Mother had worked an early shift and let the babysitter bring Lucky to meet her. But before Lucky could run into her mother's arms, Daddy had come out of nowhere—least it seemed that way to a five year old—and started yelling at Mommy. That was the last time she was allowed to work. Lucky looked at the other dancers, her vision blurred.

Daddy didn't even live with them, yet he still had ordered Mother around—worst part was, she let him.

Lucky never realized her mother must have had to quit dancing, something she loved, to stay home with her. Daddy must have demanded it.

The music began to play, the curtain opened. Lucky whispered, "This one's for you, Mama," as she lifted her leg and twirled it in a circle as she'd been taught during rehearsal.

EZ wiped the cloth inside the glass, leaned against the bar and watched the show for the first time. He'd been here before during a show, but never watched it like this—watched it because Lucky's legs had every guy in the place staring. EZ wondered if the old folks could handle the view. Maybe it was a mistake to let her dance.

Mesmerized like some hypnotized mark, EZ felt the glass slip from his grip. He caught it before he made a scene.

Speaking of scenes, this one of Lucky, black fishnet

stockings on those legs he'd like wrapped around his, a white frilly kind of slip trimmed with red—the color of hot sex—teased his senses. Hell, this was scene enough for him. Wonder that he didn't break a dozen glasses.

The other dancers moved across the stage like the unskilled help that they were, but a naturalness, a born talent had Lucky dancing as if she belonged up there.

She'd deny it, he was certain, but she actually looked as if she were enjoying herself.

The music was decent for Funland, fit right into the atmosphere. EZ made a mental note to have Lucky give the other girls a few tips on how to handle themselves. Sure, they'd fuss, but by the way they were looking at her, maybe not. Even they could see what a natural she was.

"Have any coffee ready?" Zos asked.

EZ looked up from the bar. "Oh, hey, Zos. Sure, I'll get you a cup since the waitresses don't serve during the dance number."

"And quite a number it is today. Huh?"

"What?" His gaze followed Zos's tilt of his head toward the stage. "Oh, you mean the dance number. Yeah. It's decent."

Zos sat himself on the barstool. "Decent? She's damned good, Dalton."

EZ's head flew up from pouring the coffee. The familiarity of Zos calling him by his last name was odd. No one called him that before until Lucky had arrived. "She is that," he mumbled. Lucky moved to the front of the row as the dancers rotated positions. He swallowed. "She is that."

"You two seem to be doing a damn good job of fixing this place up."

"Hm?" EZ couldn't not look. He had to watch as Lucky's leg lifted higher. He needed a cup of coffee, too. Black.

Normally he'd use some cream, but watching her, he decided—black—no sugar. No, what he really needed was *whiskey*—neat.

"I said you and Lucky are doing a good job of straightening things out."

EZ knew he was being rude to the old man, so he pulled his gaze from the stage. "Oh, yeah. Well, she's doing most of it. Damn good business sense."

"So I hear." He stirred some sugar into his coffee. "What're you doing over here today anyway?"

"I…needed to help out during this lunch show. Big busload."

Zos grinned. "I can see that, but looks to me like all the regular help is here."

"They are. Just a precaution. Doesn't hurt to please the customers. Sometimes these senior citizens can be demanding—" Oh boy. "Didn't mean anything by that."

Zos laughed. "We can be. And here I thought you'd come to see her dance." With that, he picked up his coffee cup and turned toward his table.

"I—" No wonder the guy was so good in the fortune telling booth. He was a natural at it.

EZ stuck his hands into the soapy water, pulled up a glass and started to swish it around. After he stuck it into the rinse water, he took it out and ran a cloth across the inside. This was a stupid mistake to come here today. Help out. Bullshit. Worst of all, if an old guy like Zos could figure EZ's motives out, Lucky could too.

She was one sharp cookie.

"What's it take for a girl to get a drink around here, buddy?" the sharp cookie asked.

This time, EZ dropped the glass. The shattering was magnified a hundred fold in his embarrassment. Everyone in the restaurant turned to look. He smiled, lifted the pieces up and shoved them into the garbage can. "What can I get you?"

"Coors. Light if you have one."

"It's only lunch time."

"So, I've just danced my feet off, and by the way, I won't be dancing here ever again. The others will have to make due if number seven isn't better tomorrow. Get me that beer."

EZ saw the determination in her eyes and figured it wasn't from thirst. She meant it about not dancing anymore. By the way the old guys stared at her, he wasn't about to let her dance anymore anyway. But he wasn't going to tell her that. "Well, we'll just have to see—"

"No, we won't. Come on, Dalton, I'm thirsty. Give me whatever is on tap."

He poured her a glass, making sure to have just the right amount of foam. Handing it to her, he said, "I would have been setting up that list for call-ins, but I needed to help out with this crowd over here." He waved his hands around the room as if that'd convince her.

Over the rim of her glass, she looked him in the eye. When she set it down, wiped a finger across her lip, she said, "Bullshit." Then she licked the foam off her finger.

Cripes. "Nice talk for a lady." He took a sip of his now cold coffee.

"Maybe, but I'd bet my last dime that you came here to make fun of me."

"Good thing you're not a betting woman." He looked her in the eyes. "Or are you?"

"I live in Vegas, Dalton. Where do you think I wine and dine my clients?"

"Your place?"

"I won't dignify that sexist comment with an answer. And

yes, I've been known to take a wager or two—and win."

"Well, you're dead wrong on this one."

"Prove it." She took another sip of beer, watched him.

"Okay. You said I came here to make fun of you. Right?"

"Um hm."

"Well, Ms. Lucky, seems your luck just ran out. You lose."

"You haven't proven a thing! Besides, we didn't say what we were betting."

"Okay, winner picks."

A smug look covered her face. "You're on. I say you 'volunteered' to help out just to see me dance. To make fun of me. To get some weird kicks out of seeing me make a fool of myself. And, Dalton, you have to be honest about your answer." She set her glass down, glared at him.

"Winner picks?"

"Within reason. I'm no fool you know."

"Deal." He stuck out his hand; she took it and shook with the confidence of a multi-million dollar business deal in the makings.

"So, truth time." She grinned, apparently confident in her win. "You're here to

watch me—"

He held up his hands. "I confess."

"I knew it! So I get to pick whatever I want—"

"Not so fast."

"But I won. You said you'd be honest and winner picks—"

"I came to see you, but not to make fun of you."

She wrinkled her forehead, obviously not sure whether to go with anger or confusion. "What the hell are you talking about? Why did you come to—"

"Let's just say the kicks I got out of watching you weren't weird at all. Any red-blooded male would feel the same—"

She shoved the empty glass at him. "Go to hell, Dalton."

"Hey, I won. No sore losers. Let me see—" He tapped a finger to his teeth. "What do I want to win? What *do* I want to win." He sucked in a breath, blew it out ever so slowly. "Hm, okay. Got it." He paused, tapped his damned teeth again. "Dinner—at my place. Be there seven sharp."

She blinked.

He grinned.

And another glass hit the floor.

* * *

After the last show, Lucky collapsed onto the lumpy couch in the dressing room she had to share with the other girls. Thank God no one was still here. The scent of mildew could be distinguished despite the cloud of inexpensive perfume that hovered over the room. She tried to cover her nose, but that made breathing too difficult. How'd those girls stand it here? They'd all carried on about how well she did though. Fit right in. Wouldn't she want to join them on a permanent basis?

"Not on your life," she murmured. Not only because she had a job, a life back in Vegas, but this whole mess had her remembering things about Mama that she had no desire to remember. Being back stage with Zos, brought back that horrible reality that because of Lucky, her mother had to give up her career.

No wonder Mama treated her the way she had.

Guess she'd be the same in her situation. Not that she wanted kids, though. No way. She knew her strengths and her weaknesses. Motherhood would definitely fall under weaknesses. Her feet hurt, she realized, as she pried off the fool dancing shoes. What a coincidence that number seven whoever the poor girl may be, had the same size foot. At least the shoes were broken in, and she didn't have to wear her Italian leather heels. Shoes. Dancing. Who cared about any of that right now?

Nothing could get her mind in gear except the thought of a nap. The decadent idea had her lids close as she savored the biggest waste of time that could occur during the day. With a deep breath, she smiled to herself.

"Hey, Lucky, you asleep?" Chloe's voice nudged its way into Lucky's decadent moment.

She kept her eyes closed. Maybe she'd leave.

"Lucky, hey, I caught the end of your last show. You really stood out. The girls think you are a natural and wow, did the old guys in the audience whistle and drool. EZ nearly threw one out when he called out something naughty to—"

Lucky's eyes opened. "EZ did what?"

"Oh, hey, so you weren't asleep?"

"More like dead. What did your brother do?"

Chloe pushed herself onto the couch, setting Lucky's feet off to the floor. "He went nuts when this old guy—" She started to giggled. "—the guy called out something, I don't remember, you know, like something a construction worker would call out if you walked by." She pulled her legs up and folded them under her. "Baby, yeah that was it, but in a raunchy tone. I don't do raunchy. EZ'd be too pissed."

Lucky blew out a breath and sat up before she found herself on the floor. "I'm beat, Chloe."

"I'll bet. Anyway, you know the kind of comment I mean. I'm sure you get them all the time—"

"I try not to travel in circles of construction workers."

"Ha! Good one. Anyhoo, EZ's face got redder than that ribbon on your dress, he stormed over to the guy about ready to yank him out of his chair. Good thing Zos was there—"

"Again? Zos was there at the last show?"

Chloe wrinkled her forehead. "He eats out lots. I don't

think the man knows how to cook. I see him all over at different restaurants. Come to think of it, though, I haven't seen him in the saloon before. And today, I see him here twice. But, as I was saying, good thing he was there or EZ would be facing a lawsuit...."

The kid rambled on. Lucky couldn't decide what to think about. Zos being here again, or EZ's behavior. She only had enough energy for one thought.

EZ took priority.

Sounds like Dalton thought she needed protecting and from him nonetheless. The fool. She'd donate all her assets to charity before she let him protect her. Let him? She was tired. She didn't need his or anyone else's protection. She'd fired her last bodyguard the day of Daddy's death.

"So that's that. My brother the consummate hero." Chloe laughed.

Lucky groaned. "I'm really tired, Chlo."

"You say that with the same intonation as my brother. I can see that you're pooped." She stood, grabbed Lucky's legs and shoved them back on the couch, causing her to fall back. "Rest."

"I was."

"Oh, good. Shut your eyes. We can talk as you rest."

"Since I don't have the energy to walk back to my trailer, I'm not really in the mood for talking—"

"No problem."

"Thanks." Lucky yanked an avocado colored afghan from the back of the couch and covered herself.

Chloe helped tuck her in, then sat on the floor next to her. "I'll talk. You listen. I keep thinking about what you said about getting married—"

"Not that again."

"It's important to me. I'm sure you know that. You must

remember what it was like to want to get married—"

"I also remember how wrong I was but didn't realize that until it was too late. Divorce, no matter how amicable is painful, Chloe."

"Owen and I will never get divorced!"

The girl nearly jumped at Lucky. She knew she'd never get any sleep until she got rid of Chloe. She was a darling girl, but right now Lucky couldn't take *darling*. What she wanted was *invisible*. "You say that now, and I'm sure you mean it—" She waved her hand at Chloe's near interruption. "But, I was the same as you. Maybe I had other reasons for wanting to get married—"

"You never fully explained."

Airing her personal laundry was something Lucky never did. She'd grown too private a person to share feelings. No wonder therapy never worked for her. She wouldn't talk to the damn doctor. But if a little painful background would get rid of Chloe and garner a nap for Lucky, she'd make an exception.

"Vinny was twenty-one. I was only eighteen. Your age."

"I'll be nineteen when the actual ceremony takes place."

"Don't get caught up like so many young girls in thinking of a wedding as only a ceremony. They spend fortunes on that day and forget about planning the rest of their lives together. The wedding is one day, the marriage should be a lifetime.

"But sometimes, especially when you are young and immature in your thinking, you forget that. Sometimes the thought of escaping something is so overwhelming, that you forget what the marriage is going to be like. The pain. The loneliness makes you do things that you shouldn't...."

Chloe sat mesmerized. Lucky thought of how her knees would hurt if she sat folded up like the kid, but nothing had her moving a muscle.

"So the day comes, all the white, the fancy meal, a honeymoon in Hawaii or wherever, then it's back to reality with a man, no a boy, who treats you like shit—"

"Owen would never do that," Chloe said softly.

"They're all alike. Men that is. They are takers, they want a woman, not only want her, but want to own her. Sometimes they won't even let her...work." A pain, a tightness in her throat cutoff the words from getting into her mouth. She felt a further explanation stuck in her throat. If she couldn't talk, how could she convince Chloe not to marry just to escape her father?

Oh, God.

She turned to Chloe, swallowed through the pain and said, "I told you not to ask me about...anything." The sharpness of her words had Chloe's eyes widen. Lucky could fall into the depths she'd caused by her tone. "I'm...sorry."

Chloe reached out and took Lucky's hand. "I'm sorry for you, Lucky. Don't be sorry for me. It must have been so hard living with your father...I mean, his job and all. If you can call that a job."

"My father? I was talking about Vinny and what a creep he turned out to be. He didn't want me to work, I had to be with him all the time, and he didn't even let me pick out my own clothes. A man like that can suffocate a woman."

Chloe shook her head. Lucky felt as if the kid had the wisdom of the ages behind her soft eyes. She squeezed Lucky's hand. "Maybe Vinny was a bad husband, but your father is who you were talking about. I'm not trying to escape anyone, Lucky. And you keep bringing that up. I love Owen plain and simple."

Lucky looked down at Chloe's hand on hers and said, "Nothing is plain and simple about love. *Nothing*."

LUCKY IN LOVE

Lori Avocato

Chapter Sixteen

She heard the hum of muttering before she opened her eyes. Lucky knew she was sacked out, but her body didn't care where she was only that she didn't want to move, ever. Laughter had her open her eyes to see she was still in the dressing room and by the hands on the clock across from the wall of mirrors, she'd slept for about two hours. It was nearly six now and every muscle in her legs, the legs she'd nearly danced off today, begged to stay on the scratchy brown plaid couch.

The laughter came from down the hall where she guessed it was the employees getting ready to do another show. Thank goodness it wasn't another dancing girl saloon show.

No more dancing for her.

Not ever again at any function and certainly not on stage. She'd leave that up to the other girls and her mother's legacy.

A light tapping on the door had her grab the avocado afghan, tighten it around her and say, "Who is it?"

"Zos."

Zos? Here again? "Come in."

He peeked his head inside the door. No longer dressed in his fortune-telling outfit, his appearance took her by surprise. Now he wore a black polo shirt buttoned to the top, dark slacks, matching shoes and black socks.

She sat up so quickly, a wave of dizziness had her grab onto the couch's arm.

"You all right?"

"Yes, fine." Except for the fact that you look like one of my father's cronies. One of his enemies. Did Daddy still have enemies? Owe money to someone? Remembering Salvador Giacopetti's look of anger at her father's memorial service had her grab the arm of the couch. Jesus, Lucky, that was years ago. What stupid thoughts. This place had her nuts.

Imagine thinking things like that of a nice old man like Zos? Well, she'd been sleeping, she told herself, and wasn't thinking clearly. Here was something else to think about—would these stupid thoughts ever stop? She smiled at him. "What brings you here again?"

"Again?"

She stood, folded the afghan and stuck it back on the couch. "Um, Chloe said she saw you after the last show." In the mirror she noticed her hair sticking out, one side of her face scrunched in from sleep and the theater makeup, now smudged around her eyes, looking gaudier than when Chloe had first applied it.

"Nearly dinner time. Doc's out there. We wanted to see if you had plans—"

"No, give me a few minutes to change and I'll meet you at a table." He nodded, turned and walked out. What she needed more than a meal with her two friends was a shower. No way would she use the one in this beat up old dressing room though. Not that the one in her trailer was any better, but, and here was the pathetic part, it felt like home. God help her.

She grabbed a tissue, wiped what she could get off her face and picked up her clothes from the shelf. She'd run back to her trailer and shower first.

On the way out, she headed to the table in the back where both men sat drinking beers.

"There's our little star," Doc said, standing and holding a chair out for her.

She nodded toward him. He was a sweet old man yet she

felt angry just looking at him. Damn it all, that was EZ's doing, not poor innocent Doc's. No reason to take it out on him—she'd much rather take it out on his son.

Zos scrambled to his feet only seconds after Doc. "I'll get it."

She smiled to herself at their attempts. "Actually, I need to shower and change first. Why don't you go ahead and eat. I'll be back as soon as I can." They both smiled at her. When she caught Doc's smile though, she had to grab onto the back of the chair.

Why hadn't she seen the likeness? His dark eyes, the slight smugness of his lips in the father looked like an older version of the son.

Despite the mustache and wig, they really looked a lot a like. But where a warmness of the years sparkled in Doc's eyes, sexiness usually flashed in EZ's. At least it did as she pictured him right now. Goes to show how she didn't pay attention to the likeness until she learned of the connection. She'd make a lousy eyewitness.

"Wow," she muttered.

"Excuse me? You feel all right, Sugar?" Zos said.

Again the nickname took her by surprise although she should be used to it by now. He meant no harm, and had no way of knowing why it bothered her. Actually, there was more warmth in his use of the term than Daddy could ever muster.

"I...nothing. Fine. I'm fine. Just beat from this day, I'm not thinking clearly. Actually—" She looked at Doc and felt the bond that had started when she'd first met him deepen. Although similar to his son in appearance, the man appeared frail now. "I'm so tired that I may just fall asleep after my shower. If I don't show up, don't worry and please don't wait."

She couldn't tell which one of her old friends looked more disappointed. But she could feel the bond between all of them.

Doc as a good friend, Zos more a father figure. Or maybe she only thought that way about Doc because she sure as hell didn't want EZ as a brother-figure!

With a smile, she leaned down and kissed Doc on the forehead. "I'll try, but don't hold me to anything. Go ahead and get your food." Both laughed as she leaned to do the same on Zos's head. Only he turned at the same time and her kiss ended up on his cheek. Where Doc's skin had felt paper-thin to her touch, Zos's was amazingly firm. She assumed they were the same age, but maybe not. Well, what did it matter? He was like a surrogate father to her.

And a hell of lot better at it than Daddy had ever been.

She grabbed onto the chair. Deep inside she felt her barrier shift yet again.

"Don't worry about us, Sugar. We'll be back at the trailers for our nightly game of Pinochle later. You in?" Zos asked.

"Hm. Oh, yeah." She laughed. "If I'm awake, I'm there. Got to get my money back from you two shysters."

The music started as she winked at both of them and hurried to the door. Two elderly ladies gave her a rather odd look as she passed by them. Lucky had to turn, not certain what she could have done to—

They stood next to Doc and Zos's table, flirting as if they were Chloe's age. Senior citizen jealous. How adorable.

Lucky laughed out loud, but the music camouflaged the sound as a couple did some kind of Vaudeville routine on stage while a giant horse, obviously filled with two people, danced around them.

"Lord, get me out of here."

And she didn't just mean the saloon.

* * *

Back at her trailer, Lucky stripped off the dancing girl

outfit, never gladder to get naked in her life. Not that this trailer was the Ritz, but she'd grown accustomed to the shower and stepped in as steam floated above the curtain to fog the mirror. She liked her habits, the comfort of the same showerhead, the same force of spray. It didn't take her long, as a kid, to form habits—as a means of comfort.

"Home sweet, *temporary* home."

The hot water would either soothe her sore muscles so she'd collapse until tomorrow, or wake her up and she'd get some food. Come to think of it, she was hungry. She hadn't eaten since lunch and then she'd only had some popcorn with the beer EZ had served her.

EZ?

"Oh my God!" She yanked off the faucet, grabbed a towel and jumped out. "Dinner at seven! He'll think I'm reneging on my deal." No way in hell did she want *him* to think she'd renege on any deal—especially one with him.

* * *

Seven thirteen. EZ looked at his watch, walked to the stove to see if maybe his watch was fast. Seven fourteen. He headed into the bedroom, looked at the clock radio. Seven twelve. Close enough. She wasn't coming. Lucky had lost a bet and wasn't coming to fulfill his win.

What did he expect anyway? She'd jump at the chance to wine and dine with him? Back in the living room, he slumped over the arm of the couch and asked himself why he wanted her to come?

He was hot for her body, yeah, sure. So, he could satisfy that temperature with plenty of other women. Getting a date in this little town was not an impossibility for him. Seemed there was a shortage of eligible bachelors his age, so several of the women, even Yolanda from the boutique had asked him out over and over. Maisie had nearly thrown herself at him, but after a few dates and a zillion requests for him to tinker on her car, fix the door on her house or numerous other "needy" things, he'd summoned every ounce of tact he could and dumped her. Actually, she'd taken it rather badly until, he noticed, her last meeting with Lucky. Oh well, he dated a few more before Maisie, lied that he was too busy to the others.

But, he thought, looking at the door, he really wanted this date tonight. Lucky would be furious if he called it a "date" he was certain. Okay, dinner. He wanted this dinner to happen.

As much as their relationship had started out because of their father's dealings—the revenge had dwindled as his interest in her increased. Oh she had her faults all right, but he'd never met up with such an independent woman before. He'd admit her gorgeous body was partly the attraction, okay, a hell of a big part, but the way she behaved was of interest, too.

For more years than he cared to remember, his family had relied on him one way or the other. After his mother died, he'd had to help Doc get through the sadness, which, he thought, never really happened.

Because his father took so long grieving, EZ had the responsibility of his kid sister thrown in his lap. He loved her, loved Doc, but had put his own life on hold so many times to salvage something in theirs, he'd grown exhausted. Tired of being the glue that held the family together. Tired of being both father and brother to a kid who couldn't see how she was about to ruin her life.

And, worst of all, tired of Funland.

It'd been his home since birth, and now his prison in adulthood.

Maybe part of his attraction to Lucky was her holding the key to unlock that prison.

LUCKY IN LOVE

Lori Avocato

He'd wine and dine a woman who didn't *need* him—and hoped to hell she *wanted* him—tonight.

With a chuckle, he thought of the day he'd become reacquainted with her, and how she'd jumped into the water to save him. Imagine, a woman trying to take care of him. The change was welcome, even if it had only been for several weeks.

No way would he ever forget how she looked wet either. Geez, his insides were doing cartwheels imagining the way her blouse had clung to her. Those eyes standing out with her hair slicked down by the water.

He knew this feeling in his gut wasn't hunger for his homemade spaghetti sauce but more for the lady who—

With his legs resting over the couch's arm, he shut his eyes, "You're pathetic, Dalton."

Jesus! His heart whacked against his chest. He'd never called himself that before. The shocking term, that came so naturally, had him thinking there was more to this wanting Lucky Santanelli than met his eye—or maybe then he cared to admit.

"What the hell difference does it make? She stood me up. Reneged on our bet the—"

"I've never reneged on anything, Dalton."

Jesus, again! His legs lifted into the air so fast, the next thing he knew, he was at her feet, glaring up at her. Sure he'd wanted to be on his back with her sometime throughout this evening, but not with her standing above him—laughing.

"Shut up." He pushed himself up, but caught his arm on the coffee table, sending it over, hors d'oeuvres flying onto the green shag carpet.

"Need a hand?"

"No, and stop that or you're liable to choke on your own laughter." He got up, brushed off his jeans and looked at the floor. "Damn it."

Tears wept down her cheeks as she tried to control her laughter. A crimson hue crawled up her neck. He thought she muttered something but couldn't hear in his combination anger/embarrassment. "Let it out or you'll explode."

She wiped at her eyes with her hand. "Get some paper towels and I'll help you clean the mess—" Turning toward the overturned table, she shook her head. "The cheese looks salvageable."

"Great. You eat it then."

She sucked in air, more than likely swallowing another laugh and touched his arm, "I'm sorry. It all looked wonderful. Sorry I was late, too, I—"

"That's it. If you were here on time, none of this would have happened. Don't you know to knock on someone's door?"

She pushed past him, "I called your name and heard you say something. Mumbled something that is," she said as she grabbed the roll of paper towels off the counter. "Here, wipe." When she bent to get the first wipe in, he couldn't move. Grabbed the counter. Thought he'd have been better off if she hadn't come here. And, he slouched against the wall and then thought he wouldn't make it very far into this meal if he kept looking at her.

Creamy legs barely covered by the shorts she wore were the first tantalizing part he noticed, but then she bent further over. He groaned.

"Are you going to help or cry over spilled hors d'oeuvres?"

"Cry—"

She swung her head around. Apples. An apple scent floated on the breeze propelled by her motion. She'd switched her shampoo, he thought, at first disappointed. Wait. He inhaled again. Nice. Grapefruit was more of a morning scent. Man, he was going nuts.

"Get down and help." She sat back on her legs. "I'm not doing all the work until you do."

But then I'll be closer to you, closer to your scent, your hair that looks softer than feathers and your chest—spare me, Lord—where I can almost see through your pink top. Or at least wish I could see through it. "Why...why don't you help yourself to some wine and I'll clean up. My mess. My job."

The stubborn woman didn't budge. "Since you blame me for it happening, I'll help. Although I have no idea why you blame me."

He knelt down and forced his hormones to cool off. "I wouldn't have been on the couch if you came on time. Simple as that."

She looked at him as if the cheese, ranch dip and chips had fallen over his head. "You lost me, but you're blaming me is no surprise."

With a handful of chips in one hand and the soggy paper towel in the other, he sat back and looked at her. "No, I...okay, we started off on the wrong foot—"

"You're the one who knocked over the table." She shoved her paper towel into his hand and leaned against the couch.

"Yeah, no, I mean, okay I did that, but I'm talking about the wrong foot since you arrived."

"Oh." He'd never seen Lucky at a loss for words. "You started that, too. If you'd bought me out—"

He shoved the mess into a nearby trash basket. "You know I couldn't—"

"Right. That leads me to why you lied to me about your father."

He leaned back, inhaled; let the apples jog memories of fall, pies and mom out of his thoughts. He needed to concentrate on the conversation, or he knew he'd find himself eating alone very shortly. "Let's get a glass of wine first." He reached out; she hesitated but took his hand eventually.

Bad move on his part. A man who lusts after a woman should not have any, not even the slightest contact with said woman until…if there was a God in heaven, later.

Because he was a gentleman, he helped her up, then pulled back his hand as if she were fire—he ice. It only took turning toward the wine-rack to prevent him from seeing her stunned expression. Make that maybe more like an are-you-nuts expression. Well, no matter her expression, he wasn't looking.

EZ busied himself trying to open the fool wine bottle. He'd opened a million gallons worth, but knowing Lucky stood behind him, watching, had his fingers turning to Silly Putty. Damn, he'd been alone hundreds of times with women before. Why the hell was his body and mind falling off a cliff on this one?

It really *was* a date.

That had to be the cause. They'd been alone in the office, the fortune telling booth, numerous places in the park. Public places where any number of employees or patrons could interrupt. But being alone is his trailer—maybe he should have taken her out to a restaurant.

Nah. No privacy.

"Either you're stalling for time cause you don't want to talk about your lying, or you've never opened a bottle of wine before." She came around, reached out, and took the opener from him. "A woman could die of thirst before you serve her." With that, she shoved the opener into the bottle while he held it. His insides felt as tight as the corkscrew turning in the wine bottle.

"I really didn't lie, you know." He took the glasses he'd set out earlier, poured hers.

"Semantics, Dalton. A lie of omission." She took it, nodded

a thanks and said, "Okay?"

He took a swig of his and motioned for them to sit. "Go ahead. I'll rummage up some more cheese and crackers."

"I'd say never mind, but I am famished. By the way," She took a sip of wine.

A burgundy droplet settled on her lip. Normally he had the control of a marine, but right now, maybe the atmosphere, the situation, the gorgeous woman, who knew? had him reach out and wipe it with his finger.

A slight tensing, but otherwise she remained still. "Wine," he muttered as she might have thought he only wanted to touch her. Well, he did, but again he'd go with a lie of omission.

"Thanks." Her word came out a bit throaty.

That was good. Obviously, and he chose to interpret it as such, she'd been affected by the contact, too. They stood staring at each other for what seemed like hours although he knew it was only seconds. "I'll...get those crackers."

"I'll sit down." They sounded animated, which, again he interpreted as a good sign. A lusty atmosphere surrounded them he was certain. Why hadn't he thought of turning down the already dim lights, putting on a little saxophone music?

Going with that lie of omission again.

Sure he intended to seduce her, he realized now, but he wasn't going to all out say so.

Lucky sat on the couch and took another sip of wine while EZ got the crackers. Her body wanted nothing more right now than to fall asleep. However, her mind was another matter. He looked so cute, so home-sweet-home-like pouring crackers into a basket and tearing the wrapper off an individually packaged Kraft cheese slice. The Brie he'd set out earlier had been ruined.

Taking another sip of wine, she looked over the glass's rim and told herself to watch out. She was angry with him for lying.

She couldn't let her desire for a good-looking man get in her way. Hell, she was a grown woman and could handle herself. Always had. If she wanted to jump Dalton's bones—for her own damn pleasure—she'd do it.

But she might not have the energy.

He walked over, held the plate out toward her. "This is the best I can do."

She chuckled. "It'll be fine. Whatever you've got on the stove smells wonderful by the way."

"Hope you like spaghetti." He sat opposite her on a navy plaid stuffed chair.

Obviously all the trailer furnishings were bought at the same discount warehouse. But for some reason, and she wasn't thinking too clearly in her exhausted state, EZ's trailer looked masculine. Doc's and Zos's looked, well, early senior citizen. And hers, still looked like a crappy trailer.

She had no home here even if the shower felt right.

"Look, Lucky, I am sorry about not telling you about my dad." He drank the rest of his wine, picked up the bottle, topped hers off and refilled his glass.

"Lies are something I can't tolerate. Heard too many of them from my father." She covered a cracker with cheese, handed it to him and fixed one for herself that she inhaled.

"The water is boiling. We'll eat soon." He bit his cracker. "Again, sorry about the Brie and dip. And, I understand how you feel about lying. I'm no fan of it myself—"

"You couldn't possible understand how I feel, Dalton. My father's entire life was lie. You at least grew up with loving parents, a sister—"

He shut his eyes. Suddenly she got the impression that she'd hit some nerve. "Look, I'm sorry if I—"

When his eyes opened, she noted there was sadness there.

"Doc was always there for me, especially after mom died, but he wasn't Father Knows Best, Lucky. He had his faults, too. I love him dearly, but Doc wasn't the most responsible—no, he definitely wasn't responsible. I was left to clean up after him many a time."

Lucky felt her eyes widen. Earlier she'd never have thought she could manage it with lids that begged to close. But she'd never knew, never suspected that the Dalton's weren't the Anderson's from the TV show "Father Knows Best." She could picture EZ as Bud, Chloe as Kitten. "I...my memories of seeing your family are so different. Now I remember. I always envied you, envied your life."

He leaned back, set his boots on the coffee table he'd earlier set right. "Don't get me wrong, I had a great childhood—until my mother died."

"Then you've got me beat there."

"Was it so bad for you? I mean, I remember you as such a tough kid. So independent. So spitting mad if things didn't go your way."

"I was spoiled rotten, but learned early on—maybe after my mother died like yours—to take care of myself."

He smiled. "I remember one summer when you came here and I tried to teach you how to fish. Man, you knew it all. Stubborn, I guess you were about sixteen, stubborn sixteen year old."

She laughed. "Well I remember catching a fish that could have eaten yours in one gulp." With that, she chomped her cracker in half.

He smiled. "You know, I never met your mom. I'm sorry I didn't."

Lucky felt as if the cracker would lodge in her throat and choke her. He talked about her mother as if she were any ordinary mom. The kind all the other girls in school had. The kind she wanted. She couldn't even manage a smile.

EZ continued on, "Was she anything like you? Guess I should say are you like her?"

The wine helped get the cracker moving, but her throat felt as if it had closed anyway. She shook her head. EZ set his glass down. Lifted his feet off the table. "Hey, I didn't mean anything. I sure didn't mean to upset you—"

The barrier strengthened. No one could upset her anymore. She wouldn't let them. So, she shoved the rest of the cracker into her mouth, drank some wine and said, "I'm nothing like her. She was a dancer. I may have made an attempt today—"

"A damn good one."

"I'm not a dancer, not a wife and not the type of woman to let a man run all over me. I had to learn that the hard way with Vinny—" Oh God, she hadn't meant that last part to come out. The wine, the exhaustion, had made her more vulnerable, her control slipped.

And Lucky needed to be in control.

Because she didn't have the energy to muster any up right now, she slammed her glass onto the table. It tipped, sending burgundy onto the green carpet. She grabbed a napkin at the same time EZ did. She couldn't lie. She noticed his touch, but she also couldn't stay here. "Sorry about the carpet. You know, I'm so exhausted my reflexes aren't up to par. I have to go."

He grabbed her arm before she could get up. "No you don't. I apologized. No more questions about your mom. Stay. You have to eat—"

"I have food in my trailer. Let me go."

He tightened his hold. "I don't want to."

She paused. "Don't want to?"

He stood, stepped over the table and was next to her before

she could get up. "No, I don't. I want to spend time with you—"

Oh, God. She should go. She should leave and forget that she wanted to stay. She should let her barrier shield herself from wanting to be here with him, wanting to kiss his lips as he stood inches away in the cramped trailer setting.

She'd taught herself never to become committed to a man, never become involved. She'd lost her nerve, her interest after the Vinny fiasco. Damn but she was a woman of granite in the boardroom, but here was a man she knew she could fall for, she'd turned to freaking Brie.

So, she yanked her hand free and turned to go.

EZ was on her in a second. "Okay, stay and eat. No more conversations about family—"

"Convenient way of getting out of telling me the truth about Doc." Oh geez, she was exhausted. She wanted to go, but her thoughts were so jumbled, she'd opened the door to another conversation.

He stepped in front of her. "He has early Alzheimer's."

Lucky stepped back. Not because she couldn't deal with being so near EZ, not this time anyway, but something in her had her react that way. "Alzheimer's," she whispered. It hurt to think of Doc being ill.

"He's been good lately, at least the past week. Before that I'd found him in one of the booths and he couldn't tell me why he was there. He...won't admit any of this so don't bring it up—"

"I wouldn't."

"Doc's a tough old guy and I know he's going to be...no, I don't know anything of the sorts. I've had to take care of him and Chloe for so long, I can't even admit that he may some day not even know me."

She stepped forward, reached up, and wiped the tears from EZ's cheeks.

Chapter Seventeen

Lucky placed both hands on EZ's face and captured his attention with her gaze. The tired feeling she'd been so overcome with dissipated. His shoulders began to shake as the tears increased, deep sobs filled the air. Before she could pull him closer, he leaned down, rested his head against hers.

"I...I'm sorry. I didn't mean to dump all this on you." He sucked in a breath. "I'm so tired...just so tired of it all. And that makes me feel like shit."

She lifted his head and whispered, "Let yourself be normal, human. We all feel like shit when pushed to the—" Before she could finish, she placed her lips on his. The kiss was brief, one of friendship to someone in need. But when she pulled back, looked in his eyes—it wasn't friendship she saw. He grabbed her shoulders, pulled her close and this time the kisses came from passion.

And kept coming.

EZ crushed her against his chest. She could tell how fit he was that time he'd stripped off the chipmunk costume then his shirt to dive into the sound, but feeling it, feeling him pressed against her breasts nearly had her passing out. What she'd earlier called exhaustion, could now be classified as mind-tingling desire.

He worked his lips around her, over hers, nibbling at her bottom lip, groaning in pleasure until she had to pull back for air. After a deep breath, she realized air wasn't what she hungered for right now. EZ tasted of grapes, she thought, as she lifted her head and kissed him again. This time he supported her against his solid body with his arms wrapped protectively around her.

When she inhaled, she noticed his cologne, the one she remembered from the first day, and knew she'd always remember him whenever she inhaled it—even if a thousand years had passed. Before she could think, he lifted her into his arms, walked by the stove, reached out and shut off the burners as they passed.

"I really hope you're not starving."

"I'm not," she lied, hungrier for him than the meal that earlier had her about ready to gobble down an entire plateful in seconds. She looked up into his eyes. "Are you all right now?"

He leaned back, smiled. They passed the living room. He paused at the doorway to his room and looked at her. "You've knocked my feeling sorry for myself right out of me. Now—" He leaned against the doorframe, smiled, looked past her to his room. "—are *you* all right with this?"

She followed his gaze, saw the bed, a double with black and tan striped comforter, a tiny lamp lit dimly on a bedside stand, which was all that could fit into the small room and nodded. "Um."

Again he leaned back, laughed and then leaned forward and kissed her. This time his hunger for her didn't come from sadness. He eased her down on the bed, paused and looked at her. "Last chance saloon, ma'am."

She smiled at him, ran her fingers along her shirt, and undid the buttons one by one.

EZ swallowed. He had to or else he'd choke on the saliva building up at record speed in his mouth while he watched Lucky undo her top, slowly, seductively like some siren tempting a god. Only the way he felt right now, more like an animal, say a wolf, watching the hunter setting his trap with a sweet, tender morsel. Yeah, he could do "wolf" with Lucky. He ran his tongue across his lips and knew he'd salivate like the wolf he imagined himself if he didn't get to touch her soon.

She spread the material.

He shoved his arm against the doorframe. It was either that or jump on top of her in a heartbeat.

Despite his lust, he wasn't the jump-her-bones-type. More like ease himself down. Nothing like savoring every luscious moment.

Her bra was pink. He had to smile. For some reason he expected midnight black or brilliant red. But seeing the pink, like some little girl's candy-colored ribbon took him by surprise. But Lucky Santanelli was no little girl.

In her prone position, her breasts, full, yet soft looking eased out to the sides of the material. A hint of nipple, dark like her hair peeked above the lacy pink. "I…need to…sit—"

"No." She looked him straight in the eye, control in her voice, power in her gaze. "Not yet." With that she walked her fingers along her waist headed to the center of the bra.

"God, I hope the clasp is in front—"

With a flip, the pink fell to the side, releasing her breasts, firm and begging for him to touch. Or, maybe it was his hormones; his own fingers begging to do the touching. "I want to…please let me—"

She laughed a deep throaty sound he'd never heard from her before—yet would crave the sound, he knew, over and over. "Not yet," she said.

When she lifted her hips, he feared he'd explode any second. But he didn't want to do that…until he was inside Lucky. With a few deep breathes, a grasp on the doorframe that would more than likely leave an imprint, and his jeans tightening so that he might not be *able* to move when she gave the okay, he managed to maintain an ounce of sanity.

But it wouldn't last long.

With fingers that he never knew were so deft, so nimble, she slid her yellow shorts down, revealing matching pink panties. *Give me strength*. A gasp sneaked out when she wiggled the shorts over her hips.

Lucky purred.

Damn, now she sounded like a kitten, but when he looked at her lying there in all her pink glory—all feline thoughts vanished. She was a beautiful woman, he'd known that from day one. But seeing her on his bed scantily clad in the pink lace, she was a damned fit, damned sexy woman—which he wanted more now than he could have guessed before.

"Now?" His voice cracked like a teen in the backseat of a '69 Chevy. Flames of red must have heated up his cheeks or else the trailer was on fire. Please, God, no. No way did he want to evacuate. Surely he'd shut off the stove. Yeah, a vague thought of doing it filtered through his mixed-up brain.

She lifted her finger and shook it at him all the while smiling at him. Obviously she was more of a control freak than he could have imagined. Well, he wanted independent, he got independent.

Both of her hands reached up to the waistline, the bikini line was more like it. The material set inches below her bellybutton that nestled, an inny, amongst the creamy skin that he wanted to run his tongue over. He licked his lips.

"Easy does it, Dalton."

"I'm known…for being easy."

She laughed. All it did was increase his desire as her breasts shifted, her abdomen tightened tighter, and her face, yeah, occasionally he'd glance at her face, brightened with her smile.

Actually, he couldn't stare too long at her face either. The depths of her chocolate eyes sucked him in, made him crave her sweetness like pools of liquid candy.

He shifted his gaze in the nick of time.

She slid the top of the panties down with both hands. Very slowly. Very *deliberately*. Very nice.

Lucky Santanelli was a natural brunette.

"I know I shouldn't admit this, I mean, you being the control-freak that you are, but damn it, Lucky, this is torture."

Silently, she lifted her hips, slid the material off and kicked the panties at him.

He released his death-grip on the doorframe in time to catch them with one hand. He looked down at them and dropped the laciness onto the green shag carpet before he really did explode. "I…Jesus."

She ran her hands along her naked abdomen, fingers dancing on the skin he, God, please, would be touching in seconds. But when he stepped forward, she whispered, "Unh-unh."

"You're a she-devil—"

"Ha!" She laughed gently, as ladylike as a siren could. Make that a near-naked siren. She never bothered to remove her arms from the sleeves of her top. For some reason, having her arms partly covered made her sexier looking, more difficult to keep his hands off of.

"Aren't you enjoying yourself?" she asked, winking at him.

Who knew a classy woman like Lucky could manage "naughty?" Oh, she had, in her voice, in her actions as her fingers wandered downward, rubbing across her abdomen, below her waist across the mound of brown curls, waltzing ever so slowly, so wonderfully across.

"Now," she whispered with words that yanked him from the

spot, ripping his shirt instead of bothering to undo it. He had no idea how he managed, but his jeans and boxers joined her pink lace on the Hunter green carpet.

He caught himself before he crushed her with the speed of his weight. Both hands rested on either side of her head, balancing his body inches above her. Ambivalence had him wanting to plunge into her, while at the same time wanting to keep enough distance, say a few inches, for him to keep seeing her. Looking at her. Eating her up with his stare.

With his control about to snap, he leaned down, felt her skin, warm, soft against his, and took her mouth in his. She opened her lips to let his tongue explore the tasty wetness. Wine. She tasted of wine with a hint of pure Lucky. He knew he'd never tasted anything so delicious in his life.

One hand balanced him as he lifted enough to touch the breasts that had him nearly insane, nearly bursting. Because he wanted her to be sure, he looked into her eyes and asked, "You're sure?"

She laughed, her nipples tickling against him. "Do you think anyone can make me do something I don't want to?"

"I got you to stay at Funland." He nipped at her bottom lip.

She reached between them, touched his hardness with both hands.

He gasped. Swallowed. Reached over to the end table without trying to move and grabbed a foil wrapper from the drawer.

"You never made me do anything. Maybe I *wanted* to stay," She began a methodical rub. "To save my assets—" She grabbed the wrapper from his hands, tore it open with her teeth.

"Cripes. And what assets you have." He lifted himself up enough so that she wouldn't let go, yet he could look at her, see the need in her eyes, and bend to kiss her neck, her shoulder—

one, then the other, ending up with his lips taking her nipple between them. A gentle sucking. That was his style. He started out that way but quickly sped, grew needy himself—as she sped her rubbing.

"Jesus, Lucky, I have to—"

She let go, pulled him down and commanded, "Now," as she slide the condom on him.

When he entered her, she lifted her hips to him as an offering. She swayed gently, tightened, released tightened again and again until he heard himself cry out.

But when Lucky did the same—he hit the roof.

* * *

Lucky looked up at EZ. He'd collapsed on top of her but only remained for a few seconds. Even then, he'd pushed himself up with his arms alongside her and had asked if he was crushing her.

She'd said crushing was one of her favorite pastimes.

Smiling to herself, she shut her eyes and relived their lovemaking. He'd been thoughtful, sexy, caring, and hot all rolled into one.

So unlike Vinny the "taker."

Not one second did she get the feeling that EZ was taking and not giving. Oh, he'd responded to her—appropriately, she thought, with another smile—but all along he'd tried to please her, make her feel wonderful. And he did.

"What's got you in such a good mood?" he asked in her ear all the while nuzzling behind it.

She opened her eyes. "Oh, I don't know. Maybe those fabulous hors d'oeuvres of Kraft cheese and crackers I'd eaten earlier."

He pulled back, stared and flashed her a naughty smile.

Who knew laid-back EZ Dalton could do naughty?

"Okay, you and your...um...athletic body may have put a smile or two on my lips."

He kissed her lips. "I don't taste any smile."

She slugged him in the side.

"Aye!"

"You can't *taste* a smile."

He slid his arm beneath her, leaned toward her. "No? Hm." Kissed her again. "You sure?"

She laughed. "I'm sure."

"I could swear—" He kissed her longer, slowly, deliberately this time. "—that I could taste your sweet smile."

"That's the wine, Dalton."

She was back to calling him "Dalton," but now there wasn't that sarcastic tone in her voice. Nope, more like something more personal. Of course they'd just bared their nakedness to each other. Couldn't get anymore personal than that. He smiled to himself. Lucky had changed in a matter of minutes.

She called him "Dalton" as a term of endearment now. He like that, he thought as he ran his hands over her breasts, squeezing with a gentleness that had her moan and made him do it again.

"I'd love to start that again, but in a few minutes my stomach is going to embarrass me with a growl of hunger."

He leaned over, rested his head against her abdomen. She laughed. Her breasts tickled his ear. He licked one, then the other.

"Hell, Dalton. I want spaghetti. Now!"

He flew up, grabbed her into his arms, and lifted her off the bed. "Yes, ma'am!"

As she giggled, he walked toward the door.

"Wait! Put me down so I can get dressed."

"No time." He carried her out to the living room. "I heard

the grumbling and, believe me, there is no time for redressing." He set her on the counter.

"Damn! This is cold."

"Oops." He grabbed a towel, lifted her, stealing a kiss with the motion, and set the towel beneath her. With a flip of his wrist to the burner knob, the flame shot up below the pot of water, the hiss of the gas filled the air. "You like your spaghetti soft?"

"Puleez. I am Italian."

He leaned near, nudged himself between her legs. Flicked a finger across her nipple. "So you like it stick-to-the ceiling done?"

She laughed. Took his finger into her mouth and sucked.

He moaned, leaned near and kissed her. When he pulled back, he stood with one elbow resting on the counter and stared at her.

"I'm not going to sit here buck naked for you to ogle."

"You're not?"

She pushed off the counter. "Fool."

He grabbed her, pressed her soft nakedness against him, and let go. "That'll have to hold me until after dinner. That is, don't be surprised if I rush through dinner, until dessert." He growled like a tiger.

On the way out, she said over her shoulder, "Who said *I* was dessert?"

"I—" He collapsed against the counter and moaned.

She swung around, ran forward.

He grabbed at his heart. "I have to have you again, or I'll die."

Christ, the woman was ready to save his sorry butt again. Man, he loved independent.

She slugged him in the gut. Not hard, but enough to get his

attention, make her point. "Bullshit."

She turned, walked out.

He shut his eyes and locked the vision of her naked butt into a secret corner of his brain.

* * *

Lucky leaned back to snap her bra. If anyone had told her she'd be redressing herself here in Dalton's trailer, she'd have told him or her that they were nuts. Nevertheless, here she was, redressing.

And loving every minute.

The tension that had started out between them seemed to have eased off. She was getting Funland in order, what he wanted, and she was almost done here, what she wanted.

At least that's what she thought.

Her fingers fumbled on the snap. She couldn't get it. Did she? she wondered. Did she want to leave soon? When she looked up, EZ stood in the doorway. Still naked, he wore an apron that said, "Yankees" across the chest.

She shook her head. "I've decided to set up a temporary office here."

"In my trailer?"

"No, silly. In mine."

"Hm. An entire office in number seven. Don't think there's a phone jack in that trailer. No. I'm sure there isn't." He came closer, leaned down, kissed one breast then the other, took the two ends of the bra and snapped them together.

She'd never been clumsy, even as a kid. What the heck was wrong with her? "I'll make my office somewhere else. The gingerbread house."

"No." He leaned over and kissed her cheek. "Don't think it'll be possible."

She pulled her shirt together and started to button from the top, he buttoned from the bottom. "Sounds as if you don't want me to—"

"Oh contraire, Ms. Santanelli, what I am so badly saying is—stay here with me, Lucky. I have phone jacks galore."

Her gaze flew up from watching his fingers to his face. The darkness in his eyes reminded her of a midnight pool, one she felt like diving right into.

"I'm not following—" She dropped her gaze to his fingers once again as they worked their way down to her waist and wrapped around her.

"Move your stuff in here. Then you'll have trailer seven as, I don't know, a getaway." He tipped her chin upward. "Please."

"I...don't know. This was fun, wonderful fun today, but—"

"But?" Again he grabbed his chest. "You've hurt me to the quick."

She pushed him and sat on the side of the bed. "What the hell is a 'quick' anyway?"

A look of confusion covered his face. "Got me, but you've hurt it. Now kiss it and make it better."

She leaned over, lifted the apron and kissed his abdomen. It only took her lifting the apron to get him thinking of doing again what they'd done earlier. Only this time longer.

"I...think my 'quick' is a little lower."

She chuckled, leaned over and kissed him on the lips. I'd gladly oblige, but I'm starting to feel faint from hunger. For food."

"You're trying to change the subject."

She lifted his apron again, peeked under and said, "No, *you* are."

He laughed, scooped her up, dropped both of them onto the bed and amid their laughter, kissed her several times until a siren-like sound had him jump up. "Shit! Smoke detector!"

She flew off the side of the bed running after him only to see the water had boiled out of the pot of spaghetti and was now smoking enough to set off the alarm.

EZ grabbed a towel and yanked the pot off, dropping it into the sink where he shoved on the cold-water faucet. "Open a window, the door, something!"

She ran for the door then looked to see his bare bottom. "I'll get the window."

After a few seconds the smoke had cleared, the alarm stopped and EZ proceeded to scrape the top layer of macaroni from the pan. "I think this is salvageable. Hope it doesn't taste burnt."

She looked over his shoulder. "Shouldn't."

"Thanks for the vote of confidence." He scooped up a ladle full and served it onto a plate.

"No problem," she said as she pinched his butt.

"Aye!" He set the plate down, and grabbed her arm. "No fair! My hands were full."

She sneaked one more in and said, "Haven't you ever heard that all's fair in—" Their gazes met. She froze. What the hell was she talking about? Sure they'd made wonderful, fabulous, I've-never-had-it-so-good love making before, but they weren't *in* love. She couldn't be in love with anyone—because she didn't *know* how to love.

"All's fair in what?"

She pulled free and turned toward the table. "Nothing in life is fair."

* * *

EZ watched Lucky scrape the last strand of spaghetti from her plate. A woman with a healthy appetite. He loved that. But she'd remained rather silent throughout the meal after her comment about life. He figured she'd had a dilly of a one and probably most things that had happened to her weren't fair.

But, despite what she'd said, she turned out great. Wonderful. He'd seen little hints of her "human" qualities, but he'd also seen how quick she was to barricade her emotions from anything or anyone.

But since she'd arrived here tonight, he'd managed to at least peek around that barricade. If he could get her to stay with him, she might remain here longer—and drop it completely.

She slurped up the last strand, leaving a droplet of sauce on her lips. "That was wonderful, Dalton. How'd you manage it? Prepared sauce?"

He let out a comical gasp. "Prepared?"

She laughed, took a sip of wine and looked at him over the rim.

"I'll have you know my mother was a full-blooded Italian."

Her eyes grew wider. "Really? You're not fooling?"

He shook his head. "Nope. Josie DiMaria. She taught me how to make the sauce from scratch when I was about eleven."

Something in Lucky's eyes darkened. Envy? Sure, she'd be envious of someone whose mother spent time with them. Damn. He shouldn't have said anything. But then again, she was the strongest willed woman he ever met. Maybe it didn't bother her? The only way he'd find out was to ask. "Does my talking about my mother bother you?"

She hesitated. "No." She sighed. "I've long since taught myself not to be jealous of other's families. As a kid, it used to kill me. The girls with mothers who took them shopping, took them to school, even to church. They complained. I'd have given anything to go to church with Mother. She had been so busy with her career; she never did those things. She more or less ignored me.

"Guess that's better than her abusing me like beating the

crap out of me." She forced a laugh. "Actually, I think she was jealous, resented me. When she died, I think I missed...the *idea* of her."

He refilled both wineglasses. "Didn't she stop working—"

"Yes, Daddy made her. But she resented that, resented my father and now I know, resented me so much that she still never spent time with me. She drank, you know."

"No, I never—"

She laughed, but obviously not from humor. "I'm surprised your father never told you. Yes, Mother drank martinis like water. She wasn't a fall-down raucous drunk, more the closet-type, but I knew. She'd slur her speech—and I saw it all.

"You know, I think she really didn't want to drink. She...once in awhile I'd see her making an attempt to be more like the other mothers. But it never worked. I remember her coming to school to get me one day. I didn't expect her, so I'd gotten on my bus. She tried to get me off, but the bus driver was cautious. He'd never seen her. He wouldn't let her take me." She turned to him, held her chin high, her eyes perfectly clear when he'd expected tears. "Daddy had given strict orders, I'd found out later, that no one except my bodyguard was ever to take me from school. Imagine a bus driver not knowing who a kid's mother was? You see...*he* always ruined everything."

EZ took her hand, lifted it and kissed her palm. "I didn't think you ever wanted to talk about your father, but...since you brought him up, it must have been tough being his daughter."

She pulled her hand free. "Tough? No one knows until they've walked in my shoes. And I wouldn't wish that fate on my worse enemy. The life is glamorized on TV in the movies and books, but it's nothing like that really. People get hurt...die. Bodyguards, business meetings all hours of the night from what I can remember.

"Mostly I don't remember the daily stuff because Daddy moved out when I was really young. He visited. When I look back at it now, his visits were mostly in secrecy. So, I lived with him gone, a drunken mother—" She laughed, again not from humor. "—and trying not to think, to admit to yourself that your father was...in the business." She leaned forward. "He swore to me that he never had anyone killed."

EZ stiffened as a chill raced up his back. It wasn't because he was shirtless either. He'd thrown on shorts and a tee shirt before sitting down to eat.

No, it was Lucky's tone more so than the subject that gave him the chills.

She laughed. "How the hell could I believe that one?" She looked at him, her face blank. "As usual, talking about my father has everyone I meet speechless. I should go now—"

"No!" He leaned over, took her hand. "No, you don't have to go. Who your father is...had nothing to do with you."

"That's where you're wrong, Dalton."

Dalton. The old tone was back.

"It has everything to do with me. I am who I am because of him."

"No, Lucky. I don't agree." He stood, took her into his arms and kissed her. "You are who you are *despite* him."

Chapter Eighteen

Lucky wanted to pull out of EZ's arms. The wonderful meal she'd eaten was going to be ruined by the subject of her father. Even after death, he haunted her daily existence. Well, she'd vowed years ago not to let him bother her, and she'd become a master at hiding her true feelings. Even got so she didn't *admit* her true feelings—even to herself.

Allowing oneself to be a victim took all their power away.

Even though this night had been unusual, albeit wonderful for her, she had to take control once again. So, like a well-trained athlete, she summoned everything she'd taught herself throughout the years and said, "You've avoided the obvious long enough, Dalton. Spill about your blatant lie."

She'd taken him by surprise, which was good. Surprise always gave the initiator the advantage.

"I...oh, yeah, Doc."

She pushed against his chest. "Your *father*."

"Sit down. More wine?" He headed to the counter. The bottle was empty but he opened the cabinet for another.

"None for me."

He hesitated. "Soft drink? Beer?"

"I'm fine. Spill."

He grabbed a beer from the refrigerator, walked toward her and, thank goodness, sat opposite her in the stuffed chair. If he sat next to her, like the effects of the wine, she'd be in danger of losing her footing again.

"Well, Doc is my father."

"That much I got."

"And the sorry-I-lied-to-you-part was already covered although I still argue that it wasn't a direct lie, only an omission of a fact."

"Semantics, Counselor."

He stiffened.

"Hey, I was only joking. You sounded as if you were making a final argument—"

"Guess I'm tired, too. So, anyway I didn't tell you up front because...well, truthfully it didn't seem necessary. Doc is Doc no matter who his kids are."

"But he owns this place. Didn't you think my temporary position of running it would be of interest to him?"

EZ's eyes glazed over. "No."

"He doesn't care about Funland?"

"With all his heart he cares. But some days, he forgets things, even important things, people."

"I never noticed—"

"Since you came here, he's been better. Actually much better. There were only a few times, guess you weren't around to see them. But, yes he does care about Funland.

"He...and your father that is...started this place—" He swallowed and looked at her. "You already know that part."

"Actually, I don't. I only know I came here a few summers as a kid. I had no idea back then that Daddy owned it."

"Wow. He never...no one ever said—"

"Tell me how it all started."

He took a swig of beer, sat back. The ever relaxed pose of EZ Dalton. Even telling an emotional story—and she guessed by his expression that is was emotional—almost painful for him to tell, he could slouch into the most tranquil of positions. She envied him that.

"After World War II, my father and yours—" He set the beer down. "You know they grew up as kids in Hartford. Right?"

Since she'd never had personal conversations with her father, she shook her head.

"Damn. Okay, the beginning goes back to them growing up in the same neighborhood. Went to grammar school at the local parochial...let's see. Saint Anthony's. No, Saint Aloysius. Yeah, that was it. Anyway, I guess my old man and yours became friends early on. Your dad...he didn't have it great growing up. So—"

She sat forward. "What exactly is 'not great'?"

"I...doesn't seem I should be telling you about your own father."

"Then who will?"

"Shit." He hesitated, looked at her. "All right. You never met your grandfather on your father's side?"

She bit her lip. It was like listening to a story about someone else. That's the kind of thinking that got her through life. How often she pretended things as a kid. "Neither set of grandparents."

"All I know about is your father's. Don't take any of this as gospel, and please don't be offended. All this comes from my memory of what my father had told me as a kid. I could be wrong."

"Go on." EZ was intelligent. She knew he'd remember verbatim what his father had said.

"Okay. Your grandfather must have left your grandmother...they never married. He shipped off to Australia during the war, never wrote. Left her with your father."

Lucky grabbed the nearest pillow. She'd been so alone all her life. No cousins, no aunts only one uncle on Mother's side that died years before. Maybe.... She held her breath. Could she even ask? Slowly the air cleared from her lungs and she asked, "Did...she have other children?"

He shook his head.

"I figured."

"Life was tough for a single woman with a kid back then, hell, still is. But, she tried. My father once told me she sold her shoes to by bread and milk for your dad. One hell of a woman as far as—"

Daddy's greed. Now she understood why. He'd been so poor as a kid, money became his passion. Lot's of people were poor, but honest. But he'd gone about making money so very wrong. She couldn't forgive him that. The pillow slipped out of her hands.

"So, your dad hung out with my father's family—they had seven other kids and what was one more?" EZ chuckled until he looked at her. She tried to smile, but couldn't. "Want me to stop?"

"I get they were best friends. Tell me about Funland."

"It was started as a dance place back then. Maybe that's where your father met—"

"Doesn't matter. Go on."

"When places like that went out of style after the war, they turned it into an amusement park. All the post-war kids born and all. Two parent families back then."

"Do you know whose idea that was?"

He shifted in his seat. "Doc's."

How she'd wanted him to say Rosario came up with it. To hear that he at least had one legal idea in his life. Her heart rhythm remained in sync, never flickering, never speeding. Numbed.

"So, they had this business. Thriving business. I can remember moving into a new house not far from here. It was huge. Big yard, Jungle Gym for Chloe and me. But…then things changed."

She straightened on the couch. "Define 'things.'"

"Easy money. Running numbers. Look, Lucky, you're exhausted, we both are. How about we finish this some other—"

"Finish it."

"I'm not responsible. Remember. Well, what I understand is that your father had been getting into things my dad wasn't interested in." He paused, looked up. A rather flat appearance had dulled her face. It was as if he sat across a twenty-foot boardroom table, making a million-dollar deal with a stranger. Only when he inhaled, he inhaled the scent of apple.

He guessed Lucky didn't care what she looked like right now. Internally she had to be in pain, but on the outside, Lucky would remain true to form—and hide her feelings.

"My father, and, listen, I'm not saying Doc was a saint. Far from it. What I am saying is—"

"I understand that this is all information passed down, Dalton. I'm not thinking you're giving your opinion."

He nodded toward her. "Rosario made some fast money—apparently wanted more and liked the opportunity. Doc claimed he tried to get Rosario to watch out for certain men. Men known to be in, well—"

"I've never believed my father was a simple businessman. Okay, so Doc tried to talk my father out of the life, they had this business then what?"

"Your…Rosario emptied their joint bank account. All they had…big chunk of change for two guys from their neighborhoods. Moved out to Vegas. It all happened so fast, Doc was thrown into a deep depression. Once he told me what hurt worst was being betrayed by a friend.

"After Chloe was born. My mother had to get a job. She

couldn't even stay home to raise us. Doc spent his time trying to run Funland, but, as I'd said before, he wasn't the brain behind the finances. I was left to take care of myself and Chloe—"

She looked him straight in the eye and without any more expression than before, said, "I'm sorry."

"Somehow that doesn't make up for us losing our house, having to move into these crappy trailers, and my mother having to clean the damned stuck up Yankee women's houses."

Lucky got up. "I should go."

EZ caught his anger before it spilled into the night, ruining what they'd had. What they'd just shared. "Look, I'm the one who's sorry. Didn't mean for that to come out. At least not like that." He stood, took her by the shoulders. But she pulled back so he couldn't hold her.

"My father ruined your family's life. What the hell are you apologizing for, Dalton?"

There was that tone again.

"You're right. I'm not sorry, but again, it was Rosario Santanelli, not Lucky Santanelli that did all that."

She looked into his eyes and this time couldn't hide her pain. Like liquid coffee they filled to a glaze, yet never spilt over. Never were allowed to. "We started out this relationship by me having to pay for the sins of my father. Seems I owe more than I thought."

She turned to go.

He pulled her back.

"Leave me alone, Dalton."

"Stay with me."

"That will never work. Every time you look at me, you're going to think of that little kid who had to face all that responsibility so early one. About your house, your mother." She looked him straight in the eye. "It was only sex you know. Plain, yeah sure, fun sex."

It was then he realized Lucky was a whiz at business deals, but she would stink at gambling no matter what she'd said. He knew that because she'd out and out lied to him just then—her pupils gave her away. "Believe what you want, I'm not going to argue about what I lived through." He reached out to her.

"No, I have to go—"

He'd never used his strength with a woman before, and didn't intend to now. At least not to force himself on her. But what he did need to do now, was save Lucky from her past, her fears.

Back to responsibility, back to being someone else's savior.

With that thought telling him he should let her go, yet wanting her to stay, he grabbed both of her shoulders. She yanked back. He stepped closer until the wall was behind her, he fenced her in with one arm on each side of her shoulders. He looked down, noted the defiance in her arms and thought of stepping back, but only for a second.

Instead, he slid his arms behind her and eased her near—as gently as he could.

She tensed.

He tightened.

She relaxed into his hold.

And stayed there for what seemed to be hours.

* * *

His arms around her took the place of the barrier she'd built inside her heart. When EZ leaned a bit closer, she knew all was right in their little world. Outside trailer number eight was another matter. But, with the strength from him, she could at least make it through the night—to forget it all tomorrow.

Back to tucking all the pain neatly away.

He looked down at her. Gave her his best laid-back smile.

"Your not pulling away mean you'll stay?"

The gentleness of his words had her want to yell, "Of course!" but she merely looked into the depths of his eyes and nodded.

He leaned near, kissed her cheek, then her forehead. "Good." With that, he moved his arms from beside her and in one swift motion, lifted her into his arms.

"Put me down. I can walk—"

"No doubt. What I'm trying to avoid is you walking out that door." He nodded toward the front door.

"I said I'd stay. I always keep my word."

"No doubt." He nuzzled her neck as he set her onto the bed like a china doll.

Not that she could picture someone like EZ even holding a china doll. No, with his size he'd more than likely break the thing, but he was gentle with her. "I'm so exhausted, Dalton."

He started to undo the buttons on her blouse. "No doubt."

She shook her head, sighed. "I may not be able to get up for work on time—"

Without her noticing, he'd managed to unhook her shorts and the snap on her bra. "No doubt." He grinned.

"I really am not in the mood—"

"No doubt," He leaned down, kissed one breast, then the other. "I can change that."

"EZ—"

He slid her top off, pulled the bra to the side and tossed both onto the dresser. "I only want you comfortable. In case you want to...you know." His grin reminded her of this adorable little boy on a Cheerio's commercial she'd once seen on TV. "I'll be right next to you. If not...there is great comfort in just holding one another."

"Let's start with the comfort part." Actually, she hated

having to be comforted by someone, a man. Too foreign a position for her. It wasn't as if she'd ever had a man who wanted to only hold and comfort her either. Sex was always foremost in Vinny's mind. Boys in high school and college always went for a quick feel—until they learned whom her father was. Talk about a turnoff. Then, she'd become a piranha who no one ever wanted to touch.

EZ slipped off his jeans, sent his shirt to join her clothes on the dresser and started to pull his boxers down over his obvious arousal. "This holding thing may not be as easy as I thought."

His humor brought a smile to her face, a jolt to her heart. Not to mention making her hormones doing a jig of their own. But when his story about their fathers reminded her of the empty feeling in her gut, all she could manage was the smile.

He reached for the sheet, covered her and slid in next to her. With his hand tucked beneath her shoulders, he leaned near, and kissed her ear. "My little token of comfort."

"I appreciate it."

"If you're up for it, I really didn't finish...about our fathers."

Lucky sighed. Could she listen to anymore tonight? It wasn't as if she hadn't heard horrendous accusations about her father before. Hell, Vegas's local news station had something on him practically every month. Rumors floated around her office on a daily basis. Thank goodness she'd made a name—a clean name—for herself. Not that it was easy to do being named Santanelli. But she did. And she tried to ignore any mention of her father, until she realized deep inside that he was always there. Always would be her father. No matter what.

She had to believe he never had a hand in anyone's death though.

If she found out otherwise, the old wounds she'd ignored

would fester and bleed.

Bleed her blood for his sins.

Still, what EZ had to tell her wouldn't cause more hurt. She knew he wouldn't tell her if it did. "I'm exhausted, but go ahead."

"It can wait."

She turned to him. Earlier he'd reached over and shut off the little bedside lamp. A shaft of moonlight illuminated the tiny room enough for her to see him. His hair now ruffled by leaning on the pillow gave him that boyish look again. But his squared jaw, deep brown eyes, and five o'clock shadow said he was all man.

And even in the dim lighting, she could see concern in his eyes.

She'd never seen concern like that in her life.

"I want it all out now."

"You're the boss." He looked at her and smiled. "A damn good one, too, if the books I looked at this afternoon are any indication."

"We're heading toward the black."

We're. A few weeks ago this woman wanted nothing to do with this place, with him, but now she'd included them together. EZ felt his heart beat against the inside of his chest, hers gently thudding on the outside as he pulled her closer. "Comfortable?"

"Um. Go ahead."

"I'd already told you that Rosario's actions effected all our lives. I imagine yours, too."

She blinked, nodded.

"For years Doc tried to make a go of this place, but he had no money to update the rides or the attractions. Places like Six Flags and Disney World became more and more popular. How could he compete with them? He couldn't. But he never gave up. He—"

EZ looked across the empty room, obviously at nothing, yet he seemed to see something in his mind. She reached for his hand, took it and held tightly.

"Rosario had been the brain behind the business, Doc the creative one."

"Rosario? I...he'd always made such lousy business deals. I can't tell you how many times I had to bail him out of some mess. Not with my finances, but my knowledge." Maybe guilt had him losing his touch. One could only hope.

"You know, even then he'd call me secretly. That was fine with me, though. I had no desire to lose clients over my association with him. Think that he had me in mind all along?"

EZ could only look at her.

"Ha. Fat chance. But he used my skills for damn fucking sure. Always said how my brains were worth every penny of Harvard tuition."

She had no idea what a heart attack felt like, knew women had different symptoms than men, but right now if she wasn't sure of her health, she'd swear she was having one. This was all too painful, she told herself.

It was then she decided she had to leave Funland—much sooner than planned.

EZ turned to her. "What year did you graduate?"

"Hm? Oh, ninety-three."

He looked at her. "Ninety-three? Let me see, you're three years younger. So you'd be—"

"Thirty now. I...didn't go to college until after my divorce."

He pulled her closer. "That's right. Vinny."

She pushed up on one elbow. "I don't remember telling you

about—"

EZ shook his head. "*People* magazine. There was an article about you a few years ago—"

"And you remembered reading it?"

He grinned. "Took it out of the library two weeks ago to refresh my brain."

She slapped his chest.

"Hey! I had to know what…who I was dealing with here. Besides, that's how I learned you were such a dynamite businesswoman. I figured…when you showed up that day that you had the bucks and would pump some of them into this place. But until I read about you being the only female VP at Hartwell, I had no idea what a set of brains you possessed."

She shook her head, laughed. "Brain. I only have one."

"Not according to the article. It said you were so smart that you might have more."

"You, Dalton, are full of shit. Get back to Doc now."

"Hm. The lady doesn't like compliments."

"Too foreign a concept for me. How did Doc manage to keep Funland open all those years?"

"That's a mystery to me. When I went off to college—Harvard class of eighty-eight—"

"You're full of shit!"

"Again? Actually, I'm not. We missed each other by a year. I graduated when you entered. Anyway—"

"What'd you major in? Amusement park…no, wait. You've been doing such a crummy job, that couldn't be it."

"Ha. Ha. Actually—" He grew serious.

She could feel his arm tense behind her back. "Sorry. That was a low blow."

"You can blow—"

She punched him in the chest. "I was serious."

He pinched her nipple, not painfully, but enough to make it harden. "So was my attempt. But, back to Funland. Doc managed somehow to keep the place afloat. He…on one of my last visits home I noticed he kept forgetting things. Oh he denied it was happening, but when I extended my visit to observe him longer, well, the rest you know."

"You moved here to help out."

"This place has been his life and as long as he's alive, Funland stays open."

Lucky shut her eyes, bit her lips. Before she drew blood, she knew she'd have to say the words that sat on the tip of her tongue. She'd say them for Doc.

"I'll move my stuff in to your trailer tomorrow and buy some office equipment."

He turned toward her, looked into her eyes, and said, "Thanks."

* * *

EZ's soft snore wasn't what kept her awake. It was all that had happened, all that they'd talked about. She'd said she would move in here, but now, in the darkness of night when one's mind often played tricks on them and things seem much worse than they were, she decided she couldn't.

She'd have to leave Funland instead.

Chapter Nineteen

The next morning Lucky hung up the phone, and tucked her MasterCard back into her wallet.

She didn't have the balls.

Instead of calling for her limo, rebooking her flight as she'd planned to do in the middle of the night, here she was dialing her office back in Vegas to have her work sent out. Despite how crappy she felt, she never could get Doc out of her thoughts throughout her restless night. If she left now with Funland only knocking on the door of profitability, surely the place would go back to square one.

She couldn't do that.

She looked out the window of the trailer to see EZ sitting on the steps of number seven, legs outstretched, hat tipped back, a box of her business papers on the step next to him. The dear must be exhausted after last night.

She should be, too, with merely three hours of sleep and ruminating about her life in-between, but what must have exhausted EZ, revived her. Three times they'd made love after her claims of exhaustion. EZ's claims of comfort in *just holding each other* were overtaken by desire. She smiled.

And what fun they'd had satisfying those desires.

Sex wasn't only sex with him; it really *was* making love. Despite how her heart beat faster when she watched him through the screen, she told herself that love couldn't enter into this. Even though she was setting up a temporary office—temporary being the operative word—she would eventually be moving back to Vegas, to her life, in a few more weeks. In the meantime she had to pay some attention to her business. Mark had kept her up on all the deals that had closed, but she needed her hand in it or faced losing her footing. She didn't trust any of her male peers as far as she could throw the jerks.

The West Coast office in LA would have an opening for president in the next few months when Michael Gaffe retired. She intended to have that position.

And she would move out of Vegas faster than the Air Force's F-16s broke the sound barrier above the surrounding mountains to take the position. She punched the buttons on her cell phone and cursed that the damn trailer didn't have a phone hookup.

"Ms. Santanelli's office," her assistant, Ned Baxter, said.

"It's me, Ned."

"Lucky? Are you home now?"

Sometimes she wished this was home. She watched EZ shift his hat as the sun moved. "No, I'm still in Connecticut, Ned." She smiled as EZ stretched out his legs. "My impromptu vacation, as it were, is over, but I'm going to be here longer than I'd hoped. I have to set up a temporary office. Fax me the latest business transactions, mail me out the Beachner's file and tell Mark I'll be here longer." No way did she want to discuss the reasons why she was staying longer with him. Taking a paper out of her pocket, she read him EZ's phone number. "I'll be at it for faxes, too."

After she gave Ned all the pertinent details including address, she hung up, leaned toward the window and wondered if she'd just made a huge mistake. By the things Ned had told her about her peers, she belonged back in Vegas. Especially Harry Fortune, her main contender for the West Coast position. She started to curse the way things were turning out. Then she saw

EZ push up to stand.

Well, maybe she'd hold that curse for now.

Doc came up to his son, and they started to talk. She could tell by Doc looking at the box of her stuff that EZ was having to do a bit of explaining. As quietly as she could, she moved next to the window, eased to the side and listened.

"Well, Lucky is...you know who Lucky is, Doc?"

"Hell's bells, son, I haven't lost it all upstairs yet."

Lucky winced.

"I know that, Doc."

"By the way, where is she? Zos and I held the Pinochle game as long as we could last night. Beat the living pants off of him I did." His hearty chuckle floated on the sea's breeze along with the ever-present pungent scent of the marshes behind the trailer park. She'd grown to tolerate, no, to expect the scent. Gave her a homey feeling.

Vegas had no scent.

"Lucky has to start working here to keep up with her business back home, so she's moving her stuff into my trailer for an office."

Silence.

She moved over enough to look out the window without being seen. Doc ran his fingers across his mustache. He'd dressed in full costume today including the wig. Both men had the same build although EZ stood several inches taller. Doc smiled.

"Good for you, son. Good woman there."

She'd never seen EZ blush before. How cute.

"No, it's not exactly like that. Well, there isn't a phone jack in number eight—"

Doc touched EZ's arm. "Of course there isn't."

She leaned against the wall and choked back a laugh. It really wasn't fair to spy on the men—EZ having a hard time of it and all—so she stood, looked out the window and called, "Hi, Doc."

He swung around, lifted his Stetson off and waved it toward her. "Missed you last night. Guess...er...you two were busy."

She laughed. "Stay there. I'll be right out." She ran to the door without shoving on her sandals and stepped down the stairs in time to see EZ yank his Stetson further down his face. More blushing?

Doc sat on the step and looked at her. "The boy—" He waved his hand toward his son.

Her heart jolted. He couldn't remember his name. She looked at EZ who remained silent.

"He tells me you'll be here longer," Doc finished.

"A few day...yes, longer."

"Good. Tonight's Thursday—"

"No, Dad, it's Friday."

Her heart tightened. She'd never heard him call Doc that.

"That's what I said, Friday. Draws a big crowd at the saloon for the show." He started to stand. EZ reached out his hand, Doc looked down then took it. "Yep. Good crowd. Old timers and young ones. They all love that Vaudeville show we've been putting on since, oh, I guess around the fifties. Legs ain't what they used to be, though. Gout in this one." He balanced himself, let go of EZ's hand, and looked down toward his right leg. When he looked up, he said, "You'd be too young to remember when it actually started." He smiled at Lucky. "Coming?"

"I wouldn't miss it."

Doc tipped his hat toward her and socked EZ on the arm. "I'm off now."

"See you, Doc," EZ said.

Lucky started to say her goodbye, but Doc kept walking and said over his shoulder, "Almost forgot. Leo and his wife, you know the two who wear the horse costume, had to head out of town for some grandkid's party."

EZ groaned.

Lucky swung around toward him. "No way."

Doc paused, turned. "Could make some regulars real unhappy if the horse, they do love that animal, doesn't show up."

"Like father like son," she murmured.

* * *

"How the hell am I going to see in this getup?" Lucky yelled.

EZ lifted the heavy tail end of the horse costume off her shoulders. "What's to see besides my gorgeous butt?"

"As appealing as that sounds, how about where I'm going?"

"Simple. You hold onto my waist, like we're on a motorcycle, and follow my lead."

"I'll fall and break something important."

He leered at her. "Would I let you break something important? Arms and legs would be okay, but anything in-between—no way." With that, he leaned over, aimed his lips at her.

One swift hand movement had her pushing him against the dressing room wall. "When I said I'd stay around to help out because of Doc, I had no damn intention of being a…a—"

"Horse's rump?"

"I can't do this." She stepped out of what remaining costume was left around her. The windows were all opened, but inside the furry material felt as if the sun hung way too low today. She swiped her hand across her forehead. "Look at this. I'm sweating to death. Twice around the stage and I'll disappear in a puddle."

He took her into his arms, despite her efforts to pull back.

"I wouldn't do this for just anyone you know, so mark this date on the calendar. You, Ms. Santanelli, can be the horse's head." He grinned like a schoolboy who'd just presented what he thought was an *A* report.

"Big fuc—"

EZ whinnied before she could finish. "Remember this is a family show not some Vegas act—"

She slugged him in the gut. "So I get to be the head and lead you around?"

He nodded. "EZ Dalton, the horse's ass."

She couldn't help but laugh. He looked so darn sexy, yet so boyish at the same time. Had to be impossible, she knew, but that's how she saw him. "More than appropriate."

He chuckled. "Besides, I love an independent woman who can lead me astray...er...lead the way."

She shoved the horse's backside at him. "Good. That's what I am. Now put this on."

He whinnied again as she set the horse's head over her shoulders. Between the heat and hardly being able to see out of the mesh "eyes," she sighed. "This may not be any better."

EZ looked directly at her through the mesh. "It'll have to do. I don't have anymore horse's parts to trade."

She chuckled despite the fact that she felt like a fool in any part of the horse. "I'm only doing this for Doc, you know."

"Me, too," he said softly.

It was then she knew she'd do her best to make this show a success.

* * *

"Pick up your feet faster!" EZ muttered to Lucky as they, in their horse's costume, galloped across the stage.

"We're gonna fall into the orchestra pit if you keep pushing me," she complained.

"You're in control here, lady."

"Yeah." She pulled left so they didn't fall off the stage. The dancers quick stepped it out of their way as Lucky led them toward the back of the stage. "Sorry!"

The audience started with a grumble of laughter when they'd pranced out onto the stage. Now they were in hysterics.

"We're the laughing stock of Funland, Dalton." She swung around toward the right so they didn't end up behind the curtain. That was the curtain? Wasn't it? Her vision had gone downhill after EZ's weight pulled the costume so far back that the mesh eyes were nearly on her forehead.

"No one knows we're in here except Doc. He'll never tell." He tried to follow her lead, but the woman was all over. Sweat poured down his forehead, making him glad that he took the backend. Lucky would have been falling all over him if she had to maneuver without seeing where they were going. He thought the inside of the costume would reek of well, a horse, but what kept him going and not passing out was the ever fresh scent of *grapefruit*.

Lucky's butt kept smacking into his face, as she'd make a quick turn. "We must look like a drunken horse," he said, but couldn't deny that his position was becoming more favorable with every sway.

"I'm…trying my damnedest, Dalton. Stop pulling back or I'll—"

He hadn't meant to pull back. One foot seemed to have a mind of its own and before he knew it, Lucky, horse's head and all were in his lap.

The audience silenced.

Lucky cursed in what he guessed was Italian.

And he reached around to fondle her breasts and said, "I would have waited until later, but this is rather cozy."

She tried to pull away but ended up twisting the costume so he couldn't stand. After several minutes, he managed to get up and they headed off the stage while the audience cheered and howled.

Backstage she yanked off the front end while he pulled off the back. "That was all your fault. Listen to them making fools of us!" The look in her eyes boiled like delicious chocolate with her furry.

He paused, set the costume to the side and looked at her until their gazes met—then he cracked up.

"What? How can you—" She dropped the costume to the side. "God, I'm such a perfectionist. Even being a lousy horse has my blood pressure up."

"You did fine." He wrapped his arms around her. "We couldn't have been that bad. Listen to them." With one hand he pulled the curtain to the side so they could see the audience clapping. "I think they want an encore."

"Not on your life."

He let the curtain fall, leaned forward and kissed her on the lips. "I'd be your horse's butt any day, Santanelli."

She shoved at his chest. "That job you can handle on your own." She swung around and started to leave.

Fast on her heals, he reached out and took her by the arm. "Are you upset with me or more at yourself because we weren't perfect?"

"I...it's a tie."

"Unfair. We did our best, and I won't let my woman keep beating herself up for not being perfect—"

She froze, glared at him. "Your *what?*"

Oh, geez. "That slipped out." Knowing how independent she was, he could bite his tongue off right now.

"I'm not *your* woman or anyone else's. Never will be

either."

"Okay. Okay. Like I said, it slipped out. I just didn't want you beating yourself up over a stupid horse act. Cut yourself some slack. I'm sure you strive for perfection in business, but, Jesus, Lucky, it's only a Vaudeville routine."

Her chin raised, her gaze locked onto his and she said, "If I'd cut myself any slack I'd never be where I am today. And, yes, I do strive for perfection." With that, she swung around and walked toward the dressing room.

What am I getting so upset about? Lucky thought. EZ was right, it was only a stupid act. The need for perfection had been her childish hope that she'd impress her parents—get them to love her—for so many years it even spilled over to a dumb horse routine. She stopped, turned. "Look, don't ask me to fill in for Leo and his wife ever again and...we can be friends."

He walked up, took her by the shoulders. "Friends? Hm—" He kissed her on the lips. "We can be more than friends. I'll get that call-in list done first thing in the morning."

His lips tickled against hers as he spoke. Every fiber of her body wanted to stand here and return the kiss, but the middle of the hallway with employees all around was not the right place. She eased back. "You still haven't done that list yet?"

"Oops."

She swatted his arm. "I'll give you 'oops.' You sure will do it. I'll see you in the office at eight."

"Wait a minute. You told Doc we'd join him—"

"Damn it. I really want to go take a shower—"

He grinned. "We can do that later."

She grabbed his arm. "A quick bite and I'm outta here. Alone."

"Ouch. Wounded me to the quick again."

She pinched his butt as they walked down the stage stairs.

"Don't start that 'quick' thing again. You'll embarrass yourself."

"Over here," Doc called.

Lucky looked to see the table with Chloe, Owen, Zos, Doc, and two empty seats in between. She waved and headed toward them.

Zos jumped up and held her chair when she'd expected EZ to do the honors. But the older man had been too quick. Maybe EZ was still exhausted from last night. She smiled to herself.

Zos leaned near, "Wonderful show."

She groaned.

Chloe started to rattle on about how great it really was and how she'd never heard the customers enjoy themselves so much. When she said, "Lots of them said they'll be back soon," Lucky saw dollar signs flash through her thoughts.

"Just what we need, Chlo, more customers."

"I know, things have been going so great around here. Last year at this time the saloon was half-empty. Look at the people. Just look at them. Eating, laughing, filling every seat in the house!" She swung her arms around. "There's standing room only!"

With a look of pride in his eyes, Owen leaned over, kissed her cheek. She giggled like the schoolgirl that she was. Lucky had to smile at EZ's parental look of disapproval. If the guy scrunched up his forehead any more, he'd permanently wrinkle. Doc sat oblivious to the whole thing. How sad. EZ seemed to be responsible for more than the finances around here.

"I'll get your food, babe," Owen said, kissing Chloe once more.

"How the hell do you know what she wants?" EZ growled.

Lucky kicked him under the table.

"Ouch!"

Chloe turned a lovely shade of crimson. "Don't start,

Edmund Zachary Dalton."

Oh, boy she'd used his full name. By her look of defiance and EZ's look of anger, it had to mean she was dead serious. Hm, maybe EZ didn't wear the pants in that family after all. No, Chloe was filling her youthful role to perfection. EZ taking on a role much older than his years.

Owen turned to EZ. Lucky readied to stop a punch if need be, but the kid merely nodded and said, "Sir, I know your sister very well. She loves beef, hates pork. If something has too much salt, she won't eat it. Ice cream, um, plain vanilla is her favorite. Never put nuts on her vanilla. Vegetables are okay as long as they have cream sauce on them. She doesn't drink soft drinks, only iced tea with—"

"Two lemons and one Equal," EZ finished.

Lucky felt her eyebrows rise. Stifling a chuckle, she said, "Sounds like the kid does know—"

EZ glared at her. "Go get the food, Owen." When the boy walked toward the buffet table, Doc and Zos excused themselves, too. Chloe remained glaring at her brother who turned toward Lucky. "I'll handle the situation with my sister."

Chloe leaned over, punched him in the arm. "There is no *situation*. Owen and I know each other so well because we are soul mates, destined for eternity together."

"Cripes."

"You can swear all you want—"

"Cripes isn't swearing. You want swearing? I'll give you swearing—"

"I don't care what you say, I don't need you anymore, EZ. Besides, I have Lucky to talk woman to woman...."

Lucky felt her eyes widen. She'd never seen such a look of pain than the one in EZ's eyes right now. But when he turned toward her, the look changed. Disgust? Anger? No, maybe jealousy.

Chloe stiffened and continued, “I’m marrying Owen—”

“Over my dead body.”

She turned to Lucky. “Know any good undertakers?”

Whatever Lucky wanted to say was silenced by EZ’s look. She shook her head.

“Seems to me, Lucky, with your father’s line of work, I’d think you knew—” EZ looked more shocked at his words than either Chloe or Lucky.

Actually, as she felt her face heat up, she thought anger was a much stronger emotion than shock.

“That sucked, Edmund Zachary,” Chloe said.

“Jesus, Lucky. I’m sorry.” He ignored his sister and tried to take Lucky’s hand. She pulled away. He repeated, “I’m so sorry. You...know I’m not thinking clearly being this beat and all.”

The same exhaustion had her eyes tearing when normally she wouldn’t allow herself to slip like this. Damn him, she would not cry. Lucky Santanelli was lots of things, but a hysterical female was not one of them. Still, she had to bite her lip until she could make certain her words would come out with the firmness she intended and not with a shaky inflection. With a deep breath let out slowly, she deliberately softened her voice, “I told you he never had anyone....”

If she had taken the butter knife off the table and stuck it into EZ’s chest, she didn’t think he could have looked anymore wounded. It wasn’t as if she hadn’t had years of experience dealing with hurtful comments about her father. Oh, yeah, she had years of it. Most were true anyway. EZ really wasn’t a malicious person. And, what bothered her most was that she hated seeing the hurt she’d caused on his face.

Caring led to pain, she reminded herself.

“Lucky, I am so sorry—”

"Forget it. Really." She smiled and felt it came out as sincere as she could make it. Years of being her father's daughter also gave her plenty of practice to hide feelings, camouflage true facial expressions. "I know you didn't mean to hurt me."

He leaned over, kissed her cheek. "Never. I would never hurt you intentionally or otherwise."

Because she'd be lying if she told herself that she didn't buy that, she turned, kissed him back.

"Now that's more like it," Chloe said, ending with a romantic sigh.

Owen returned with Chloe's and his food. "There weren't any vegetables with sauce on them, babe, so I brought you extra salad with only olive oil."

She looked at EZ as she said, "*Exactly* the way I like it."

Lucky studied them throughout the meal. Owen knew everything Chloe wanted—almost before she did. He waited on her without a thought. Memories of Vinny yelling, "Get me the fucking beer now!" had her realizing that this couple was very different.

Owen had love in his eyes and caring in his voice with every word he spoke to her. There was gentleness, a maturity about him, despite having such a youthful zest for life. He and Chloe fit perfectly.

She sputtered on about the summer, their school plans, he at the University of Connecticut at Storrs, she commuting to the nearby campus of the University's nearby branch. They couldn't afford for her to live on campus.

When they chattered on about their trip to New Orleans, Lucky could taste the beignets, smell the chicory coffee and envied the time two had shared. So many things. So many wonderful things Chloe talked about that Lucky thought the girl must be more exhausted from talking than Lucky felt from making a fool of herself on the stage earlier. Still, there was something adorable in the kid, something Lucky never had at that age.

A vibrancy for life.

She was lucky to make it from one day to the other, from one rotten living arrangement to the next.

And Daddy always called her "lucky."

Showed how much, no, how little he ever knew about her.

Maybe it was because she was bone-tired, but she found EZ's dagger-looks toward Owen both amusing and adorable. He loved his sister so much, that was obvious as he did his father, but the guy didn't cut the young couple any slack. She watched him lean back, probably tempted to shove his booted feet on the table, and wondered why EZ was so set against them getting married. She'd give anything in the world to have a family to worry about.

Envy had never been in her vocabulary, a wasted emotion, until now.

She envied EZ's family. She envied the unsullied love of Owen and Chloe. And, worst of all, she envied Doc's relationship with his two kids who would obviously do anything for their father.

Even give up their lives, their careers to save a rundown amusement park for him.

Lucky looked down to see a hand touch her arm even before she felt it.

"Someone was off in thought," Doc said, then chuckled.

She smiled. Zos was staring at her along with Doc. EZ had gotten up to check on how the staff was refilling the buffet tables. "Guess I'm just beat."

Doc winked at her, and she knew he was thinking of her being with EZ last night. Zos had a more concerned look on his face.

The two were adorable in their own ways.

Doc remained in his Western getup although his last show had to have been hours ago. His wig, now probably hanging from some lampshade in his trailer, had matted down the fine hairs, what little there were, on the top of his head. Still, as tired as he seemed, his eyes sparkled.

Zos on the other hand didn't have the wear and tear of age on his face. Funny, she was no expert, but if she was a betting woman, she'd bet he'd gone under the knife a time or two. What an odd thought for someone like him. A loner. Maybe even a drifter with no home to go back to. Even some professional who'd fallen on hard times.

And he'd been vain enough to have the wrinkles removed from his face. It still unnerved her that he chose to wear all black when out of his costume. She told herself that she was foolish to even compare such a gentle natured old man to any of her father's cronies, or him for that matter.

Zos looked as if he might be of a nationality much like the gypsy fortuneteller he played. Maybe Turkish. Maybe Russian, with his dark hair and dark mustache. Flecks of gray nestled amid the black. Smiling to herself, she wondered if he dyed his mustache as he obviously did his hair.

"If you are so beat, Sugar, maybe you should head back to your trailer? I'll gladly walk you over," Zos offered.

She winked at him. "Thanks, but I'm having too good a time with everyone." And she really meant that. For the first time she felt as if she had participated in a family-type meal along with the laughter, the concerned big brother, and even the caring fathers.

Imagine, she told herself, weeks ago she had only the memories of a father she wanted to forget—tonight she had two living, breathing father-figures—who she couldn't imagine never seeing again.

Her heart thudded.

Because she'd told herself she and EZ didn't belong together, had no right to be together, she had convinced herself that leaving in a few days would be the thing to do. But tonight, the situation, the people, actual friends had her questioning—no fearing—having to leave.

"Doc, tell me about my father." Jesus! The words sneaked out without her brain ever having a inkling of what she was going to say.

Sure he was taken aback, but took a long sip of his beer, set the glass down and gave her a smile that warmed her inside better than any liquor could.

"Be glad to. What exactly do you want to know?"

Lucky took in a deep breath to organize the millions of questions that suddenly appeared in her thoughts like the stars outside the saloon on this warm summer night. "Well, let me see—"

Before she could finish, Zos, looking suddenly pale, stood. "You know, I'm beat myself. No Pinochle for me tonight. I'll see you tomorrow—"

She jumped up and grabbed his arm. He stiffened, but this time she wouldn't let him pull away. "Are you all right?"

Doc looked as concerned as she felt, but he chuckled and said, "More than likely an excuse so he doesn't have to lose his shirt to me again tonight. That it, old man?"

The color returned to Zos's face beneath the bushy mustache that Lucky had at first thought was as fake as Doc's wig. But at this close angle she could see it was real and felt relieved to see his color less pale.

There was, however, no doubt that this kind, elderly gentleman had had a facelift. How cute. The guy was obviously a ladies' man.

"Ha! You old bugger, you only want to take advantage of me being tired." Zos patted Lucky's arm. "I'm fine. He's the one you'll have to watch out for if he bamboozles you into a game."

"Shit," Doc grumbled.

Because the two old friends seemed to be back to normal, she released Zos's arm. "I wish you'd stay, but I understand—" She yawned. "—tired."

He leaned forward. She lifted her cheek to meet his kiss.

But he merely nodded at her and turned.

She touched the spot. For the first time this evening, Lucky felt all alone once again.

Chapter Twenty

EZ came up behind Chloe and Owen in the doorway of the saloon. Once again the "lovebirds" were staring into each other's eyes as if they were the only ones in the damn room. Puppy love. Couldn't they see that was all it was? If it were the real thing, hell, they'd be arguing. At least that was his take on real love.

Then again, he was no expert.

He readied to tell them to take it outside, thought better than to encourage the horny kids and looked up to see Lucky. With lips set, eyes focused forward, her usual vibrancy had dimmed. Quickening his pace, he had to get to her to find out what the hell took the usual sparkle out of her eyes.

She looked as if someone had taken away her favorite doll.

Hell, Lucky probably never played with dolls, but it didn't matter. The sadness on her face made him want to hug her.

Doc moved closer to Lucky. EZ came up behind in time to hear him ask, "You sure, Lucky?"

"Sure about what?" EZ asked.

Lucky turned around. "I asked your father to tell me…more about mine."

"Jesus, Lucky."

She touched his arm, smiled at him, but he could see it was only on the surface. "I want to know what he was like when your father knew him. Doc, I know what he did was despicable, with the money and all, but can you see past your anger and tell me more about him?"

Doc smiled, reached over and patted her hand. "Anger's a wasted emotion at my age."

EZ straddled the chair next to her. She'd have laughed about how it reminded her of their "horse" escapade and all, but she wasn't in the mood for laughing. Earlier she had been, but as if a curtain had fallen on the wonderful show she'd been living through, a melancholy feeling had her gut tighten, her heart slowed. Strange. She really wanted to hear about Daddy, yet when Zos didn't give her the fatherly peck as expected, her wonderful night had shattered.

EZ took her hand into his after Doc moved to take a sip of his beer. "You really want to put yourself through this?"

"I'm not putting myself through anything." Her tone came out too defensive, she knew, but she couldn't do much about it. She felt that way. Felt as if only she could make up her mind. No need to have anyone tell her what to do, what to feel. She wasn't Chloe and didn't want EZ trying to run her life, too.

"Then why do you look—"

She pulled her hand free. "I don't know why I look however you're going to say I do, Dalton. I only want to hear, maybe learn more about my father from someone who knew him before...his life went to hell." She didn't like the feeling that had come over her before and didn't want to feel it ever again.

Doc placed his hand on EZ's shoulder. "I wouldn't hurt her for the world, son. And, I'm not sure I've ever shared some of the stories about the two of us with you either." He nodded. "I won't hurt her."

EZ sighed. "I couldn't change her mind if I wanted to anyway."

Doc chuckled, lightening the mood. "Stubborn like her old man, and independent as hell, too. Just like him."

She would have expected to bristle at Doc's accusations,

but a warm feeling started deep inside her, making a smile form on her lips that seemed to come out of nowhere. Maybe Doc's tone, maybe the fact that she believed he wouldn't hurt her, or maybe her hopes that she could hear some redeeming qualities about her father had her feeling more alive. More like Chloe.

Lately Lucky'd been more open to parental feelings—since coming here. After all, Doc was a darling and her relationship with Zos had her missing her old man. Hell, if anyone had told her she'd miss him, she'd have called them a fool. But, fool or not, Zos brought out her need for being loved by a father. He was one special man.

"You bit my head off once for saying you were like your father, but—" EZ said, interrupting her thoughts.

"But your dad is telling the truth from what he knows, not from gossip. Let him go on."

EZ wanted to argue, but she'd leaned against his shoulder in a way that only said *I can handle it, but I still want you near.*

His heart jolted at the thought.

There wasn't time to keep thinking of his feelings, though. No time to think about another person, someone he cared about, needing him. If he did, it would smother his feelings for that person. For Lucky.

Doc took a long sip of beer and started out way back when Rosario and he had met. Most of his stories EZ had in fact heard, but coming from Doc they seemed like a salve to Lucky.

He'd listen to a million repeat stories to see the interest in her face, feel her body relax next to his.

"And," Doc laughed. "We used to go to that Hartford neighborhood every afternoon when the baker would put out the pies to cool. I saved the money I earned from shinning shoes, and Rosario would deliver goods for the baker to get the leftovers. Blueberry was my favorite—"

"Apple was his," Lucky muttered.

EZ looked at her.

"I...I have no idea how I knew that. I guess I saw him eating them. Odd. I really can't picture...wait, I remember he ordered apple pie when we went to a restaurant once. But I was very young. Could be wrong." She looked around the table, even though some seats were empty now, sadness filled her eyes as if she were looking for a family of her own. "What I don't remember are any family meals together."

EZ winced. About to offer his words of comfort, he caught her gaze that said not to say what she already knew. Lucky didn't need or definitely didn't want sympathy.

"Anyway, Doc, go on."

More than likely carried off into the past, Doc rambled on until he and Rosario were in their early twenties—the years they started the dance hall that would become Funland.

Lucky settled in against EZ's shoulder. He couldn't help himself as he placed a protective hold around her. Old habits die hard, he mused. Not that he thought she'd need protecting from Doc's words, but Lucky was one complicated woman. EZ had no idea what might upset her and what wouldn't. Jesus, remembering about apple pie nearly had her in tears.

Not that he was any expert, but he'd bet that Lucky had gotten herself stuck somewhere within the grieving process—and would never be happy until she completed the necessary journey.

"Oh, at first we tried to make the place a regular Disney World. Big ideas. Big dreamers we were—"

"Both of you?" she asked.

Doc hesitated. EZ guessed he was carefully considering his words so nothing would hurt Lucky. He smiled to himself. Doc had his moments. Thank God there were still plenty of them.

"In our own ways, yep, we both were big dreamers. Your daddy was the brains behind most of it in the beginning. Had the street smarts. Knew all the angles—"

Lucky tensed.

Doc touched her arm. "That is he knew how to get the work done on time and to our best interest. He also knew a hell of a lot about an amusement park. Why he always argued with me that the theme rides, you know, like the Haunted Mansion had to stimulate all five senses of the customers. I argued until I was blue in the face that we could get away with only them seeing things, maybe a bit of scary music. But, Rosario, insisted and, I want to tell you, in its day the Mansion was the most popular ride."

Lucky felt a twinge of guilt at her and Zos making fun of the place. But she didn't let it fester because that was a long time ago, and customers were very different. Today's sophisticated people, brought up on the high-tech entertainment of TV, videos, and movies did want all five senses involved—and fast. Could Daddy have been ahead of his time?

"But—" Doc leaned forward, took her hand again and smiled. "His greatest accomplishment was the old roller coaster."

"He had it built?" EZ asked.

"No, son, that thing's older than me. Built in the golden age of the twenties. Folks thrilled when the wild, wooden coasters were built back then."

"I don't understand. My father wasn't even born until the late twenties—"

Doc ran a gnarled finger through his hair. "I'm not being clear. The coaster was there on the land from years before. Wasn't a true amusement park like it is today, more only a restaurant and The Big Dipper. I wanted to tear the old wooden thing down. Actually had the wrecking crew lined up, but Rosario wouldn't have it. No siree, he said she'd be a real draw—still is today. One of the oldest in the country, you know. True classic."

"I knew it was old, but a classic?" Lucky said.

Doc laughed. "Hell, they even got criteria for roller coasters. Have to have traditional lap bars so folks feel as if they're floating above the seats, and they can't have a bucket seat. No way. Folks have to sway from side to side. There's a few more things, but The Dipper meets them all."

"We should publicize this, EZ." She pulled herself up and looked at him. "It could be a major drawing card for business. I've got a friend back in Vegas that does independent filming. I'll get him out here to do a documentary on The Dipper. We'll air it on public TV, call the media, and the cable stations throughout New England." A feeling of excitement, much like the ones she felt when making a multi-million dollar deal, surged through her. Of course, Doc's excitement had to be contagious, too. He loved this place.

"Cripes. A film." EZ leaned over, kissed her on the cheek. "I never would have thought of that."

With reddened cheeks, she turned to Doc. "I'm sorry, go on."

"Don't you see, Rosario got this place together. I was more the entertainer," he said, tweaking his mustache. "Still am. Your daddy got the backing and, well, as the young kids say, 'The rest is history.'"

Lucky sighed. "We all know the history my father engineered."

EZ could see Doc getting tired by the minute. So far his thoughts had stayed clear, but EZ feared if he tired too much, he'd ramble on and it wouldn't be of any help to Lucky. "Maybe we should call it a night."

"No!" Doc grabbed EZ's arm. "Don't you see the girl needs to know."

Lucky stiffened. She pushed away from EZ and slid on the empty seat next to Doc with her heart thudding so loudly she thought the customers would soon complain. "Know what, Doc? What about my father—"

Doc looked away, across the room as if no one were there. "I...he was a good man when I knew him. We were friends for so long, I knew he had to have a good reason for why he did what he did."

She grabbed his arm more tightly than she wanted to. EZ jumped up and placed his hand on hers. "Sorry," she said. "Please go on." She released her hold on Doc but her hand found EZ's arm and she locked a grip onto it that had him wince. "Why did he take all the money?"

Doc turned to her, wiped a finger across her cheek. "He loved you in his own way."

A tear escaped her barrier and ran singularly down her cheek.

"Please," she whispered, praying that the old man would not have a moment of forgetfulness.

"You want to know why he stole from me, left me to fend for my family, to keep up this place, although I've done a lousy job of it—"

EZ grabbed his father's shoulder. "You did your best, Doc."

Doc chuckled. "Thank goodness for sons who ride in like the Calvary to save their old man's hide."

EZ remained silent.

Lucky gripped tighter, her breath held until she knew she'd either pass out or Doc would tell her what she wanted to hear. With her lungs feeling the heaviness, she waited.

Doc eased free of his son's hold, shook his head, stood and kissed her on the forehead. "He must have had his reasons." With that he turned and walked out.

Lucky jumped up.

"Let him go," EZ said.

"No! No!" She shoved at EZ until he fell back on the seat. "He didn't finish—"

EZ jumped up and grabbed her into his arms. She fought him, but he held tight.

"But...he...he didn't tell me—"

"How could he tell you what he doesn't know?"

* * *

Lucky spent the rest of the week walking around like a zombie, attempting to work. Sleepless nights tended to do that to her. After Doc's story about The Big Dipper, she had the film crew here and gone, a local television station airing the clip, and every nearby radio station notified of it, too. A group of some Coaster Classic Club booked the place and a wealthy Greenwich millionaire rented Funland for his kid's birthday because of the show.

All in all, she'd done a damn good job despite the way she felt.

And how did she feel now? she asked herself as she settled onto EZ's couch where she'd taken to spending her days doing both jobs of saving Funland and climbing the Hartwell corporate ladder to president. She twisted her head side to side to attempt to stretch out the sore muscles of her neck, then took a huge sip of coffee. The bitter taste warmed her inside, made her realize just how tired she was. But as much as she longed for the night to come to recover her lost sleep, she knew damn well her thoughts would keep her awake.

Maybe she could catch a short nap here before Ned faxed

her more work. Exhaustion was not good for deal making. She needed a clear head.

So, she told herself to shut her eyes and forget that Doc couldn't solve the mystery that ate away at her. Forget that maybe her father might have had a legitimate reason to swindle his best friend and leave him to fend for a wife and two kids.

Forget that Daddy was...Daddy.

Looking into the black liquid of her mug, she said, "You might be able to make up fortunes, but you sure as hell can't do the impossible."

"What's so impossible?" EZ asked from behind.

"Falling asleep with you here." She set the mug down, shut her eyes.

"Sleep?" He came around the couch, sat on the edge. "It's not like you to waste time during the day sleeping." He touched her forehead.

She pushed his hand away. "I'm not sick."

He leaned down attempting a physical examine with his gaze. "No? Then why a nap?"

"Don't stare at me like that. It gives me the creeps. You don't have x-ray vision, Dalton. I'm tired. Haven't you ever been tired?"

"Yeah, but I sleep—at night."

"And I would, too, if my mind would let me."

He took her hand even though she tried to pull away. "You still can't get over what Doc said the other night." It wasn't a question, but a hell of an observation.

"Could you if you were me?" She really didn't want an answer, so she shut her eyes.

But damn it if the interfering fool didn't say, "If I were you, Lucky, I'd let myself feel. Let myself—" He grabbed her and pulled her off the couch.

"What the hell are you doing?"

"Come with me. Humor me for chrissake."

At first she tired to fight him, but in reality she had neither the strength nor the energy. Sinking into his arms she said, "What the hell do you want from me?"

EZ softened his words. "I want you to get on with your life, Lucky. Forget the past that is eating you up."

She looked at him, tears filling her eyes. Hell. Control slipped from her grasp with every bleary vision of his face. "How?" her voice shook. One thing exhaustion managed to do was to let her barriers down enough so EZ could sneak in. And sneak in he did with his arsenal of know-it-all suggestions.

"How? Well, first of all, let me hold you."

"Brilliant, Dalton. You should be a shrink. If only the ones I'd paid tens of thousands of dollars had only held me—I'd be cured."

EZ wouldn't allow her sarcasm to stop him. He'd made another trip to the library a few days ago, but this time not to get a *People* magazine but a book on death and dying. He may not be a shrink as she'd accused, but he'd faced his mother's death and all four grandparents' and knew there was a process. A process one had to go through or they couldn't heal from the loss. A day didn't go by that he didn't think about his mother, miss her, but he'd learned to deal with that. Everyone had to.

Even someone like Lucky.

She pressed her face into his chest. He ignored the inner voice telling him that once again he was the caretaker. The one who had to deal with Doc, Chloe, Funland and now Lucky.

Could he do it one more time?

"I still feel like shit."

"Because you've never completed the grieving process for your father."

She shot out of his arms, slammed a fist against his chest. "Grieving? Why the hell would I grieve for *him*?"

EZ hesitated. Her hair had flown about her head with the swift movement, and he'd only now noticed dark circles beneath her eyes. She looked more as if she'd lost a loved one right now than a furious woman about ready to slug him again. With a Herculean effort he softened his voice although he'd much rather yell back at her and said, "Because he was your *father*."

That took her by surprise. Thank goodness he didn't go with the anger she'd revved up in him. If she'd continued with her punching, he would have entertained the idea of walking out.

"Big fucking deal."

EZ smiled. "It was. Because no matter what you want to think Lucky, you are who you are, in the position of life that you now hold because of that fact."

"Bullshit."

EZ shook his head. "I need a beer. Want one?"

"It's not even lunch time."

He opened the refrigerator, took one out, flipped off the top and held it toward her. "I'm taking that as a 'no.'" After a long slug he set the bottle down on the counter amid the now neatly stacked mail. She'd only been sharing the place as her office a few weeks, but she'd done a little organizing of his stuff, too. "Anyway, we all are products of our parents—"

"Okay, I'll give you he was a sperm donor." She slumped against the counter, resting on one elbow and glared at him. Reminded him of Chloe in her defiant teen years.

"Products of our environment. If your father had been...oh, let's say a factory worker making silverware in some rural Connecticut town, you have to admit your life would have been different."

Her lip curled. "No shit, Sherlock."

"You're vocabulary is going downhill fast. Let me get to my point before you doze off on me or your speech becomes X-rated."

"That idea, the nap that is, has crossed my mind a few times in the last few minutes." Had the dark circles deepened?

"Look, I'm trying to help—"

"And that would be because—"

He wanted to take her into his arms and kiss her, but with her glaring anger at him, he thought better than to touch her right now even though he knew, in addition to her problems with her father—Lucky was a lonely woman. "Because, despite what you want to hear, and sometimes despite what I want to admit, I care about you."

I care about you.

Lucky heard his words and couldn't shove up her barrier fast enough before they had a chance to strike her heart. Strike directly to the center, the very core of her being. The anger she'd earlier wanted to strangle him with, evaporated to allow her the admission that she liked hearing his words—and more importantly—returned the sentiment.

He cared about her!

"I'd do the same for any friend," he said.

Friend! She shut her eyes. Sleep threatened. But she allowed herself the thought, why should she be surprised? Why should she feel as if he'd kicked her in the gut? Why would EZ Dalton care about her in any way other than a friend, a good lay?

"Okay, *friend*, cure me."

"Lucky, if you'd give me the benefit of the doubt and at least go along with my idea that you are stuck in the grieving process, I really think it would help."

"Okay, what stage am I at?"

"Hostility."

"Ha! I've got the best god dammed reason to be hostile. My father was a fucking gangster! I was practically raised by bodyguards, *friend*.. Do you know how little time I spent with my father, my mother for that matter?"

"No... I—"

"No... I...of course you don't cause you really did grow up in the Beaver Cleaver existence. You had a father who cared about you, a sister who despite your stupidity and narrow-mindedness loves you. I'm guessing your mother was a lot like June. And what did I have? Hostility? You bet your ass I'm hostile toward my old man. Toward his fucking memory even after seven years!"

"Jesus. You've held all this in—"

"Been stuck in my 'hostile' stage for seven years. Yeah." She wiped her sleeve across her face. Her bangs stood up, her eyes had grown swollen and red, and her tongue kept running across her lips as if she were parched.

He still wanted to hold her. Kiss her.

And he wished like hell she would stop calling him "friend."

"Lucky, tell me about how your father died."

"The gory details?"

Cautiously, he made it close enough to reach out to her. But he raised one hand slowly. She flinched, looked down as if he held a snake out toward her. "Can I at least hold you?"

"As opposed to fuck me? Isn't that what friends are for?"

He ignored that. Hostility didn't mix well with anger, with pain. So, he took her into his arms, guided her to the couch and sat them both down. He grabbed the afghan his mother had crocheted for him when he'd gone off to his first sleepover camp and covered them both with it. "Was it an accident?"

She chuckled, but not from humor. "As opposed to

someone blowing his brains out on the red and white checkered table cloth of some Italian restaurant like in the movies?"

He nodded although she faced away from him, her body resting in his.

"He was boating on Lake Meade. I told you before he drowned."

"But seven years ago and you only came here now? Wait, when you first came here you said there were legalities."

She laughed. "You thought I was more organized with my business than to wait seven years to dump this place. Ha! Goes to show you. I had to wait all this time for him to be declared legally dead. No body and all. The DA even investigated the death. Thought he might have been whacked. Didn't even believe the testimony of the crew. No one saw him go overboard since it was nighttime. Nothing was proven."

She adjusted her position, pressing her butt into him. This wasn't the time to get aroused, but when she'd shifted, her hair whisked across his face. He inhaled grapefruit and knew breakfast time would never be the same.

"I'm so exhausted, Dalton, sarcasm seems to be the only emotion I have left."

"Or you chose to hide your others."

"Low blow for a nice guy like you. My old man's body never was recovered. The crew swore he fell overboard, even took lie detector tests, but the DA wasn't going to let him get away with anything. He'd been on the rotten end of too many deals."

"Shit. Did they think you were involved?"

"Although the idea would have been tempting, no, they thought *he* was involved once they got past him not being killed."

"I'm not following."

She shook her head. "You've led too sheltered a life in this amusement park. They thought he faked his fucking death before his enemies could whack him. His last business deal with Salvador Giacopetti went real sour. Even I couldn't help him. Damn him for making me feel guilty—that I might have wanted him dead."

"You know that's not true."

She yawned. "I don't know what I know. Neither did the DA."

"They really thought he'd faked his death? Hell, how did you deal with that?"

"All I knew was he wasn't around anymore to call me to come get him out of some rotten deal. Relieved. I'd say I felt relieved although you'd say I was *hostile*."

"In the stage of hostility."

"What the hell's the difference?"

He turned her around as much as he could without getting him more aroused and looked into her eyes. "I'm guessing even as a kid you hid your feelings inside. Anger, pain, even love—"

"How can someone know love if they've never experienced it?"

"Jesus. I am sorry, but you need to go on now. When your father died, you were so angry with him, you never expressed it. Never got past it to reconcile his leaving, feel the relief of accepting his passing."

"His passing isn't the part I wanted to accept."

"You lost out on the opportunity to save yourself from hating being his daughter when he died. Maybe you're grieving for your lost childhood, your lost family—"

He never meant to draw out the tears she'd hidden away most likely for years. But as he pulled her close, droplets ran along his cheek, down his neck. Her body shook as sobs filled the trailer.

"I only wanted what all the other kids had. What you had. Was that so wrong?"

"No," he whispered. "No, it's normal to want all that, but you need to get past this stage or you'll never be able to have it with your family."

She lifted her head. "I'll never have one of my own."

EZ shut his eyes, hoping the pain he'd caused would go away. Who did he think he was interfering in her life? Yanking out memories that she'd so neatly tucked away for her own sanity. He'd grown so tired of being the caretaker of his family yet here he was now trying to take care of Lucky—and all he managed to do was cause her more pain than any person should ever face in a lifetime.

"Shh." He ran his hands through her hair, shoving it from her eyes. "Shut your eyes and try to sleep now."

"I'm…so tired." She yawned. "I…couldn't sleep…if you…."

Her soft breathing, the silence, had him shut his eyes and pray that she'd be spared of any dreams right now—ones that *he* would have caused by dredging up her past.

Chapter Twenty-One

Lucky blinked. Her eyes didn't want to open; yet she knew she'd somehow made up for all her lost sleep. The day? Well, that was another matter. The time? She had no idea except that it was light outside by the shadows on her eyelids. Hopefully, she hadn't wasted a whole day of work...wherever she was lying, was too bumpy to be a bed. She shifted, heard a soft snore and realized she was neatly tucked into EZ's embrace.

Her eyelids flew open.

Yep. His trailer. Four by the clock above the stove, and he was asleep beneath her. Shit. What a position to be in—

Their conversation came back to her.

She shut her eyes a second, opened them and wiggled herself off of him. He stirred but didn't wake. Silently she stood there looking at him.

Her *friend*.

That part she did remember along with the hurt the one word had caused. All the stuff about Daddy wasn't nearly as painful—at least that's what she told herself.

Could EZ have been right? Could she still be in some grieving process for a man she barely knew? Didn't love?

Maybe she really did love him and felt angry for...not being able to have it returned. "Oh God, my head." She groaned only to look down and see EZ staring up at her.

"Hey, you all right?"

He looked adorable with sleep keeping his eyelids half shut, his body more relaxed then usual if she could imagine that, and a pinkish wrinkle across his cheek where a pillow of Niagara Falls had pressed into him.

"I'm all right."

"So you slept? Good. What time is—" He shifted his head, looked past her. "Four?"

"Sorry you couldn't get up—"

He pushed up, grabbed her hand before she could move away. "My pleasure. Do you remember anything we talked about—"

"I fell asleep, Dalton. Not into a coma."

He grinned. "Back to normal."

She sat on the couch next to him. No point in trying to move away, the jerk would only follow. The fax machine held nearly a ream of paper in the holder. Ned must have been busy; she'd need to work late into the night reading it all. "Yeah, my usual wonderful self. Thanks and I'm going to have to excuse myself to perk up with a shower—"

He motioned toward his bathroom. "Shorter walk."

"I prefer my own."

"Why? Because I don't have grapefruit shampoo?"

Grapefruit? She looked at him, but obviously he didn't pay much attention to the fact that he'd just admitted noticing the scent of her shampoo. She only wished she didn't care that he noticed.

Damn him.

"But I do have a brand-spanking new, not even out of the package shower brush. Be my guest—"

"I want to change, too."

He leaned over, kissed her cheek. She sighed while he worked his lips across her neck to the spot behind her ear that had her nearly fall into that coma when he kissed it. "Change later. We can put my new brush to good use. One hand washes the other and all."

She pushed him away. "Hands aren't all that would be involved."

He grinned. "Exactly."

She wanted to. She wanted to get naked, jump into the shower, wash whatever made them feel good and follow up with lovemaking that would knock the soap out of the dish.

Friend.

She could not get the stupid term out of her head—even when she told herself it was an excuse, a lie. What she couldn't get out of her head, either, was how she felt about this man, and how he admittedly felt about her.

Loss of power leads to pain.

She had to stay in control. If she wanted pure, consenting adult sex in the shower right now, she'd go for it. But she didn't. The niggling feeling that she wanted some kind of strings attached had her slam the barrier up once again.

"Okay," he said, pulling back. "No shower right now. I promised I would help you get out of the stage you're in, and I will—" He stood up and grabbed her hand.

"I've had enough of your help—"

"Hey, I got you to fall asleep. Besides, I'm not letting you go out of here until you make one attempt for me. Humor me, Lucky."

"If I do whatever the hell you have in mind, you promise me you will not ever bring it up again? No mention of my father, his death, stupid hostility. Nothing."

"Nothing with a capital *N*."

"I'm too smart to agree to anything until I know what it involves."

"No kidding."

His smile said he had her best interest in mind. Just as Doc's did when they had talked that night at the saloon. Not for one second did she doubt EZ. Her feelings, her own reactions were another matter.

How long could she shove them back inside?

"You guarantee it'll help?"

He softened his tone. "There are no guarantees except I'll give it my best shot."

"What do I have to do?"

He reached out his hand.

She looked at if for several seconds.

"Lucky?"

When she felt his fingers wrap around hers, a sense of security, safety started inside her. EZ wouldn't hurt her.

When he yanked her toward the refrigerator, pulled out the ice tray and hurried them toward the door, she wasn't sure.

"What the hell are you doing?"

"Trust me, Lucky." Once outside, he looked around. Thank goodness the trailer park was empty. Near trailer number twelve, the last one in the row, was a concrete wall dividing the trailer park with the rest of Funland. The Dumpster set to one side, filled with boxes and trash. He guided her as far to the left as he could. That end of the wall buffeted against the fence than ran along the beach. Three seagulls sat at the juncture, looking as if they thought he and Lucky were nuts.

"Shoo!" He pulled Lucky closer, handed her an ice cube. "In the book I read, it says to throw it against the wall to get out your anger."

She looked at the cube melting in her palm then up at him. "You're nuts." She dropped it to the ground and turned to go.

He yanked her around. "You promised."

She shrugged loose. Anger starting to build in her eyes. Good. That was good. Even if she let a few cubes go with him in mind, at least she'd be expressing *some* emotion.

"I didn't promise to be made a fool of."

He held up his chin, said, "I am not making fun of you. If you can think of all that's hurt you, everyone that's hurt you in the past, hell, release any frustration, you can, the cubes shatter away the pain as they hit the wall. And no mess." He gave her his best smile. Maybe coercion would get her going.

She grabbed a handful of ice cubes and threw them at the wall. "Dalton's a jerk! There. I feel better."

"I can't help you if you don't want to help yourself."

She swung around toward him. If she had the handful of ice cubes with her, he knew she'd have logged them at him. "Help? Haven't you done enough?"

"You tell me, Lucky. Do you feel as if I have? Have the demons of your past been exorcised from you?" He leaned near for effect. "How do you feel about your *father*?"

He winced at the pain that flashed before the anger in her eyes. Seemed the only way to get her into this was to make her once again angry with him. He'd gladly bear the brunt of shattered ice if it would only help her.

"You son of a bitch."

The words came out so deadly, he hadn't been able to reach out fast enough when she yanked the tray of ice cubes out of his hand. Like a major league player, she hefted another handful toward the wall. "You freaking son of a bitch, Dalton!"

"You have to do one at a time."

She swung around, glared at him then picked up an ice cube like a lady reaching for a tea-sandwich. "Like this?"

He nodded.

Who knew ice shattering could make a sound?

"You have a lot of nerve!" She lobbed another, followed by three more. "You think you can make me relive...you think you are helping me? You're a son of a bitch, with your wild ideas. You think you are so smart. You think I don't feel pain?" Her hands shook, her shoulders stiffened. As if mesmerized she screamed, "You think you could get away with leaving me...leaving me without a family no matter how pathetic. You think it didn't hurt. A kid, a little girl with no one..."

He watched the ice run down the concrete wall, as the tears ran down her cheeks. As if a damn had broken loose, tears spilled over her chin into the empty tray she hugged to her chest.

"Your fucking code of silence was more important than your family..."

* * *

Lucky's energy drained from her body as tears ran down her face. She'd slept for hours but this emotional upheaval had her legs collapse beneath her. The pain she'd felt in her heart tore deeply. No way could she even lift another ice cube let alone throw it.

But as the pain ripped into her heart, anger spilled through the hole, leaving her momentarily numbed.

That's when she collapsed into EZ's arms.

"Lucky. Lucky," he soothed. "I'm so sorry for putting you through that. I had no business...I only wanted to make you feel better."

Because he held her so tightly, she had to push back to manage to lift her face to meet his gaze. "Thank you."

He glared at her, most likely wondering how she managed to get out the words in such a weak voice. "I...do you feel better?"

She managed a chuckle, felt her body against his. "*Better* is a long way off, Dalton. But I will tell you something clicked, changed. I don't think I'll get to that relief stage anytime soon, but I'm not angry anymore."

He kissed her on the lips, his warm touch soothing momentarily. She moved back and said, "You know, I always wondered if...maybe if I was a better daughter, he would have loved me, stayed with us—"

EZ shoved his fingers against her lips. "Don't you ever say that. You heard Doc. He said Rosario loved you in his own way. You had nothing to do with how he acted. That was his choice."

"I know you're a big strong jerk, but even you couldn't carry me back with my heart feeling like a lead weight. I have to sit."

He led her to the trailer where she stumbled up the stairs and fell onto the couch. "I'm getting you a glass of wine whether you want one or not."

"I want one."

As he poured a Chardonnay into a plastic Yankee's cup, he grabbed a can of Budweiser from the refrigerator. She could barely move, but her gaze followed him around the room. With a sigh she told herself no matter how she felt about him, she'd never find a better friend.

"Here." He handed her the wine. "Take a big slug."

She did as he'd suggested, nearly choking. When she could swallow and speak she smiled at him. "Thank you for forcing me to get that all out."

She'd expect him to look more pleased with himself. "What?"

"I—" He sat opposite in the brown stuffed chair, drinking his beer.

"Off the subject, but do you have Dixie beer around here?"

He gave her an odd luck. "No. Isn't that found down South? Why?"

"Yeah. No reason."

He shrugged. "I think it's great what you did so far. A start as you say, but you need to get it *all* out."

"Aren't you ever satisfied until you get your own way?" She lifted her chin. "No need to answer that. Besides, I can't. Not tonight."

"Lucky, I'm so tempted to say that's fine, just go back to sleep, but you've come so far, you need to go on...or you might never."

"Damn you, Dalton."

He nodded. "I know. Maybe if you tell me why you think you did something wrong...you won't get stuck in the guilt stage."

With the plastic cup to her lips, she took a sip, looked at him over the rim. "I...maybe for the same reason kids feel they're the cause of their parents getting divorced. I know my mother treated me differently when my father forced her to give up the career she loved, to stay home with me. I don't know why he did it, but she grew distant to me.

"And Lord knows he'd never been close as it was. Actually—" She chuckled. "I already told you he'd moved out—had his other 'family' business to attend to. But in the late seventies and early eighties things changed nationwide in *that* business."

"After Sammy The Bull ratted on the late John Gotti."

She looked at him. "You've read your history. Yeah, after that, and I remember seeing a news clip about it, my father changed. He, and I'm sure all the other members grew leery of everyone. They didn't know whom they could trust, who would sell them out. I think that's when Daddy grew more distant if that were possible. He didn't even call me secretly anymore.

"I lived with bodyguards outside my door and although I wondered why I needed them, at least they were like friends. But do you know how humiliating it is to go on a date and have these 'suits' following you around?"

"I know how humiliating other types of dates were, but, no, not like yours."

She chuckled. "Thanks for trying to lighten the mood, Dalton. I see why you make such a good big brother, although you are a pain in the ass."

EZ smiled but couldn't get past the reminder. If she only knew how he'd grown tired, actually hated, his roll as the responsible Dalton, she wouldn't be saying that. But he couldn't tell her or anyone else for fear it would get back to Doc. Not that he thought Lucky would tell him on purpose, but a slip, a word, and he'd hurt his father so deeply EZ would never forgive himself. "Thanks for the compliment."

Holding the Yankee's cup toward him, she nodded.

"You have to be able to see though, Lucky, that your father, just like mine or anyone else's made their own decisions, were responsible for their own actions. No matter what we did as kids or grownups for that matter, we couldn't make them act any differently."

"I've always been the most logical person I know, and what you say, I hear. I hear it, buy it, but don't *feel* it yet."

"Give it time."

"Please hold me," she whispered.

He stood, walked around the coffee table and sat, taking her into his arms. "You know, I remember a time when you came to visit one summer and—"

"My father used to just leave me here and go to Atlantic City. Right?"

He pulled her closer. "Look at it this way, he knew you were safe here and the Dalton family would take damn good care of you."

She looked at him, paused. "I'm going to try to believe

that."

"It's true. Remember when we took that boat out and the offshore breeze came along?"

"We had to be towed back by a boat with a water-ski line."

"Right. But what I remember is, your father sent the bodyguards back that very same day, earlier than expected, when Doc told him about it. He was worried about you, Lucky."

"You could have fooled me." She curled her lip. "Okay, maybe. But I also remember he had me whisked back to Vegas that night as if he could remove me from any potential situation. Back then I wondered, hoped was more like it that he would have come to get me himself. Why the hell are you sticking up for him anyway?"

"I'm not. All I want is for you to grieve for him no matter how you felt about him and get on with your life. Not to blame yourself for something you had no control over."

Lucky leaned back, shut her eyes. He wrapped his arms tighter around her, his breath a reminder of the comfort she felt right here, warming her cheek. She didn't want to move. She turned to him and said, "Make love to me now, Dalton."

* * *

Lucky watched Chloe prancing down the pathway toward EZ's trailer. Thank goodness Lucky had caught up with all the faxes from Ned since last week she'd never even gotten to them. Making love with EZ had been a salve she desperately needed after the tumultuous time they'd spend talking.

And the pure sex wasn't bad either.

They'd gotten closer the days that followed. Vegas became a distant memory, and funny, but she looked forward to the marsh scent each day when she woke.

She and EZ had spend hours together working on Funland. With the film of The Dipper released throughout the East, attendance was at an all time high. Two more millionaires from Greenwich had booked the place after hours for private functions. The Griswald's daughter's sixteenth birthday party and Benjamin Rosenblatt's son's bar mitzvah. Benjamin owned the largest jewelry store in Connecticut.

That and EZ getting all the past due bills paid back, sent Funland roaring into the black.

She could leave any day now.

"Hey, Lucky." Chloe bounded into the trailer.

"What's going on?" Lucky knew she'd need to focus, forget that she didn't want to pack, because it took a lot of energy to follow along with Chloe.

Chloe opened EZ's refrigerator, grabbed a cola, held one out toward Lucky. She took it before the girl hoisted herself up onto the counter. "Owen and I are thinking of eloping."

Lucky laughed, twisted off the top of her drink.

The girl's eyebrows drew together. "Where's my brother?"

"Showing a prospective customer, a huge group from New York City, around. Apparently they thrive on classic roller coasters."

"Then he won't be back soon. Good." She hopped down, sat her hip on the edge of the table directly above Lucky.

Lucky felt her eyebrows draw together. "You're not kidding."

"Nope. Owen and I have been talking all night—"

Lucky waved her hand in the air. "Don't give me any details about being together all—"

"We're both still virgins."

Lucky spilled her cola. "Shit!" She jumped up and grabbed a towel off the hook left of the sink.

Chloe moved to the side, the cola seeping into her white shorts.

"Sorry, kid. But you—"

"Swear you won't tell my brother. I like having him think—"

Lucky laughed. "First of all it's good to hear young people having their own moral values and second of all, I wouldn't tell EZ anything you didn't want me to. But, please don't involve me in any elopement plans. I still think you're too—"

Chloe grabbed her arm, sending the soaked towel flying off the table. "I'll get it later. You were young, you know how it feels to be in love—"

"No, Chlo, actually I don't. My marriage was an escape from my father. I didn't love Vinny and he was no Owen. Vinny treated me like something he owned. I told you this. I had no life, really, I was like some trophy for him to show off. But, I can't condone your marriage."

"You've seen Owen and me together. Can you honestly say that we don't belong together? That age really makes a difference? You just admitted your situation was different. I really want to know…because you're like the mother I miss so much."

Lucky winced.

Chloe tightened her hold until it hurt.

Lucky tried to pull away. Chloe grabbed her and pulled back. "Jesus, Chloe, you're not being fair."

Chloe chuckled. "Just like a real mother-daughter argument. Isn't it?"

As if Chloe had moved her hand from Lucky's arm to around her throat, she felt a tightening from the outside, a knot form on the inside. The comment had her mute. She couldn't breath.

Like a *mother*.

Would it ever really be possible? Could she raise a child and have it grow up to be someone without all the problems she'd had? Ever have a normal happy life?

"Please, Lucky," Chloe whispered, releasing her grip.

Lucky took her into her arms, pulled her close. Feeling as she did right now about EZ, she couldn't imagine not being with the one you loved. And she did, in fact, have feelings. Oh my God! As if the proverbial lightening bolt had struck, she realized she loved the jerk. "No, I can't. I can't honestly say that you don't belong together. You're right. It is very different. But still. I don't know. Well, I...perhaps you're getting married is the right thing to do."

Lucky'd always wonder how a growl could overtake the yelp someone like Chloe could produce. But she didn't need to wonder who the growl came from. She turned around.

"What the hell are you trying to pull with *my* sister?"

LUCKY IN LOVE

Lori Avocato

Chapter Twenty-Two

Chloe moved away from Lucky's embrace although she was tempted to pull her back—as a shield. But, she wouldn't use the girl like that despite the fact that EZ looked as if he wanted to kill Lucky.

"Get out of here, Chlo."

She stood defiant.

"Now!" he shouted.

"I said I don't need you anymore, EZ. And don't take your anger out on Lucky—"

"I'll talk to you later. Leave now."

Lucky nodded at Chloe so she turned and marched out all the while mumbling about her narrow-minded brother. Lucky wanted to smile, but she was no fool. EZ wasn't just angry, he was pissed—at her.

"Can I get you a cola?" she asked.

He glared at her.

"Beer? Arsenic?"

"What the hell gives you the right to interfere in a family matter? *My* family?"

That stung, but she refused to go with the pain he'd shot at her. Here she thought they'd grown so close, they were almost family.

God, had she even entertained the idea that they might be a family some day?

"She asked." Flimsy answer, but if she let herself say what she wanted, she might never get out of here alive.

"Oh, she asked. She asked. A teenager asks for your blessing to make the biggest mistake of her life and you say, 'sure, kid, go ahead.'"

"It wasn't like that and you know it."

"Then what was it like, Santanelli? Oops. Forgot you don't know how the workings of a family should be—"

"Low blow even for you, Dalton. Maybe I'm not part of this or any family—"

"Jesus. I'm sorry. I didn't mean—"

"The hell you didn't. I'm *not*. I know I'm not part of any family. But Chloe wanted my opinion as a woman—" She refused to tell him how flattered, touched she was that Chloe looked at Lucky as a mother-figure.

"Fuck it."

"That's what you think of my opinion?" She pushed past him to leave, heard his footsteps, felt his arm grab her.

"What I meant was, some days I wish the hell I never had the responsibility I do. First Doc, all the employees around here, even Zos, Chloe, then—"

She froze. "Me."

"I didn't mean—"

Because he was much stronger, she knew she couldn't pull free of his hold. But she used her smarts, placed her hand gently over his. Bingo. His grip loosened. When he reached to take her hand into his, she yanked it away and grabbed the door.

He reached out.

"Don't you dare. Don't you dare touch me, Dalton." He pulled his hand back, softened his face. "I'll be leaving on the first flight I can book."

EZ stood and watched the woman who he'd come to care about walk out the door. Damn it all! She'd been wrong, though, to encourage Chloe to marry. He'd straighten that out later. Right now, he had to find Lucky and tell her why he'd come over here in the first place.

The door to the trailer swung on its hinges after Lucky had stalked out. He ran down the four steps and looked around. She must have gone right into number eight. Slamming the door behind him, he hurried across the short distance—and told himself that this wasn't going well.

He might have blown the best chance in the world for his happiness.

He knocked several times, but she never said anything. "The screen door's unlocked, Lucky. I can hear you back there. Let me in."

"Yes, ma'am, I'd like to book the first flight to Las Vegas—"

He hurried inside and yanked the phone from her hand. "Hang it up."

"Funland is in the black, I'm guessing you can find yourself some manager to help you keep it that way. I have no business here any longer, Dalton."

"Yes, you do."

She clucked her tongue, told the woman on the phone she'd call back and slammed it down. "Say what you came to tell me then get out."

"The Bank of Seagrove just called. Seems a balloon note is past due. Doc had re-mortgaged the place. I only found out about it—"

She jumped up and slugged him in the gut. "You bastard! Will you never stop finding ways to keep me in this prison?" After her "exorcism," she'd long given up hiding her feelings, her emotions. Tears flooded her eyes.

"You can't do this to him, you know. You can't leave him, this place." What he wanted to say was "don't leave me" yet he couldn't get it out. He feared her anger—feared her lying to him about her feelings as she had about their lovemaking—because she was striking out at him. So, he aimed low and hit her emotions.

She swiped a hand across her cheeks and said, "Fine. How much?"

He shoved a hand in his pocket, pulled out a note and handed it to her.

She blinked several times. Blurry vision had her hoping at first that she wasn't seeing the six-figure amount correctly. "God damn it. God damn, you."

"I didn't *know* about it?"

She believed him, but said, "Like hell."

He grabbed it from her hand. "Think what you want, but if you leave, the place goes under. Your assets will be affected and my father—"

"You son of a bitch. You hit below the belt without a thought."

"No, Lucky, I don't usually. But my father will always come first where Funland is concerned."

He might as well have put his hands around her neck and squeezed—because that's exactly what she felt he was doing.

She really was only a short-term 'friend' where he was concerned. She pushed away, headed toward the door.

Why had she ever let him tear down her barrier?

Now she'd lost another family.

* * *

Lucky ran past the long lines of guests waiting for the Great Zosimoff to tell them their fortunes. Clearly she had no idea how she got all the way over here from the trailer park. EZ's news, the pain he'd caused, had her so confused, she longed for an old friend to talk to.

LUCKY IN LOVE

Lori Avocato

She longed for Zos.

EZ had chased her most of the way, but when she stopped by the cotton candy booth and let him have it, he raised his hands in surrender and turned back—but not before telling her they weren't through yet.

Through with what? Saving this prison that had ripped her life apart?

Or, and she knew long shots had the worst odds, through with *them*?

Did they have a chance together?

Hell, she didn't even want a chance with a jerk like him. Someone who could make such passionate, earth-shattering love to her, then break her heart with his words.

A woman hollered at her for cutting in line, but Lucky ignored her and the rest who mumbled about cutting in, shoved open the door and stood there.

Zos's head swung up from looking at the crystal ball. "Lucky...Lucky what is wrong?"

She hoped she didn't look as foolish as she felt. "I'm...sorry. I didn't mean to interrupt."

Zos pushed up, shoved the ticket of the woman who sat in front of him at her and said, "Please excuse us, Madame. You will get a double session if you come back in an hour."

She looked at Lucky. "Double?" the woman said, nearly salivating.

"Yes, ma'am," he said, ushering her out the door.

Lucky collapsed into the seat, the cushion warm from all the day's business so far and heard him say to the people in line, "Excuse, me. The booth will be closed temporarily. Please forgive the inconvenience, an....emergency. Check back later. Thank you."

Lucky set her elbows on the table, her face resting in her

palms until she felt a touch on her shoulder. At first she tensed. Had EZ come back? But she turned to see Zos standing above her.

A look in his eyes had her hear nearly stop.

Something so familiar, so touching filled his eyes. But his wrinkled forehead said he was worried. She sniffled, wiped her nose with the tissue he handed her. She realized then that she needed him, not Doc or anyone else.

"What is wrong?"

"I shouldn't have bothered you—" She started to get up.

A gentle touch had her sit back. "Something serious has you upset."

"I'm leaving Funland—"

His grip tightened.

"Ouch!"

"I—" He released his hold, sat opposite her. "I am so sorry."

"It's all right, Zos. I'm the one who's sorry. Sorry for having come here to bother you. Sorry for having…to help out at this stupid place." The sobs started. The words barely came out in an audible whisper, "Sorry for having been born—"

"Don't *ever* say that, Lucy!"

Her eyes widened. "*What?*"

"I—" He stiffened. "Don't ever say that, Lucky."

"No. No, you…didn't call me that. What did you call me?"

"Lucky."

"No, I'm sure you didn't—"

"Goddamnit!"

How unlike Zos. That tone. Had her ears been playing a trick on her because her sobs were so loud? No one, not EZ, not Doc new her real name. Yet….

"I called you Lucky." Zos sat back, now looking like a man of about seventy-eight that she guessed he was.

Rosario Santanelli's age.

God, she was going nuts here. Even from the grave her father had his tentacles on her. Made her insane. Here she was accusing this wonderful man, her friend.... Her face sunk down into her palms again. She blamed it all on EZ, too. When she looked up, Zos sat staring. She pulled herself up, shoulders high, chin straight. "Please, again. What did you call me?"

"*Lucky*."

How she wanted to believe that, but she couldn't let it pass. "No, no, Zos. You called me—"

"Lucky." His voice came out determined, but so was she.

"I thought we had a better relationship than you—not telling me the truth. You called me 'Lucy.'"

He got up, turned his back on her. Lucky's hand shook as she touched the crystal ball.

"You misunderstood, Sugar. How would I know...you were so upset, you didn't hear me correctly, *Lucky*."

She got up and walked toward him, having no idea where she got the strength. "No one knows my given name. I demand you tell me how you knew it!" Her tone even surprised herself, but she had to know. Was he someone from her father's past? "Oh God, you're... one of the Giacopetti men. You've come to hurt...take me. Don't hurt the rest of--"

Zos turned around waved his hand at her. "Lucy Marie Santanelli."

Her hand flew to her mouth.

Zos reached out, she pushed him away. "Don't, Lucy!"

"Oh God!" She froze. How many times had she heard that tone when she was a kid? Sure the voice was different—*altered* surgically now she realized—but the tone came through loud and clear. Daddy wasn't this tall...hell, lifts, she figured. He grabbed her by the shoulders. She kicked his leg.

LUCKY IN LOVE

Lori Avocato

If she thought she was having a heart attack that time with EZ, now must be the real thing. She clutched at her chest, felt the pounding on her fingers. Sweat beaded on her forehead as nausea welled up her throat. With all her strength, she kicked him again. Damn her heart.

"Damn it, Lucy, stop that!"

"No. No. No!" She had to get away. This wasn't really happening. No way. She wasn't in this godforsaken booth with—*him*. The scream came out on a whoosh and continued without any effort. Of course it came easily after suffering such a shock.

Zos looked at the door, pushed her up against the wall, pining her in-between his arms. "Stop it! Stop it, Lucky! I order you to stop!"

When he put his hand over her mouth, she shut her eyes, readied for the worse. But he leaned near, his warm breath on her cheek. "Please, Sugar, don't scream. We'll all be in danger. We need to talk."

The screaming stopped. He released his hold. She swallowed against the pain in her throat, too confused, overwhelmed to think of what was really happening. All she could do was sink against the wall and look into his eyes. Contacts. He'd changed the color of his eyes with contacts.

A stupid thought for such a traumatic revelation, but who could think clearly when they looked at a ghost?

Zos, no *Rosario*, whispered, "I am so sorry for all of it, Lucy."

She shut her eyes. Tears filled them when she opened her lids. Once when she was about five, she'd fallen off her horse and Daddy happened to have been there—the one time she remembered him comforting her. He used the same tone right now. Because it was the only memory she could think of, she didn't run.

He was as slick after death as he was when alive.

"I had to do it, for you. For *you*." Tears now filled his eyes, too.

She'd never seen her father cry, never thought him capable. Damn it, she told herself looking at him. This wasn't Daddy. She couldn't get past looking at Zos. Past the exterior. He was Zos the man she'd grown to love, like the father she never had. Betrayal hurt worse of all. He'd lied to her—the worst lie he ever could.

"But you'd drowned." How stupid, but nothing was clear anymore. "You died. And now you've killed Zos for me, too." One father she never had stood before her, one she had grown to love, now gone in the revelation. Numbed, empty, she remained still.

"Please sit down."

She shook her head.

He sucked in a deep breath, let it out so slowly she thought her mind would explode if he didn't finish explaining soon. If she could, she'd collapse into a heap at his feet and never get up.

But, looking past the exterior of the fortuneteller, she knew she wouldn't collapse. Because he was Rosario—she'd never allow him to see her crumble.

"Things had been going down for so long—"

She curled her lip at him.

"I know I wasn't the best father, but I...it was all I could be. I was a bastard where you were concerned. I know it. Knew it then. My life meant nothing to me, you have to believe that."

She felt like spitting in his face, but that wasn't her style. "Go on."

"You know how the families had crumbled, the business, the Giacopetti family targeted my business. That bastard

Salvador...he ordered me whacked."

She gasped.

"But the worse thing, Lucy, the reason I had to engineer my death, cut up my face and put it back together, get my larynx cooked with a laser...was because the bastard threatened...*you*. I learned early on to distance myself from you—not that I wanted to—but so they wouldn't think you were the most precious thing in my life. My most vulnerable possession."

"You made Mommy give up her career."

"Because she'd been drinking for years. I thought she'd stop if she stayed home with you—"

"I don't believe you! You made her stop."

"I did it to save her from humiliation. She...hated me. Hated the secrecy. It drove her to the bottle."

He looked down to see the ring Lucky wore. Was that a hint of a smile?

"Because of her working, I couldn't keep up," he continued, "I'd let down my guard one time before and paid the price. She was never happy. I knew it, I couldn't change that. I never should have secretly kept in contact with you—but I got selfish."

Tears dripped from her chin. He gave up everything, left his life, the life he'd only known—for her.

"I know you can't forgive me for this, but we've gotten so close—"

"Zos. I got close to Zos."

He cursed. "I *am* Zos."

She shook her head. "No. No. You'll never be Zos."

"Don't you see, I finally could love you without fear of someone harming you. I had to do it," he said, sounding so unlike the father she knew.

All she could think of was the Dixie Beer. Now she knew why Zos drank it. He must have had Chloe bring it back from

New Orleans. Jesus. She couldn't take it anymore.

She started to push at his arm. No longer could she stand here an emotional heap. His voice had softened, almost weakened. He was an old man now. Her heart broke looking at him, when all she wanted to do was kill him.

He looked her in the eye. "They would have kidnapped you *again*."

Again? "What the hell are you talking about?"

Zos—Rosario glared at her. "You and I...we were never close...."

Despite the fact that his voice had been altered, he sounded exactly like Rosario right now. She shut her eyes and listened to him say how sorry he was for all of it.

"I wanted to be there for you, but couldn't."

"Because you had another family, a more important family. Your fucking code of silence."

"Omerta."

She cursed. "All I wanted was for you to spend time with me and not some bodyguards following me night and day."

"I knew everything about you. I was there when you never new. I made sure safe, loyal people surrounded you. That's why I left you this place. You'd save it for Doc, not for me. And you and EZ...I'd watched you both grow up. Knew you two could belong...." He sucked in a breath. "I was there for your high school graduation. College. Danny had to take out a loan for your tuition—"

She gasped. He had paid for her schooling? Things were so unbelievable, and ironic. Danny had paid for her education—and her business skills had saved this place.

He shut his eyes. "I never had a head for business once I left here. No banks would lend me money. For all of it, I'm sorry."

"Sorry doesn't erase the pain, Daddy," she spat. Before he

could grab her, she shoved him out of the way.

"Lucy, you can't tell anyone. Not even EZ."

She froze. "I'm not a liar."

"They'll find me...you and *he* will be in danger."

"You bastard."

"I don't deserve you. I know that. Don't let my actions ruin your life though. I've watched you become independent—made me proud, but you've also locked away your emotions. I am so sorry. But I don't expect you to forgive me, Lucy—"

She swung around. "In the future, don't *ever* call me that."

He chuckled but not from humor. "I don't have much of a *future*. I have cancer—"

She gasped. "Daddy."

"Ironic. Isn't it? I come alive to you and...years of Camels have caught up with me. Spread to my spine and soon my brain if the doctors are right."

How she wanted to go. How she wanted to run, to get away from all these explanations that tore her into a million pieces. But she turned. "How...long?"

"Five, six months."

"Oh, God—"

"Even afterwards, you can't say anything. Giacopetti has a long memory. My underboss found out Giacopetti had his spies out and saw us together on more than one occasion. Even after seven years he'll make you pay for my sins."

"The daughter shall pay for the sins of her father."

"I won't allow it."

"You're a little late."

He touched her hand as Zos often did during their nightly Pinochle games and shut his eyes. "I am sorry."

She pulled free. "I'm going back to my trailer, *Zos*, do not follow me."

He nodded.

She grabbed the doorknob and hesitated. When she turned, she noted the sallow coloring beneath his eyes, on his cheeks. He'd worn makeup to cover it, she now knew. Tears had streaked down his cheeks. Although she vowed to herself right here that she'd forget every word of their conversation, she had to first ask, "Why? Why did you do it to Doc?"

Zos looked up, "You never remembered."

"Me? I had nothing to do with you stealing from your best friend—"

"At the age of three, you were taken…I know I was a rotten businessman, overspent, so I didn't have the money…you were taken for chrissake."

"Ransom. You stole to cover my *ransom*."

He nodded.

"Why the hell didn't you just ask Doc for the money? Too proud?"

A tear worked its way down his cheek. "I couldn't involve him. You know their arms reach very far."

Their. The mob. Daddy'd lied to protect Doc and his family.

When she walked out the door, she stopped with a hand on the doorknob, shut her eyes. She could only picture the pain on his face, the pleading look of forgiveness in his eyes, as she walked past the laughing children.

Chapter Twenty-Three

She couldn't pull herself away.

All Lucky wanted to do was run to her trailer, be alone forever.

But she couldn't get her feet to move her away from watching the laughing children. The young boy giggled so loudly, she thought the kid would tumble beneath the Ferris wheel in front of her, but his mother had a firm hold on his hand. The blond little girl, obviously the sister, stood by rather shy, one hand clutching the mother's shorts.

Both children trusting the mother not to let them get hurt.

Trust, she thought with a jolt.

Both kids laughing along with her, as if only they knew the secret they shared.

Secret. She, too, had a secret that would never pass through her lips. Hers, no doubt, would never bring a smile to her face. Yet on some level, some plane of her existence, she felt a weight lift from her—the grieving process continued on.

"Mommy, look at how high it is!" the little girl with the golden hair and dusting of freckles across her nose screamed.

Lucky's emotions soared higher than the Ferris wheel.

I want that.

I want what that woman has, Lucky thought.

It was then she turned to go, stopping only to see the line forming outside the fortune telling booth. She watched it a few seconds...then smiled.

* * *

LUCKY IN LOVE

Lori Avocato

EZ dropped the folder onto his desk, leaned back in his office chair and shut his eyes. Right now he had no idea what to do. Lucky had left in such a huff, in such pain, all he wanted to do was run after her, but she'd put a stop to that. Anger at himself had him bite his bottom lip. It took all the control he could muster not to go searching Funland to find her, whether she wanted him to or not. He looked at the folder.

Why hadn't he told her the real reason he'd come after her earlier?

Before he'd found her with Chloe, he'd sworn to himself that he wouldn't tell her about the balloon payment being due for several days—when he could break it to her gently. He'd thought if need be he'd find the money somehow or refinance since the place was doing so well.

But she'd angered him into it.

If she hadn't stormed off...hell, she had every right to. He'd made a mess of everything. If only Chloe hadn't gone to Lucky—was he jealous that she had? Was Chloe's action only a reminder that he would never be both a substitute mother and father to her?

Damn it, he *was* jealous.

Jealous that Lucky had interfered into his position of caretaker when he'd convinced himself that all he wanted in his life now was *not* to be responsible for anyone but himself.

Her actions made him see that he actually wanted the cherished job. He'd been too protective of his sister, and Lucky had made him realize that now.

"Damn her."

"I'm guessing you're talking about me, Dalton."

He swung around. Lucky stood on the other side of the screen door. Without an invitation, she pushed it open and walked in.

LUCKY IN LOVE

Lori Avocato

"You look like hell," was all he could say.

She curled her lips, walked closer. "Flattery will get you nowhere."

He started to get up.

She pushed him down.

"You know I didn't mean—I'm concerned about you," he said.

"Ha. Never know it by our earlier conversation."

"About that. Let me explain." He shifted to stand, she glared at him. "Can I get up? I can't think straight sitting here—"

"No. I'm going to be doing the talking." She opened the small refrigerator near the file cabinet, took out two beers, handed him one. "First, I've had a revelation."

He took a sip of beer, watched her. Watched the sparkle slowly return to her eyes. He knew a miracle had just occurred.

"Revelation?"

"Um." She sipped the beer, sat on the edge of the desk above him.

"Well, are you going to keep me in suspense?" She'd changed, he could see it yet not put his finger on what the difference was or what had caused it. But he sure felt good about it.

She took a long slow drink, set the bottle on the pile of papers on his desk. Hopefully she noticed how he kept it much neater these past few weeks.

"I don't know how long I was standing by the Ferris wheel watching a mother and her two kids—"

He downed the rest of his beer, stared at her above the can.

"Don't look at me as if I'm nuts."

"I'm not...go ahead."

"I intend to."

She leaned closer; he inhaled her scent and knew, he just

knew that everything was going to be fine. Perfect.

"Anyway, I watched that family, and, you know what, Dalton?"

"I'm guessing you're going to tell me."

"I decided I want that."

"That?"

"That family. Well, not that particular one, but I want what that woman had. A boy. A girl with hair the color of winter wheat and a dimple on both sides of her cheeks. I want a boy who holds my hand so tightly; my fingers will turn blue. I'll know he trusts me...."

She looked at him, knowing a glassy film covered her eyes. God she wanted to tell him. Tell him about Zos, Daddy. With a sigh, she told herself that if she really cared about EZ, no, if she really loved EZ—and she did—she *couldn't* tell him. Now she knew how ruthless Daddy's enemies could be. No way could she involve EZ or any of his family in this mess. So, she tucked the knowledge she'd just gained from her father into the deepest recesses of her mind, admitting that sometimes a lie was necessary, and said, "I want all that, but...."

EZ couldn't move. All he could do was stare at her, waiting for the tears. Waiting for her to say although she wanted all of it, she'd never have it.

He didn't know if he had it in him to comfort her any more.

Was there anything anyone could say to take away Lucky's pain? He'd give his life to know. He sighed.

She leaned down, grabbed his hand from his lap. "I want it all with *you*, Dalton."

"I wish I could say something to take away your pain...what the hell? What'd you say?"

She pulled him from the chair, smacked him a good one on his lips. "You jerk. I just proposed."

EZ pulled back. He had to get a good look at her to remember this moment. "Jesus. Your eyes, that sparkle...I should have known." He leaned near. "Don't take this wrong, I mean I'm thrilled, Lucky. But why now? What happened to—"

She touched his hand. "You'll just have to trust me."

"I always did." He let out a whoop that had a group of guests outside his office window turn and stare. "I'm getting married!"

Lucky grabbed him, danced him around. "I'm taking that as a 'yes' and you can't go back on your word."

He kissed her this time, long and slow, knowing there'd be millions more in their lifetime, but this one, on the day she proposed would be tucked into a special corner of his brain. "Okay, if you put it that way, I'll marry you."

He'd said it in his most matter-of-fact, easygoing tone—pure EZ Dalton style. "You jerk." She punched his chest. He grabbed her hand, kissed each finger.

"So, you about ready to head to my place and start...what? You want the boy or girl first?"

"Well—" She gave him her sexiest smile. "I'm organized, smart, independent, but not fussy. Whatever."

"Ha! You are the damnedest independent woman I've ever known, and...don't ever change."

She turned around, knocked the folder off his desk.

"I'll get that later," he said, grinning. "Right now we've got—"

But, Lucky being the organized woman that she was, had already bent to pick up the papers that had fanned themselves across the floor.

He saw it before she did—and shut his eyes.

Those kids would never be conceived.

"What is this?"

LUCKY IN LOVE

Lori Avocato

He opened his eyes to see her holding his diploma.

"Law school? You went to law school?"

"Didn't I ever mention that?" He laughed, but she stared, face firm.

"No, Dalton, you never mentioned that you were a lawyer." She stared at the diploma as if it would talk to her. "I'm guessing you passed the bar?"

"First try."

"Then you...damn you. You knew the law from day one. You knew if Funland went bankrupt, it would no longer be part of my father's estate." She shoved all the things off the desk with a swift force—and left them there. "It'd go into a separate bankruptcy estate that a trustee along with the courts would liquidate it." Lucky felt as if she were discussing a deal with one of her colleagues.

But never during any business deal did her heart break in two.

Maybe he really hadn't known. God, she hoped not.

"Your practice...what kind of—"

"Commercial real-estate."

How she wanted him to say malpractice, personal injury or patent for chrissake—anything but real estate. "God damn you. You knew Funland should have been liquidated, creditors paid off—"

"Yeah, I did know all that, Lucky. But I also knew I wanted revenge—"

She winced.

"Revenge against the Santanelli family. Only I found out the hard way that the old cliché isn't as sweet as someone who's been hurt might expect. I found out I couldn't hurt you, because somewhere between paying bills, telling fortunes, and dancing around as a horse's ass, I fell in love."

Her gut tightened. The windows were opened, she looked to make sure, but the air, the air smothered her. A wave of dizziness had her about to pass out. All because the man, the only man, she'd ever truly loved, had admitted he loved her too.

Yet, she had to turn and leave.

When she did, he grabbed her arm. "Even criminals are considered innocent until proven guilty."

She grabbed his diploma and threw it at him. "Case closed, counselor. Now I know why you reacted so strangely that time I'd called you that. What would you have looked like if I'd called you—*liar*?"

Pain had been a part of her life for as long as she could remember, yet she'd never felt it so deeply, so sharply as now when she looked at his face. She'd caused the pain in his eyes with her words.

How she wished she could change it all now.

"I did lie to begin with. Hell, I didn't know you as an adult except for your father's reputation and what a hell of a businesswoman you were. I used that knowledge to get this place back in order. The fact I did it for my old man, *may not* be enough to get me an acquittal, but those are the facts, Lucky. Along with me loving you."

She couldn't move.

"You can walk out of here and I'll never contact you, or you can understand that what I did then and what I feel now are two very different things and, in my opinion, shouldn't be held against me."

"You risked my businesses. If Funland was foreclosed on before you filed—I could have lost—"

He bent down, grabbed an envelope from the papers on the floor, held it out toward her. "I'd drawn up a contract to let you out of any financial responsibility because I would have bought out your share first. My friend in Hartford had his office draw it up."

"Hartford?" Confused, she couldn't think of anything else to say. She'd never let emotions get in the way of business, but it seemed love had a way of making the famous businesswoman rather stupid.

"I have...had a place there. My office would have done it, but I closed it before moving here—"

"Along with selling your house. You put all you had into Funland already."

"I never had anything near what *People* reported you were worth."

"You planned to protect me." She had to smile. First, because he'd been so noble for his father, and second, because he was being honest with her now—and that's what apparently mattered. He didn't love her when he'd started out the lie, and now she understood his love for his father prevented him from telling her long ago.

She thought of Zos.

A tiny seed of forgiveness had been planted in her heart when she'd looked back to see the line for the fortune telling booth. Could the seed grow fast enough to forgive Dalton, too? Maybe, she realized, she no longer had the energy to be angry or hurt. All it ever did was ruin her life. Maybe she'd take a dying man's advice.

"Okay, here's the deal, Dalton. I'll forgive you...well, because apparently I have no choice. If love means forgiving, then the verdict is acquittal." He reached out, she pushed his hand away. "I'm not done. We'll agree to two joint ventures, refurbishing Funland until it's so in the black it'll be a major attraction throughout the country. If I can't be president of Hartwell's West Cost office, I'll be president of the East Coast's most famous amusement park. We'll renew the partnership of the Santanellis and Daltons. Only this time on a marriage certificate. Besides because I find you so fucking attractive, I want my son to look like a miniature Dalton."

He took her into his arms, kissed her cheek. "And your father thought you were the lucky one."

"Seems Daddy had been wrong giving me that nickname—until now. Now that I am lucky in love."

* * *

The funeral had been small, only a handful of Funland employees and the Daltons. Chloe came back from college, now that Funland was doing so well, and they could afford to let her live in the dorms.

Lucky sat on the beach alone, insisting to her husband that she needed a few minutes. He'd seemed confused that she'd didn't want him to share her sorrow, her grief that they all felt for a beloved friend.

Zos never made it past October.

The last few months were the best of her life, she thought. Thank God she'd found it in herself to forgive Daddy. She had a family. A real family with all the joys, the sorrows, the pain of a dying father. Even the responsibility of a child, albeit a teenager. She never knew if it was her doing or not, but Owen and Chloe set their wedding date for four years from now—after they graduated from college.

Of course, EZ had insisted it was his influence.

Doc was never his jovial self once his good friend had died, and she'd always wonder if he really knew. But he seemed so pleased to see his Funland back on the map the idea obviously got him through day to day.

EZ spent most of his time working in his half of the gingerbread house's office on his law practice since commercial property in a shoreline town like Seagrove sold at an all-time premium. She happily ran the park from her desk by the window.

They'd argued who'd get the view.

She insisted she should since she had to monitor the park, but truthfully she wanted to sit there each day—to be able to smell the marshes.

The crisp sky held no clouds today. Thank goodness. She didn't want Zos's funeral to be on a dreary day. When she shut her eyes, she opened them to see a seagull fly off above the water, and knew her heart would never need to hold the secret any longer.

Sometimes a lie *is* necessary.

Although her father lied to her, it was because of him that she'd forgiven EZ.

Beyond the sand, beyond the squawking gulls, she noticed a familiar figure against the brilliant sky. A silhouette with broad shoulders that at times she knew she'd need to lean against—and other times she'd merely wrap her arms around in love, in joy.

He stood there, only yards away, watching, waiting, loving only her.

ABOUT THE AUTHOR

After serving in the Air Force as a registered nurse, award-winning author, Lori Avocato, decided to give up her nursing career to write fiction. The award-winning author has sold nine contemporary romances. Lori lives in New England with her husband, her two boys and their little dogs, Kirby and Spanky. She's the past president of the Connecticut Chapter of Romance Writers of America and has served on the Board of Directors for four years. She is still an active member of the Romance Writers of America and attends various conferences throughout the year.

She is also a member of Mystery Writers of America along with several RWA chapters. Lori writes full time with the focus of her work running from humorous contemporary stories, often with medical professional characters, to military romances. She currently has completed a novel with a female fighter pilot heroine, and continues working on her humorous crime-solving series of a burned out nurse who becomes a medical fraud insurance investigator.

Lori loves the idea of romances having happy endings in which characters overcome immense odds--often at great emotional prices. These books, she feels, in today's world can help women see that there is always that proverbial light at the end of the tunnel--or they can just be a great entertaining read.

While taking Lori in a new direction, the crime-solving series is a great medium for her quick wit and amusing characters. However, her romance background lends itself to creating believable, engaging character relationships sure to have readers begging for more.

Lori has won numerous writing contests throughout her career and teaches fiction writing in several Adult Education programs. You can visit Lori's website at: www.loriavocato.net